DESTINY CHALLENGED

MARJORIE JOSEPH

Scripture taken from the HOLY BIBLE, NEW INTERNATIONAL VERSION®. NIV®. Copyright © 1973, 1978, 1984 by International Bible Society. Used by permission of Zondervan. All rights reserved worldwide.

Higher Ground Books & Media
P.O. Box 2914
Springfield, OH 45501-2914
www.highergroundbooksandmedia.com
1-937-970-0554

ISBN (Paperback): 978-1-955368-19-3

Printed in the United States of America 2022

DESTINY CHALLENGED

MARJORIE JOSEPH

CHAPTER ONE

Luke had to take a moment away from the fanfare and celebration of his latest victory. He sat in his office, holding his phone in deliberation. The urge to call Melody was overwhelming. There was so much he wanted to tell her. So much had happened in the past few weeks, and his head was spinning.

Luke was still skeptical of the events. After having worked for Body Electric Era for a little over three months, his programs were in negotiations with a number of software companies out in California. Those companies were willing to pay millions for his groundbreaking technological innovation. One program held their interest in particular. Luke had worked on it for a few years, and it was almost perfected.

He was still in process of tweaking the ***Dimension Four*** Program. The technology surpassed much of today's most advanced programs. It also topped the tools available through social media, and other applications utilized by computers and phones. ***Dimension Four*** was pioneering in the field of travel and transport. It was the latest in biometrics-capable of *faxing* people from one place to another. That was the way Luke viewed it anyway. It was sort of like the "Beam me up, Scottie" solution for the 21st century.

Dimension was literally being handed the world on a silver platter. Not only could a person speak to their loved ones in any part of the world, but they could also share in their experiences. ***Dimension Four*** offered limitless vacation possibilities. That meant, not having to deal with the red tape of booking flights, baggage checks, claims and security checkpoints at local airports.

Luke smiled and shook his head in incredulity. He was still having a difficult time wrapping his head around the concept. Stephen Sanderson and the other execs were holding a luncheon in his honor on that very afternoon. Later, there would be a celebration at a ritzy restaurant called *Rossetti's*. The establishment was located in the affluent sector of the upscale town of *Pinewood*. Luke didn't want to discourage the festivities. So, he'd agreed to pop in for a *minute*. In light of all he'd recently gone through, he thought it best to stay away from alcohol for a while. In fact, his resolution for the upcoming year was to no longer use drinking as a crutch.

Alcohol had temporarily numbed the pain of losing the love of his life. However, every morning when he woke up to face the day, the pain bit back with a vengeance. The hurt would always be there-just as potent as his love for Melody remained. Luke toyed with the phone in his hand in indecision. He thought about calling Melody. She was the only person he wanted to talk to at that point. No one else knew how drastically his life had just changed. Luke hadn't yet told his family, or his best friend Sean. All he wanted was to hear Melody's voice.

Tears shone in his eyes, and his throat felt scratchy. Based on all Sean had told him, Melody's life had changed drastically as well. For starters, she was dating Clarke Vale. Sean had said that Melody even seemed happy. The realization that Clarke Vale was moving in on Melody, was a knife to the heart for Luke, because he loved her more than ever.

Given the circumstances, Luke had even more doubts about returning to Sands Port in order to make things right. He perceived that even if he did go back, Melody would want nothing to do with him. She was all wrapped up in Clarke Vale. All things considered, Luke couldn't blame her for moving on. He was the one who'd made the irrevocable decision to walk away. Timing was everything. He would inevitably accept one of the offers from the software companies vying for his program. When that happened, it would probably mean a move out to California.

As his thoughts raced, Luke involuntarily dialed Melody's number. A light rap simultaneously came to his office door.

"Hello, hello…," Melody's voice pealed over the phone.

Luke sat there feeling totally immobilized. He was poised to speak, but no words issued from his mouth. "Melody, I love you! I miss you so much, and I'm miserable without you, baby," he muttered inaudibly.

"Luke, is that you?" Melody questioned, surprised.

It had been a while since Melody had received such a phone call, and she couldn't help thinking it was Luke. Her heart lashed in ambiguity. Even now, if Luke called and said he wanted to reconnect, Melody couldn't see herself turning him away. It was like she'd climbed the most daunting mountain, and had made it to the very top. Now, nothing would ever bring her back to that place again. That pinnacle had only been reached with Luke.

She was both wary but overjoyed that the call was from Luke. *Maybe he still cared. Maybe, he was operating with half a heart in the same way she was.* Melody could only hope. She wanted to scream into the phone how much she still loved him, but things were different now. Clarke was in the picture. Even if she couldn't say she was *in love* with Clarke, she still had to respect the fact that he cared. *How had something so simple become so convoluted?*

Luke closed his eyes in resignation. He quietly shut down the phone, and strove to hold it together. "Come in…," he called out, trying to sound normal.

Luke pasted a smile to his face the moment Arianna Ward's face came into view. "Hey, Ari!" he welcomed.

"Is it alright if I come in?" she asked diffidently.

Luke's smile brightened, because he actually liked Arianna. She was a sweetheart. "Of course it is." He gestured.

"What are *you* doing in here?" she teased. "You're the man of the hour at this luncheon, and *you* pull a disappearing act?" Her bright blue eyes, and golden hair smiled along with her.

Luke pushed out of his chair, stood to his feet, and walked around the desk. Standing directly in front of Arianna, he easily towered over her. The contrast of height was their ongoing joke, because Arianna was petite. So, Luke tried to look and sound intimidating. "I guess, *somebody* noticed I went missing."

"Well…" Arianna's face twisted in mischief. "Just saying… if they're *honoring* someone with a luncheon, *they* should show up." She shrugged. "Just saying…"

Luke laughed. "You just might have a point there. You *think* they noticed I'm missing?"

"I don't care if they noticed, but *I* definitely did." Arianna stared reticently up into Luke's eyes. She reckoned that he had absolutely no idea that she was crazy about him. Luke was so special-so different from anyone she'd ever met. He was also very kind.

"Oh, so *you* noticed…" Luke gave her a quirky look and winked. "So, you've come in here to drag me out of my office, and *force* me to return to the party? Are you going to *force* me to dance, party police?" He set his right hand introspectively on his chin, and his brows furrowed in waggishness.

"If that what it takes," Arianna said glumly. "Word has it that you're leaving BEE, and that you're going to become some hotshot millionaire out in California." Arianna's face changed. She couldn't even *pretend* to be happy for him.

"Is *that* what you've heard?" Luke set his hand gently on her shoulder, and urged her to look at him. Arianna was doleful.

"It's what everybody's talking about around here. Is it true, Luke?" she prodded searching his eyes.

"That I'm leaving or the *hotshot millionaire* thing?"

"Luke…," Arianna raised her voice, exasperated. "Is it true?" Her face strained in angst.

Luke smile sadly. "Several offers have been made, and I am *thinking* about it," he admitted.

"Oh…?" Arianna's head slumped. "No big deal. I'm just losing my new best friend around here."

Luke cupped her chin. "Even if I do decide to make the move, we'll always be friends, Ari. You can text and call me whenever you want to." Luke gave her a heartening smile. In a lot of ways Arianna reminded him of his baby sister Rachel.

"It's not the same. Luke, don't leave," she pleaded. "This

place was so drab before you came along. You're like *Sunshine Man* or something."

Luke set his clenched fists on his hips, and pushed his chest out like a superhero. "*I'm* Sunshine Man. I'm able to dry up raindrops at a single bound-able to make Mr. Harrison in accounting show some teeth, and able to bring peace to all water cooler wars…" Luke liked that Arianna was laughing.

"You're such a mess. I'm going to miss you so much!" She instinctively threw her arms around Luke's neck, and crushed him lovingly.

Luke gave her a loving squeeze. "I'm not going anywhere yet. Don't be in such a hurry to see me off."

Arianna hesitantly released her hold on Luke. "You don't have to worry about that. *I'm* the one who's trying to get you to *stay* for as long as possible."

Luke smiled earnestly. "That's sweet. Truth be told, nothing's set in stone…at least not yet."

"So, about the honors party tonight, you *do* plan on being there, right?" Arianna frowned in uncertainty.

Luke was both stirred and surprised by Arianna's display of affection. "I *might* drop by for a minute." Luke nodded. "I hadn't planned on…"

"How could you not attend your *own* party?" Arianna shook her head, incredulous.

Luke laughed. "I guess, I *can* put in an appearance, and then cut out really fast."

"I'd like for you to save the first and last dance for me, okay?" Arianna's eyes momentarily wandered away in timidity. .

Luke was touched and extremely flattered. Arianna was so young and sweet. At twenty-three, she was one of the youngest employees for BEE. "Okay." Luke surrendered to a slow nod.

"Okay, that you're attending your own honors party, or that you'll dance with me tonight?"

Luke met Arianna's hopeful eyes affirmatively. "Yes…I'll drop by, and *show* you how to dance."

"You'll show *me*? Oh, it's *so* on right now." Arianna clasped her hands together like a little girl about to say her prayers. She then stared dreamily into Luke's eyes. "Yay, I get to have the first dance with a hotshot millionaire."

"No, Ari, you'll be dancing with *me*." Luke winked at her.

"I *know*." Arianna winked back.

She then turned on her heels, and veered towards the office door. She was just a few feet away, when the door opened up. Arianna was taken aback when she saw her bosses and supervisors bustle in looking for Luke.

Luke shook his head humorously over the matter. As much as he'd wanted some alone time, he realized he couldn't hide away forever.

Arianna was standing by the door, when the execs literally began dragging Luke away from his desk.

He looked at her and mouthed the words "*Help me…,*"as they were hauling him out of the office. Arianna laughed to see Body Electric Era's top men romping around like children. She couldn't say she blamed them for celebrating the company's latest and greatest achievement. That was, bringing Mr. Lucas William Bryant aboard.

***

Luke lingered inside his SUV after pulling into a reserved parking spot at Rossetti's Restaurant. It was close to eight p.m. So, he was indeed fashionably late to his own honors party. He'd thought extensively on the matter, and figured that if the execs of BEE were honoring him in this way, the very least he could do was to show up. He'd already dialed Melody's number twice. Both times he'd frozen up, and had remained speechless.

Things were happening so fast, it was difficult to keep up with the changes. However, the one thing Luke knew would never change was his love for Melody. It killed him to know that Clarke Vale was the one holding her, kissing her, and he was her last phone call every night. Luke felt insanely jealous.

"I love you! I never wanted to walk away. I was backed into a corner, and taking that awful deal seemed like the right thing to do at the time. Not a day goes by that I don't want to hop on a flight back out to Maryland to see you again. What I wouldn't give for another weekend like the one you, me and Cupid shared in May of last year. There isn't anything I wouldn't give to have a night like the one we had when I returned from Rhode Island," Luke's voice was croaky, as he rehearsed the things he wanted to tell Melody.

He now owned a luxury Lexus SUV. After having his vintage forest-green Jeep for over a decade, Luke finally had a brand new ride. He was baffled by the opportunities coming his way. Mr. Sanderson had updated him on the latest in respect to his breakout program *Dimension Four.* There were dozens of other companies wrangling to own the rights. They were all ready to top, or double the amount of money being offered by the competition.

Luke was both overwhelmed and totally nonplused. He kept thinking how different life would have been, if those offers were on the table back in the spring, when things were financially shaky for his family. If those opportunities had been set in place, he would not have had to endure the humiliation of taking money from Clarke Vale. Neither would he have had to give up the love of his life. His integrity would have remained intact, and Melody would be by his side.

Luke tried not to give in to discouragement. "Melody would

be with me tonight, and we would be celebrating together. None of this even matters, if she isn't here to share it with me."

Just then, he was reminded of God's faithfulness through it all. If God hadn't kept him alive, he would have undoubtedly given in to despair. God was the one who'd opened up the door with Body Electric Era. God had also carried him to where he was now. So, Luke trusted God's fidelity and would adhere to Romans 8:28. He would choose to believe that all things would somehow work together for his good.

Furthermore, if God wanted Melody back in his arms, no one-not even Clarke Vale, would be able to stand in the way. There were times he lost perspective. And, Luke always had to depend on his Heavenly Father to help him see the bigger picture. So, if having wealth meant nothing to him *personally*, it would certainly mean a lot to all those little guys out there who were at the mercy of men like Clarke Vale.

Luke didn't want to be presumptuous. However, he grasped that God was giving him an opportunity with the potential to bring Clarke Vale down. The thought of exposing Vale as a liar and a fraud, brought a smile to Luke's face. "You were *never* good enough for Melody, and I'm going to make sure she knows exactly who you are."

The restaurant had been rented out for BEE's execs and employees. There was a large private room which included; pool tables, a vast selection of beers, wines, champagnes and the very best appetizers. On an isolated table was a huge green and white cake. It was designed to look like a million dollar bill. In the center it read: *Congratulations Luke!* Dimmed amber lighting created an ambiance of flair. The walls were covered with sports-themed memorabilia. Luke loved the atmosphere, and he didn't regret showing up.

He couldn't believe this celebration was in his honor. Stephen Sanderson, his boss, and BEE associates, kept toasting to the man of the hour. "To the best decision this firm has ever made! We took a chance on you, kid and you didn't disappoint us!" Those words set the theme for the entire night.

Luke felt obligated to say a few words. He was immensely grateful for their support and admiration. "Stephen, Ben, Tom, David and Harvey, I can't thank you enough for taking a chance on a kid with literally no experience in the field." Luke laughed. "This was just a hobby for me, but you've turned it into a career. I am forever in your debt," his voice broke.

He hated getting all choked up, but couldn't seem to help it. At that point, Luke figured that all of BEE's execs, knew just what a big old mush he was. Melody used to call him a mush all the time. She loved teasing him about being sappy. Luke smiled to remember how much she loved messing with him. In the thick of the festivities, Melody was all he could think about, as applause resonated throughout the vast room.

"Just *one* more dance before you leave?" Arianna kept her arms territorially about Luke's neck. She refused to let go, even if they'd been dancing for a while now.

In light of Arianna's behavior, it occurred to Luke that she probably had a slight crush on him. It was cute, and he was immensely flattered. Arianna was a beautiful, highly intelligent and very sweet girl.

"Okay, so *this* will be our last dance, Ari. You and I have been dancing for the past hour," Luke razzed on her. "Not to mention the fact that you wouldn't let anyone else cut in." Luke stared all about the room. Three of his coworkers had requested dances, but Arianna had staunchly forbidden it. Luke wanted to be friends. However, he perceived that Arianna wanted more.

Arianna frowned in disappointment. "All right, this will be our last one. Are you going to dance with any of them?" Arianna indicated the three young ladies who were standing by waiting to pounce on Luke. They were all giving her the death stare. Arianna wished they would go away. This was probably the last time she'd get to be close to Luke before everything changed. It was her chance to tell him how much she liked him. "I'm going to miss you so much!" she said straightforwardly.

"I'm going to miss you too, Ari. Don't let anyone put out that fighting spirit. I *do* realize how hard it is to be heard sometimes." Luke smiled at her.

"You've impressed me so much, Luke Bryant. You encouraged me to be bold in such an intimidating environment. No one's ever done that for me." She stared yearningly up at him. "You're very special, you know that?"

"Thank you. I think you're quite special as well, Ari. You made the transition so easy for me when I first got here, and I'm grateful for that. I will never forget your spark." He gave her a warm hug.

When Luke pulled away, Arianna tiptoed, and bridged her mouth to his. She tenderly coaxed his mouth, as she avidly tried to extract the honey she desired. She brushed her fingers through his curls, and moved in for a deeper kiss.

Luke felt totally numb. Something had shut down internally. It was automatic whenever anyone tried to get close to him. It wasn't that he didn't like Arianna, because he liked her a great deal. The problem was that he was madly in love with Melody, and his heart wouldn't let anyone else get close. So, in an unassuming manner, he pulled away from Arianna's firm grasp. He pressed a quick kiss to her cheek. "I have to say goodnight, Ari." His face crinkled in remorse.

Hurt spread over Arianna's face like jam on warm toast, and tears gleamed in her eyes. "Night, Luke."

She watched Luke turn away, and rush out of the party lounge. Inwardly, she knew Luke would never intentionally hurt her, but she felt the sting of his rejection just the same. She hadn't held back in expressing her feelings. However, he'd made it abundantly clear he wasn't interested. And yet, Arianna couldn't bring herself to be angry at him. She also couldn't blame him, because Luke was such a good guy.

Although mortified, she realized there was nothing malicious about Luke's reaction. It seemed to be the story of her life. All of the good guys always seemed to evade her. For one reason or another, she'd thought it would have been different with Luke. Nonetheless, Arianna knew that she'd been wrong. Even so, she knew Luke had a lot going on. So, once she was able to work past the shame, she would probably call him, and apologize for coming on so strong.

***

It was after 1 a.m. when Luke rolled out into the highway from the honors party. It had been a great party, but he still felt conflicted about Arianna's kiss. Luke kept thinking he'd overreacted. He wondered if he'd always have a meltdown, whenever women expressed an interest in him. Arianna was a sweet girl. So, their kiss *should* have been the most natural thing in the world. That would have been the case, if he still wasn't hung up on Melody. Luke couldn't even imagine being with anyone else. And yet, as a result of his poor choices, he knew he'd probably never be with her again.

Nothing mattered to him, not the money, the titles or the status. Without Melody in his life he wanted no part of it. His heart knew the truth all too well. He would never love anyone else. Knowing Clarke Vale was moving in on Melody, broke his heart. His thoughts were racing just as speedily as his SUV.

As he contemplated his lost love, the song, *"She's out of my Life"* from Michael Jackson's *Off The Wall* album played over the radio. That song brought the pain home, and hit like a bulldozer. Hyperventilating, Luke wanted to pull over. However, he had to keep moving, because it wasn't the safest area.

Luke prayed for God's strength to get through such a rough patch. He wanted to shut the radio off, because hearing that song was like a hatchet to the heart. In spite of the pain, remembering his and Melody's first kiss, after their Karaoke duet, made him feel in some way closer to her. However, his nostalgia was short-lived.

At that instant, what felt like a freight train rammed into his SUV. Stunned, Luke made an instinctive turn, and saw the black 4x4 speeding up again for a repeat performance. Bewildered and outraged, he pressed on the gas pedal, in an effort to lose the psycho who'd just crashed into his new ride. But, the truck shadowed him at an incredible speed.

Luke swerved, and shifted in and out of his lane in order to get away. But, wherever he turned, the aggressor followed, and had sideswiped him several times. Accessing the automatic phone feature for his car, Luke commanded the feature to dial 9-11. "Yes, I'm eastbound on Highway 9. There's someone out here driving a black 4x4 shadowing me. They've rammed up into my car several times. I think they're trying to run me off the road," Luke explained. "No, I've never seen the truck before..."

Luke's heart was in his throat, as he turned to get a look at the license plate number. Straining, he tried to see who was behind the wheel, but it was too dark. So, Luke pushed down on the gas in order to lose the truck. Moments later, he veered yet again to see if he was still being followed, but the vehicle was nowhere to be found. Relieved, he decided to get off at the next exit. It wasn't the exit he needed to get home, but he decided to ditch the routine. There was no telling if the maniac who'd just tried to hurt him would continue tailing.

Travis Connors worked for Clarke Vale. The man had been paid to issue a warning strike at Luke. It was Clarke's way of reminding Luke to keep his distance from Melody Maxwell. Travis now had to reach out to Clarke, and let him know that the mission was accomplished. After having put the fear of God into Luke Bryant, Travis exited the highway. He'd been operating a stolen car, and he was almost sure that Luke had probably read off the license plate number to the police. Travis heard sirens from a distance. So, he left the stolen truck on the service road off the highway, and took to running.

***

Luke finally managed to make it back to his apartment complex after 2 a.m. He was still traumatized over the incident on Highway 9. The back bumper of his brand new SUV was dented, and also the left rear passenger's side door. Luke had taken every precaution to ensure no one had followed him home. In light of the way things had played out, he was grateful to be alive and breathing. He'd feared that his car would have been shot up. Even if he wasn't hurt, he was peeved that the incident had occurred at all. It seemed so random and pointless.

Clarke Vale excluded, Luke couldn't think of *one* enemy. The more he thought on the matter, the more it seemed feasible that Clarke was behind the attack. Perhaps, Clarke had discovered that he and Sean had been looking into his criminal activities out in Central America, the Philippines and the Caribbean. Sean had gone down to the DR. Of the many things he'd discovered, was that many poor locals had died after taking generic drugs manufactured by Vale Pharmaceutical subsidiaries

Also, Clarke's fixation on Melody was totally twisted. All the same, Luke wondered why Clarke was coming after *him*, when he was no longer a part of Melody's life. He'd held up his end of the bargain, and had done everything Clarke had asked. To imagine Clarke trying to rub him out, made Luke so angry he was ready to declare war on the man. If Clarke *was* the one behind what happened earlier on, Luke had to return to Sands Port to tell Melody who they suspected Clarke Vale *really* was.

Melody had to know that Vale wasn't the gentleman he was masquerading around as. Sure, he dressed the part, and had mastered the vernacular. However, underneath his refined veneer was a cruel, heartless monster-even a mafia lord, who only cared about getting what he wanted. Clarke didn't care who got caught in the crossfire in his quest for the almighty dollar, or when it came to having the woman he wanted.

"It stops here, Clarke. I'm *so* done with you." Luke shook his head senselessly over the matter, as he slipped into the building elevator. "I'm going to get Melody away from you, if it's the last thing I do," he avowed. He was so outraged, he thought he'd jump right out of his skin. So many things were happening all at once. He was on the cusp of leaving Body Electric Era, pending offers for his program, and a possible move to California.

Still, Luke resolved to return to Sands Port. He *had* to warn Melody about Clarke. She had to know that the man she was dating, was nothing more than a common criminal. Luke had to set the record straight, because Melody meant everything to him. He felt *personally* responsible for leaving her exposed to wolves. Not only was Clarke himself dangerous, but his associates were just as lethal.

A man like Clarke Vale irrefutably had his share of enemies. Word that had it that Clarke's then girlfriend had been gunned down on the balcony of their hotel suite out in the Dominican Republic. No doubt, she'd been murdered as an act of revenge. Hundreds of people had suffered-and some had even died, as a direct result of non-tested generic drugs manufactured by Vale Corp. So, it was anybody's guess as to the person who'd murdered her. Her death was undeniably payback for the pain and misery Clarke and his lackeys had caused in that region.

Still, because Clarke was obsessed with Melody, Luke couldn't imagine him or any of his associates doing anything to hurt her. However, what was to stop Clarke's enemies from taking revenge on his loved ones? Luke had to step in, and warn Melody of the potential dangers. For that very reason, before his pending trip to California, he had to try to make Melody understand who they were dealing with. If Melody heard him out, Luke would feel in some way vindicated. At that point, he'd be forced to let her go once and

for all. He couldn't imagine that she had any feelings left for him.
Coming to terms with that reality only deepened the comprehensive
wound in Luke's heart.

Stepping off the elevator, Luke was ill-prepared for what
happened next. Turning the usual corner in order to get to his place,
someone grabbed his arm, and pulled him into a supply closet.

"What on earth?" Luke blared at the man wearing a gray
trench coat, a baseball cap, black jeans and boots. The man's salt
and pepper hair matched his beard and moustache, and he looked
totally disheveled. "What is this? Who are you, and what do you
want from me?" Luke shifted back, and positioned himself for a
fight.

The man disarmingly removed the baseball cap from off his
head, and his face came into plain sight. Luke immediately
recognized him. Despite the weight gain, it was undoubtedly Carter
Stephens. The bloodshot eyes were a dead giveaway.

"Carter? What are you doing here? Are you in some way
connected to the lunatic who tried to run me off the highway?" He
instinctively grabbed Carter by the collar.

Fearful and bewildered, Carter baulked from Luke's forceful
grasp and piercing eyes. "Someone tried to drive you off the
highway?" He flinched in shock.

Luke dauntingly closed in on Carter, and lowered into his
eyes. "Don't even pretend you don't know what happened. Were
you out there?" Luke's face reddened, and veins pulsed at his
temples.

"Nah, kid, you got it all wrong. I came out here to *warn*
you." Carter kept shaking his head in denial. "That kind of thing
just ain't me."

Tenseness drained from Luke's fired up features. "You came
here to *warn* me about what, Carter?" Luke stared warily at him.
"Why would you *need* to warn me? We made a deal back in the
spring. Your shady boss…"

"He's losing his marbles, Luke. Now more than ever, he's convinced that you are in contact with Melody. You haven't been in contact with her have you?" Nervousness spread over Carter's face like syrup on a stack of pancakes.

Tears stung Luke's eyes. "No… No. I *have* kept my end of the deal," his voice broke. "I walked away from her and everything we had. I haven't spoken to her since the day before I left Sands Port." Pain permeated within Luke like helium in a balloon.

Luke was irritated. "I did what I was *supposed* to do. Now what's going on? I haven't gone anywhere near Sands Port since that day." Luke couldn't bear to say Melody's name again without falling apart. "What the hell does Vale want with me?"

Carter's face warped in fear and dread. "Luke, Vale's losing his mind. I don't think things are going as well as he hoped with…the girl…" Carter realized how difficult it was for Luke to keep saying and hearing Melody's name. "So, he called me the other night ranting about how he suspects that *the girl* has been in touch with you…"

A spark of light flickered through the gloom of Luke's misery. Things weren't working out in as far as Clarke's plan to be with Melody. Luke could only hope and pray Melody wouldn't give her heart to him, because the man didn't deserve to have her. "So, he thinks I'm *not* holding up my end of the bargain?"

"I told him he was wrong, Luke. I told him to leave you alone, and to back away from the situation. But, he got it in his head that Mel…*the girl* is not warming up to him, because she's still in love with you," Carter said plainly. His anxious eyes searched Luke's.

After all Luke had gone through that morning, those words sparked hope in the embers of his despair. He nodded with a sense of satisfaction. "But, you told him that I *haven't* contacted her?" He lowered into Carter's eyes.

"Yeah, I told him. But, he don't care, kid. When he ask me to come out here to scare you, I said no." Carter paused for a moment and looked away. "It was wrong for Clarke to split the two of you up." Carter's eyes bridged to Luke's again. "Anyhow, I really don't think he gonna be happy, until you're out of the picture."

"I'm *not* in the picture, Carter," Luke argued, befuddled. "I moved to another state."

"No, Luke, I mean until you're *gone*…for good. Believe me, it wouldn't be the first time. You need to go to the cops, and ask them to watch over you, kid. What happened to you out on that highway was a warning. That's how it starts. He warns you he's coming after you. He ain't messing around, and he don't play fair. I took a chance coming out here myself."

Luke's brows furrowed in wariness. "How do I know *you're* not here working for Clarke?"

"Cause, I don't work for him no more. After the last job I did, I said I wasn't gonna work for him. He set me up to take a fall. If I didn't have that alibi, I would be in jail right now serving a 20 year-sentence. It ain't worth it to work for Vale no more. I'm trying to do things right. I got enough cash to move out of the country, and start a new life for myself. I don't need no more connections to Vale and his goons.

"Anyway, kid, what I'm trying to say is that I'm risking my neck being here this morning. You a good kid, and you got your whole life ahead of you. Clarke already stole a whole lot from so many people. So, I don't want to see you be his next victim. Understand?" Carter stared intently into Luke's eyes.

Luke nodded compliantly, and sensed that Carter *was* probably risking his life to be there. "I'm sorry." Luke's expression softened. "It's just hard to know who to trust nowadays. I really appreciate what you're doing, Carter. I never thought I'd *ever* be glad to see *you*. No offense…"

"I ain't offended, kid. I get it. The first time we met, I didn't make a very good impression. Just watch your back, and stay as a far away from Sands Port and *the girl* as possible. I wouldn't wanna see you get hurt."

Carter opened up about a lot of Clarke's illegal practices. He disclosed how Clarke had had a number of people *rubbed out*. However, being who he was, and with his incredibly deep pockets, he'd managed to cover it all up. Clarke seemed to be above the law, because he had others doing his dirty work. Luke was grateful that Carter was taking the time to confirm much of his and Sean's suspicions about Clarke.

"Would you be willing to testify against him in a court of law?" Luke quizzed, still reeling from the events of the morning.

"I would probably testify against Vale, if I get immunity."

"I'm sure you'd be granted immunity, if you agreed to help them bring down someone as powerful and evil as Vale."

"I guess, that's a bridge I'll cross when I get to it."

"You might have to cross that bridge sooner than you think." Luke stared critically into Carter's face.

"Listen, kid, I gotta get going. I got an early morning flight to Negril, Jamaica. I have some friends out there. They got my back, in case Vale comes looking for me. Watch your own back and." Carter's face wrinkled in seriousness.

Idly looking down at the Persian-styled carpeting out in the hallway supply closet, he pointed a liable finger at Luke. "Maybe *you* can't go talk to Melody right now, but you should have someone out in Sands Port talk to her. Get her away from that man. When he *keeps* a woman she is his *property*. He's the jealous type, and can be violent if pushed." Carter continued to stare nervously about.

Luke flinched upon hearing those words. He *had* to find a way to get Melody away from Clarke. However, he had to do it in a way that wouldn't endanger both of their lives. Luke plowed his fingers through his curly mane in jeopardy. His heart jumped when Carter opened up the closet door, and looked both ways. Then, the man circumspectly slunk down the hallway. Opening up the heavy emergency door down the hall, he took the stairs rather than the elevator. Luke himself decided to wait a few minutes before stepping out of the supply closet. Paranoid, he also looked both ways before stepping out into the hallway.

Moments later, he was standing in front of the apartment door. Like music to his ears, he heard Cupid panting on the other side. Luke's smile was irrepressible, as he let himself into his place. Before he even got a chance to shut the door closed, Cupid was on top of him. The dog was overjoyed that Luke was finally home. Luke playfully rubbed his collar and mane, and couldn't help laughing. He hadn't spent much time with Cupid the day before.

Between the luncheon over at BEE and the honors party, they'd barely gotten half an hour together at the park. It was hard whenever they spent most of the day apart. "I guess, you *really* missed me." Cupid buried Luke in tongue-dripped kisses, and wagged his tail feverishly. "I missed you too."

Luke bounded back to his feet, and crossed over into his bedroom. Cupid was glued to his calf, even as Luke changed out of casual party attire, and slipped on comfortable sweats and a T-shirt.

When Luke pulled back the covers on the bed, Cupid immediately jumped up on it-as if Luke had fixed the bed for him. Luke shook his head comically, tickled by his nutty dog. Noting else but Cupid's antics could have brought a smile to his face, after the kind of morning he'd just had. Before slipping into bed, Luke got down on his knees to pray.

There was a lot he needed to verbalize to God. He wanted to take a moment to thank God for all of the blessings coming his way. So many doors were opening up by God's grace and providence.

Furthermore, he had to thank God for keeping Melody safe, even in the midst of danger. Luke prayed for God's continuous protection over her. She was-and always would be his heart. Luke also opened up about the hopefulness he felt, because of Carter's visit. Luke estimated that even if Clarke Vale was doing everything he could to *buy* Melody's love, the plan didn't seem to be working in the way he'd hoped. Lastly, Luke thanked God for protecting him out on Highway 9. He lifted his hands up in praise to God, and avowed to trust on a deeper level.

Luke wasn't afraid, because God definitely had a plan and purpose for his life. Melody had always called him a *child of destiny*. So, Luke was assured that God wouldn't allow the enemy's schemes to prosper or to prevail. He had yet to come into the fullness of God's plan. So, Luke was certain of one thing. Until God's plan was fulfilled in his life, he wasn't going anywhere.

As he prayed and waited in God's presence, he was reminded of key scriptural truths. Isaiah 54:17 which reads: "No weapon formed against you shall prosper, and every tongue which rises against you in judgment you shall condemn. This is the heritage of the servants of the Lord, and their righteousness is from me." (NKJV). Luke meditated on those words.

Psalms 91 also came to mind, and Luke read it aloud just before slipping into bed. He was confident that God would carry him through every difficulty. Suddenly, the peace of God washed over him. There was a glimmer of hope that God would also make a way for him to have Melody back in his arms. He found it humorous that Cupid was already asleep. Cupid had waited up for him, and now the silly dog was finally free to rest. It had been a long day, and an even longer morning for both of them.

CHAPTER TWO

The Sands Port Tower Restaurant had been closed out for the night. Ornamental lights glistened on the evergreens out in the lobby, and inside the expansive, upscale bistro. Luminescent white lights created an enchanting flower garden. Every table held clear flower vases shaped like lanterns, and the entire room smelled of Lilacs. Melody wandered around the place like a little girl. She couldn't believe that Clarke had set up such a virtual wonderland.

Clarke had asked her to meet him at the restaurant that evening, but Melody had no idea he'd planned a private affair. The restaurant had one of the most picturesque views of the city's skyline and of the *Onyx River*. Melody strolled over to the back end of the restaurant in order to take in the scenery. The backdrop reminded her of a Christmas concert set. She drifted further out towards the balcony. However, she stopped short when she saw Clarke standing out there with his back pressed up to the verandah barricade.

He looked extremely handsome and charming in his designer black suit. Melody smiled, and shook her head in incredulity. She couldn't help thinking Clarke never did anything halfway. Everything had to be grand scale. "Clarke... What is all of this?" Melody gestured to her surroundings.

Clarke didn't speak at first, because he was utterly mesmerized. Melody looked like a dream in a rust-colored dress with sequined flower patterns. She had on matching heels, jewelry and makeup. Her radiant hair shone like meshed copper against the play of lights all round, and her angelic face was luminous. Clarke's smile was satisfying as he ogled.

"Clarke, I'm waiting for an answer." Melody walked out to the balcony to join him. "I thought *we* were having dinner here tonight." She was swept away.

Clarke eliminated the space between them. He was completely enchanted as he stared down at Melody. "We *are* having dinner here tonight, my love. But, I guess I forgot to tell you that it's a private dinner." Clarke slipped his arms around Melody's waist, and pulled her avariciously to himself. "You are the most beautiful creature I've ever seen!" He pressed in close to whisper in her ear, and covered her face and hair with tender kisses.

Melody surrendered to his embrace. She draped her arms about his neck, and plowed her fingers through Clarke's thick dark hair. "Clarke, you're too much. What are we going to do with all this space?" She looked all around. "You really don't know the meaning of keeping things simple do you?"

"There's nothing *simple* about you, Melody Maxwell, and there's definitely nothing simple about the way I feel about you." Clarke hunched down, bridged his lips to hers, and kneaded them avidly.

Melody reciprocated Clarke's kiss automatically. At that point, she was *conditioned* to respond. But, she found herself still reserved. She doubted that Clarke realized that she was collaterally damaged. Melody had already resigned to the fact that no one would ever have her heart in the way Luke had. Luke had brought out the very best in her. Moreover, he'd shown her things about herself she'd been oblivious to. Melody loved him fiercely and always would. Even so, Luke was gone, and Clarke adored her. So, Melody assented to making an effort at being an active participant in their relationship.

Melody smiled up into Clarke's eyes, when he finally released her. "So, are you planning to *feed* me tonight?" She gave him a quizzical look.

Before Clarke could respond to Melody's query, a waiter breezed out to the balcony, and asked if they were ready to come inside for champagne. "Does that any your question, pretty lady?" Clarke winked at her.

"It *does*. So, you *are* going to feed me after all?"

"Yes, I *do* plan on feeding you." Clarke pulled her to himself once again. His arms tightened around her waist, and he pressed a quick kiss to her lips. "Are you cold?"

"No, actually... I'm fine, but this is way too much."

Clarke hushed Melody by pressing a finger up to her lips. "You are so worth it."

Melody realized how futile it was to argue with him. All that seemed to matter to him was that she was appreciative of all of the effort he'd put into making the evening possible. "I love it, Clarke! This is amazing!"

"Shall we go in for appetizers and champagne?" Clarke linked his arm through Melody's.

"That sounds good." Melody pursed her lips to speak, but desisted, as Clarke led her over to their special table inside of the spacious, yet deserted restaurant.

Their table was ornately set, embellished by brick-colored candles in a sizable clear glass cylinder as the centerpiece. Champagne on ice was brought over soon after. As Melody and Clarke engaged in conversation, management closed the balcony's glass partition. They were told that the doors would reopen after dinner. A variety of appetizers were brought over to their table, including Hors d'oeuvres, Caviar, and an assortment of the most delectable breads and cheeses.

Melody was surprised and impressed by how Clarke had pulled out all the stops to make their night special. Their friendship had blossomed in the past few months. So, Melody was a little bit more *hopeful* of a breakthrough. However, it was difficult to be emotionally available after the heartbreak she'd suffered with Luke.

The lights were dimmed as she and Clarke had dinner. The entire room looked like a star-filled night, only a hundred times brighter and more wondrous. After dinner, Clarke led Melody back out to the balcony. He held her protectively from behind, as they took in the diamond-studded sky, and the shimmering river beyond them.

"Clarke, this is so beautiful!" Melody scrutinized the sable and diamond-crusted night sky.

"You're so beautiful!" Clarke turned Melody around to face himself. His arms still encircled her waist. "I've never felt this way about anyone, Melody!" His eyes searched hers ponderously. "I want to see you every day. When I wake up in the morning, I want you next to me. I want to take care of you." Clarke's expression was sentimental.

Melody was breathless, and rendered temporarily speechless. When a man poured his heart out to a woman, they expected reciprocity. Melody's eyes fastened to Clarke's piercing gaze. She resolved to be as truthful as she could. For months, she'd asked God to show her his will in respect to her relationship with Clarke. However, Melody was still unclear, even if Clarke had attended church with her in past weeks.

It seemed there wasn't *anything* he wasn't prepared to do, just for the asking. All the same, Melody needed to know for sure that Clarke had a relationship with Jesus Christ. Even if he *said* he did, she still had to figure out what that *meant* to him. There was no doubt she was in Clarke's life for a purpose and vice versa. What that purpose was remained to be seen.

"Clarke, I'm touched that you feel so strongly about me…"

"I'm in love with you, Melody!" Clarke declared. "I love you!"

Melody's heart melted. It was the very first time Clarke had said he loved her. She smiled, reached up and sensitively brushed his cheek. "Clarke, that means so much to me!"

"*You* mean so much to me, Melody." Clarke looked cautiously around to ensure they were alone. "I rented out this place, because I wanted to be completely alone with you." Clarke smiled mischievously

"Okay…?" Melody was perplexed. "It's been the perfect night! Thank you so much."

"I'm glad you're enjoying our intimate night together. I'm hoping for many more nights just like this one."

Melody nodded and smiled. "Okay…," she said quizzically.

Clarke released his hold from about her waist, and

genuflected to one knee. Melody cupped her mouth in shock. "Clarke, what are you doing?" She gasped.

"I'm doing what I've wanted to do for such a long time. Melody, you mean the world to me, and I can't see a life apart from you. Will you marry me?" Clarke removed a wine-colored jewelry box from the inner pocket of his suit jacket.

Melody cupped her mouth yet again in utter amazement. It was the very first time anyone had ever proposed, and she was beyond swept away by the gesture.

"I understand if you need time. I know this is all so sudden…"

"Yes," Melody said. She wasn't sure what had gotten into her. Maybe, it was because she'd waited for such a long time for a proposal. She was overwhelmed. And perhaps, she wasn't insanely in love, but she was *fond* of Clarke. Melody evaluated that in life a person had to make concessions. No one could have it all. Even if it seemed as if she'd had it all with Luke, their relationship was short-lived. To Melody, it seemed as if the passionate stint she and Luke had shared, was for the sole purpose of teaching her the difference between fantasy and reality.

Plausibly, in this life, it was enough to share a connection based on values, mutual respect and a solid commitment. Love was overrated, and had let her down. Now, it was time to plant both feet firmly on the ground. Melody had to get her head out of the clouds. A good-looking, rich and powerful man *loved* her, and that was a lot more than most could lay claim to.

Melody thought about Serena and Dane. Dane *was* wealthy, but he and Serena were madly in love and happy. Waves of self-pity threatened to rise up on the inside, but Melody suppressed them. There was no time to feel sorry for herself, or to be envious of her best friend. This was a once in a lifetime opportunity. Heaven knows, she had waited long enough! The circumstances weren't perfect. All the same, she deduced, waiting for an ideal set of circumstances, meant never taking any risks. So, by faith, Melody was jumping in, hoping for the best. She smiled till her face hurt, as she helped Clarke back up to his feet.

"Did you just say *yes* or did I dream it up?" Clarke's face radiated, and his eyes were blue lightbulbs of hope.

"I said yes," Melody softly reiterated, as she draped her arms about his neck.

Clarke pulled her possessively into his arms and held on. He celebrated, swaying Melody's body in a quiet rhythm. "I just got my wish. I guess, wishes really *can* come true." He squeezed her potently, and didn't let go for a long time. With his arms securely enfolding Melody's waist, he prompted, "Let's not wait, pretty lady. Let's do it right away." Clarke stared intently and excitedly into her eyes.

Shocked, Melody pulled back for a moment. Not wanting to falter, she kept a firm grasp on Clarke's arms. Confusion blanketed her face. "What...? You mean like in a week or two?" Melody's heart pulsed in angst.

"That's exactly what I'm saying, my sweet girl. I mean, just tell me what you want...sky's the limit. Tell me your dream wedding, and I will make it happen." Clarke bent down, and began nibbling the corners of Melody's mouth.

Melody felt out of sorts and apprehensive, because things were happening so quickly. "Clarke," she said in between his fluttery kisses, "a girl needs time to plan these things out. For starters, my mom would have to come out to Sands Port...not to mention my brother Calvin..."

"Melody, my love..." Clarke pulled back to look into her eyes. "You can do whatever you want. In fact, we can call on the best wedding planner I know, so that you can start planning our wedding as early as tomorrow." Clarke caringly caressed her face.

"As early as tomorrow...," Melody's voice trailed, as she uneasily internalized the matter. She couldn't even protest, because Clarke refused to stop kissing her. She tried to find a way to buy a little time. "Can we do a month instead of two weeks?"

"We can do whatever you want." Clarke stared at her with involvement. "I'm a very longsuffering man. I've waited *this* long to be with you. So, what's another few weeks?" Clarke had a clement expression on his face. "Just as long as it *is* just a *month*, because I can't stand not having you next to me for much longer." Clarke closed in on Melody. He crushed her in his arms, and pelted her with a hailstorm of kisses.

Melody had consternations, but wasn't sure what exactly she was holding out hope for. Yet, in the back of her mind, she knew it wasn't *what* but *who* she was holding out hope for. Melody still dreamed of Luke riding back out to Sands Port on his white horse to get her. He'd tell her he still loved her, and they would live happily ever after. That was the *fantasy* but *reality* was staring her in the face.

Reality was a handsome, well-off man, who consistently demonstrated how he was willing to do anything to have and to keep her. Melody was resigned to the fact that life would never be one hundred percent. Everything was a tradeoff. She could only hope that her feelings for Clarke would grow over time. God was ordering her steps, and she had to believe he had a plan.

So, she kept a smile plastered on her face, as Clarke lavished her with kisses. Melody estimated that there were worse things. Still, she had to try to find a way to reconcile her heart and mind with the pressing offer Clarke had made. Opportunities of this magnitude rolled around maybe once-if a person was lucky. And even if the prospect of marrying Clarke was *frightening*, Melody was determined not to miss the boat.

***

"Hey, Sean, is that you?" Serena approached the blond-haired man standing just outside the sporting goods store at the mall. She wasn't sure, but from the back he looked just like Sean. When the young man turned to face her, Serena's suspicions were confirmed. It *was* Sean.

"Hey, Serena! How are you?" With the most welcoming

smile, Sean wrapped his arms around her in greeting. Sean carried shopping bags which crinkled and swished, as he and Serena hugged.

"I'm doing well," Serena said pleasantly. "How are *you*? I don't think I've seen you since…"

"The wedding," Sean filled in. "It meant a lot to me and to Nicole to have you and Dane there."

"It *was* a beautiful wedding!" Serena smiled. "But I *really* thought we'd all get the chance to hang out after the honeymoon. Is everything all right?" Serena moved to the side of the entryway of the store to avoid being shoved around by the mob of mall patrons.

"I'm good," Sean said trying to sound upbeat, but his face creased in awkwardness. Sean tussled with feelings of uneasiness, because he was keeping secrets from Melody and Serena. "What are *you* doing out here?" he evaded.

"You *know* how much Melody and I *love* to shop. Ah, but before you judge me too harshly, I'm actually here to purchase a gift for my amazing husband. We've been married a whole year now!" Serena had a mawkish expression. Her face and eyes radiated like street lamps on a dark night. Still, she perceived something totally off. Sean was being weird. If she didn't know better, she would have thought he felt uncomfortable around her, and that was totally unlike him.

"That's amazing, Serena! Congratulations! I'm so happy for you and Dane." Sean gave her a heartening smile.

"Thank you. I love Dane more today than I did on the day we got married." Tears of affect shone in Serena's eyes.

Sean smiled again, and forced a smile. "That's truly wonderful! That's the same way I feel about my Nicole." His eyes wandered away from Serena's intent stare. And, he kept looking nervously about the congested mall.

"Something wrong, Sean?" Serena frowned, as her eyes finally connected to Sean's wandering ones.

Sean's expression was that of befuddlement. He set his hand on his heart in an effort to explain things away. "I'm fin..." Sean sighed, and shook his head apologetically.

Serena took hold of his arm. "Are you okay? Is there something you want to tell me? Have *you* been in touch with Luke?" Serena's eyes narrowed in suspicion.

Sean sighed again, and steadied his gaze into Serena's piercing eyes. "Yes... Luke and I have been in touch."

Serena set her free hand on her forehead in jeopardy. "Sean, you've been in touch with Luke and...?"

Sean kept shaking his head contrarily. "Serena, believe me, I wanted to tell Melody... I wanted to tell you, but..."

Tears shone in Serena's eyes. "Sean, how could you *not* tell her? Melody hasn't recovered from what happened with Luke last year. I don't care how many gifts and trinkets Clarke Vale has given her. She just doesn't feel that way about him. Sean...?" Serena kept shaking her head in denial. "Melody's shattered, and you didn't tell us?"

Sean tried to make Serena understand. "There's a lot you *don't* know, Serena."

Tears rolled down Serena's cheeks. "Then, tell me what I don't know, and *make* me understand, Sean." She stared pleadingly at him.

"Come with me." Sean guided.

He led her away from the crowd, and kept his hand on the small of her back, as they pushed through the throng of mallgoers.

Serena powered through the bustle with whizzing thoughts. She couldn't believe Sean had been in touch with Luke, and had kept it a secret. She was so angry she felt like screaming, but mostly she was hurt. Knowing how devastated Melody had been over Luke's departure, there was no viable excuse for Sean to have kept this secret from them. Serena understood that Luke and Sean were best friends, and that Sean's loyalty was primarily to Luke. All the same,

Serena felt as if Sean should have said something.

Sean ushered Serena into *Bix's Bar and Grill*. The restaurant was cool quiet and dimly lit. Sean took his and Serena's bags, and rested them to the side of their table.

"Do you want anything?" Sean offered. It was hurtful to see the taut and frustrated expression on Serena's face.

"I'm fine," Serena said shortly. Her fiery eyes connected to Sean's, and she shrugged, bewildered. "Sean, I realize how close you are to Luke, but I also know how much you care about Melody. How could you be around her for months, knowing how much she was hurting, and not tell her that you'd connected to Luke?"

Remorse shadowed Sean's features. "There's a lot you don't know. First of all, when Luke reached out to me, he didn't even want to tell *me* where he was. He was wary of giving *me* his phone number, Serena. We've been best friends since middle school."

Sean kept shaking his head apologetically, as he explained the circumstances surrounding Luke's sudden departure from Sands Port. He'd promised his buddy never to speak of the matter to anyone-least of all to Melody's best friend. However, his promise seemed immaterial in light of how deeply Melody was hurting. Even if Luke got mad at him for talking to Serena, Sean resolved that it was high time they all knew the truth.

Serena was tangled up in offense, and she'd been shocked by Sean's initial revelation. However, as she heard him out, she softened a bit, and realized why he couldn't tell her. She was astonished to hear about Clarke's offer. It validated all of her suspicions about him. So many times before, she'd *tried* to tell Melody that Clarke was behind Luke's departure from Sands Port. Luke taking Clarke's money for *any* reason, was something Melody could not have conceptualized.

However, Serena concluded that both she and Melody had judged correctly. Melody had been right to assess Luke's character. She'd judged that Luke wouldn't have taken Clarke's money for the sake of personal monetary gain. However, Serena had been right to assess that Clarke had made Luke an offer he couldn't refuse.

Furthermore, Clarke had seen to it that Luke was backed into a corner. He'd found a way to take Melody away from Luke. Now that Serena knew the truth, Luke's love for Melody resonated. Luke *did* and *always* would love her.

Incredulous and befuddled, Serena pushed back into her seat. "Poor Luke." Her thoughts whizzed. "I can't believe any of this, Sean. Clarke is an even more horrible person that I'd imagined."

"Serena, you have absolutely no idea who Clarke Vale is..."

Sean decided to hold his tongue. The less Melody and Serena knew, the less danger would follow. So, he didn't want to go into the details of what he and Luke had discovered about Clarke Vale and Vale Corp. "Serena, I will say this. The further away Melody stays from Clarke, the safer she'll be."

"Sean, what are you saying? Is Melody in danger?" Serena's face warped in apprehension, and her eyes cut through Sean's like lasers. "If she's in danger you *need* to tell me."

"What I *can* tell you is that Clarke isn't a straight shooter. You've got to tell Melody that Clarke used the Bryant's financial and medical worries against Luke. I sincerely doubt she'll want anything to do with him after she hears the truth. Luke has been absolutely miserable without her, and he hasn't moved on at all."

Sean eluded discussing Clarke's criminal involvements with Serena, because he refused to put her and Melody in that kind of danger. He hoped that all he'd disclosed to Serena so far, was enough to make Melody want to sever all ties with the man.

"Sean, you're saying Luke still loves her?" Jeopardy veiled Serena's face.

"He loves her more than ever. He was *forced* to walk away. He never wanted to."

"This is totally messed up. Timing is everything. Melody's *marrying* Clarke. In fact, in a matter of days."

Sean felt as if the wind had just gotten knocked out of him. "You're kidding right?"

"Sean, I wish it was all one big joke, but Clarke asked her to marry him a while ago, and Melody said yes. The wedding is this upcoming Saturday. What are we going to do?"

Sean was stunned and speechless. Serena telling him that Melody would be marrying Clarke, was a direct hit to his own heart. He knew how hard Luke was working to set things straight. There wasn't anything he wouldn't have done for a second chance with Melody. So, Sean felt the sting for his buddy. If Melody married Clarke Vale, Luke would never recover.

Serena's voice roused Sean from sulking. "Sean, what are *we* going to do? I can tell Melody how Clarke pushed Luke into a corner last year, but I don't know if that will be enough to make her call off the wedding."

Sean was fully alert at that point. He reached across the table, and gripped Serena's arm "Serena, you've got to make Melody understand." His eyes flickered in jeopardy. "No matter what happens, she *can't* marry that man. He's all wrong for her."

"She'll hate me if I ruin this chance for her, and she'll probably never forgive me." Tears shone in Serena's eyes.

"Serena, she'll be grateful you stopped her from marrying a cold, calculating monster. You've got to let her know what he did to Luke. If you explain to her how Clarke used Luke's family's vulnerability against him, it will be a total game-changer."

"What if she doesn't believe me, Sean? I've made no secret of the fact that Clarke isn't my favorite person. My heart dipped down to the floor, when she showed me the ring he put on her finger."

"Serena, I can be there with you when you talk to her. Whatever the case, she just *can't* marry that man." Sean's expression was pleading, as he searched Serena's eyes.

Serena was still trying to process everything she'd just learned. She was confused, but she knew Sean was absolutely right. She *had* to tell Melody how ruthless Clarke was. He'd made it impossible for Luke to stay in Sands Port.

"I just hope she believes me and leaves Clarke alone."
Serena frowned in concern. "I worry that even if Melody ends the
relationship, Clarke won't leave *her* alone."

"Luke and I will handle that part," Sean said plainly. "If he
gives her a hard time, we'll be forced to step in. So, don't worry."
Sean reached for Serena's hand. "Your part is to make sure Melody
knows how much Luke loves her, and that he would do anything in
his power to set things straight."

Tears escaped the corners of Serena's eyes. She swallowed
the chunk lodged in her throat and nodded compliantly. "She's
never stopped loving him. It'll mean everything to Melody to know
that Luke has never stopped loving *her*. Thank you, Sean." Serena
set her free hand on Sean's. "And, thanks for offering to back me up
on this. Hopefully, all you've just told me will change everything. I
can only hope Melody doesn't hate me for telling her these things
just days before her wedding."

Sean nodded affirmatively. "She'll be grateful you stopped
her from marrying a man who has no conscience and no personal
integrity. I doubt that Melody will want to marry a man who thought
so little of her feelings that he forced his way into her life…" Again,
Sean pulled back before making any more unnecessary disclosures.

"You're right. It's the only way." Serena smiled through the
tears. "Thank you," she acquiesced. "I'm so glad I ran into you
today."

"I am too." Tears glimmered in Sean's eyes. "I've been
living with this secret for far too long," his voice broke. "I'm so
sorry I couldn't…"

"It's all right, Sean. I get it now." Serena gave him a
sympathetic look. She hoped that Sean would be able to let go of the
guilt he'd carried around for months.

Serena and Sean talked through the entire matter. Both of
them concluded that it was best to tell Melody right away. They *had*
to stop her before she made the worst mistake of her life. Melody
also had to know that the faith she'd placed in Luke had been totally
on point. Luke hadn't failed her. He'd sacrificed his great love for

her in order to save his family. Melody had to know that she had a choice.

***

Serena wrung her hands, and nervously paced in her living room. She settled in front of the expansive bay window. Drawing back the curtains, she stared outside, and fretfully bit her bottom lip. She wasn't sure how to tell Melody about Clarke's wager with Luke. Melody would be by any minute with her matron of honor gown. Melody had picked out the dress for her, and Serena hadn't argued. Melody was excited about the gown, the makeup and jewelry. However, Serena couldn't have felt any less disconnected from her best friend's wedding.

It was high time Melody knew the truth about Luke's sudden departure from Sands Port. Bumping into Sean earlier on had changed everything. Serena had consternations about telling Melody, but time was of the essence, and she could no longer put it off. Serena prayed for God's wisdom, and for discretion, when she told Melody that the man she was about to marry, had run the man she loved out of town.

Serena had always sensed something seedy about Clarke. However, she'd never quite grasped why she'd always felt so ill at ease around him, even if he seemed to be the epitome of polished and cosmopolitan. There was another reason why Serena knew she had to bring Melody up to speed. Dane had just come home from a business trip in Denver, and he'd learned even more disturbing news about Clarke. Dane had met an entrepreneur at a business conference. The man's name was Edgar Steele. Dane and Edgar had talked for a while. Apparently, there had been an incident, which had resulted in the death of Edgar's good friend, Arthur Banks.

Arthur had died a year ago from complications linked to liver damage. Allegedly, prior to his death, the man had been on a generic form of a popular medication manufactured by Vale Corp

Pharmaceuticals. A key side effects of the drug was high enzyme levels. And so, the man had been yellower than a piece of copier paper right before he'd died.

When Dane told Edgar that his dear friend was engaged to marry Clarke Vale, Edgar had asked Dane to check on Vale Corp's history of lawsuits, past and currently set in place. Edgar also told Dane that Arthur Banks knew Clarke Vale and his *friend* Darien Stiles.

So, out of concern for Melody, Dane had questioned Edgar extensively about Clarke. What Edgar told Dane was both sobering and alarming. Clarke Vale was nothing but a mafia lord in covert. There had been so many underground drug deals out in Central American, the Philippines and in the Caribbean. Moreover, there were inflated prices for some of their medications in the poorest sectors of those countries.

Every time Clarke's name was implicated in a libelous suit, someone else always wound up taking the fall. And, Clarke himself, always came up smelling like roses. In addition, anyone who challenged him either disappeared, or were silenced by monetary settlements. There were also lots of payoffs to wealthy underground dealers, who used Vale Corp's drugs for their illegal practices. Serena had nearly passed out when Dane had explained the matter.

Dane had to stop at some point, because Serena was so distraught. Now, she was a bit more composed. Her voice no longer wavered. Serena considered it her personal responsibility to stop Melody from marrying Clarke Vale. All the same, things seemed to be going from bad to worse.

She felt guilty because she'd encouraged Melody to go out with Clarke after Luke had broken her heart. There was so much regret and shame there. Serena grasped just what a huge mistake she'd made by not telling Melody to steer clear of the man. Contrarily, Serena assented to the fact that Melody had made the right judgment call by kicking Darien Stiles to the curb. All the same, how could Melody know that she was jumping out of the frying pan and into the fire?

If anything happened to Melody, Serena knew she wouldn't

be able to forgive herself. Maybe, it was too little too late, but Melody had to be warned about her fiancé. Melody had to see Clarke for the cold, cruel, calculating and selfish monster he truly was. Serena determined to only tell Melody about Clarke's payoff to Luke. She didn't think Melody needed to hear about Clarke's criminal involvements. Serena prayed that the truth would be enough to make Melody rethink her decision, and to call off the wedding.

"Hey, baby." Dane found his wife staring blankly out the window. Tears were in Serena's eyes, and she couldn't stop shaking. Dane gently directed her to face himself. He collected her in his arms, and held her comfortingly. "It's okay, honey. It's all going to be all right. I promise." He pressed a kiss to her forehead.

Serena broke down in his arms again. "What am I going to tell her, Dane? Melody's going to be devastated, but we've got to get her away from Clarke. What if he winds up hurting her?" Serena pulled away to look into her husband's eyes. She rested her hands on his chest so that she wouldn't falter.

Tears shone in Dane's eyes to see his wife so upset. "We're going to find a way, honey. We *will* get Melody away from him, but we have to be extremely cautious. Vale's shrewd and he doesn't mess around. Word has it that every woman who's ever walked away-or tried to… Well, they're no longer around to talk." Dane rubbed caringly on Serena's shoulders.

"She doesn't deserve this, Dane." Serena shook her head in dismay. "I didn't think things could get any worse. She falls in love with Luke, then *Clarke* uses Luke's family's financial troubles against him. So, Luke winds up leaving her…and now *this*."

Serena scowled in misery. "I feel directly responsible, Dane. I had my suspicions about Clarke. I always got the sense that he wasn't right for her, but I *didn't* discourage her from going out with him. Not only is he not *right* for Melody, but he's downright evil. Lord, why is this happening to Melody? She trusts you with her whole heart." Serena sobbed.

Dane held his wife acquisitively, and tried to pacify. "Baby, everyone picks up negative vibes. However, it's a totally different story to have those feelings validated. You had no way of knowing, sweetheart. So, please stop blaming yourself. That's not going to get us anywhere right now. We have to do everything we can to protect Melody." Dane made Serena look at him. "Okay, baby?"

Serena nodded. She buried her head in her husband's chest, and tried to take heart. The two prayed together. They direly needed God's wisdom and strength. There had to be a way to break things down to Melody without detailing too much. What Clarke did to Luke last year would be enough to break Melody's heart.

"I don't know why this is happening. Believe me, I wish I had the answers but I don't." Dane cupped Serena's chin. "What we *do* know is that Mel is going to be here any minute. Melody's strong, and she has her faith. So, God's got her. Is there any way of contacting Luke?"

Serena pulled away to connect to Dane's eyes. "Luke's still out in Virginia, but Sean's in town. He said we could call on him if we needed to."

"If we *do* need Sean, we will bring him into the mix. But for now, *we* need to figure this out on our own." Dane grasped Serena by the shoulders in sustenance. "You and I have got this, and we will walk Melody through it."

Serena acquiesced and nodded. "Okay... But do we *have* to tell her that Clarke and Darien are friends and working associates? That will kill her."

Dane sighed, and looked away for a moment. "Baby, listen to me. I know you're trying to protect Melody by not telling her about Clarke's criminal activities, but between you and me, I think Melody should know it all. She has to know that Clarke and Darien are tied into the same criminal ring. It's quite possible that Clarke and Darien forged a plan for her. Maybe, Clarke *asked* Darien to step aside, so that he could have Melody for himself," Dane speculated. "Whatever the case, we can't keep that from Mel."

Serena acceded. "You're right. As much as I hate all of this..."

"I'll be with you every step of the way."

Serena grimaced in sorrow. "I'm going to need your help when I talk to Melody. I don't know what I would do if you weren't by my side."

Dane held his wife protectively. "Baby, that's the way I feel every single day. I'd be totally lost without *you*. I love you!"

"I love you more, Dane!"

Serena tried to get her bearings, because Melody would be there any minute. Her bestie would undeniably be excited about the wedding, and she had to be the bearer of horrible news. And yet, Serena knew Dane was right. Melody had to know it all in order to make a wise decision. Serena couldn't help feeling as if she'd failed Melody, by not discouraging her relationship with Clarke. So, she solemnly resolved not to fail her best friend again.

CHAPTER THREE

Luke met Sean in the restroom of a gas station in Pennsylvania. Their plan was to throw whoever had followed Luke out of Virginia off track. Luke and Sean had devised a plan, when Luke had told Sean he was being followed. They would swap clothes, then Sean would take Luke's SUV. Luke, in turn, would drive Sean's Tahoe in a completely different direction. They figured that it was one sure way of confusing Clarke Vale's lackey.

Luke would exit through the back door of the station, wearing Sean's winter green baseball cap. Then, Sean would drive around for a few miles in Luke's SUV, until he made a rest stop. Hopefully, that would throw the sleaze off Luke's trail. When Sean eventually stepped out of the SUV, the lowlife would realize he was following the wrong guy.

As planned, Luke and Sean made the switch. Luke continued east in the direction of Sands Port, Maryland. He couldn't afford to waste another minute. Melody undoubtedly needed his help. Even if he realized that she would probably never take him back, he had to do what he could to ensure her safety. She was by no means safe, because any affiliation with Clarke Vale was skirting with danger.

The plan seemed to work because the black Toyota SUV, which had followed Luke out of Virginia, suddenly vanished. Luke was grateful for this much. "I guess, Clarke needs to hire smarter guys," Luke joked over the phone with Sean.

"You *think*?" Sean shook his head inanely. "That clown's tailing *me* right now. I just pulled over on a local street and guess what? When I got back on the road again, there he was. Won't he be surprised when I stop in at a McDonald's Drive-thru, and he sees that I'm not the guy he thinks I am?" Sean chortled. "All joking aside, watch your back, Luke. Clarke's not playing any games."

Luke had passed through Rhode Island, but was now headed out to Sands Port. It felt strange not having his frisky best friend in the car with his furry head sticking out the window. Luke hated being away from Cupid, but he had to be for a while. There were so many pressing matters to handle. Luke had stopped by Arianna's the day after the honors party. He'd felt the need to apologize for his behavior at the party. Gracious as always, Arianna had apologized to him as well.

Arianna also made Luke promise to stay in touch, after he moved out to California. When Luke told her that he'd needed a sitter for Cupid, she'd offered to keep the dog for a little while, and refused to take no for an answer. Luke was immensely grateful that Arianna was doing him such a huge favor. Furthermore, she was doing an awesome job with Cupid. Whenever they Face-timed, Luke saw how happy and well-adjusted Cupid was with Arianna and her family. Luke would forever be indebted to her for such a tremendous sacrifice.

Also, Luke seeing his parents after such a long time was a total gift! True to his word, Clarke had indeed restored the old house, and it looked better than new. In fact, contractors had added additional space to the kitchen and the living room. They'd also converted the old yard shed into a walk-in apartment, as a means to generate additional income for the aging couple. Luke was both grateful and impressed by all of the work done on the house.

However, what impressed Luke the most was seeing his father again. In spite of the strained speech and feeble right hand, William Bryant was doing one hundred percent better. Luke was actually able to shake his dad's hand, and carry out a conversation. That was a lot more than he could say a year ago, after his dad had suffered the stroke. Luke was moved to tears when his dad had emphasized how proud he was of his accomplishments. William Bryant also thanked his son for the time he'd spent with them last spring. All things considered, Luke could only thank God for His faithfulness.

Luke had decided not to tell his parents about the multimillion dollar offers pending out in California. He doubted they were capable of handling such news. What he *did* tell them was that he'd been offered a very prestigious, well-paying job out in California, and that he was considering it. Gradually, he would break it down to them that they were probably never going to have to worry about money again. It was taking Luke a *minute* to process the information for himself.

His hands were full. There were still a lot of loose ends to tie up in the next few days. Those matters had to be resolved before he flew out to Burbank to accept an offer for his groundbreaking work. However, the most important matter at the moment was seeing Melody again. She had had to hear the truth from him. Luke hated that Sean had told Serena about why he'd left Sands Port. Luke felt he should have been the one to tell Melody and her friends the truth.

Luke's heart was in knots, because Melody probably knew everything. He hoped she wouldn't judge him too harshly, or label him void of integrity and scruples. However, Luke had no idea how Melody perceived him at that point. Even if she did judge him, he had to stop her from marrying Clarke Vale. The wind had gotten knocked out of Luke, when Sean had told him of Melody's plan to marry Clarke. Luke's hopes were completely dashed.

How to find a way to turn things around was something he was working on, while trying to find some modicum of hope. As much as he loved Melody, he was willing to accept the fact that *her* feelings had in all likeliness changed. Still, Luke felt it to be his responsibility to ensure she didn't marry a man without a conscience, and a murderer several times over.

Luke tussled with shame, and regret, because he'd played into Clarke's game. Both he and Melody had paid hefty prices as a result of that awful bargain. Luke felt directly responsible for putting Melody in harm's way. And now, it was time to make it right. In a matter of hours, he would be back in Sands Port, and Luke was determined to face Melody, in spite of the risks. By then, he hoped that Sean would have found a way to catch up to him.

Just five hours away from Sands Port, Luke felt confident that he'd make it. The authorities were aware that he'd been followed out of Virginia. They were also aware of the highway incident back in Virginia. However, for lack of evidence, they were unable to charge anyone for the infraction.

Luke hoped that he and Sean would have enough evidence against Clarke, by the time he reached Sands Port. This time around, there would be no scapegoats or patsies to buffer Clarke's fall.

Luke enjoyed the explosive sunset as he breezed through parts of Pennsylvania. "I know Clarke's watching every move I make. There isn't anything he wouldn't do to keep me away from Melody," Luke spoke to Sean on the phone.

"Carter already *told* you Clarke's looking to rub you out. For Clarke, getting rid of you would be all in a day's work. He wouldn't even bat an eyelash, if he ordered a hit on you, Luke," Sean told him. "Maybe, you should let *me* go and talk to Melody."

Sean was jetlagged, because he'd just gotten back from the DR. There, he'd uncovered even more damning evidence in respect to Vale Corp's shady practices. The only problem was that Clarke's victims were still too afraid to come forward.

"I can't let Clarke Vale intimidate me, Sean. And, it's high time that I spoke to Melody for myself. It's been over a year now, and it's *my* fault things got this far. She's planning to marry a murderer, and *I* handed her over to him on a silver platter." Luke shook his head in skepticism and remorse.

"Luke, you've got to stop beating yourself up about what happened. At the time, you were doing what you thought you had to in order to help your family. It wasn't your fault. You didn't know who Clarke Vale was… none of us did. He comes off clean as a whistle, and he even hob-knobs with politicians. So, he's got everyone fooled."

"If Melody gets hurt because of me…" Luke couldn't even bring himself to finish his train of thought.

"Melody's going to be just fine. You'll see." Sean sighed. "Again, I apologize for telling Serena about your bargain with Clarke before *you* got to. Keeping that secret from them was killing me. Serena's heart was broken for Melody."

"Sean, there's no need to apologize for what happened. *I* should have come clean with Melody from the outset. Maybe, things would be different if I'd told her from the beginning. Maybe, we'd have a chance right now." Luke pounded his fist angrily against the steering wheel. "Sean, it burns me to up consider how far this has gone."

"Don't worry, buddy. We'll find a way to get Melody away from him."

"I can't help thinking that she might not even talk to me. She has every reason to hate me."

"But she doesn't, Luke. Just as you haven't stopped loving her, Melody hasn't stopped loving you. You *do* get that right?" Sean kept checking the rearview for his stalker. The man was faithfully following behind him with a few cars between them.

Luke nodded, and tried to take heart. "I pray you're right."

"You *know* I am. Now, stop the pity-party, go out there and fight for your girl. The police are already aware that Clarke Vale poses a threat. So, when you get to Sands Port, promise you won't go *anywhere* without me. Clarke's ruthless."

"He's a heartless hardened criminal…and he's with *my* girl." Luke's thoughts were all over the place. There were a hundred different scenarios of all that could go wrong, but Luke tried to rule them out.

"What if she doesn't trust me anymore, Sean? I misled her and turned away."

Sean commiserated. "I know, Luke. Listen, we're going to take one step at a time. If she doesn't hear you out, then *I* will talk to her. And for the record, Luke. It doesn't matter how close you think Melody has gotten to Clarke, he's just not *you*. I remember the look on her face and in her eyes when you left. She hasn't, and she never will stop caring about you."

Luke tried to sound brave. "Okay… Okay… I have to believe that things will work out." He tried to still his drubbing heart, as he whizzed out on the highway. "Thanks, Sean. I don't know what I would have done without you this past year."

"Luke, we're brothers. It's not like you wouldn't do it for me. I got your back. Take it easy out there. Make sure you get to Sands Port in one piece. If you run into any trouble, let me know."

"I will. Thanks, man."

"I got your back. Oh, and Luke…? Don't worry about Melody. She's going to be just fine."

It hit like a ton of bricks for Luke how he'd jumped the gun by taking Clarke's offer. In a matter of days, he would be signing a multimillion dollar contract. Luke thought about how things *could* have played out, if he'd waited a few months, and had stalled the bank. He would have undoubtedly been able to keep his parent's home from going into foreclosure. He would have also been able to help his brother Branden. However, he'd panicked, and had taken the only viable option at the time.

Luke deliberated on how much it cost him. He'd paid the ultimate price, and had forfeited his heart. Still, he prayed that it wasn't too late to make Melody see just how wrong Clarke Vale was for her. Luke never imagined that things would have gone this far. As it would seem, Clarke was on the verge of getting everything he wanted. And, Luke felt as if he was about to lose the war.

Based on all he and Sean had learned, Vale Pharmaceuticals was using people in the poorer sectors of the world as guinea pigs to test out new medications. Many test subjects had died as a result of unsafe and unethical allocation of those drugs. In addition to making poor test subjects their guinea pigs, Vale Corp subsidiaries practiced selling drugs to the highest bidders in those regions.

So, those with wealth and power, could withhold medicine from those who couldn't afford to pay for them. As a means of control, they forced those in need to pay obscenely high prices. Because of compromised regulations, reps from the pharmaceutical company used the drugs as bartering tools, and sold them at inflated prices. So, in certain parts of the world, medication that could be obtained with a minimum copay in U.S. pharmacies, could potentially cost thousands of dollars. Needless to say, those unable to afford those inflated prices for themselves, or their loved ones-more often than not, were overtaken by illness. Many succumbed to death.

Luke and Sean also knew of Darien Stiles' connection to Clarke Vale. They were frat brothers, and Darien Clarke's top crony. He, along with a hosts of others were paid handsomely for their part in exploiting the poor out in the Philippines, the Caribbean and Central America. The seedier aspect of their *work*, was underground drug deals to private buyers, who used the meds to lace other drugs.

Sean had gone down to the DR and in some parts of Haiti. Some of the families whose loved ones had been murdered as a result of Vale Corp's underground activities, had come forth. Some had agreed to meet with Sean in secret, because they'd feared being targeted by members of the ring.

There were still missing pieces to the puzzle. However, Luke had enough of the pieces to conclude that Clarke Vale was a *very bad* man. All of his associations made for a nightmarish situation for anyone linked to him. Luke realized what a terrible lapse in judgment he'd made, and regretted giving Melody up, so that Clarke would have a chance with her.

But that was all about to change. Even if took the rest of his life to right his wrongs, and even if it meant sacrificing his life in the battle, Luke was resigned. Melody had to understand just how much danger she was in. The further he drove out east, the more Luke prayed for strength to face the woman he loved. Luke needed for Melody to give him a chance to set the record straight, because their lives depended on it.

***

Melody tried to focus solely on the wedding. The only thing left to do at that point was to make sure all of the bridesmaids had their gowns. Melody had Serena's matron of honor gown all prim and pretty in a garment bag, hanging on a hook in the back of her SUV. She was excited about the dress she'd chosen for her bestie.

It was a shimmering sand-colored sequined gown, and Serena would *slay* in it. Now that all of the alterations had been made, Melody couldn't wait for Serena to try it on. Being immersed with wedding details was a good thing for Melody, because it kept her from obsessing about Luke. In the quiet moments, he was all she thought about. As a result, she found herself constantly second-guessing her decision to marry Clarke.

Clarke had kept his word, and had hired the most coveted wedding planner on the planet. Misty Sims was an elite planner, who usually worked with celebrities and socialites. Melody was honored that Misty had worked so diligently in creating the dream wedding.

Because she was marrying Clarke Vale, the affair would be covered by the press. There would even be coverage from the local news stations. It was the kind of wedding Melody had always dreamed about as a little girl. However, she wasn't a little girl anymore. The wedding promised to be the biggest event of the year, but she wasn't very impressed by the impending fanfare.

Wine-tasting, picking out bridesmaid and matron of honor gowns, flowers and a cake, had kept her preoccupied. Still, in spite of the activity, Luke remained with her. Now more than ever Melody missed him. There wasn't anything she *didn't* miss about him. There were moments where the tactual sensation of his kiss was so palatable, Melody cried because she wanted to have him close.

God seemed silent those days. Melody wasn't sure what his *perfect* will was in the matter, but she trusted him to lead and guide her. Marrying a man like Clarke Vale was a once in a lifetime opportunity. No one had ever asked for her hand in marriage, so Melody was determined not to mess things up. She couldn't allow fantasies to cloud good judgment, and keep her from making a very practical decision.

Melody sighed, as she pulled up into the Hennessey's driveway. Serena and Dane's expansive house never failed to impress her. They kept the grounds immaculate, and the array of flowerbeds coming up in the garden were absolutely delightful! Melody was proud of the way her friends maintained their property. She also loved Serena and Dane to death, because they were such great people!

Admiring the house, made Melody think about house-hunting with Clarke. The plan was to buy a brand new home. Melody had agreed to live at the penthouse out in Waverly Falls for the time being. And yet, nothing was set in stone. Melody felt conflicted about the move, because she loved her house. Nonetheless, it was difficult to imagine Clarke moving into her starter ranch. There were so many decisions to make, and very little time to work with. So, Melody felt a little overwhelmed.

She smiled as she perused her shopping bags. Mischief colored her cheeks, because she'd just bought her bestie the most elegant diamond jewelry set. Melody couldn't wait to show Serena the dress and the jewelry. There was a fleeting sense of satisfaction, as Melody considered that her upcoming wedding promised to be the event of the year. She sat out in the car for a moment for a breather, after running a gazillion errands. She also took a moment to allow everything to sink in. In a couple of days, she would be Mrs. Clarke Victor Vale.

"God, my life is in your hands. *I* don't know much, but you know all things. I do believe that you will order my steps, and keep me from making a mistake." Melody choked back tears. "I love Luke, and I always will, but Luke walked away from me. It's been a year since he left…"

Tears were in Melody's eyes, because the one-year anniversary of meeting Luke out on Mooney Beach had passed. Melody laughed as she remembered how Cupid had hunted her down just to love on her. Luke had apologized up and down for Cupid's behavior, and he'd followed her up to the boardwalk. Melody was still baffled by his bold initiative to invite her out to breakfast without first asking for her phone number. Perhaps, she considered, Luke had faith that they'd see each other again. Memories of the love they shared overpowered Melody.

Nevertheless, she had to find a way to tuck in all of those feelings. There was no looking back. Her commitment was now to Clarke, and she wasn't a doubleminded woman. Sadly, she wasn't in *danger* of any infidelity to Clarke, because Luke had permanently removed himself from the equation. So, she *had* to honor her commitment to Clarke. Melody had to keep reminding herself that people seldom got what they *wanted* in life. It was enough that Clarke loved and wanted her.

Melody smiled and tried to take heart. "I'm getting married! I'm going to marry Clarke, and he adores me."

Before walking up to the Hennessey's front door, Melody tried to pull it together. She didn't want Serena and Dane to see her sad just days before the wedding. Melody gathered the garment and shopping bags in both hands, and gingerly stepped out of the car. She scurried up the walkway, stood at the Hennessey's front door, and rang the doorbell. Holding all those bags was a balancing act. So, Melody positioned herself not to drop any of the items.

Serena opened up the front door, and saw how overburdened Melody was. In addition to a thousand shopping bags, her bestie held a garment bag high up, so that it wouldn't touch the ground. "Oh my goodness, Mel, let me help you with all of this stuff." Serena took some of the items out of Melody's hands, and hauled them into the house "Did you buy out the entire mall?" Serena's smile faintly, as Melody followed her into the living room.

"That's your gown in there, Reena." Melody excitedly pointed at the garment bag. "I picked it up yesterday afternoon, and I couldn't wait to bring it over!" Melody was so giddy she bustled about like a child. "Serena, don't you want to see it?"

When Serena said nothing, Melody walked around to connect to her. Melody's enthusiasm waned seeing the dispirited expression on Serena's face. Disheartened, she dropped the garment bag to the side of the elegant ivory-colored sectional.

Serena couldn't even bring herself to look at Melody. Melody's heart thrummed in apprehension, and her face creased in dread. She took hold of Serena's shoulders. "Reena, what's wrong? You've been crying… Your eyes are all red and puffy."

Serena's listless eyes connected critically to Melody's. "We need to talk."

"Okay…" Melody nodded compliantly. "Okay, Reena, I *get* that we need to talk, but you're *really* scaring me. What's wrong?" Melody cross-examined, daunting Serena's eyes to wander.

Serena sighed, and tried to gather up her strength. She motioned for Melody to take a seat, and Serena deliberately sat down beside her. "I'm sorry, Melody. I'm really not trying to scare you, but there are some very important matters we need to discuss."

Dane stood out in the living room entryway and listened. He assented to allow his wife the chance to speak to Melody first. He would step in to support her, if she needed him to.

Tears were already in Melody's eyes, her heart whipped erratically, and her thoughts whizzed. "Did somebody die and you're not telling me?" her voice sounded warped, as if she was forced to speak while submerged in water.

"No, honey, it's nothing like that," Serena said plainly. "But, you need to hear me out."

"I'm listening, Serena. Please, just tell me what's going on." Melody tried not to panic.

"Okay… So, I ran into Sean earlier at the mall…," Serena began to say.

Melody's heart flagellated, and she was suddenly out of breath. Her face warped in shock and hurt. "You ran into Sean at the mall? I haven't seen Sean for a while. Is everything all right? Did something happen to Luke?" Tears automatically formed in Melody's eyes. "Luke *is* okay isn't he?" Her breathing grew even shallower.

Serena's eyes gleamed with fresh tears. "From what Sean and I talked about, Luke is fine. He moved out to Virginia last June."

Melody sighed in relief. "Luke's okay…" She baulked. "Wait a minute. Sean told *you* where Luke is?" Melody's expression was of both shock and hurt. "He told *you*, but he never said anything to *me*. Did he say he's known all along?" Offense emerged like crashing waves of the ocean. Melody's chest ached, as she gasped to catch her breath.

Serena held her hands out in a halting manner. "Mel, please don't get upset. Listen to me. Don't be angry with Sean. You need to hear the whole story."

Melody strove not to fall apart. Regardless, she was crushed. Sean had known of Luke's whereabouts for close to a year, and had kept it from her. The concept was too cruel to imagine. There was a fire rising up on the inside. The components of her heart which had died when Luke had left town, were now sparking back to life. Heat permeated her entire body, and it felt as if she'd be consumed by the conflagration. Melody's world was spinning. Even if she'd heard Serena's voice, she found it hard to decipher what her best friend was saying. "I don't understand." She shook her head feeling disoriented and confused.

"Mel, you have to know why Luke left last year. He wrote you that letter saying that he didn't want to go away but that he had to," Serena interpreted. "Mel, stay with me." Serena took hold of Melody's shoulders, and gave her a gentle shake. "This involves Clarke too…"

Serena disclosed how Clarke had propositioned Luke during the Bryant family's crisis. Serena tried to break things down with as much wisdom and caution as she possibly could. It was difficult to know what was going on in Melody's head, because she seemed to be in a daze.

Melody was trying to process everything Serena had just said, but she kept shaking her head in denial. "*Clarke* forced Luke out of town?" That much she was able to interpret, and tears pushed through her eyes.

"I'm afraid so, honey. That's why Luke left so suddenly. You were right by the way. Luke wouldn't have taken one red cent from Clarke. He was pushed into a corner, because his family was in trouble. In fact, Clarke offered Luke money for himself, but Luke didn't want any of it. Luke loves you so much it killed him to walk away. He did what he had to help his family, but what Clarke did was to benefit himself."

Melody closed her eyes, and kept shaking her head in disbelief. "I know Luke. Unless he was out of options, he wouldn't have accepted anything from Clarke. And, here I was thinking he left, because he didn't want to be with me. In that letter, he'd emphasized how much he didn't *want* to go," Melody murmured, with tears in her eyes.

"Why would Luke *ever* walk away, when he loves you so much? Sean says he's been miserable without you. "

"*I've* been miserable without *him*. Not having him in my life this past year has been torture. Why, Luke? You didn't have to go to Clarke. You should have come to me…," Melody considered in hindsight. "I can't believe any of this. I can't believe Clarke would do something so…"

"Reprehensible," Serena filled in. She wanted to say a lot more, but held her tongue. She had to give Melody a chance to process this new information. So, Serena would pace herself before citing Clarke's other sins.

Melody was in a world all her own. Stunned, it felt as if she couldn't seemed to get enough air to her lungs. She just kept shaking her head in utter doubt. When she *did* try to speak, her breathing was spasmodic and her words choppy. "You didn't have to go, Luke. We could have worked it out together." Melody's face wrinkled in misery. "Why didn't you come to me? We didn't have to spend an entire year apart. I haven't been the same since you went away…"

Serena felt helpless. It broke her heart to see Melody so crushed. Melody was obviously still trying to process the fact that her fiancé was the one responsible for Luke's departure. Serena had no idea how to help Melody through such an upsetting set of circumstances. "I'm so sorry, sweetie. I'm sorry to tell you all of this just days before your wedding."

"Where in Virginia does Luke live?" Melody asked, frenziedly. "I've got to see him. I judged him so harshly. I didn't know the truth. I thought he left because he thought *we* were moving too quickly. He was under so much pressure, because his family was in trouble, and I had no idea…" Melody's face warped in sorrow.

"Luke is very proud. He didn't want to ask you, or even Sean for help. He truly thought he was doing the right thing, Mel," Serena supported. "Luke moved out to *Berkshire*, and found work at another elementary school. But, Sean says he doesn't work for that school anymore. He was recently hired by a software company out there."

Melody smiled through the pain. "I'm so proud of him, Serena. He's a genius and super talented! I knew it was only a matter of time before others stumbled upon his gifts." Melody's thoughts were still scattered. Mostly, she was outraged that Clarke had thought so little of her feelings. He'd disregarded her wishes, and had forced his will on her.

His controlling behavior had cost her the most precious relationship she'd ever had. Clarke's lies had kept her and Luke apart for an entire year. Clarke had reassured her that he was capable of identifying with the pain of her breakup. However, he'd failed to tell her he was the one responsible for it.

"All along, Clarke kept telling me how sorry he was about my heartbreak. He said he understood how it felt… All this time…" Melody seethed. "*You* knew something was wrong too, Serena." Melody direly searched Serena's eyes. "You said Clarke was the reason why Luke had left town. My head was in such a fog. So, it was hard for me to see how right you were." Melody cradled her head in her hands in jeopardy. It was all she could do to keep from pulling her hairs out. Her life was now one big mess.

"*I* was only right about Clarke paying Luke off. *You* were right to assess that Luke would not have *sacrificed* what the two of you shared for monetary gain. Luke loves you so much! He's never stopped."

Melody trembled, and felt as if she would erupt like a volcano. "We were happy, Serena. We were so blessed and so in love… Clarke took all of that away." Melody was so angry she was heaving, and her thoughts were jumbled. "He destroyed the best thing in my life. And, he has the *nerve* to say he loves me?"

Melody scowled in outrage, as she stared down at the sizable engagement ring on her finger. She yanked it off, and tossed it angrily across the room. She then buried her face in her hands, and wept inconsolably.

Serena wrapped her arms around Melody, and held her in comfort. "It's okay, honey. It's all right," she hushed, "It's going to be all right."

"How could someone be so cruel? I agreed to marry him, Serena. I had no idea who he *really* was. I thought he was a decent man." Disillusionment and dread caked on Melody's face like clay. "I need to see Luke. I *have* to find him, so that I can tell him I know the truth. He doesn't have to stay away from me anymore. He doesn't have to honor any deal he made with Clarke."

Melody tugged away from Serena's grasp, and stood defiantly to her feet. Her eyes were crimson, and she felt as shaky as a wet strand of hair. "Did Sean say that Luke was coming back out to Sands Port?" Melody had a thousand questions.

Serena stood up as well, and followed Melody out to the center of the living room. "Sean and I didn't discuss that. What he did tell me was that Luke hasn't moved on because of you."

"I've got to find Clarke, and tell him that it's over."

Serena's face changed from anger to angst. "You *do* have to tell Clarke that it's over, but we don't think you should tell him right away." Terror flashed on Serena's face and in her eyes.

"What do you mean, Serena? I can't spend another minute around him. He ruined my life. He made me think his intentions were pure, while he was pulling the strings to have his way all along."

"Melody you can't…" Serena's face furrowed in dismay. It was then she realized that Melody deserved full disclosure. Serena wouldn't have wanted anyone to keep those kinds of secrets for her, if she'd been in Melody's position. So, she had to come clean with Melody.

"Serena, what's going on here?" Melody shrank back, with a bewildered expression on her face. "Why are you telling me that I can't break up with a man who's manipulated me, and has kept me away from Luke?"

Serena's face veiled in remorse. She gently and supportively took hold of Melody's shoulders. Melody would undoubtedly need all of the support in the world. "Because, Mel… There's a lot more you should know about the man you agreed to marry," Serena said demurely, as her mournful eyes searched Melody's. She pursed her lips to speak, but it was challenging. However, after a few attempts, Serena discreetly began to divulge all she'd learned about Clarke Vale and Vale Corp to her best friend.

"You're wrong, Serena," Melody argued, once she'd heard the sordid details. "I can't believe any of that." Her face shriveled in denial and hurt. "Clarke might be the lowest of the low for running Luke out of town, but he's no murderer." Tears brimmed over in her eyelids, and rolled weightily down her cheeks like mercury. Melody felt vertigo, and could no longer maintain physical equilibrium.

Serena tried to sustain her, but didn't have the strength. Melody teetered, and her body leaned heavily to one side before her legs gave way. Luckily, Dane rushed out, and caught hold of her before she crashed to the floor.

"It isn't true, Dane," Melody muttered, distraught. "Tell me none of that is true." Melody felt as if she's slipped into another realm.

Serena was grateful Dane was there to break Melody's fall. Serena herself felt totally powerless and immobilized. She was frozen, and had no clue what to do or say to make things better. She immediately regretted telling Melody about Clarke's criminal involvements. Serena was crumbling, but she had to remain strong for both Melody and Dane. Dane didn't need two floundering women on his hands.

Dane sustained Melody, and held her in his arms in comfort, while Melody sobbed with abandon. She couldn't get the world to stop spinning. "I'm so sorry, Mel. It's all right," Dane pacified, "I'm really sorry about all of it."

"It can't be true, Dane. I didn't agree to marry a *murderer*." Melody's body went limp.

"Dane, help me get Melody into the guest bedroom. She needs to rest for a minute." Serena panicked. She set her arms around Melody's waist, while Dane supported Melody by the shoulders to keep her from passing out.

"I'm fine, Serena. I'm fine. I just need to go home to figure this out," Melody disputed, seemingly still in a stupor.

"You're in no shape to drive home right now, Mel, and it's an even worse idea for you to be alone," Serena argued.

"Serena...," Melody whined, but no longer had the strength to argue. Someone had pulled the rug right from underneath her. She felt like a total invalid, as Serena and Dane led her over to the bedroom. She was too paralyzed to resist. Serena and Dane laid her on the bed, and wrapped her up in blankets.

Serena sat on the bed at Melody's side, and maternally stroked her face and hair. By then, Serena's face was veiled in dried tears. "You rest, sweetie. Don't worry about anything. It's all going to work out. I promise." Serena's eyes felt raw from crying, but she still found herself blinking back fresh tears.

"I *have* to go home, Reena. I've got to talk to Clarke..."

"Melody, you can't. You've got to continue pretending that you know absolutely nothing. Do you understand me?" Serena's face strained in conflict and alarm. "Did you hear what I said? Women who've been romantically linked to him, and defied him in one way or another, have all *mysteriously* disappeared."

"I have to talk to him, Serena." Melody scowled, shuddering. "I agreed to marry him." She kept shaking her head in the negative. "I've got to take that back."

"You *will* be able to talk to him, Mel. Just let the ongoing investigation on Clarke wrap up. Once that's done-"

"*Investigation…?*" Melody's eyes widened in shock, as if she'd never heard the word before.

"Yes, Mel. Luke and Sean have been conducting an investigation on Clarke. And in light of what Sean told me, the authorities are also watching his every move. Luke and Sean had their suspicions about Clarke from the outset. They've both been so worried about you."

Fresh tears pushed through Melody's eyes again. All she wanted was to find Luke, run into his arms, and hear him say he still loved her. But, she'd made a mess of her life. "The authorities are keeping tabs on Clarke? All this time…" Melody had a faraway expression.

"Bottom line, until *Clarke's* hand is found in the cookie jar, none of the accusations will stick. He's a master at remaining above the law."

"He's *never* been implicated, in spite of all he's done?" Melody was still trying to wrap her head around what she'd just learned. She'd agreed to marry a murderer, and her best friend kept telling her she couldn't break off their engagement. Serena had warned her not to abruptly end the relationship with Clarke. Melody screamed on the inside, but felt powerless to make a sound.

"Mel, Clarke is insanely rich. So, that kind of money and power means it's a lot easier for other people to take the fall for his crimes. We're not talking about this right now." Serena set her hand to the side of Melody's face, and stroked it fondly. "Mel, please trust me when I say to act as if nothing's changed with Clarke."

"The wedding's on Saturday, Serena," Melody coughed out. She had to make Serena see how implausible it was *not* to tell Clarke she'd changed her mind. "Reena, I've got to tell him that it's over," Melody settled.

"Yes, honey. I totally agree. You *do* have to tell Clarke it's over. But, blurting out *why* you've changed your mind, would be a mistake. You have to break it off with him cautiously. You're upset right now, Mel. So, if you talk to him, you're bound to be an emotional wreck. You need a day to yourself to process and to calm down. Then, Dane and I will drive you over to the penthouse…," Serena placated.

"You *really* think Clarke would hurt *me*?" Melody frowned in apprehension and uncertainty. However, even in the midst of the fear and confusion, she was reminded that God was still in control.

Serena's expression was of urgency. "We can't afford to take that risk, Mel. *We* will drive you over to the penthouse tomorrow. You *need* a day to yourself to process everything."

"I can't believe any of this, Serena. I can't believe how Clarke has lied to me. He drove Luke out of town, and made me think Luke had commitment issues." Melody swallowed the chunk lodged in her throat, as she quivered like a wet leaf on a rainy and windy night. "Clarke's a *murderer.*" Melody huffed and sobbed.

Serena wrapped her arms around Melody, and cried along with her. "I'm so sorry, Mel. I wish I could take it all back. I wish I could give you back the year you lost with Luke. I wish Clarke was *never* in the picture." Serena rocked Melody gently in her arms as Melody cried. Melody breathed spasmodically, as Serena tried to get her to remain calm.

"Luke…" Melody grimaced in hurt. "*He* took you away from me. I've died every day thinking you didn't want me. Luke…" Melody's hands cradled her lower abdomen.

"I've been dating a man without a conscience, who has no fear of God, and no regard for human life. God, why is this happening? How could things go so wrong for me? Lord, I trusted you every step of the way. How did things get so off course?" Melody's heartbreak poured out in torrents. "Please, help me. Show me what to do. Please, help me find a way to make things right with Luke…," her voice was frayed.

Serena gently swayed Melody in her arms in pacification. "It's okay, honey. It's going to be all right. I promise. God is still in control. He will carry you through this."

"Reena…," Dane's voice was hoarse. "I made Mel a cup of

tea." He stood in the doorway of the bedroom holding a tray. He floated into the room. Walking around the bed, he gingerly set the tray on the nightstand next to Melody.

"Thank you, Dane," Melody said faintly.

"I would do anything for you, Mel. Listen, I want you to take the Tylenol and drink a little of the tea. Hopefully, you'll feel better." Dane hunched down, and pressed a kiss to Melody's forehead.

"Thank you for doing that, baby." Serena smiled at her husband through the tears. Watching Dane's interactions with Melody, confirmed what a great man God had blessed her with.

"I have your bag." Dane reached just beyond the door for Melody's pocketbook. He walked around again, and rested it to the side of the bed. "There must be at least five missed calls from Clarke." Dane's eyes shifted from his wife to Melody. "Are you ready to talk to him, Mel?"

Serena zeroed in on her best friend. "You don't have to call him back, if you're not ready."

"If I *don't* call him back, he'll know for sure something's wrong."

"Mel, if you *have* to talk to him, you can't sound angry. Remember, you're not supposed to know any of the things we told you today. Understand?" Serena's tone and expression were stern.

Melody flinched but nodded in agreement.

"Now that you know all about Clarke's past relationships, Mel, you've got to tread cautiously. Anyone who's tried to walk away from him…"

Serena's eyes flashed at Dane, to relay that he not say another word."

Dane gave her a discerning look, and agreed not to go down that road.

Melody was still in disbelief over the circumstances, but she tried to resist giving in to fear. She looked over at Serena, and then at Dane. "How did this happen? How did I *not* see Clarke for who he is? I've been so naïve." Melody pouted.

"Mel, stop. It isn't your fault. Clarke is a master manipulator, so don't you go beating yourself up over this. God is showing you who he is *now*, so that you don't make the biggest mistake of your life. God is also showing you why this man-no matter how many times he's attended church with you in the past few months-is not his will for your life."

"Melody, you don't have to worry. Serena and I will be closer to you than your own shadow. We won't let anyone hurt you," Dane avowed.

Melody buried her face in her hands in an effort to shut out the world. She had to find a way to acclimate to her new set of miseries. Now more than ever, she wanted to take a flight out to Virginia to see Luke. She craved the sensation of his immuring arms around her. However, she had to step back in order to process the fact that her fiancé, was nothing more than a glorified mafia lord. The level of Clarke's depravity was staring her in the face. Clarke was indeed a monster, if he'd compelled Luke to choose between loving her and helping his family.

Serena and Dane stood by refusing to leave Melody alone. Serena held Melody in her arms, until she was certain Melody was strong enough not to fall apart again. At Dane's request, Melody took the pills, and drank a bit of the herb tea. After a while, she lost the power to cry, and surrendered her weary head to the pillow propped up to her back.

"Is there anything I can get for you, honey?" Serena stared sympathetically at Melody.

Melody shook her head contrarily. "No. I'm okay."

Just then, Melody's cell phone rang, sending shockwaves throughout the entire room. Melody froze as she stared at the object.

Serena grabbed the phone from off of the nightstand, and

confirmed that it was Clarke. "You don't have to talk to him right now, Mel," she whispered.

"I'll handle this one, Reena." Melody sat up on the bed, and Serena handed her the ringing phone. Dane stood to the side, and watched on anxiously. Melody's face stretched into an unnatural smile, as she tried to work up the courage to speak to her *fiancé*. Her heart lashed in terror. "Clarke...?" her voice pealed like tiny bells.

"Where have you been, Pretty Lady? I've been calling you for hours. I was really getting worried for a minute there."

"Clarke, I'm so sorry. I've been running around all day tying up loose ends for the wedding." Melody tried to sound energetic, but knew she was probably failing miserably. "I didn't get a chance to even *look* at the phone until now. I'm so sorry."

"It's okay, baby. All that matters to me is that you're all right. I couldn't stand it if anything happened to you."

"I'm fine, Clarke. Just a little tired from everything...," Melody said, with a little more strength. She warily looked from Serena to Dane. *They* were even more engaged in her phone conversation than she was.

"Baby, I hired Misty, because I didn't want you stressing yourself out before the wedding. I want you nice and rested, pretty lady."

"Okay, Clarke. I promise to stop rushing around. I'm just really tire-"

"I miss you so much! Do you miss me? I just want to feel you in my arms right now," Clarke coaxed. "Can I come over tonight...just one kiss...?"

Melody laughed in irony and shock, but tried not to sound too freaked out. "Clarke," she put on her best siren voice, "I will come by in the morning. Maybe, we can do breakfast if you're not too busy."

"Okay, baby. I understand that you're tired. I can't be too selfish. After all, in just a matter of hours, you'll be all mine."

"Right...," Melody's tried to keep her voice from wavering. Her face was a mask of misery, but she feigned total aplomb with Clarke. "Breakfast it is..."

Clarke sighed. "On Saturday night, you're all mine, Melody. I feel as if my fondest dream is about to come true. I'm about to marry the most beautiful woman in the world!"

Melody laughed nervously. "You're so dramatic. I'm *all right*, Clarke."

"You *are* the most beautiful creature I've ever laid eyes on, and don't you ever forget that!"

"I won't," Melody squeaked. Tears rolled down her cheeks. Dane and Serena hovered protectively over her, as she exchanged words on the phone with Clarke.

"You sure I can't come over?"

It occurred to Melody that Clarke was probably under the impression that she was at home. She was puzzled, because she was almost certain he followed her every move. Or maybe, he just *wanted* her to think he thought she was at home. Melody concluded not to offer up any unnecessary information. "Can I offer you a raincheck?"

"I will go with whatever you want, baby doll. And, Mel...?"

"Yes, *honey*?" Melody squirmed.

"I love you!"

"Me too, Clarke," she said generically, cringing.

"Pleasant dreams, my love."

"Pleasant dreams, Clarke." Melody shut down the phone, but couldn't stop shuddering. Her chest rose and fell violently. Her breathing was labored, as the tears started up again.

Serena encouraged her to try to get some rest. She stroked Melody's hair and brushed caringly on her arms. Serena had no clue what to say to her dearest friend. All she could do was to cry along with Melody, until their strength was spent. Serena hated that Clarke Vale was even a part of their lives. She prayed over Melody, and petitioned God's wisdom, strength and protection. She comforted and quieted Melody until Melody fell asleep.

It was just after 11 pm when Serena dimmed the lights in the guest bedroom. Melody had been asleep for quite a while now, and Serena had stopped in to check in one last time. She gently adjusted the comforter over Melody before shutting the bedroom door. Serena veered in the direction of her bedroom to join her husband. She'd been under the impression that Dane was already asleep. However, she found him waiting for her out in the hallway.

Serena didn't need to say anything at all, because her husband undoubtedly understood. Dane pulled her into his arms, and crushed her to himself. In Dane's secure grasp, Serena was able to release the crippling fear she'd tried to conceal from her best friend. Dane pacified and quieted her in the same way she'd done for Melody. Dane also didn't need to say a word. He just guided Serena over to their bedroom. They slipped into bed, and held each other in silence. It had been one the hardest few hours they'd ever faced together.

Melody's eyes sprang open. She sat up on the bed, gasping for air, after having one of the worst nightmares. She squinted her eyes in the dimly-lit room, as she tried to decipher her surroundings. It was then it occurred to her that she was indeed living out her worst nightmare. She was over at Serena and Dane's in their guest bedroom. Hours ago, she'd learned that Clarke had forced Luke to leave Sands Port. Moreover, Clarke was using his pharmaceutical company to exploit the poor, and to support illegal drug trafficking in third-world countries. However, the most defamatory aspect of Clarke's sins, was that he was a murderer. Not only had he himself killed before, but he'd probably ordered hits on countless people.

Internalizing who Clarke *really* was sickened Melody to the core. She and Clarke had gotten close. They'd touched, kissed, and she'd agreed to meet him at the altar in a wedding gown. Melody winced, and she was tremoring again. However, this was hardly the time for self-pity, or to play the victim. She had to take action as quickly as possible.

Melody thought about calling Sean. However, when she looked over at the alarm clock at her bedside, it indicated 12:20 a.m. So, it was a little late to call, or text Sean to ask for Luke's phone number and address. What Melody wanted was to run away, and to find Luke. And yet, she was completely aware of the dangerous implications of contacting him. There was no telling what Clarke would do, if Luke returned to Sands Port.

Furthermore, Melody grasped that *she* would also be in danger if she tried to reconnect to Luke. There was trouble on every side. Whatever the case, she refused to put Luke in a position that meant he had to deal with Clarke Vale. Melody couldn't even consider a reconciliation with the man she loved, until the matter with Clarke was settled.

Still, she couldn't give in to self-pity. And, in the interim, there had to be something she *could* do to free herself from her illicit involvement with Clarke.

"God, I thank you for showing me the truth about what happened with Luke last year. I judged him so harshly-not realizing that he would have never intentionally hurt me. I also thank you for revealing the truth about Clarke. I've been so naïve-so trusting and now I'm in trouble. Please, make a way for me. Make a way for all of us. Clarke is dangerous but your word says that no weapon formed against your children shall prosper. (Isaiah 54:17).

"Please protect Luke out in Virginia, and relay to him in one way or another that I've never stopped loving him. Even now, I just want to go to him, but I know it isn't safe. I love him far too much to put him in that kind of danger. If Clarke even *suspects* that Luke reneged on their deal, he will find Luke and hurt him."

Melody's face contorted in distress. "I can't let that happen. I can't allow this man to go on hurting, manipulating and murdering innocent people. Show me what to do," Melody prayed.

After pouring her heart out to God, she pushed back the covers and jumped out of bed. Silently, she moved around to set things in order. The room's lighting was faint, but Melody noticed that Serena and Dane had set her pocketbook and her phone on the nightstand. Lifting the pocketbook off of the table, revealed her sizable engagement ring. On instinct, she wanted to throw it away again. However, Melody grasped that she had to take Serena and Dane's advice. She had to play it cool, until they found a way to tie Clarke into *some* form of criminal activity.

Melody found her jacket. Serena had hung it up in the closet. Then, Melody slipped her sandals back on her feet. There was too much happening for her to sit still. The last thing she wanted was to make Serena and Dane worry about her. They wanted to be around when she confronted Clarke. However, Melody realized that time was quickly running out for her to undo her unholy bond with him. Melody slunk quietly out of the bedroom, and wandered into Serena and Dane's huge kitchen. There was an olive green key house right next to the built-in microwave.

Melody had a plan. She would borrow Serena's SUV instead of driving her own. That way, if Clarke *was* following her, the change of automobile, could possibly throw him off…at least for a minute. Perhaps, Melody figured, Clarke would recognize Serena's car by association. However, it was a chance she was willing to take.

She felt compelled to go over to the penthouse. Melody wasn't sure why, but she knew she had to follow through. She snuck out of the house, and made it outside to the driveway. Using the car sensor, she opened up Serena's smoke-gray Lexus SUV. Accessing Google Maps from her phone, she put in the address for the Waverly Building, and silently rolled away from the Hennessey's.

CHAPTER FOUR

Melody was blocks away from Clarke's penthouse when her phone rang. Her heart lunged into her throat when she saw that it was Clarke's number. She pulled over onto a quiet street, and just stared at the phone for a moment. The object had been shoved into one of the car's cup holders. Melody's chest hammered, as the phone continued to ring. Fear crippled on the inside, and she had misgivings about answering. She'd spoken to Clarke earlier on. They'd said goodnight, and Melody had told him that she'd see him in the morning.

What could he possibly want now? It's almost one in the morning..." Melody was more than upset and decided not to answer. She could always tell Clarke she'd fallen asleep, and had missed the call entirely. She decided to let Clarke's call to go straight to voicemail. When the phone indicated one missed call and message, Melody shakily picked it up in order to listen to Clarke's message. Her grasp was so tremulous, she almost dropped the device.

Melody allowed the message to play. Her heart whisked, as she strained to hear what Clarke had to say. *"Just calling to say how much I missed you today, pretty lady. I feel as if we missed the entire day together, and that's something I hate. I want to be with you every waking moment. I realize you're probably asleep, but I just wanted you to hear this message when the sun comes up. I can't stop thinking about you, and I can't wait to have you in my arms again... Sleep well, my love...*

Clarke's voice was always resonant and soothing. He just had one of those voices, but on *that* particular morning, for the first time since she'd known him, Melody heard something different in his tone. Up until that moment, she'd been completely unaware who she was dealing with. However, what issued after Clarke's romantic message, made Melody's blood run ice cold. There was no way Clarke had meant for her to hear any of it, and she kept shaking her head in denial.

"Did you get the flight information for that coward, Carter

like I asked you to?" Clarke nefariously contrived.

*"Yeah, Mr. Vale, I got his flight information. His flight gets in later today at 8 a.m. We'll be sure to **get him** once he's off the plane. He probably won't even get to make it to baggage claim."*

"Good, because I want him eliminated. He's dead weight to me now. And, he knows way too much... He's also got to learn a very important lesson. No one double-crosses Clarke Vale."

*"We'll grab him, and take him for a nice, **long** ride. Only, it'll be the last ride he ever takes."* Debauched laughter pealed in the background, and made Melody cringe.

*"You got that right, Tom. Now, if that Luke kid manages to make it out to Sands Port, and goes anywhere near Melody, make sure you listen in on their conversation. You **did** make sure those cameras I set up over at her place are working properly like I asked you to?"*

"Yes, I did, Mr. Vale. I checked the feed, while she was out of the house. She's been out all day."

"Melody didn't go home tonight?"

"No. She's spending the night over at her girlfriend's."

"Good. So, even if Bryant comes looking for her, he won't find her at home. Listen, if he connects to Melody in any way, and there's the slightest indication she wants to take him back, see to it that you follow him when he leaves that house, and kill him. If she sends him away, we may not have to take care of him. Still, I want you to follow his every move."

"I understand, Mr. Vale. If she says she wants him back, take care of him. But, if she says it's over leave him alone...?"

Melody figured Clarke's phone must have locked up at that point. No doubt, he thought he'd ended the call to her number after having left a voicemail. Melody should not have heard Clarke's exchanges with his crony, Tom. *Why had she been made privy to their exchanges?* What a colossal error Clarke had made. But, now she was afraid he would figure out his blunder, and then come after *her.*

Melody was so jittery, she could barely touch the icons on her phone. Her fingers suddenly turned to Jell-O, and she couldn't stop the tears from spilling over in her eyelids. How on earth could this be happening? Surely, she was in a nightmare, but yet Melody knew she was wide awake. Clarke had slipped up, and had inadvertently recorded a conversation with one of his cronies on her phone.

Melody's thoughts raced, and she had no idea what to do next. It was taking a moment to internalize just how truly dangerous Clarke was. He'd killed before, and he was obviously planning to again. Melody sat in the automobile feeling like a block of ice. It felt as if her entire body had cramped up, and her limbs had fallen asleep. She was terrified to go anywhere near the penthouse at that point. She had to try to avoid Clarke at all costs, until she and her friends had enough evidence to have him put away for good.

Also, whoever *Carter* was, had to know they were planning to rub him out when the sun came up. Melody figured that Luke or Sean might know something about that. Perhaps, Dane would be able to help in that regard. Someone had to make sure to warn *Carter* that he would be apprehended, and murdered the moment his plane touched ground. Clarke had to be stopped and put away, and his murderous spree had to end.

Recounting the closeness she'd shared with Clarke in months past, made Melody cringe in disgust. She'd been in his arms, they'd kissed repeatedly, and he'd said he loved her. Melody couldn't wrap her head around his split personality. She couldn't reconcile how sweet and loving Clarke was to her, while finding a way to compartmentalize his inner mercenary.

Melody held her head in her hands in conflict, as she tried to figure out the next move. "Lord, I don't understand any of this. I don't know what to do. How am I supposed to even face this man? How could you let me get close to someone so evil? Why wasn't I able to see who he was all along? I've been so wide-eyed, and only saw what I wanted to…" Overwhelmed, Melody breathed spasmodically. She wanted to stop the emotional roller coaster, but had no idea how to.

In spite of the danger, Melody couldn't seem to suppress her instinct to go out to the penthouse. So, she took the drive over to the Waverly Building. Maybe, something would come of it. Then again, it wasn't outside of the realm of possibility that her efforts would prove to be in vain. All the same, Melody pressed on the gas, and drove away from that serene street.

Melody parked Serena's SUV a few blocks away from the Waverly Building. She jumped out of the automobile, and took to walking. She pulled her hair back, zipped up her jacket, and draped the hood over her head. It was chilly at that hour, so she picked up the pace. One block down from the building, she shifted over to one side of scenic landmark, and brushed up against the sizable evergreens. Staying near the brushes made her feel a bit more secure. Making it over to the front of the building, Melody deliberated.

What are you doing? Why are you here? Don't you know how dangerous it is being around here at this hour? I guess, there's still that part of me that wants to believe in that suave, seemingly cosmopolitan fellow who calls me 'pretty lady.' Get it through your head, Melody, he's **not** *that man. He's an evil, scheming murderer... and he wants to hurt Luke. I can't let him hurt Luke..."*

Melody wrapped her arms about her waist so that she wouldn't falter, and shakily walked up to the front door. Trying not to look suspicious, she pulled off the jacket's hood, and brushed through her hair. She took a quick peek through the set of glass doors. There was a new watchman at the desk-one Melody didn't recognize. She only knew Oliver, who usually occupied the desk during the hours whereby she'd visited. Then again, she'd never been out there so late. Melody pasted a superficial smile to her face, and geared up for the performance of a lifetime.

Confusion wrinkled the face of the middle-aged Caucasian gentleman, but he stepped away from his post and came to the door. "May I help you, Ma'am?" he asked politely.

"Yes, I'm Clarke Vale's fiancée, and I seemed to have misplaced my key."

"Oh, you must be *Melody*," the gentleman said plainly.

Bewildered, Melody asked, "Have we met?"

"No. We have not, but Mr. Vale has spoken of you. It's nice to meet you, Melody!" He smiled, and extended his hand. "I'm Miles."

"It's nice to meet you, Miles," Melody said nervously, and shook his hand.

"Is Mr. Vale expecting you? Should I tell him you're here?"

"No, that won't be necessary." Melody smiled up at him. "I wanted it to be a surprise. We're getting married on Saturday, and I'm sure you're familiar with tradition. Apparently, the groom can't see the bride twenty-four hours before the wedding." Melody gave Miles a knowing wink.

"Oh…" Miles nodded in agreement. "You don't have to say another word. I understand. Quite soon, the two of you will be newlyweds."

Melody smiled until her face hurt. "I just wanted to steal a few moments…"

"Of course…" The gentleman ushered Melody into the building without hesitation.

"Miles, may I impose on you for a favor?" Melody turned back to look at him just before he floated back over to his post at the front desk.

"Yes, of course," he gladly welcomed.

"Can you please *not* tell Mr. Vale I came by here tonight without my key? He would absolutely kill me." A chill rippled through her body upon saying those words. No doubt, Melody considered, Clarke was *capable* of doing just that. "He's told me a hundred times not to misplace it."

Miles smiled at the beautiful young lady. There was just

something about her he liked. Moreover, he couldn't fathom why such a seemingly nice girl would want anything to do with Clarke Vale. Sure, the man was insanely rich, but he was extremely arrogant and condescending. The only reason why he himself was affiliated to such a rogue, was because he was paid handsomely. He had no allegiance to Clarke Vale, and really didn't care to speak to the man-let alone disclose that his fiancée had come by the penthouse to see him after losing her key. "Your secret's safe with me, Melody."

"Thank you, Miles. I really appreciate it."

"Not a problem." He winked impishly at her.

Melody's face veiled in dread, and her heart raced, as she veered and headed for the elevator.

"Melody...?" Miles called out.

Miles' voice carried out into the lobby, and made Melody jump, as she turned to address him. It felt as if her heart would pop right out of her chest. "Y...e...s...?" She turned towards him.

"I thought you should have this." He handed her a copy of the penthouse key.

Melody sighed in relief, and she looked heavenward to thank God. "Thank you so much, Miles! Mr. Vale would *really* be mad at me if he knew I lost his-"

"Well, he's *not* going to hear it from me." He gave her a reassuring smile.

"Thank you again," Melody said in earnest. The elevator doors opened up. Melody slipped inside, and pressed the up button.

"Be careful, honey," Miles said concerned.

"I will be, Miles..."

The elevator doors shut, and conveyed her up to the floor below the penthouse. Melody would take the stairs the rest of the way up. Then, she'd slink quietly up to Clarke's place. She couldn't risk going all the way up to the penthouse. The elevator opened only feet away from Clarke's door. Melody felt shaky. Her heart flagellated like a bass drum with every step. She wasn't sure why she was even there. The last thing she needed was to run into her lethal fiancé. If Clarke found her there, she'd be in no position to explain things away.

Melody came to the top of the stairs, and pried the heavy metal door opened on the penthouse floor. She slipped quietly out into the hallway, staring anxiously about, and listening for bustle or activity. Clarke's door was just down the hall. There was a gym and spa positioned almost next door to his place. There was also a separate minibar directly across from the penthouse's door. There wasn't a physical bartender, but the fixings for a variety of drinks were refreshed on an hourly basis.

Melody was a few feet away from Clarke's place, when she heard commotion and voices beyond his door. On instinct, she scurried over to the bar. Hunching down, she stayed pinned to the corner wall, hoping not to be detected. Melody's heart thrummed so loudly the rhythm pulsed through her entire body. Once again, she quivered like wet strands of hair after a vigorous shampooing. Knowing God was with her everywhere she went, Melody prayed. He had his protective hand on her. All the same, she was beginning to see what a huge mistake she'd made by coming out there.

Nevertheless, there was no time to rethink her decision, because the voices she'd heard beyond Clarke's door were becoming more audible. The door opened up abruptly, and Clarke issued from the apartment. Stunned, Melody gasped, because she couldn't have imagined the person Clarke was keeping company with at that hour. In her position near the bar wall, she had a side view of the men. Melody's heart lurched in shock to see the second man. It was the man who'd strung her along for months. There, right in front of her, was Darien Stiles, chatting it up with Clarke.

Melody refused to react. Rather, she tried to keep her wits about her. She cupped her mouth, and hoped that the sound her initial gasp had gone under the radar. It was bizarre seeing the two men together. They were very handsome and bigger than life. It was also startling to see them both in dark dress suits at two am.

Melody wondered if either even owned a pair of jeans or wore T-shirts. Horrified, she tried to quiet herself long enough to listen to their conversation.

"Congratulations, Clarke! You're a better man than me. You won Melody's heart!" Darien's face radiated in both shrewdness and mischief.

Clarke's smile was cunning. "It's very generous of you to congratulate me, Darien-as none of it would be possible without you. No hard feelings?" Clarke's insidious expression matched Darien's.

"Look, all I did was what you asked. I stepped aside, so that *you* could have her. Easiest five million I've ever made. Melody is indeed beautiful, but there *are* others out there. I still don't understand-"

Clarke shot Darien a menacing look. "You don't *have* to understand it, Darien. I made it worth your while, didn't I?" Clarke snapped. He scowled irascibly, as his eyes knifed through Darien's.

"Sorry, boss, I didn't mean to upset you. And, yes… You definitely made it worth my while."

"Don't *ever* say a negative word about Melody again, and you better keep your mouth shut about our agreement." Clarke's eyes were lasers piercing through Darien.

Melody felt the chill from where she was balled up to that corner of the bar. She couldn't believe what she'd just heard. Clarke had *paid* Darien to step aside. It was then she realized that *Clarke* had been pulling the strings from day one. She wondered how long he'd been manipulating the circumstances to work in his favor. Fresh tears brimmed over her eyelids, and her throat felt scratchy, as she continued to listen. She was nothing but a chess piece in their power play. Clarke had paid five million dollars to have her. Melody wondered how much money it had cost Clarke to keep the Bryant family from going under.

"I'm sorry, Clarke. I didn't mean to... You know that I'll take that secret to the grave. You must really *love* this woman," Darien assessed.

Clarke didn't answer. Rather, he gave Darien a dismissive look. He neither confirmed nor denied Darien's observation. "So, you and Tom know *exactly* how you're going to dance this twostep at the airport in a few hours?" Clarke evaded.

Melody felt like an object the two men had bid on. Apparently, she'd gone to the highest bidder. Just then, she remembered that her phone was secure in the pocket of her hoodie. However, Serena's car keys were also in there. Melody had to find a way of getting the phone out of her pocket without rattling the keys. No doubt, Clarke's fixation with her would turn deadly, if he knew she was there-privy to his defamatory exchanges with Darien.

So, with wavering hands, she cautiously tried to pull the phone out of her pocket. The keys rattled just a bit. Instantly, Melody saw Darien's head whip in the other direction. He looked suspiciously around, but seemed to dismiss the notion that he'd heard something. Melody sighed in relief, and decided to try for the phone again.

She waited for the men to reengage in conversion before making a second attempt. This time around she was successful. She instantly accessed the camera icon. Melody turned on the camera, and began recording Clarke's interactions with Darien. Although, she only had a side view of the men, their faces were visible. Moving past tangled feelings of hurt, betrayal and exploitation, she went on to listen and to record.

"It'll be a walk in the park. Carter's too dense to suspect a thing. I always thought he was just a little too *nervous* to work for you," Darien joked.

Clarke didn't even flinch. "I want him gone by morning. He went out to Virginia to warn that kid Luke I was hot on his trail. Tom also *knows* what to do with *Luke Bryant*."

Darien smirked. "Is there trouble in paradise, Clarke?" Darien felt a certain sense of satisfaction. In spite of his wealth and power, Clarke had obviously failed in some way. Apparently, Melody had met this Luke kid right after *he himself* had stepped aside for Clarke. It was quite possible that Melody had even fallen in love with Luke. It was both *unsettling* and *gratifying* to see the mighty Clarke Vale vulnerable, to the point where he felt threatened by some kid. Darien thought that it served him right.

"Not that it's any of *your* business, Darien, but Melody and I are just fine. It might have taken a little while to change her mind, but make no mistake about it, the *best* man won. She loves me."

"If you're so sure of that, why do you feel the need to rub this kid out?" Darien pointed out.

Clarke smiled temperately. "I'm nothing if not *thorough*. I don't leave things up to chance. *You* of all people should know that. Now, just like I told Tommy, Luke doesn't have to get hurt, if Melody plays her cards right. If she reconnects to him, and wants to pick up where they left off, the minute he steps out of her house, he meets his maker. However, if she upholds the integrity of *our* relationship, then all is well. Luke will be too crushed to even stay in town. So, he'll pack up, and return to wherever it is he's been hiding.

"See? Any way you look at it, I win." Clark scowled insidiously.

Seeing the expression on Clarke's face, and hearing what he'd just said, Darien didn't say another word on the matter. Clarke was obviously out of his mind, so Darien wanted to drop the subject as quickly as possible.

"You *do* have what we agreed on last night?" Darien segued.

"Yes, of course I have it." Clarke reached into the inner pocket of his suit. He pulled out a cream-colored pouch, and handed it over to Darien.

No doubt, Clarke was paying Darien for his part on the hit ordered on Carter. Melody recorded the important details on her phone. She paid close attention to their exchanges before the pair shook hands and called it a night. It was actually after two in the morning at that point. Melody saw Darien turn to leave. She followed his gait all the way down to the elevator.

Now, it was just Clarke standing out in the lobby. He lingered, seemingly indecisive about going back inside the penthouse. Melody got a chance to size him up. Clarke was an *image* in his dark designer suit. He was great at creating the illusion of a proper gentleman, who enjoyed the finer things in life.

Yes, he was indeed skilled at playing the role of a man of integrity and wealth. However, he was nothing more than a street thug. Any misapprehensions Melody might have had were fading away. She would no longer be taken in by his pseudo charm and polished manners. He was a ruthless, heartless, and a controlling murderer.

In light of everything she'd just witnessed, Melody knew that God had led her to come out to the Waverly Building. It was necessary for her to be in the *know* of the nature of Clarke's relationship with Darien Stiles. It was also God's way of showing her why Darien could have never been a part of her life. Her Heavenly Father was empowering her to do what needed to be done about Clarke. Now that Melody had the closure she'd needed, she was free to go to the police with the evidence she'd accrued. Every bit of affection or fondness she'd once felt for Clarke had evanesced.

There were no more emotional hindrances. However, first and foremost, Melody had to get out of the building alive. Now more than ever she feared for her life. Clarke veered, and began ambling over to the bar. Melody immediately slumped underneath the counter. She was surprised to see how much room she had. Her heart pulsed to the point of pain, as she listened to Clarke moving about to fix himself a drink.

Melody heard him putting ice into his glass. She also deciphered him stirring something into his drink. Even if it was only a few minutes, it felt like an eternity. She held her breath until Clarke went away. Before long, Melody heard him taking steps away from the bar area. She followed his stride back over to the penthouse, and she was extremely grateful when she heard the door shut closed.

Logically, she realized Clarke was back inside of his place, but Melody was still petrified. She couldn't will her body to move from that spot. All she'd seen and heard had left her totally debilitated. She wasn't sure how long it took for her legs to work again. But, at some point, she managed to skulk silently back towards the emergency door. Pulling it open, she gingerly went down the stairs in order to make it to the floor below.

Melody didn't want Miles seeing her make a getaway. So, she purposefully created a scenario to get him to move away from the security desk. She stood right in front of the metal door leading out to the main floor, and put in a call to the front desk. Disguising her voice, she pretended to be a guest staying in the building. Melody told Miles that there was a disturbance on the third floor.

"I'll be right up, ma'am," Miles said pressingly.

It was music to Melody's ears. With the door ajar, she watched Miles secure the building's glass front doors before he rushed away.

Melody knew that she could let herself out without any trouble. No one could come in from the outside, but someone from the inside could leave without setting off an alarm. So, she glided over to the front door, cautiously undid one of the compartments, and pushed the right door open.

Rationally, she grasped that the alarm wouldn't go off, but Melody flinched all the same. The early morning air against her face felt soothing, and Melody breathed in deeply. Rushing away from the Waverly Building, Melody praised God every step of the way. Sprinting a few blocks over, she found Serena's SUV just where she'd left it.

Melody jumped into the automobile like a woman on fire, and warily shut the driver's side door. She got the car going, and rushed away from that location. Her mind was already made up. She wasn't going back over to the Hennessey's. In her estimation, it was a lot safer if Clarke thought she was in her bed asleep, and that *Serena* had taken a late night drive. Dane and Serena would be upset when they realized she'd left the house. All the same, after all she'd just witnessed, Melody knew she'd made the right call.

There were other matters to tend to. So, she would continue using Serena's truck as a decoy. Melody had to go to the police. First, she had to tell them about flight 307 scheduled to land in Sands Port at about 8 a.m. Someone had to warn *Carter* that Clarke's men would apprehend him just as soon as he got off the plane.

Moreover, Melody had to turn over the evidence she had against Clarke. Having solid evidence against Clarke was something she couldn't wrap her head around. At a red light, she took a moment to examine her phone. She checked it to ensure that she'd indeed recorded Clarke and Darien's interactions. The images and the words were clear, but the experience still felt surreal.

Melody figured that the authorities probably had their eye on Clarke for a while. So, she couldn't believe she'd gotten damning evidence against him. Melody realized she couldn't take any credit for it. God had led her to the right place at the right time. For that very reason, she had to act on the matter quickly. Clarke had evaded the law for far too long. Despite of the crippling fear she tussled with, Melody determined to take the proof she had to the police.

***

It took all of twenty minutes for Melody to pull into the parking lot of the police precinct. The locale out in Amber Woods was eerily quiet. Her hammering heart was audible, and Melody had prayed for God's strength and protection every step of the way. Taking a few deep breaths to still the whisking inward storm, she finally hopped out of the car, and careened over to the front doors of the station.

Even if activity seemed nonexistent outside of the station, the pace was quite lively on the inside. There was a police officer positioned at the front desk. He was an older Caucasian man with a head of silver hair and a boyish face. Melody marched over to the desk with as much courage as she could muster.

"May I help you, young lady?" the officer asked.

Melody's hands quavered, as she handled her phone. She

held it up as a visual. "I'm Clarke Vale's fiancée, and I think that I might have come across evidence that could be considered conspiracy…" Melody's face changed, as a result of the officer's reaction. The man appeared to be completely stupefied.

"*You're* Clarke Vale's fiancée, and you brought in evidence against him?" His face rumpled in perplexity, and he stared at Melody as if she was the main attraction at the circus. Abruptly, he stood to his feet, and rushed around the desk to connect to her.

Melody was confused when the officer put his hand on the small of her back, and began ushering her along. "*You're* his fiancée?" he asked again

"Yes, Clarke Vale and I are engaged," Melody said impatiently.

Officer Ronan guided Melody away from the front desk. "You need to come with me."

"Alright…" Melody stared all about in uncertainty.

At that point, Melody began to rethink the decision she'd made to come out to the precinct at that hour. As it would seem, dropping the name Clarke Vale had a greater impact than she'd originally assessed. It was sobering to see how others reacted whenever someone said they were tied in to Clarke. Melody felt as if she was the *only* one who'd been living in a glass bubble for the past year. Everyone seemed to know that Clarke was bad news. Melody felt like a naïve little girl, as the officer marched her through the station.

Even so, Melody had to thank God for his grace. He'd kept her from becoming a casualty of Clarke's illicit lifestyle. Officer Ronan brought her into a cramped, private room. Melody figured it was an interrogation room. She warily examined the dingy, bland light gray walls.

"Have a seat, Ms. Maxwell. I will be right back," Officer Ronan told her.

Melody didn't say a word. Rather, she nodded in compliance. Even if she herself hadn't done anything wrong, she couldn't help thinking that she'd be arrested, because of her affiliation with Clarke. She prayed for the ability to speak unwaveringly, as she obediently set down on a plain dark brown wooden chair.

There was a cold, drab feeling to this place, and it smelled of industrial-sized cleaning products. The decorator in her was always at work. Melody's eyes skimmed over how she would have tackled such a dismal looking room, in order to make it look aesthetically more appealing.

Minutes later, Officer Ronan returned with two other men. "Melody, this is Lieutenant Valentine and Sergeant Griffith."

"Hello," Melody said generically. She was leery, and prayed that she wouldn't be the one in the hot seat. It was paramount for the authorities to understand that she was in no way tied into Clarke's illegal practices. All the same, she wasn't oblivious to how things looked. No doubt, her presence there had stirred things up. It made no sense for the fiancée of a nefarious criminal to show up at a precinct in the middle of the night, stating she had evidence against him.

All three men huddled into the room and shut the door. Sergeant Griffith sat down at the table across from Melody. Lieutenant Valentine stood to the side of the table, while Officer Ronan stood by the door.

Sergeant Griffith folded his hands cautiously, as his eyes affixed to Melody's. "Ms. Maxwell, you've stated that you've come across evidence of crimes committed by your fiancé Clarke Vale?" Skepticism wrinkled his clean cut features. His pale blue eyes were a direct contrast to his dark hair.

"That's what I told Officer Ronan. Mr. Vale and I are supposed to be getting married tomorrow," Melody explained. "However, last night I discovered who he really is. Apparently, he uses his pharmaceutical corporation to…"

"We know *all* about Clarke Vale. In fact, we've been

monitoring his activities since he moved out here a year ago. His MO is to drift from one state to the next, whenever he wants to avoid bad press from action suits brought against Vale Corp. We've been trying to pin something on him for a while now, but it's been like coming up a brick wall.

"Vale has a way of always coming out squeaky clean. He has a name around here. We call him *invalable*. That means, he's both invisible and invincible. Authorities in the US and abroad have been jumping through hoops trying to get this guy." Suspicion changed Sergeant Griffith's face. "So, what's *your* stake in this? Why would you want to implicate your own fiancé the day before your wedding?"

Tears of frustration were in Melody's eyes, because they were clearly mistrustful of her. She sniffled, and wiped the tracks of tears from off of her face. "I had no idea *who* I was dealing with. I don't want anything to do with him. I came here this morning hoping that the evidence I've gathered is enough to help you to put him away for good.

"He has to be put away, so that he can't hurt anyone else. I feel like such a fool, because as it would seem, *I'm* the only one who didn't know who he truly was." Melody's eyes shone with fresh tears. She found it exacting to say another word, so she pulled her phone out from her pocket, and accessed the voicemail Clarke had unintentionally left on it. "I realize you might not trust or believe me, but there's no denying this." Melody allowed the message to play. She then showed them the video of Clarke's exchanges with Darien Stiles.

Melody sat there, and examined the three men, as they reviewed the evidence over and again. Their expressions were critical.

After reviewing the video for the umpteenth time, Sergeant Griffith addressed Officer Ronan. "Get me information on all flights coming into Baltimore/Washington International this morning. Also, have the airlines fax us a copy of the names of all the passengers on those early morning flights. We've got to make sure they don't grab this *Carter* guy."

"I'll get right on it." Officer Ronan rushed out of the room.

"Ms. Maxwell, are you sure Mr. Vale was unaware of your visit over to the Waverly Building a little while ago?"

"I was extremely cautious, but it's hard to know," Melody admitted, fighting back feelings of apprehension. It was possible Clarke *did* know she'd been over at the building. Maybe, he was waiting to *deal* with her the moment they were alone. However, Melody couldn't afford to entertain those thoughts.

Both Lieutenant Valentine and Sergeant Griffith stared at Melody incredulously.

"You're one brave young lady, Melody," Sergeant Griffith said.

"I was scared out of my wits being there. I wasn't sure what I was looking for. I just stumbled upon Clarke's conversation with Darien Stiles."

"Well, you were *very* brave,' Lieutenant Valentine emphasized. "You *really* have no idea who you've been dealing with." The lieutenant went on to share only a few accounts of murders out in the Caribbean and in Central America. They were hits suspected to be masterminded by Clarke himself.

Melody wasn't surprised at that point. She was grateful that the veil had lifted, and she could clearly see who Clarke was. "So, are you going to make sure that *Carter Stephens* is not harmed?" Melody asked, concerned. Carter Stephens was the only *Carter* who would be on Flight 307.

"We will handle the matter."

"Will you arrest Clarke and his men at that time?" Melody asked, rattled.

"No," Sergeant Griffith said.

"No? What do you mean no?" Melody's face rumpled in agitation.

"Melody, listen to me. What you have here is evidence no one has ever been able to garner against Vale. So, we need to play this out cautiously. That's why we need for you to go on pretending as if everything's just peachy. Vale has to know that you're moving forward with the wedding tomorrow afternoon. He's an extremely shrewd man. We can only apprehend him in a public setting, where he won't be able to escape as he has in the past." The sergeant's face strained in concern for Melody. However, his involvement wasn't strong enough to make his recant what he'd just told her. .

"What…?" Melody was flabbergasted and hesitant. "*I* have to keep up the pretense that we're getting married tomorrow? I don't want to go anywhere near the man after what I witnessed earlier, and you're telling me to play along?" Melody was outraged.

Sergeant Griffith set his hand on Melody's in pacification. "Melody, listen to me. We will be monitoring every move he makes. So, we're not going to let you go through with exchanging vows with the likes of Vale. The plan is to overtake him right then and there. My guess is that his *colleague* will also be there?"

"Darien Stiles is definitely *not* on our guest list, but it shouldn't be too difficult to find *him*." Melody shook her head censoriously over the matter.

"Melody, for your safety, we need for you to act as if nothing's changed. Try not to make any waves, and play along with whatever Vale says. If he suspects that you're aware of his criminal ties, it could mean a world of trouble for you." Sergeant Griffith's face wrinkled in jeopardy.

Melody grudgingly agreed. "I hate this." Her vulnerable eyes met the Sergeant's. "The thought of being anywhere near Clarke makes me feel sick to my stomach."

"Melody, you've been extremely brave, and you took a huge risk to obtain this evidence. All we're asking is for a chance to trap Vale in a public place."

"A public place like the wedding…," Melody deduced.

"A wedding is the perfect setting to bust a man, who's

evaded arrest and prosecution for decades."

"He's got to be stopped. He's hurt too many people," Melody established.

"And *you* have the power to stop him in the palm of your hand, Melody. So, can we count on you to give the performance of a lifetime?" Lieutenant Valentine asked. "We will guide you every step of the way. Even when you think you're alone with him, we will be close by." He sighed in relief, and a kind smile spread across his face. "You have no idea what you've done. You garnered solid evidence against a man we *never* thought we'd snag. Thank you." His eyes searched Melody's with hopefulness.

"I can't take any credit for it. Still, none of us will truly be safe until *I* see Clarke carried away in handcuffs." Melody's expression was militant.

"We're sorry for the runaround earlier," Sergeant Griffith offered earnestly.

"Look, I get it. I'm engaged to the man. So, it might *seem* as if I'm onboard with all his activities. I'm sorry I couldn't be more interesting. I've been such a fool..." She shook her head contrarily.

"Don't be so hard on yourself, Melody. You're dealing with an extremely smooth operator." Lieutenant Valentine rested his hand on Melody's shoulder. "But thanks to you that's all about to end."

Melody didn't say a word. Her thoughts were a million miles away. There was so much at stake, and danger at every given corner. It evaded her as to how she was going to act like everything was copasetic with Clarke. She also had to take into account the threat Clarke had made against Luke. Melody prayed that Luke would stay away, until this mess was all cleaned up.

The thought of anything happening to Luke threatened her sanity. Still, Melody resolved to trust God now more than ever. God had carried her thus far, and he wouldn't let her go now.

She also kept reminding herself that Luke was under God's

care and protection. So, she tried not to entertain the worst. Like
Sergeant Griffith and Lieutenant Valentine had said, she had to get
ready for the performance of a lifetime. That meant, she had to
focus, and not leave anything up to chance.

"Melody…?" Lieutenant Valentine tried to get the young
lady's attention for the umpteenth time.

Melody was a million miles away, but she was finally alerted
by the lieutenant's voice. He was all up in her face, and had startled
her. "I'm sorry. My head's all over the place." She finally
connected to him.

"That's understandable. Listen, honey, we're going to need
to borrow your phone for a little while."

Melody nodded in compliance. "Be my guest."

"We're also going to need for you to sign an official
statement. We're about to get started on the paperwork. So, hang
tight, while we get the documents ready."

"Sure," Melody agreed. She slid her phone over to Sergeant
Griffith without saying another word.

He rolled back in his chair, and stood to his feet. "I'll be
right back. Are you going to be okay?" Sergeant Griffith stared at
her, pertained.

Melody nodded absently. The men left her alone in the
room. Apprehension tried to creep in, and she felt shaky again.
There was so much to do, and so many loose ends to tie up. Not to
mention the fact that she owed Serena and Dane an explanation.
After all, she'd taken Serena's SUV. Melody felt as if she'd
deceived her closest friends. Even now, Melody presumed, Serena
and Dane were probably under the impression she was sound asleep
in their guest bedroom.

Half an hour later, Sergeant Griffith returned to the room
alone. He had Melody sign a number of documents. Melody gave
her official statement. When she got done, Sergeant Griffith brought
Lieutenant Valentine back as a witness.

They drilled Melody on what to expect, and how to act around Clarke. She was also reassured that they'd be keeping tabs on her at all times. Moreover, they promised to send someone out to her home in covert. This would be an expert in detecting planted recording devices. The cameras Clarke had set in place in and surrounding Melody's home, would be detrimental to their case.

Melody was leery when she stepped outside of the station. The predawn sky was clear, and the air still brisk. The sun would be up in just a little, and everyone would be about their day. However, *she* didn't know how to act as if nothing had occurred, when *everything* had changed.

Staring nervously about the precinct parking lot, Melody cradled her phone in her right hand. She was grateful to have it, because she honestly believed that the authorities would have held on to it. Wearily, she climbed into the SUV. She sighed, and took a moment to process the morning's events. Seeing the ring on her finger brought tears to her eyes. Melody sobbed and gasped until she had no more strength. Internalizing it all, seemed much too heavy a burden to bear.

She would go home and keep up the charade. Because she was driving her best friend's car, Clarke would probably think she was Serena. However, there was very little she could do to trick Clarke, once she stepped out of the car, and went into her house. There were cameras all over the place, and Melody had no idea where they were planted. All the same, driving around in Serena's car would secure the illusion for a little bit longer.

Melody tried to pull herself together before driving away from the station. Before she drove away, she dialed Serena's number. She apologized for deceiving them, and asked that they trust her for the time being. She also promised to explain things just as soon as she could. Melody kept a vigil of prayer all the way back home, because God was the only one *truly* capable of protecting them all.

CHAPTER FIVE

It was half past 4 a.m., when Melody pulled into her driveway. She was drained in every sense of the word. Listless, she stumbled into the house, and hauled into her bedroom. There, she dropped down to her knees at the foot of her bed. Melody wept in the presence of her Heavenly Father and cried out for help and strength.

"Lord, I'm sorry. I'm so sorry that I couldn't see what you were trying to tell me. I missed the mark completely with Clarke. In retrospect, you *did* tell me not to move ahead so quickly. You used Serena and others to tell me not to give up on Luke..." Melody panted. "It killed me when Luke left.

"So, I would have done anything to stifle voice of pain on the inside. But what a mistake I've made!" She shook her head contrarily. "I might have taken a detour, but Father God, please lead me back to where I'm supposed to be. Please, see me through this. Please, protect Luke. Don't let anyone hurt him... I couldn't handle that. Your word says we should trust in you when we're afraid (Psalms 56:3). Well, I'm going to trust you now. This is a very precarious set of circumstances, so I'm going to trust you to bring us all out of it safely..."

She lingered on her knees, and allowed the Spirit of God to calm her rattled mind. God was with her. He wasn't letting go, neither would he allow any of her loved ones to become casualties of Clarke Vale's crimes.

After a while, Melody got up off her knees. She had no idea if she could quiet her mind long enough to get an hour of sleep. Now that she knew that Clarke was monitoring her every move, she no longer felt comfortable being there. Melody's privacy had been violated, so it no longer felt like home.

Melody moved about the house like a total stranger. She wanted to change out of her clothes, but couldn't find the strength. So, she drifted out into the kitchen. Despite feelings of despondency, she had to feign cheerfulness. After all, Clarke was watching. She had skipped both lunch and dinner the day before, but food was the last thing on her mind. Melody grabbed a water bottle from the fridge, and tried to project a normal demeanor. Just then, the doorbell rang. She was so startled that the water bottle went crashing onto the kitchen floor, and splashed all over the place.

The hammering heart returned, and she trembled like a wet leaf on a stormy night, as she moved deliberately towards the front door. *No, it can't be Clarke. He can't be the one calling on me at this hour. What if he knows I was over at the penthouse? What if he knows I went to the police...? What if he's here to kill me? Oh God, I need your help so much right now...* Melody's limbs locked up only feet away from the front door.

Hesitant and quivering, Melody resolved not to live in fear. 2 Tim 1:7 "For God has not given us a spirit of fear, but of power and love and of a sound mind (NKJV)." God would carry her through this, and she would be stronger for it. So, with a great deal of fortitude, Melody crossed over to the front door. She undid the lock and opened it up. However, she was astonished to see the person on the other side.

For a moment she found herself stunned and speechless. Melody cupped her gaped mouth in shock, and her eyes dilated to the size of silver dollars. She wanted to speak, but words evaded her. She kept shaking her head in disbelief, but she knew she wasn't dreaming. The moment was real. *He* was real. She'd dreamt about this moment for an entire year. After all of the heartache and misery, Luke was standing at her door.

Melody had the tremors again, and fresh tears flooded her eyes as she took him in. He was even more perfect than the first time she'd seen him out him on Mooney Beach last year. His hair was highlighted, and his skin was almost olive. The tanned skin was an indication that he'd been out in the sun a lot. Luke tanned easily, and his hair was always lightened by the sun.

Also, his captivating eyes looked aqua in contrast to his coloring. In jeans and an ice-blue colored sports shirt, he was more than appealing. Luke was slightly thinner than she remembered, but that took nothing away from his toned physique. It took a great deal of restraint not to express her heart, but Melody knew she couldn't afford to revisit. She had to pretend as if she didn't care until they were out of danger.

As her eyes fastened to his, it was difficult to perceive what Luke was thinking. Remorse strained on his perfect face, and his beautiful eyes were imbued by sorrow. Luke seemed to want to say something, but the words weren't readily accessible. Melody seemed to be suffering from the same speech impediment. There were so many thoughts and impressions, it was difficult to verbalize them. Melody pursed her lips to speak, but couldn't seem to find the words.

Looking into Luke's eyes again, made Melody realize that nothing had changed. She loved him now more than ever. The past no longer seemed to matter. She just craved the tenderness of his touch, and the honey of his kisses. Instinctively, she found herself leaning into him. However, Melody reflexively pulled back, when she remembered the kind of trouble they were in.

Luke was spellbound, as he explored Melody's eyes early Friday morning. He'd face many dangers, but against the odds, he'd made it out to Sands Port. Luke had evaded and had tricked Clarke's lackeys all the way down to Maryland. Sean had risked his own neck, and had helped Luke every step of the way. Now, Luke stared yearningly into the eyes of the woman he loved more than life itself. In that moment, he knew that he would have braved anything to see her again.

After months of misery, he was seeing her angelic face. Melody's hazelnut skin was creamier than pudding, and she looked flawless in an off-white colored top and dark jeans. She had on adorable flip-flops, designed in a pattern of red and peach colored beads.

Her well-manicured toenails were painted burgundy, and her strawberry and cinnamon-streaked hair, tumbled loosely over her shoulders, and accentuated her garnet brown eyes. Melody was even more breathtaking than the day he and Cupid had found her out on the beach. And yet, Luke couldn't escape how sad she looked.

Melody's eyes were red and puffy. He knew unequivocally that she'd been crying.

Automatically, Luke moved in to touch her. However, *he* pulled back when he remembered he no longer had the right to. *He* was the one who'd walked away, and had left her alone for a year. He doubted Melody even wanted him there. Still, Luke knew he had to try. He *had* to warn her about Clarke-that was if she didn't already know. Perhaps, she would want nothing to do with him. Nevertheless, the only way Luke was going let her marry Clarke Vale, was over his dead body.

Luke tried to form words again, as he stood there gaping at Melody. It difficult to pull it together, when he was utterly fascinated and more in love than ever. He gulped nervously, and tried again. "Melody, I'm so sorry for coming over here so early," Luke said thickly. Tears of regret shimmered in his eyes. He found himself unconsciously drawing closer, because he wanted her in his arms so badly. He had to find a way to make her understand that he'd never wanted to walk away.

Melody wanted to tell Luke that what happened last spring no longer mattered. She wanted to throw her arms around him and never let go. However, just as she would have to put on a performance for Clarke, Melody knew she had to do the same for Luke. All she cared about was keeping him safe. She had to pretend not to care, even if she was inwardly jumping for joy to see him again.

Missing Luke was like spending a year on a very high elevation with thinning air. *Finally*, there was enough air, and she could breathe again. Even so, she couldn't tell him how much she loved and missed him. Not being able to touch or kiss him, was like trying to resist a magnetic pull. Worse yet, Melody had to hurt him in some way. Doing so was the only way to ensure that he'd really stay away. He couldn't be in Sands Port until it was safe. Tears glimmered in Melody's eyes, and she swallowed the chunk lodged in her throat before she jumped into her act. "What are *you* doing here?" her voice wavered.

Luke shook his head contrarily. "I needed to see you.

There's a lot I have to tell you."

"Are you serious? You disappear for an entire year. Then, you show up at my door at five in the morning on the day before my wedding, because you need to see me?" Melody's tone was full of venomous reproach. Her eyes delved into Luke's critically, but her heart sank, because she clearly saw how broken he was.

Luke's head slumped in shame, and his tan cheeks flushed. Despite feelings of mortification, he *had* to power through the pain. Luke held his hands out in a halting manner. It was his way of relaying he wasn't there to argue, and that he'd do whatever she asked. "Melody, I know I'm probably the last person you want to see. I get that I have absolutely no right to be here...not after what happened last year."

Melody didn't know if she had it in her to follow through with obliterating him. However, when the realization hit that their lives depended on it, it sparked a righteous flame on the inside. "You're right," she said in an accusatory tone. "You have *absolutely* no right to be here. What do you want?"

"I don't want anything." Melody's demeanor and her word, added yet another puncture wound to Luke's bleeding heart. "Can I come in for a minute? I'd like to talk," Luke said meekly. Even now, it took restraint not to take her in his arms.

Melody's expression was taut and unyielding, but she didn't say a word. Rather, she stepped aside and allowed him into the house. She looked both ways before shutting the front door closed. *Lord forgive me for what I'm about to do. It's the only way I know for sure that he'll be safe."*

She stepped back inside, and followed Luke into the living room. For a moment, she stood in the entryway, and just stared at him. Luke was undoubtedly edgy, as he brushed his fingers nervously through his curly bed of hair. Melody knew Luke was in habit of brushing through his hair whenever he was extremely stressed.

She hesitated for a moment. Her heart was an open sore, and she ached to decipher Luke's body in the folds of her arms.

Nevertheless, she shoved all of those feelings away for the greater good. With her arms crossed over her chest, she stared at him in contempt, feigning totally aloofness. "Can you tell me why you've come here? Why would you *ever* show up here after what you did?"

"Melody..." Luke floated over to face her. "You're right. What I did was terrible. I walked away from us. I'm not sure if you know why that happened." Tears meandered down his cheeks.

"Why don't you tell me?" Melody frowned in leeriness and recrimination.

"My family was in trouble. My parent's home was falling apart and pending foreclosure. There was a mountain of medical debts, and my brother had been laid off from his job," Luke explained. His cheeks flushed red in embarrassment to even talk of the matter out loud. "Clarke Vale offered to alleviate my family's burdens, providing I did him a small favor."

"No, I'm not hearing this..." Melody kept shaking her head in denial. She couldn't let on that she was already aware of the proposition, because Clarke was watching. She had to pretend it was the very first time she was hearing about it. "That's not right. Clarke would never...," she argued.

"Melody, *I* would *never* lie to you. Clarke agreed to take care of the family's medical worries, pay all outstanding mortgage debts and restore the house. He also promised to get Branden a job. All he asked in return was that I walk away from us." Luke's face wrinkled in indignity to relive the humiliation.

"Clarke told *you* to walk away from us?" Melody's face warped in outrage and doubt. "He propositioned you to leave me, so that I would turn to him?" Heavy tear drops teemed over in her eyelids. She looked up into Luke's face from her stupor. "Why didn't you tell me any of this? What right did you *or* Clarke have to make that kind of an agreement?"

Overwhelmed by guilt and shame, Luke momentarily closed his eyes. "You're absolutely right. It was totally unfair to you, Mel. I was desperate, and there seemed to be no other choice at the time."

"You *did* have a choice, Luke. You could have come to me. We could have worked it out together," she reproached. "If what you're saying is true, Clarke's behavior was reprehensible. *Still*, it didn't have to be the way you made it." Melody glared at Luke. She tried to turn a blind eye to his crestfallen expression. "You have any idea what you did to me?" she censured.

The tears shining in Luke's eyes, only emphasized the mask of regret he already had on his face. "I know that I hurt you, Mel. You're right. I should have come to you. I wanted to come to you, baby... I really did, but I was still dealing with so many insecurities about my financial status. I just didn't..."

"It must have been an *awful* financial burden for you, but you didn't even *try* to talk to me about it. You made the decision for both of us."

Luke nodded. "Yes, you're right. *I* made that horrible decision. At the time, I didn't realize just how selfish it was of me." His dolorous eyes searched hers. "Keeping that part of my life a secret, and walking away from you was never my intention. I was so wrong, Mel." Luke set his hands on Melody's shoulders. "I was wrong to leave you...wrong to walk away from us. What we had was the best thing in the world. It was stupid to take anything from Clarke Vale."

Melody shrugged away from Luke's addictive touch. "You didn't trust me enough to tell me the truth. You shut me out." Melody had to look away for a minute, because she couldn't bear to look into Luke's face. All she wanted was to feel his arms around her.

Luke kept shaking his head contrarily, as he tried to make Melody understand. "I was wrong on so many levels, baby. I get that you're probably never going to forgive me." He flinched. "But, I do need for you to listen to me. As much as I want you, Melody- and I always will want you, I didn't come here to try to win you back. I'm here to try to stop you from making the biggest mistake of your life. You can't marry Clarke Vale. Mel, he's not a good man."

"What are you talking about, Luke? My wedding's tomorrow afternoon. And, for the record, Clarke *is* a good man.

What he did was horrible. He might have made mistakes-"

"He used my family's misfortunes as a means of getting what he wanted. He knew I was in a desperate situation, and he preyed on that. He manipulated the circumstances, because he knew he couldn't have *you* any other way. Is that the kind of man you want to marry? Melody, please…"

At that moment, Melody realized that she was going to have to make things crystal clear. She couldn't allow Luke to say one more recriminating word against Clarke, because all of their interactions were being monitored. She had to silence him quickly. The less he spoke, the more of a chance he'd have to leave Sands Port alive. "Clarke's a perfectly great man, and he loves me. I won't have you saying one more disparaging word about the man I'm going to marry."

Luke gently grasped Melody's shoulders again. He brushed sensitively on them, because it just came so naturally. His eyes delved into hers portentously. "Melody, you don't know what you're saying. Clarke isn't the man you think he is. Please, hear me out, honey. Marrying him will be a huge mistake." Luke's face strained in hurt and frustration.

Melody fiercely shoved away from him. "Here you are telling me Clarke isn't the man I think he is…" She turned away to say what she was about to. "Well, *you're* not the man I thought you were either." Melody trembled, and perforated her own heart by saying those words. She could still feel his intuitive touch, and the desire to feel his hands on her again was overpowering.

Luke balked in shock after hearing Melody say those words. "You don't mean that, Mel. You *know* me. You know what we shared was *real.* I *love* you!"

Melody shifted back to face him. "*Do* I know you, Luke? You keep talking about how Clarke made you an offer. Granted, what he did was selfish and controlling, but I understand why he behaved that way. He felt cornered. He's not a *bad* guy. I've gotten to know him in the past few months, and he's a lot more vulnerable than people realize."

"Do you even *hear* yourself right now? Clarke is as vulnerable as a fox. Is it okay for him to take whatever he wants, and to leave a string of casualties behind? He's-"

"He might have pushed things a little too far, but at least he was there for me after…" Melody's eyes sank to the floor just then. She swallowed hard before she went on. She then decisively stared into Luke's eyes. "Clarke is the man I'm going to marry, and I *can't* have you talking that way about him," she argued.

"You asked, what kind of man *makes* an offer like Clarke did? Well, Luke, what kind of man *agrees* to take such an offer?" Melody saw how clearly crushed Luke was. He seemed lost and devastated, as he blinked back more tears.

Melody vicariously felt the sting of her words to Luke's heart. She realized how difficult it must have been for him to come out to Sands Port. And, Melody hated herself for ripping his heart out. She looked away from his pitiful expression, because it was too much to bear.

Luke gulped with a heavy heart. It was all he could do not to fall apart. He'd known that it would have been difficult to see Melody after being apart for a year. However, he was ill-prepared to handle what she was throwing at him.

In spite of the suffering, he bravely marched over to Melody and cupped chin. "You asked *me* what kind of man would agree to such an offer. Well, I'm going to tell you. It's a man who felt desperate and backed into a corner.

"It's a man who felt powerless to help his family, when they were facing financial uncertainty. That man did what he thought was best to keep his parents from losing their home," Luke's voice broke, as he stroked Melody's skin, and explored her eyes. "I've died every single day because of that awful choice. I can't see a life apart from you. I'm the kind of man who would do anything to make sure you're safe. I love you, Melody! I've never stopped."

Melody felt splintered on the inside. She wanted to tell Luke she understood the decision he'd made, and that she didn't blame him for it. She wanted him to know she'd died too when he'd left

Sands Port. However, Melody realized what had to be done. She loved Luke too much to put him in harm's way.

She couldn't even let Luke *hint* at anything having to do with Clarke's criminal involvements. It was killing her, but Melody loved Luke enough to let him go. She hoped she'd be able to undo the damage, once the dust settled. Her relentless eyes connected critically to his grim ones. "Well, *I* don't love *you* anymore, Luke."

Luke set his arms around her waist, and buried his head in her chest. He refused to let go. It was too hard, and he'd missed her to the point of insanity. "You don't mean that, Melody. Please, say you don't mean that. For me there's just no one else…" Luke sobbed into her chest. "Please, don't make me go back to living without you. It's such a dark place. We belong together. You're my honey baby. I realize how much I've hurt you. I messed up in the worst way, but please give us another chance. You *can't* marry Clarke!" Luke pleaded.

Melody yanked forcefully away in an effort to break free. "Let me go, Luke." As she tried to emancipate herself from Luke's possessive hold, she burst into tears, because the circumstances were tearing her apart.

Luke held on and refused to let go. He was ready to beg her if he had to. He just couldn't be without her anymore. "No, Mel, don't do this. Don't give up on us."

"Luke, please let me go. This isn't helping anyone. Please, stop it," she pleaded as her heart went up in flames. It was sheer torture having him this close, and not be able to show him how much she cared. She had to push him away, when being close was all she wanted.

"No, Melody. You can't marry him. I know you love me. Don't do this, baby. Please," Luke implored. His heart throbbed, and burned almost to the point of combustion.

Shakily, Melody pried herself from Luke's potent comprise. Her listless eyes transfixed to his sorrowful ones. "You need to get it through your head that we're over. We've been over for a year now. I don't love you anymore. I *love* Clarke, and we're getting married. I don't even know why you came here, because I don't want anything to do with you. Do you understand me?" Melody's face wrinkled in conflict. "I don't want you anymore, Luke.

"Whatever we *had*, ended on the day you decided to walk away. I don't love or want you. We're history. In fact, I don't even want to see your face in this town."

Melody moved away from him, and retreated to a corner of the living room. She couldn't be in close proximity to issue this final and defining blow. "The best thing you can do is to pack your bags, go away and never come back. I wouldn't even want to run into you at the supermarket or the mall. I love Clarke!"

There was a crazed expression on Melody's face, which daunted Luke to challenge her. Melody didn't know where she was drawing the strength to annihilate the man she loved. All the same, it was a powerful force she didn't even know she had. There wasn't anything she wouldn't have done to ensure his safety.

Luke shook his head contrarily. "Melody, you can't mean that."

"Oh yes I can. When you turned your back on me to play hero to your family, Clarke was the one who helped me pick up the pieces." She set her hand on her heart. "You didn't think about me...about us. So, now I've got to do what's best for *me*. I want you out of here." She pointed in the direction of the front door. "You being here will only complicate matters, and I want to put as much distance between us as I possibly can."

Stunned, Luke could hardly find the strength to speak. Up until that moment, he hadn't fully grasped the extent of Melody's bitterness. He couldn't say he blamed her. His heart was an open sore. For all intents and purposes, it was being operated on with an icepick, and without any anesthesia. It thumped and ached in a brand new way. 'You want to put as much distance...' Luke rehearsed, baffled. He kept shaking his head in disbelief. He stared courageously into Melody's eyes. "You want me to go?"

"Yes. I want you to go. And, don't you *ever* come back here looking for me." Melody turned to face the living room curtains.

She couldn't even look at Luke anymore. Having him there in her living room had brought back so many memories. It was the room where they'd first kissed. It was also where they'd shared the scrapbook, and had said I love you for the first time.

Unable to say another word, Luke tried to gather up the shards of his broken heart. Yet, he lingered there staring at Melody. His gaze was strong enough to burn a hole through her. How was he supposed to let her go? He'd scarcely survived the year without her. So, how was he supposed to survive *this*? He'd never loved anyone in the way he loved Melody. Luke hadn't allowed anyone else to get close to him. What would he do if he couldn't see her again?

Yet, even if it was destroying him, he had to respect her wishes. He loved her so much he just *had* to find a way to stop her from ruining her life. In order to protect her, Luke realized that he was going to *have* to step in. He couldn't allow her to marry a murderous mafia lord. Then, when he knew for sure that she was safe, he'd do exactly as she'd asked. He would leave Sands Port for good.

If Melody no longer loved him, there was no reason to remain in town. He wouldn't have much of a life without her in it. Luke had tasted life without her for an entire year, and it was something he never wanted to palate again.

"I'll go… I'll go, only because it's what you want, but I will never stop loving you." Luke wanted to shout. He wanted to tell her there was no way he was going to stand by, and watch her marry Clarke. However, he didn't want to upset her any further. If *he* couldn't make her see reason, maybe Serena, Dane or Sean could.

Melody wouldn't even turn to look in his direction. So, Luke mustered up the strength to walk away. Before he turned away completely, he looked over at her one last time. "Goodbye, Melody." Luke felt totally lost.

Melody stared out the window, and refused to look at him. So, he felt as hollow as an empty cardboard box. Yet, he lugged over to the front door with his quavering limbs. He let himself out and shut it behind him.

The early morning light assaulted his crimson eyes, as he walked outside. Luke felt so disoriented, he couldn't remember where he'd left his car. He walked blocks over, and managed to find it. Luke hopped into the truck, and turned the key in the ignition. He wanted to drive away, but felt too despondent to move. He thrust his head repeatedly against the steering wheel and agonized.

"God, I messed up… I messed up, and it cost me everything. She doesn't love me anymore. I didn't know it was going to be this hard. I can't live without her, and she doesn't want me. She says she loves Clarke. Help me, Lord.

"I don't know how to fix this. It's *my* fault. I left her all alone. I handed her over to this monster on a silver platter. Please, help me to make it right. Please, help me clean up the mess I've made. Seeing her again only confirms she's all I want. Please, stop the pain screaming on the inside…"

Luke prayed for God to step in, and do the things he couldn't do for himself. In spite of his dashed hopes, he was reminded of Psalms 50:15. It read: "Call upon Me in the day of trouble; I will deliver you, and you shall glorify Me." (NKJV) Luke actually found strength in those words, as he drove away from the area. He had to find Sean. It still took a minute for him to process that his greatest fear had become a reality. He'd lost Melody for good.

Melody was numb while standing in front of the living room windows. The sun pierced through the curtains, and assailed her tear-filled eyes. She couldn't believe what had just occurred. It still felt like an out of body experience. She kept shaking her head in denial about the circumstances. How on earth had she just taken a hammer to the heart of the man she loved? Had it actually happened? Melody couldn't escape Luke's crushed expression and doleful eyes. The image still stabbed at her heart.

Reliving the moment Luke had taken her in his arms, and refused to let go, tormented Melody. The tears flowed ceaselessly down her cheeks, as she moved away from the living room. She had to keep reminding herself that Clarke was watching her every move. So, she couldn't even allow herself to be distraught over breaking Luke's heart. Melody had to act as if everything was just *great*, and pretend to be totally in love with a murderer several times over. She also had to feign excitement about their upcoming wedding.

Melody shifted deliberately about the house, and wandered into her bedroom. She shut the door. Not having the strength to do much else, she had to find a safe place to cry. She changed out of her clothes, and put on a comfortable pair of sweats and a T-shirt. She then went into the closet, and pulled out one of her favorite comforters. It was by no means cold, but she felt chilly, and kept shivering like a stray dog outside on a frigid winter night. She threw the comforter over her blankets, and pulled them back

Melody slipped quietly into bed, and took cover under the blankets and the comforter. She lounged there spiritless and trembling. It was in the quietness and shadows of this immuring cave, she was able to allow herself to weep with abandon. She couldn't have fathomed hurting even more profoundly than on the day Luke had left Sands Port, but Melody was wrong.

The heartache was so crippling, she felt like a wounded animal screaming out in the middle of the forest. No matter how loudly she cried, no one could hear. Melody couldn't seem to find any words, neither was she able to draw enough strength to keep breathing. So, in an effort to self-pacify, she set her arms about her own waist, and gently rocked back and forth. "Luke…" She kept repeating his name over and again. "Luke…"

***

Tom stepped out of the taxi at the airport terminal after paying the driver. He took a quick glance at this watch, and it indicated half past seven a.m. Flight 307 would be touching down on the tarmac soon enough. He and Darien would wait until Carter stepped off the plane, then they would grab him. Everything was going according to plan. Tom made his way through the crowd, and pushed towards the terminal's glass doors, but stopped short.

"Are you Thomas Haynes?"

"Who wants to know?" Thomas blustered, and scurried inside of the airport.

"Authorities-that's who," an older detective with a salt and pepper head of hair answered, while two other officers apprehended him. They B-lined Tom right out of the airport.

"You're coming with us. We have reason to believe that you're an accessory in a conspiracy to commit murder," the older detective told Thomas. "Not to mention the fact that you have a bit of a rap sheet, Mr. Haynes."

"I want to see a lawyer. You have nothing on me," Tom resisted, as they walked him over to a midnight blue sedan. In a very clandestine manner, they cuffed him and coerced him into the vehicle. "You have no right to do this to me. You haven't told me what I've done."

"I guess *conspiracy to commit murder* went right over your head. Besides, by the time we get you down to the station, we'll be able to list all of your credentials," another one of the detectives said flatly.

"I *need* my attorney."

"What you **need** is to keep your mouth shut. Look, *Tommy Boy*, you're not fooling anyone. We know why you came out here this morning, and it wasn't for a breath of fresh air," the same detective argued.

"Does the name *Clarke Vale* mean anything to you?" the older man spoke up again, as he slid into the passenger's side seat next to Thomas.

The third detective who hadn't spoken to Thomas at all, took his place behind the wheel, and slowly pulled away from the airport terminal."

"I want my lawyer," Tom bellowed, irate.

Hearing Clarke's name, was enough of a reason for Thomas to keep his mouth shut. He realized that the authorities had in some way discovered the scheduled hit on Carter Stephens. *But how on earth could they have known?* Thomas started sweating profusely, and he was frustrated that he couldn't even loosen his tie, as they drove him away from the airport.

Even so, he vowed to remain silent. Tom knew all too well that the last thing he *should* do was to implicate Clarke Vale. Falling into the hands of the authorities was a lot safer than falling into Clarke's. So, he would play it by ear, and feign coyness for as long as he could. He understood that he would in all likeliness wind up taking the fall for this one. To incriminate Clarke or Darien was like a death wish, because they were both cutthroat.

Darien looked anxiously about, as he stood at the appointed gate at Baltimore Washington International Airport. Flight 307 had landed minutes ago. All passengers were now off the plane, and Carter Stephens was nowhere to be found. "I don't see him anywhere, Clarke," Darien said, annoyed.

Clarke walked out of his bedroom in his wine-colored robe. He'd barely gotten four hours of sleep, but he'd been up for a while now. He was chomping at the bit to hear that Carter was out of the way once and for all. Clarke's face suffused to the color of his robe, as he ambled into his den with his morning coffee. "What are you talking about, Darien? What do you mean you don't see him? He was supposed to be on that flight." Clarke grimaced in rage.

"He wasn't on the flight, Clarke. I should also tell you that Tommy never showed up. I'm the only one out here," Darien informed.

"Now I *really* don't know what you're talking about," Clarke roared. "What do you mean you're out there alone? Is Tommy *looking* to be the next Carter Stephens? We talked about this, and made extensive plans. He also has my money. I paid him upfront to make sure the job got done today. You don't think he would be stupid enough to…?"

"No, Clarke. Tommy knows better than to pull a fast one on you. I haven't heard from him since earlier on. He was calling me with updates up until a couple of hours ago. So, I know he was headed over this way."

"Listen, you morons don't get paid as much money as I pay you to slip up. Now, I need for you to find out why Carter wasn't on that flight and find Tommy. Otherwise, *I'm* going to find him myself, and things could get messy. Are we clear, Darien?" Clarke growled. "I need answers, and I need them *now*. So, don't call me again until you have them."

Darien didn't even bother responding. He quietly shut down the phone. He bit his bottom lip in jeopardy, as he walked through the airport. He couldn't understand how such a failsafe plan had been botched. Carter wasn't anywhere to be found, and neither was his partner in crime. Darien *had* to come up with an explanation, as to why Tommy had pulled a no show. He needed to find Tommy, and warn him that if he didn't *pop* us soon, he'd never *pop* up anywhere else ever again. Clarke wasn't taking any prisoners.

***

Clarke was miffed, and paced agitatedly around in his den. He couldn't believe the incompetence. But something was wrong. The men he'd hired were trustworthy, and usually got the *job* done. He'd already put in the necessary phone calls in order to play damage control. No one had seen or heard from Tommy in the past few hours. Clarke had sent *people* over to Tommy's place to check to see if he was hiding out, or planning to sing like a canary to the authorities.

Clarke picked up the phone again to dial one of his associates. However, a knock to his door, made him reconsider making the call. Clarke immediately crossed over to answer.

"Your breakfast is here, Mr. Vale! Will you be taking it in your den, or would you prefer to sit out on the patio this morning?

The weather's lovely!" Mason usually served Clarke his breakfast and dinner.

Clarke's smile was elastic. "Thank you, Mason. I will have it in the den."

Mason wheeled the silver tray and cask into the den. He also poured fresh coffee into a cup, and added cream and sugar.

Clarke tried to keep a temperate expression on his face as Mason lingered. Once the older gentleman left, Clarke put in a call to another one of his people. However, he wasn't getting an answer. Clarke was frustrated for a number of reasons. Still, he had to hold it together. He was getting married. So, Retribution would need to take a back seat. Clarke shut down the phone and sighed. A genuine smile stretched across his face, when Melody came to mind.

He'd worked so hard to have her, and his hard work was finally about to pay off. Images of being with her out on the beach, with clear blue waters and stretches of silver sand on their honeymoon, temporarily took the edge off. Clarke knew exactly how, and when to deal with his enemies. However, for the time being, Melody consumed his thoughts. Making love to her for the first time was all he could think about. Clarke shook his head comically, as he considered all the hoops he'd jumped through to have her.

Clarke had even attended church, and submitted to lengthy Sunday morning sermons. Religion was a waste of time in Clarke's estimation. He'd crossed a certain line, so God no longer acknowledged him. That meant, he was far beyond saving.

However, because of Melody's faith, he'd even agreed to remain *sexually pure* until they were married. *Purity* in any form was a foreign concept to him. So, the entire situation was ironic. However, Clarke realized that his sacrifices only solidified how much he truly loved Melody. There was no way he would have gone through so much for anyone else.

"Tomorrow's your wedding day, Clarke. Lighten up. You'll deal with these buffoons after your honeymoon." He took a couple of deep breaths, and walked over to the breakfast tray. Clarke lifted the silver cask, and took a hearty bite of his Western Cheese Omelet. Soon after, he took the breakfast tray over to the small sitting area.

Clarke accessed the latest recorded feed in and surrounding Melody's home. He had to see if there had been questionable activities, since he and Melody had last spoken. It still bothered him that she'd missed a number of his calls the day before. Melody had alluded to being busy, and handling last minute details for the wedding. All the same, Clarke hated not hearing from her for hours.

Clarke detested it even more when Melody was unavailable to him. He wasn't crazy about Melody spending the night over at her best friend's. However, he was trying to tuck in his controlling tendencies. In time, Melody would come to understand that he needed to know her whereabouts at *all* times.

Clarke enjoyed his breakfast, and sipped from his coffee cup, as he accessed the video feed. He wasn't expecting anything out of the ordinary. Nevertheless, he was quite surprised when he saw Serena's SUV pull into Melody's driveway after four a.m. "What the…?" Clarke was riveted. *What was Serena doing at Melody's at that hour?* However, it didn't take very long for him to get an answer.

He saw his fiancée jump out of the gray SUV. Clarke's face was masked in confusion, as he squinted his eyes to make sure he was seeing correctly. Melody was indeed the person who'd opened up the front door, and walked into the house. Now, Clarke was perturbed. *If there was something wrong with your car, you should have called me, baby. I don't like you having to depend on anyone else.*

However, Clarke was even more put out to see how tired and stressed Melody looked, once she went inside the house. "What's the matter with my girl? She looks upset." Clarke shook his head defiantly. "I hope Bryant's got nothing to do with it, because he's just one breath away from seeing his maker." He slammed his fist angrily on the table.

Cameras had been planted in Melody's living room, in her kitchen and the work area beyond the dining room. There were a few limited access feeds throughout the rest of the house, but her bedroom and the bathroom were off limits. The next time Melody came into view was when she floated into the kitchen. Clarke watched her open up the fridge, and grab a water bottle.

"Why would you be coming home at that hour in Serena's car, Melody?" Veins pulsed at Clarke's temples, and his face reddened in irritation. "And, who's the man approaching her door? No…no… It can't be…" Clarke seethed when he recognized Luke at Melody's front door. But, where was Luke's car, and how on earth had he managed to make it to Sands Port in one piece? Clarke had pulled out all the stops so that Luke would be diverted.

Now, it dawned on Clarke why Melody had looked so stressed. Clarke hoped Luke Bryant wasn't making her life miserable. If Luke *was*, Clarke was prepared to remedy that infraction without any hesitation. Clarke took a few deep breaths in order not to lose his cool.

"Melody, why did you tell me you were in bed-too tired to have me come over?" Clarke doubted. However, when he saw Melody drop her water bottle on the kitchen floor, he rethought the matter. *She probably went over to the Hennessey's, because she was trying to get away from Luke.*

He watched Melody diffidently gravitate over to her front door. She seemed wary of opening it up, and Clarke totally identified with her angst. When Melody *did* open up the door, she looked stunned and scared. Clarke stood to his feet, and drew closer to the monitor. "I can't believe you came out here, Luke. I guess, you must have a death wish."

The way Luke Bryant stared at his fiancée, made Clarke burn in jealous indignation. At first glance, Clarke thought he saw the same awestruck expression on Melody's face. However, her expression changed rather quickly. He observed how indifferent Melody was to her former beau. She wouldn't allow him anywhere near her.

Clarke was worried when Melody finally did allow Luke into the house. But, as he continued to monitor Melody's interactions with his nemesis, he felt less threatened. A victorious smile stretched across his face. "Now, *that's* my girl! That's *my* fiancée.

I can't wait to have you all to myself tomorrow night."

Nevertheless, when Luke took Melody in his arms, Clarke felt nervous and irritated. He also didn't appreciate the way in which Luke had tried to vilify him. Clarke was, however, quite impressed by the way Melody handled herself. He was amazed to see how staunchly she'd defended him to Luke. Her loyalty made him love her all the more.

Clarke laughed uproariously when Melody pointed to the front door, after telling Luke she never wanted to see him again. It suddenly occurred to Clarke why Melody had chosen to switch cars with Serena. It was obvious that she'd done so in order to evade Luke. Perhaps, Luke had reached out to Melody to let her know that he was coming to town. Thus, the reason Melody had chosen to go over to the Hennessey's.

Clarke had it *all* figured out. "You're such a smart girl. You make me so proud, baby!" Clarke cheered when he saw Luke go through Melody's front door. He was bordering euphoria, watching Luke walk away from the house until he disappeared.

Clarke was stirred beyond words. No one else had ever championed him in the way Melody had. He kept replaying the part of the video where Melody said she loved *him*, and no longer loved Luke. "Now, I *know* for sure she loves me. I've never heard her attest to loving me so boldly. Just goes to show… If you jump through enough hoops, and make enough sacrifices, it eventually pays off."

Clarke celebrated Melody throwing Luke out of her life for good. He must have watched that part of the video a dozen times. The look of dismay on Luke's face after Melody told him to take a hike, brought about a sense of vindication. Luke was probably still *in love* with Melody. No doubt, he was devastated over her rejection. So, Clarke couldn't imagine Luke staying in Sands Port to watch the woman he loved marry another man.

Recounting Luke's dauntlessness and audacity the day he left Sands Port, only heightened Clarke's satisfaction. Luke had threatened to come after him, if Melody was in any way hurt. And now, Melody no longer loved or needed him. "I might not have to kill you after all, kid. Pulling you and Melody apart this past year, was the best decision I've ever made. Thanks for accepting the payoff."

Clarke heartily ate his breakfast. He kept rewinding the video to the part where Melody had said she loved him, and that she *no longer* wanted Luke Bryant. It was music to his ears. Lord knows, he'd waited long enough to hear those words. All the same, Melody's declaration could not have come at a better time. As of tomorrow, Melody would become his wife. Once they tied the knot, Luke Bryant would truly be a footnote in a very insignificant chapter of their lives.

Still, every rose had its thorns. Melody knew the truth regarding why Luke had left Sands Port last year. She had indeed kicked Luke out of her life. However, Clarke had no idea how Melody felt about the wager he and Luke had made last spring. All things considered, he wasn't afraid of losing her. If Melody broached the subject, Clarke planned on explaining things away, even if he had to lie. At this late stage in the game, losing Melody just wasn't an option. Whatever the case, Clarke was confident that Melody would be his, locked, stocked and barreled come Saturday night.

CHAPTER SIX

Luke sat in Sean's truck out in the parking lot of a development not too far away from Melody's house. Behind the cul-de-sac was a very posh high rise. So, Luke deemed that it was a safe place to rest until Sean showed up.

That spot was the closest he could be to Melody's house, without being considered a stalker. Through the car GPS, Luke had a view of Melody's. There seemed to be a great deal of activity outside of the house that morning. Unsettled by the flurry, Luke determined to shadow Melody's every move for the next twenty-four hours.

His heart was frayed like a worn piece of cloth, and he couldn't stop the flow of tears. Regardless, he avowed not to abandon Melody. Despite the fact that she would never forgive him, Luke couldn't budge an inch, until he knew for sure she was safe. Keeping her out of harm's way was the mission. And, if that meant making a scene at the wedding on Saturday afternoon, Luke was all up for it.

Sean had texted him about an hour ago, and had told Luke he'd made it out to Sands Port. He'd driven Luke's Lexus SUV down to the city. Luke was more than relieved that Sean was all right. He and Sean had gone through a lot trying avert Clarke's lackeys on their way down to Sands Port. And yet, Luke was so disheartened, he didn't notice when Sean pulled into a parking space not too far away from his.

"Luke, what's up, man? Why'd you ask me to meet you out here?" Sean seemed confused as he hopped into the truck, and sat next to Luke. He frowned in concern. "You okay? I know you got down here before I did. You only beat me down to the city because I had to take that annoying detour." Sean smiled waggishly, as he alluded to tripping up Clarke's men.

Sean had pulled some mischievous pranks on two of Clarke's henchmen. While the two men had stopped into a rest stop for a bite, he'd rewired their car cables. Messing with the car had set them back for hours. Sean was amazed to see how dense Clarke's employees were. He shook his head amused and laughed over the matter. However, he stopped short when he realized Luke was in a totally different headspace. Sean stared over at him pertained. "Luke, what's wrong?"

Luke swallowed the chunk lodged in his throat. He tried to speak, but was barely able to open up his mouth. And yet, in spite of the pain he felt, he had to pull it together for Melody's sake. "I saw her," he said thickly. His sad red eyes fastened to Sean's befuddled expression.

Sean hit his forehead with the base of his right palm, nonplused and irate. "Luke, you have any idea what a huge risk you took by going to see her? What if Clarke and his men were waiting for you over at her place? I told you *we* don't go anywhere near Melody, unless we're together," Sean censured.

"I'm sorry, Sean. I just couldn't stay away from her for another minute. I know I took a huge risk, but I needed to see her so badly." Luke kept shaking his head contrarily.

Sean nodded understandingly, and set his hand on Luke's arm. "Okay… So, I'm guessing things didn't go well. What happened, man?" He frowned in commiseration.

Tears blurred Luke's vision again. "She doesn't love me anymore," his voice broke. "My worst fear has become a reality." Luke brushed tears from off his face.

"No, that can't be right, Luke. Did she *say* she didn't love you?" Sean shook his head in denial.

Luke's heart was an open wound, as he relived what happened over at Melody's earlier on. All the same, he disclosed even the most harrowing aspects of their interactions, even if his heart refused to stop pulsing and bleeding.

Sean remained momentarily silent. He was both confused and saddened by Luke's experience. Luke looked like he'd just sustained the worst beating of his life. Sean couldn't remember ever seeing his buddy so crestfallen.

Even when he and Luke had reunited out in Virginia back in December of last year, and Luke had looked like the posterchild for world hunger, there was still a spark of hope that he could win Melody back. However, looking into Luke's eyes that morning, Sean realized that the tiny spark of hope they'd held onto was gone.

Even so, Sean refused to let him give up. "Luke, I *know* how much Melody loves you. I don't know why she said those things, but I've gotten to know her this year. It doesn't *sound* like Melody to judge you for helping your family." Sean held his hand up, and gestured point number one.

"Melody would also never make you feel financially incompetent. Number three, she would never...*ever* tell you she wants you to leave Sands Port, or that she wants to put as much distance between the two of you as possible."

"That's what she said, Sean. She said she wants *nothing* to do with me. *I* wasn't there for her but *Clarke* was. She told me she understands *why* Clarke put out the bribe. She understands *his* side," Luke said disconsolate, as he brushed his fingers agitatedly through his curly bed of hair. "The entire experience felt so surreal. It felt as if I was caught up in some nightmare. At any minute, I kept thinking that I'd wake up. Honestly, I can't say that I blame her. What I did-"

"Luke, what *you* did was noble. It pulled you away from the best relationship you've ever had, but you put it all on the line to give your family a fighting chance. And, I don't care what she told you. I know Melody would never make you feel bad for doing that. She might be hurt because you didn't tell her, but... Something's not right." Sean frowned in bewilderment.

"None of it is right, Sean. That's why I can't walk away. I'm worried about her. When I know for sure she's safe, then I can leave Sands Port."

"I see you're monitoring her house." Sean examined the details on the GPS. Luke had access to the activities taking place outside of Melody's.

"I can't let her out of my sight, not until we stop her from marrying that sleaze." Luke tried to shake off the sadness. His heart was broken, but it didn't matter what it cost him personally. He couldn't stand by, and watch Melody marry Clarke Vale. "I need your help, Sean." Luke's face strained in uncertainty.

A mischievous smile broke across Sean's face. "Now, *that's* my boy. We don't give up without a fight. Whatever you need, I'm your man."

"Thanks, Sean." Luke nodded. "No doubt, Clarke knows I'm in town. He probably also knows that I went by to see Melody a little while ago."

"Did you park the truck in front of Mel's?"

"No, I parked it a few blocks over and walked. I'm going to need decoys for all of today and tomorrow." Luke's thought were going.

"You mean, you need to create as much fog for Clarke and his men as you possibly can, so that they can't pin down your activities?" Sean grimaced in introspection.

Luke liked the way Sean got him. He never really needed to expound on very much for Sean to follow his train of thought. Luke had to work past the initial hurt of Melody's rejection, so that he could focus on saving her life. "I'm going to need someone to play the role of *me*- headed for the airport, boarding a plane back to Virginia. Clarke *has* to think I've completely thrown in the towel." Luke's face wrinkled in urgency as he contrived a plan.

Sean nodded with a clever smile. "Yes, I believe that can be arranged. I think I also might know just the person to pull it off. Coworker about your build…" Sean created a scenario.

Luke laughed. "So, you're going to drive this kid out to the airport in my SUV. Would you say he looks a *lot* like me?" Luke stared warily at Sean.

Sean examined Luke for a moment. "He has your build and the curly hair. We can work on the face, and even throw in a pair of shades to the mix. From the back, he looks like you. His name's Josh."

"You think Josh is up for the challenge?" Luke couldn't afford to leave anything up to chance.

Sean smiled waggishly. "He's a really cool guy. So, I'm sure he'll play along, once I tell him it's to pull the wool over the eyes of a dirt bag like Vale."

Luke suddenly felt encouraged. "That's really good to know. It *has* to be convincing, Sean."

"We'll be *so* convincing that your own mother will think it's you. Josh will be the one going through security and baggage checks. Trust me, Luke. For all intents and purposes, *you'll* be the one boarding that plane," Sean settled.

"Good... That's exactly what has to happen. I need to be free to follow Melody around without Clarke and his thugs knowing I'm still in town. I like that you get me, Sean." Luke smiled faintly.

"If *I* didn't get you, I really don't think anyone else would, Luke." Sean ruffled Luke's curly mane.

Luke laughed a bit. "You're certainly right about that, man. I'm going to call the car rental company. I'll be switching up car rentals for the next twenty-four hours or so. Clarke and his men will probably notice if *one* particular car is tailing wherever Melody goes. However, if it's a different car every time, it'll definitely throw them off. And, we've already established that Clarke's men aren't the brightest bulbs in the box."

"Yeah...no they're pretty dense." Sean nodded in agreement. "Okay, so you work on the car rental thing. How many cars are we talking about?"

"At least three for today," Luke said.

"So, you're also going to need a theatre dress kit," Sean said, only half-joking. "You'll need a few changes of clothes, a variety of hair, beard, moustache, the works..." Sean seemed absorbed by something on his phone.

Luke issued a genuine smile through the sadness. He knew that if anyone was capable of getting his hands on material like that, it was Sean. Luke was grateful Sean had thought of it. So, switching out his car rentals wouldn't be the only elements of change. There would also be a different man or *woman* behind the wheel every time.

"*Who* are you feeling like today, Luke? Are you feeling like a scraggly blond with straight bangs, or an older balding man with salt and pepper hair?" Sean's expression was waggish.

"I'm feeling about sixty-four and balding this morning," Luke bantered. "Can you work that out?"

"You bet. I'll bring some stuff over in just a little while. You can come over to the house to get into character."

"No, I can't leave my post. I have to stay put, so that I can follow whenever Melody decides to leave the house," Luke countered. "Besides, there's plenty of room to change in here. It also helps that you have tinted windows."

"So, you're already steps ahead. Just be careful…" Sean's voice trailed when he noticed Luke's eyes affixed to the GPS monitor. Apparently, something was happening over at Melody's. "What's going on?" Sean inched in closer to get a better look at the monitor for himself.

Luke's thoughts were whizzing, seeing two sizable service trucks pull into Melody's driveway.

"What's that all about?" Sean frowned, nonplused.

"Why would Melody have to service anything around the house the day before the wedding?" Suspicion and angst covered Luke's face.

"Maybe, she's thinking about selling the house, and has to have everything up to par…," Sean's voice trailed. He stopped trying to speculate on the matter. Luke was brokenhearted enough, without having to hear about Melody's future prospects.

"Maybe…," Luke said passively. He had a feeling something strange was going on over at Melody's, and he *had* to figure out what it was. However, he couldn't just run over there at every turn. So, Luke decided that as long as Melody remained secure inside the house, and Clarke was miles away, he could more or less handle the little annoyances.

Luke also had to move quickly on his idea. "So, Sean, you're holding on to the SUV, because you'll be driving Josh, alias *me*, over to the airport. I'm gonna book the next flight out to VA. If they check the names of passengers for that flight, *my* name will be on the list."

"You seemed to have covered all your bases, buddy." Sean smiled hopefully.

"I'm really trying to."

"I'm going to drive *you* out to the airport, because *you're* much too distraught over Melody's rejection to stay in Sands Port. You're also much too upset to *drive* back down to Virginia. That's why you decided to fly out instead. You've decided to leave the SUV with me, but you do plan on having it shipped down to Virginia sometime later." Sean winked.

"That's right. I'm taking the first available fight back to Virginia today, because I can't bear the thought of Melody marrying Clarke…" Luke's voice trailed, and his throat got scratchy. "I really can't you know." His face twisted in misery. "I can't stand that she's with him."

"I know, buddy… I Know…" Sean patted Luke's arm fraternally. "We're not going to let Melody marry Clarke. This **will** work."

"It has to, Sean, cause I really don't know what I'll do if it doesn't." His desperate eyes locked to Sean's.

"One way or another, we're going to stop that wedding. More importantly, we're going to stop Vale."

Luke tried to take heart. He'd prayed extensively for God's intervention in the matter. So, Luke was certain God would work it all out, and do what was best for all involved. However, for the time being, he had to continue following every move Melody made. His wounded heart belonged to her, and that would never change.

***

Melody's eyes suddenly sprung open. Only a few hours after she'd dozed off that Friday morning, she was in a cold sweat and shivering. She sat up on the bed, and gasped trying to catch her breath. Staring all about her bedroom, reality kicked in. She was currently indeed living out a nightmare. Luke had indeed returned to Sands Port after a year's time, and the impact of it all was devastating.

Taking what was left of Luke's heart, and chopping it up into tiny pieces, was also part of the horrible equation. Melody grimaced in remorse, as she buried her face in her hands. Not only was her breathing erratic, but her heart thumped. "Oh, Luke, I'm so sorry. I'm so sorry about all of it." Melody strove to pull it together, but the pain was a huge mountain staring her in the face. "I would never hurt you…never judge you. I love you so much! I'm sorry."

Melody had cried herself to sleep earlier on. So, needless to say that her quality of rest had been compromised. All the same, she was resigned to the misery, until Clarke was apprehended by the authorities and the FBI. Until that happened, she had to go on pretending she was totally in love, and couldn't wait to get married.

"God, I need your help now more than ever. Please, carry me through this and protect Luke. I told him those horrible things, so that he'd leave town. He can't be around as this mess unfolds. He would be a sure target for Clarke's rage. I only hope Luke took me at my word. I couldn't handle it if anything happened to him. Thank you for the gift of seeing him after all this time.

"Seeing him again, only validated the fact that I could never stay angry with him. He's so wonderful, and I love him even more now. But, I can't sit around here feeling sorry for myself. I've got to push forward. Clarke's got to be apprehended for all the pain he's caused."

Melody pushed back her blankets, and inched slowly towards the edge of the bed. Up until that very moment, she hadn't factored in just how truly exhausted she was. She lingered there for a moment, and tried to quiet her mind. So much had to be done to keep her from exchanging vows with Clarke tomorrow afternoon.

Her phone's ringtone sounded shrill. Melody was immediately on the defensive, because Clarke's name and his face were magnified on her lock screen. Her heart instantly began thrumming, but Melody strove to collect herself. She had to get into performance mode, and be good enough to win an Oscar. The lives of her friends, and loved ones were at stake. Melody willed her hands to stop shaking, as she handled the device. A fake smile stretched across her face. It was an effort at exuding joy, in spite of the sorrow she tussled with. "Good morning, handsome!" Melody said as pertly as she could.

"Good morning, Pretty Lady!" Clarke's voice resonated. It was richer than a chocolate milkshake.

"And, how are *you* doing this morning, Mr. Vale?" Melody's stomach plunged in disgust, but she powered through feelings of malaise.

"Much better *now* that I am talking to my *wife*."

"Not so fast, my love. The wedding's tomorrow," she quickly reminded.

"I know, baby. I guess, it just can't happen fast enough. I missed you so much yesterday. I was worried."

"Were you? Why were you worried about me?" Melody began to get into the groove of her performance. Melody perceived that she could successfully keep up the act, as long as Clarke remained at bay. She had no idea how she'd be able to keep up the act, if and when Clarke tried to touch her. However, that was a bridge she'd cross when she got to it.

"I was worried. You *never* take so long to call me back, baby. I don't like not hearing from you, or knowing where you are. Is everything okay?" Clarke wanted to see whether or not Melody would come clean about Luke Bryant's visit.

Melody assented to the fact that Clarke was aware of Luke's visit. Furthermore, Clarke definitely knew that she and Luke had talked about their wager last spring. So, Melody was within her rights to be angry with him. That meant, she had a legitimate reason to discourage any PDA's. Nevertheless, it was paramount for Melody to come clean about Luke's visit earlier that morning. Otherwise, Clarke would think she was untrustworthy. "I'm sorry about yesterday, Clarke. It was a *tough* day for me."

"Princess, that's what I'm here for. Why didn't you come to me? You can always come to me, when you're having a bad day. Is anyone giving you a hard time, baby? I could-"

"My ex-boyfriend came into town last night," Melody improvised. She couldn't really say for sure when Luke made it down to Sands Port.

"What...?" Clarke feigned jealousy. "What did *he* want? I hope he knows you're getting married tomorrow," he said irate. "Who does he think he is showing up here after all this time?"

"He wanted to try again, but I told him that I wanted *nothing* more to do with him." Melody's heart dipped down to her feet to even *talk* that way regarding her connection to Luke. It was desecrating, because Luke was immensely special to her.

"Did he upset you in any way?" Clarke anxiously waited for the other shoe to drop. Now that Luke had told Melody about the payoff, it was only a matter of time before she addressed the matter.

"It *was* upsetting, but I handled it. I told him it's over."

"Are you sure *he* knows it's over, Melody?" Clarke's voice took on a more urgent quality.

"Clarke, I'm not that kind of girl. I promised to marry *you*. Don't you trust me?" Melody tried to sound hurt.

"You're my whole world, Melody! Of course, I trust you. I just don't trust other men around you. You're my most prized possession, and they just *can't* have you," Clarke philandered. He was still on cloud nine, because Melody had defended him, and had expelled Luke Bryant out of her life.

"So, I'm your *possession* now?" Melody trifled.

"My most *prized* possession," Clarke's tone was sonorous. "I miss you so much! I want to see you so badly. I missed the entire day with you yesterday. Will you let me take you out for lunch later? I know that whole can't see the bride for twenty-four hours tradition. That's why I wanted to take you out before it gets too late."

"Sure. I'd like that," Melody's tone was lackluster. "It'll give us the chance to talk. There's something I'd like to discuss with you."

Clarke's heart plunged. "Everything okay, baby?" No doubt, Melody would want to discuss the payoff he'd made to Luke. Clarke hoped she wouldn't decide to cancel the wedding or end their relationship. He'd worked so hard to have her, and he wouldn't let her go. He refused to lose her just one day before their wedding.

Melody laughed nervously. "Everything's fine. We *are* getting married tomorrow, and I won't get to see you until tomorrow afternoon. So, there *are* a few things we need to cover."

"I agree one hundred percent. There's only one thing I want to *cover* right now. I want to cover your lips with mine. I'll be by to pick you up at around one for lunch. I can't wait to feel you in my arms."

Melody issued another awkward and exaggerated laugh. "You're too much, Clarke. I'll be right here waiting."

Just then, Melody's doorbell went off. Her heartstrings tightened in her chest with a sense of both dread and anticipation. She wondered if it was Serena coming by to yell at her, or whether Luke had returned. Both scenarios made her feel apprehensive.

"I won't be late. I'm going to relish every minute I have with you today."

"Me too," Melody said tautly.

"I love you!"

"Love you too, Clarke!" Melody said, almost through gritted teeth. "I've got to hit the shower, and do a few last minute things. So, I'll see you later...?" she quickly added.

"Of course, you will. Bye, honey." Clarke shut down his cell, but kept his eyes on the television monitor. Two plumbing work trucks were parked in Melody's driveway. He wondered why they were there. Why had Melody failed to mention that she'd been having plumbing issues? Clarke circumspectly continued to monitor the folding events.

Melody rushed to her front door to see who the caller was. Seeing Luke at her door earlier on had thrown her for a loop. So, she paused and took a deep breath before answering. Melody felt both a sense of dread *and* anticipation, over the prospect of seeing Luke again. However, her heart plunged when she saw the commercial trucks camped out in her driveway. Melody's face was a mask of confusion. "Good morning!" Her arms crossed over her chest to buffer the morning chill. "How may I help you?" Her face creased in perplexity.

"You reported trouble with your pipes?" The man's eyebrows furrowed in persuasion, and he gave Melody a knowing wink."

It then occurred to Melody that he was one of the detectives sent over to locate the hidden cameras Clarke had planted in and around her house. Melody nodded, and gave the gentleman a knowing smile. "Yes, of course." She pointed in the direction of the backyard. "There's a leak of some sort out in the backyard, but I called you guys last week," Melody added unrehearsed. "What took you so long? There's also a water pressure issue in the bathroom." Melody's eyes delved into the gentleman's.

"Sorry for all the trouble, Ms. Maxwell. Boys, you can start the work," he turned to address his work crew. Within minutes, drilling and rumbling noises permeated the area.

The noise level was so high, Melody could hardly hear herself breathe.

"I'm detective Dexter Walker. We're not really drilling or hurting anything out in the backyard, but we have to make it look good, Melody. Do you understand?"

Melody smiled, and felt in some way relieved. She nodded. Otherwise, she would have had to raise her voice in order to be heard.

"While the boys are drilling out here, I'm going to check around the house and inspect the *plumbing*. I'll *really* be puttering around to locate, and to get rid of those devices. So, things are going to be loud for a little while."

Melody sighed. "I'm okay with that. You can drill as many holes in the backyard as you want. I just want those cameras out of my house." Her face wrinkled in doubt. "Are you sure you're going to be able to find all of them?"

Detective Walker gave her a reassuring smile. "We *are* the experts, Melody. So, don't worry. We're also keeping our eye on Vale. Since you're in the loop, you should be aware that one of his men was apprehended at the airport earlier…thanks to you."

Melody's heart skipped a beat, and her eyes widened in shock. "You arrested Darien Stiles?"

"No. We didn't catch that big of a fish yet, but we will handle Clarke and Darien by tomorrow afternoon. Carter Stephens was diverted before making Flight 307. He is currently being kept at a safe house. He's not exactly ready to testify against Vale. "

Melody nodded absently. She was both grateful and sad. She was grateful that Carter was safe, because it meant Clarke's plan had failed. However, she was grieved, because she was tied in to both Clarke and Darien. Melody still couldn't believe that Clarke had paid Darien five million dollars to step aside. Even more tragic, was the way their business deal had affected her relationship with Luke.

Even now, all Melody craved was Luke's arms around her. In fact, if Luke stopped in to see her again, Melody knew she'd be powerless to resist his tender touch and his kiss. She only felt strong as long as Luke stayed away. She could still feel his arms around her and his head buried in her chest. The pain in his voice replayed like a horrible recording.

"You're doing the right thing, Melody. You have no idea how brave you're being. That's why we're going to see to it that you remain safe."

"Huh?" Melody looked up suddenly, roused by Detective Walker's words.

"You're very brave to do this. We're going to make sure you're okay." He smiled warmly at her.

Melody shook her head contrarily. "I'm not brave at all. Just trying to keep my loved-ones safe."

"You have *no* idea. You *are* one brave lady."

"Thanks," Melody ceased to argue. "By the way, should I leave?"

"Not necessary, as long as we keep the noise level high. We're also going to take a look at your fuse box. Is that all right with you?"

"Whatever it takes," Melody told him. "Just find those cameras."

At that very moment, Serena pulled into the driveway in Melody's BMW SUV. Serena tried to find a tiny bit of space to park in the four-car driveway, because there were service trucks parked erratically in the spaces.

Melody closed her eyes meditatively in dread, because she knew what was coming. Serena was about to give her a verbal tongue-lashing. She braced herself, as she watched her best friend jump out of the vehicle.

"Is that a friend of yours?" Detective Walker asked. Concern wrinkled his set features.

"Yes… my best friend," Melody admitted.

"So, we'll get started inside the house," Detective Walker said. "Whalen, come give me a hand in here," he called out to one of the men, who'd just crossed back over to the driveway from the backyard.

"Yeah, sure thing," Whalen said. He was a young, dark-haired Caucasian man, who seemed a lot younger than the others.

Melody followed the men's interactions, as they stepped into the house. Her home had suddenly become Grand Central Station in New York City. She pretended to be wrapped up in the detective's activities, as a way to escape Serena's wrath, but Melody knew she couldn't avoid it for long.

"Melody Christine Maxwell," Serena started. She stood in front of the door.

Melody flinched. Her face was veiled in dread, as she turned to address Serena. Her eyes connected timorously to Serena's bewildered and demanding expression.

"Serena...," Melody deliberated. However, she couldn't have foreseen Serena's reaction.

Serena burst into tears, threw her arms protectively around Melody and wept. "I thought something happened to you. Why would you do that to me and Dane? We were so worried. Dane hated that he had urgent business to tend to this morning, because he's just as upset as I am. He asked me to call him just as soon as I found you," Serena's voice wavered.

Melody surrendered to tears as well, and took refuge in Serena's arms. Melody clung to her for dear life. "I'm sorry, Reena. I'm so sorry. I didn't mean to make you worry about me." Melody pulled away, and wiped tears from her eyes. "I'm sorry for taking your car."

Melody tuned into the bustle around her. If Clarke was watching, he wouldn't be able to hear a word she exchanged with Serena. All the same, Melody felt uncomfortable being there.

"Mel, what happened last night?" Serena wiped tears away

from her eyes. She'd been certain that Melody had gotten caught up in trouble with Clarke."

Melody's face rumpled in remorse and angst. "Take a drive with me, Serena. Give me a minute to throw on my sneakers." Melody veered back towards the house.

"Okay." Serena watched her friend rush back into the house. She remained posted to the front door feeling utterly confused. She observed the men walking up and down Melody's driveway, and disappearing out towards her backyard. A few of them also paraded in and out of the house.

Melody rushed back to the front door to Serena. She'd changed, and had on jeans, a taupe-colored T-Shirt, a tan Aeropostale hoodie and her Nike's. She blinked back the tears stinging in her eyes, and kept a smile pasted to her face. Clarke was watching, so she had to pretend to be excited about getting married.

"Mel, what's going on? What's all this?" Serena examined the bustle all around her.

"Can we take *your* car out by the water?" Melody asked. It was a nice day to go out by the marina. The sun was making a slow ascent in the undimmed beryl sky. If her life wasn't such a mess, Melody could have actually enjoyed the weather.

"Of course, we can, honey." Serena frowned in concern. The look on Melody's face was one she'd never seen before, and it scared her more than anything else. Serena decided to stop censuring Melody about her disappearing act in the middle of the night. "It's a perfect day to have *breakfast* at the marina," Serena appealed. She ushered Melody away from the house, and shut the front door. "Mel, is it all right for these men to stay here while we're out?"

Melody was already opening up the door to Serena's SUV. She nodded absently. "It's okay for them to be here. They're going to be around for a while. *Detec...Derek* said he'd call me just as soon as they're done." Melody caught herself from saying *detective*.

"Okay, honey. You're okay." Serena gave Melody a

sympathetic look, as she jumped into the automobile next to her. Serena examined her best friend in utter stupefaction.

Melody tried not to speed, as she put distance between herself and the house. She couldn't stop trembling. However, she tried to hold it together, until they were out on the expressway. Too scared to look back, her eyes remained fastened to the road.

"Mel, I'm really worried. What's going on? Why won't you even talk to *me*?"

"I *will* talk to you, Reena. I just have to stop shaking first." Melody's eyes connected desperately to Serena's at that moment.

Serena was heartbroken. Tears brimmed over in her eyes again, because she didn't understand Melody's bizarre behavior. Still, she avowed not to push. Melody had gone through enough. So, she would wait until her bestie was ready to open up. The entire situation seemed to be one big nightmare.

***

The sun was high in the vista, and the cool early morning breezes wafted from the ocean, when Melody pulled up to a parking spot out in the marina. She jumped out of the car, and immediately took to walking. It was the perfect morning-if just a bit on the cool side. However, the temperature would inevitably warm up, as the gilded sun continued to knife through the teal blue waters. Seagulls hung low in the panorama, and sung their special song. So many memories came rushing back to Melody.

The marina was where she and Luke had had their first date. After having breakfast on that fateful morning, Melody had shared her faith in Jesus Christ with him for the first time. She remembered how receptive Luke was in respect to learning all he could about the things of God.

The marina was where Luke had first held her in his arms. He'd picked her up, and had playfully carried her over to the edge of the water. It would forever be a very special landmark for them, but Melody hadn't stepped foot there since Luke had left Sands Port.

As painful as it was to revisit their old stomping ground, being there made Melody feel oddly more connected to him. Luke had said he still loved her. Melody wanted to find comfort in those words, even if she'd just emotionally annihilated him. She plodded through the sand, wanting to cover as much ground as she could. Melody was a breath shy from jogging, and didn't realize Serena was having a difficult time keeping up.

Serena had to sprint in order to keep up with Melody, but she didn't complain. Rather, she decided to wait until Melody felt safe and comfortable enough to pour out her heart. Melody was undoubtedly overburdened. So, it was only a matter of time before she exploded.

Melody walked as far up on the beach as she could. Panting, she finally turned towards Serena. "I'm in so much trouble, Reena," she admitted, with a vexed expression on her face.

Serena walked over to where Melody had stopped. "Please talk to me, honey. Tell me what's wrong. I'm so scared for you." Serena pulled Melody in, and gave her a comforting hug.

"I couldn't sleep last night...," Melody began to explain. Her breathing was labored, and she spoke choppily, as she told Serena the whole story. Melody detailed the events after she'd left Serena and Dane's in the wee hours. It ripped her heart out yet again to share the details of Luke's visit.

Serena was incredulous. "Mel, they said you *have* to be around Clarke, until he's arrested over at the castle tomorrow afternoon?"

Melody nodded frenziedly. "They said that it's important for Clarke to think that nothing's changed. I have to convince him that I *want* to get married more than anything else. He can't even *suspect* that I know anything about his *alternate* life."

Serena's face was blanketed in horror. "Mel, how on earth are you supposed to do that? Don't they realize they're putting you in harm's way? This man has killed before." Tears gleamed in Serena's eyes. "Mel, you're my sister, and I'm not trying to have a funeral right now."

Melody took hold of Serena's hand. "I've got to believe God will work it out. I've got to have faith that he will guide me every step of the way. I'm under his protection." Melody took a deep breath. "Remember when you said there's purpose for what happened with Luke, and even for my involvement with Clarke?" Melody agitatedly searched Serena's eyes.

Serena nodded, and blinked back even more tears. "Of course, I remember. But, I didn't think that purpose was for you to help bring Clarke down. I guess, you're the one God *would* choose to bring Clarke's evil empire to the ground, because in his own twisted way he actually loves you."

Melody shook her head contrarily. "Love isn't compartmentalized, Reena. The same mouth used to say, *I love you*, can't be the same one issuing a hit on someone's life. The same hands that have been gentle and kind to me, are the same ones pulling the trigger to end countless lives.

"It's either you have true love in your heart or you're deceived. Someone who says they love you with their whole heart, can't be capable of committing murder. That's a total contradiction. True love doesn't do that. You get what I'm saying, Reena?" Fresh tears shimmered in Melody's eyes.

"Yeah, I know *exactly* what you mean, honey. *Some* people actually live their lives compartmentalizing good and bad deeds. You're sure right about one thing. They're totally self-deceived. I'm so sorry, honey. I'm sorry about all of it. Dane and I are *not* letting you out of our sight until the wedding."

Melody flinched. "I don't know if that's a good idea, Reena." Melody tugged nervously at her ponytail. "Clarke wants to have lunch today. He's picking me up at one."

"Okay… So, Dane and I will be waiting for you when Clarke brings you home. Mel, I don't want you alone today. You're my best friend, and I'm your matron of honor. That means, we're hanging out all day today. No ifs, ands or buts about it. *Clarke* is the one who isn't allowed to see you for the next twenty-four hours. So, it works out. *Today* of all days, I'm so grateful for that tradition.

"So, you'll be staying with me and Dane until tomorrow afternoon. Let the FBI and the detectives work everything out on their end. All *you* have to do is to show up in that wedding gown, and show Clarke how eager you are to marry him."

"I *have* to find a way to reign in my emotions when I'm around him. All he's been talking about is touching and kissing me. Serena, I can't..." Melody kept shaking her head contrarily. "And, no matter what, I *have* to address what he did to Luke last year." She stared into Serena's eyes with consternations.

"Yeah, about that...," Serena started to say.

"I'm sure Clarke watched my interactions with Luke earlier on. He knows exactly what we talked about. So, I have to make him aware that I know about the payoff. I already told Clarke that I sent Luke away this morning. However, when he called me a little while ago, I didn't bring up the bargain they'd made last year. If I *don't* bring it up, Clarke will think I'm being dishonest."

"That may not be the best idea, Melody. You're not supposed to be making any waves, remember?"

"If I leave out the part about the payoff to Luke, Clarke will know for sure I'm putting on an act, and just going through the motions. He *has* to know how upset I am about what happened. However, when it's all said and done, I have to reassure him that it doesn't change anything between us." Melody guffawed, and laughed caustically. "I have to tell Clarke what he did was *okay*."

She gulped, and tried not to fall apart. "I've got to tell Clarke Vale that running the man I love out of town was *not that big a deal.* Furthermore, I've got to tell him I understand how he felt-that he had no other choice, because he loves me *so* much." Melody kept shaking her head in denial, miffed over the circumstances.

Serena hugged Melody in comfort, and held on for a while. "I get it, Mel. Just be careful how you come at Clarke."

Melody's laughed in irony. "*Careful* has become my new name, Serena. Whatever the case, if I'm going to be convincing, I can't just sweep what Clarke did under the rug."

"You do what you need to." Serena frowned in angst. "You told Luke it was best for him to leave town, and never look back?"

Melody cautiously pulled away from Serena's grasp. "You should have seen his face, Serena. He was crushed. I'm pretty sure he thinks I'm some kind of monster, and that I hate him. I told him I love Clarke, and that I'm on Clarke's *side*." Melody's face twisted in misery.

"All I wanted was to be close to him the entire time. I wanted to be in his arms and kiss him so badly. Not being able to show him how much I missed him was the worst feeling in the world. I pushed Luke away so harshly." Melody wrapped her arms about her shoulders to avert the cool breezes.

Serena set down on a small rock. There was another one close to it, and she invited Melody to join her. "Oh, honey, I'm *so* sorry you had to go through that. But, you're only trying to protect Luke. Clarke is extremely dangerous. I still can't believe he ordered a hit on some guy at the airport this morning." Serena shook her head incredulous.

"I know it broke both yours and Luke's hearts, but you did the right thing by discouraging him. Clarke told one of his cronies to kill Luke on the spot, if you decided to take him back. Dane and I could find out if Luke is still in town. We could explain..."

"No, Serena. I want him as far away from this situation as possible. It's best for Luke to do exactly what I told him to. I couldn't handle it if anything happened to him."

Overwhelmed by the current set of circumstances, Melody cradled her head in her hands. She had no idea how things were going to play out, but she knew God was with her. She had to believe that he would make everything all right. "It killed me, but I *had* to try to get Luke to leave town. I pray he listens, and leaves Sands Port right away."

Serena smiled through the tears. "You love him even more now than before."

"I didn't think it was possible to love, and miss someone so much! I love him so much more now," Melody admitted.

Serena smiled. "At least, you know for sure Luke loves you too…that he's never stopped. Try to dwell on the positive. Nothing's changed your love for each other, not even Clarke's evil schemes. I knew Luke loved you when you introduced us at the church."

Through the pain, Melody laughed ironically. "He said he still loves me, and I love him more than ever but…"

"But nothing… When Clarke is finally behind bars, you can find Luke again, and tell him the truth."

"Now, *I'm* the one who's scared he won't forgive *me* for being so awful." Melody grimaced in sorrow and uncertainty.

"Oh, honey, if *you* can forgive him for leaving Sands Port last spring, he can definitely forgive you for trying to keep him safe in this situation." Serena took Melody's hands in hers, and squeezed them supportively. "Everything's going to work out."

Melody sighed. "Okay… I know it *has* to be all right. Even if I failed God, he won't fail me. He *can't* fail us. Thank you." She smiled earnestly at Serena. "I really needed to come out here for a little air."

"Yeah, I think we both did, sweetie. Let me give Dane a call to let him know you're all right. He's been worried out of his mind."

Melody nodded. "I love Dane! You really lucked out with him."

Serena smiled and winked at her bestie. "Count *your* blessings, sweetie. I think we *both* lucked out, Mel."

Melody sighed. She knew Serena was referring to Luke, but Melody didn't respond to the observation. "I've got to get back over to the house. Clarke will be coming by to get me for lunch."

Melody stared into Serena's face in ambiguity.

"Go have lunch with Clarke. All you have to do is to hold it together for a couple of hours. We've got your back every step of the way. The authorities are watching, Dane and I are watching. But, most importantly, Mel, God's got your back," Serena heartened.

Melody stood to her feet. Serena looped her arm supportively through Melody's, as they hauled away from the beach. Melody was grateful to God for such great friends. She also thanked God for his presence, and power in all of her circumstances. He was her victory, and it was impossible for God to fail.

CHAPTER SEVEN

"What's going on with this thing?" Clarke fiddled with the camera equipment in his private den. He'd suddenly lost footage of activity taking place in and surrounding Melody's home. So, he kept hitting the monitor. Moreover, he tried resetting all of the plugs and wires, but to no avail. He couldn't bring the images back up.

"Mr. Vale, you called?" Taylor, who was Clarke's personal technician showed up.

"I need this thing in working order just as soon as possible," Clarke blared, not even taking a moment to greet the young man.

"Will do, Mr. Vale," Taylor said perfunctorily.

"Now, I have a very important lunch date to prepare for. Get this thing going," Clarke ordered, pointing at the compromised material. He then turned, and stormed out of the den.

"Whatever you say, *your highness*," Taylor muttered. "I can't stand that man," he said quietly, but immediately started trying to figure out the problem.

Sometime later, Clarke was all dressed up for his date. This was to be his and Melody's final date before they would officially become man and wife. What he needed was to hear the good news from Taylor. He had to know that the equipment was up and working again. He popped his head into the den, and saw the young man still at work. Veins immediately pulsed at Clarke's temples. "You haven't figured it out yet?" he bellowed.

Surprised, Taylor's heart skipped a beat when he saw Clarke in the doorway. "Oh, Mr. Vale... I *did* figure it out. The problem isn't with the equipment. It's a malfunction where the cameras are planted. Maybe, there's something in the locale interfering with the feed."

Clarke tried to keep his wits about him. He remembered seeing the service trucks and workmen parading in and out of Melody's house. "Those idiots must have damaged something over there." He was livid, but there was nothing he could do. "All right, then. If that's the case, there's no reason for you to stick around here."

Taylor gave Clarke a nonplused look. "Mr. Vale, you haven't given me my check."

"Oh, yes…" Clarke stepped into the den. "Can you step outside for a moment?" he asked irascibly.

"Sure," Taylor said. He walked out of the den, and shut the door after himself.

Exasperated, Clarke took the checkbook from the top drawer of his desk. He sighed, and tried to work through feelings of frustration. In a matter of hours, Melody would be his wife. So, he would no longer have to worry about keeping tabs on her, because she'd be living in his penthouse. He concluded that the interference with the hidden cameras wasn't that big of a deal. Come tomorrow night, he would have Melody all to himself. Nothing and no one-not even Luke Bryant, would get in the way.

Clarke wrote out the check, and invited Taylor back into the den.

"Thank you, Mr. Vale. Would you like me to return later?"

"No, no… That won't be necessary, Taylor. It's fine. Thank you," Clarke said dismissively. He had way too much on his mind.

Taylor rushed out of the penthouse as soon as he got his check. He really didn't know why he put up with Clarke Vale, because he couldn't stomach being in the same room with the man. However, inspecting the check in his hand, which read five thousand dollars, Taylor realized exactly why he tolerated the arrogant and pompous prude.

Clarke refused to allow the setback to upset him. He crossed back over to his bedroom, and checked himself in the mirror. He was all set to pick Melody up for their lunch date. Clarke was both excited and anxious. He was apprehensive, because Melody had mentioned wanting to *talk*. Melody certainly wanted to address the bargain he'd made with Luke Bryant last year.

Clarke was prepared to refute *any* and *every* argument, because he refused to lose Melody. Even if he had to twist everything around, he would do just that. There was no way he was going to relinquish everything he'd fought so hard to obtain a day before the wedding.

He was just about to leave to meet with Melody, when the phone call came in from one of his men. "Vale, here."

"Mr. Vale, I guess Luke Bryant is much too *heartbroken* to stay in town after all."

"Excellent." Clarke's smirk was indomitable.

"I have it on good authority that young Luke has left Sands Port. Best friend Sean drove him out to the airport early this afternoon. He's on his way back to Virginia as we speak," Nigel's voice was both resonant and raspy.

Clarke's smile grew all the more pronounced. "That's the best news I've heard all day! Thank you, Nigel. Remind me to give you a raise." Clarke shut the phone down. He was elated. Luke Bryant's departure was the best news ever!

Now more than ever, he was confident that nothing and no one would be able to stop him from exchanging vows with Melody. *Finally*, Luke had done something right, and Clarke could not have been any more pleased. *"Good Riddance, Bryant!"* That was the song Clarke sang on the limo ride over to Melody's.

***

Luke had sat out in the parking area of the marina for the past hour. The silver Toyota sedan was the first car he'd rented for the day. The sedan was parked on the left hand side, towards the back end of the expansive lot. From that position, Luke had a clear view of the beach. He'd followed Melody and Serena there.

The marina brought back so many memories. He and Melody had frolicked on the beach on a number of occasions. In fact, closer to home, they'd spent the afternoon on Mooney Beach the day he'd returned to Sands Port from Rhode Island. Remembering it all, overwhelmed Luke with sentimental sadness. However, he couldn't afford to stay on that page. There was too much at stake. His job was to keep Melody safe, and he refused to stop until that mission was accomplished.

Even if Luke couldn't see Melody up close, from a distance, he could tell she was stressed out and sad. From his position, he had a clear view of Melody's interactions with Serena, without being detected. Too far way to listen in on their conversation, Luke noticed both were in tears.

As he watched them haul back over to the parking lot, Luke perceived that something was terribly wrong. Even now, it was difficult to hold back. It was a real challenge not to rush over and talk to Melody. She was no posterchild of a happy bride-to-be. And, Luke couldn't stand seeing her so discontent.

Luke felt silly parked out by the waterfront in costume. He was masquerading around with a bald cap of a man in his sixties. What little hair on the cap was graying and frayed. Sean had also added glued on wrinkles to his face for effect. Luke's sunglasses only made him look all the more bizarre. Despite the odd getup, he *was* on the right track, because he hardly recognized himself in the mirror. If *he* barely recognized himself, he figured others would have a hard time identifying him as well.

Because a vital part of his plan had already been set in motion, Luke felt encouraged. Apparently, his *twin* had successfully boarded a plane headed back to Virginia an hour ago. Luke couldn't have been any more pleased to hear it. In fact, he'd asked Sean to see to it that *Josh* was rewarded for his performance, and for sacrificing his time. Sean had assured Luke that Josh would be compensated. Now that Clarke was off his scent, Luke felt a lot more confident hanging about the locale to protect Melody.

Luke watched Melody and Serena hike back over to Serena's SUV. He hated not being able to connect to Melody, and offer reassurance. She was as beautiful as ever, but she seemed undeniably despondent. Her downcast expression was something Luke couldn't escape. The ladies took their places inside the automobile. This time around, Serena was the one behind the wheel. Melody sat on the passenger's side looking lost and dispirited.

Luke's eyes remained pealed to Melody the entire time. *Please, let me help you, honey. What are you doing? You **know** you don't belong with Clarke Vale. You belong with **me**..."* Such was the internal conflict for Luke, as he watched the pair roll away from the marina.

Luke lingered in the parking area, until Melody and Serena were almost back on the main road. Soon after, he pulled out himself, and continued to follow discreetly behind them. Staying under the radar without being detected was the goal. He refused to let Melody out of his sight, until he was certain she was no longer in danger.

In the meantime, Sean would finally go to the authorities, and detail some of his findings in respect to Clarke's covert operations out in the Caribbean, Central America and the Philippines. Both Luke and Sean realized they probably weren't citing anything new to the authorities. All the same, some of the evidence Sean had garnered, would undoubtedly add a nail to Vale's coffin. Every nail was essential in the battle to end his reign of terror.

***

Melody felt a lot safer at her house. Detective Derek Walker and his men, had successfully deactivate the hidden cameras in and surrounding her home. Melody was even more surprised that they'd left the house in perfect order. Nothing was amiss, and she was grateful for this much.

Having the police and the *FBI* on her side, also fostered a sense of security. Melody was encouraged to know that they were aware of her every move. More importantly, they had their eyes on Clarke. Melody also felt anchored with Serena and Dane by her side. Her friends were never too far away. However, beyond human support, God was with her, and he would always protect her. Because of the far-reaching nature of Clarke's crimes and his status, the FBI had to be brought in to work in conjunction with the local authorities. Clarke's illegal activities had spanned the globe. Melody's eyes were now opened to the full extent of Clarke's deception.

She'd gotten all dressed up for her lunch date with him. Melody had on a pretty tangerine-colored dress and matching accessories. Her hair was upswept. Loose tendrils cascaded down her shoulders, and accentuated her sweet features. Even if she was totally exhausted, she looked oddly refreshed after showering and changing. Clarke would be by shortly, and she had to get into performance mode.   Her heart lashed, as she nervously paced by the front door.

When she heard a car pull up into the driveway, she pushed back the living room curtains, and saw the sleek black vehicle. Melody's heart plunged, but she picked it up, and set it back into her chest. She was going to need a lot of *heart* to do what was necessary.

She waved as Clarke made his way up the front walk. Melody couldn't escape how handsome and charming he looked in his designer suit. His hair was cut and styled perfectly-giving him a polished and appealing look. Outwardly, he embodied all that a gentleman should be. Melody skeptically estimated just how deceiving appearances could be.

Bravely opening up the front door, her face stretched into the widest smile she could possibly offer. "Clarke!" Melody heralded, welcoming him with opened arms. However, Clarke instinctively took her by the waist, and avariciously guided her back inside. His lips bridged to hers, and he took the time to ingest every inch of her mouth. Clarke's kiss grew more intense by degrees. Melody had conditioned herself to respond automatically. Clarke's kiss felt even more foreign, and anesthetizing than the first time they'd kissed.

Melody felt totally disconnected, while Clarke could not have been any more engaged. He would have swallowed her up whole if he could. It was an intensity he'd never displayed before, but Melody felt totally detached.

Clarke pulled away enough to look into her yes, as his arms tightened around her waist. "Do you any idea how much I've been wanting to do that?" He nestled her. "I missed you so much yesterday!" Clarke found her lips again, and pelted them with fiery kisses.

Melody's eyes misted, and her heart knotted up from sheer revulsion. However, she had to find a way to move past those feelings. "Clarke," Melody teased, "you've got to let me breathe." She laughed nervously. "What was that?" She pulled away, but kept both hands pressed up to Clarke's chest.

Clarke squeezed her even more acquisitively. "That was me missing you so much it hurts." Clarke stared yearningly at her. He examined her eyes, and touched the faint dark circles underneath them. "I don't like anyone upsetting you." Clarke cupped her chin. "You're stressed out and exhausted. You're the most ravishing creature I've ever seen, but you have to get some rest later."

"I'm fine, Clarke." Melody smiled up at him. "I am a *little* tired, but I'm *really* hungry." She gently pulled away from his immuring grasp.

"Then, let's get some food into you, beautiful!" Clarke's expression was provocative, and he touched her seductively. "Melody, I'm sorry for all of the trouble your ex-boyfriend has caused for you."

Melody's heartstrings were pulled in a hundred directions. She intently met Clarke's gaze and forced a smile. "I'm *glad* he came by. Seeing him again only made me realize…well…" Melody hung her head down for a second, but then met Clarke's steadfast gape. "That's one of the things I wanted to talk about today."

Now, Clarke's chest tightened in uneasiness. He figured Melody was going to bring up the wager with Luke last year. Nonetheless, he was determined to play it cool. He was ready to deny, refute and negotiate what he wanted. There was no way Melody was going to walk away from him just hours before their wedding. "What have you realized, pretty lady?" Clarke asked with a cunning expression on his face.

"Well, I think we can talk about it over lunch." She gave Clarke a knowing wink before she turned away. "I'm going to get my bag, okay?"

"Sure, baby," Clarke said passively. Inwardly, he was stewing, because he didn't know for sure what Melody wanted to discuss. *You're not going to walk away from me today, Melody. I've worked too hard for this day. I've worked too hard to have you in my arms. I won't lose you. Now that Bryant's out of the way for good..."* Clarke fretted.

Melody stood out in the hallway of her living room in deliberation. She wanted to go back out to Clarke, but was in aversion of seeing him again. She felt nauseated about their lunch date. Her lips still seared where Clarke had kissed her-and *not* in a good way. Melody was convinced she was in danger of hurling if he kissed her again.

She pushed back tears, and pasted the paper smile back to her face. There was just no way around it. She had to play it out until the very end. Melody took heart, because the charade was quickly coming to an end.

Still, the ball was in her hands. She *had* to see to it that the story ended with Clarke behind bars. And, Melody wasn't about to drop it. She'd already dropped it once-taken in by Clarke's good looks, wealth and charm. But, that was a mistake she planned to rectify.

Clarke couldn't go on sulking, because Melody suddenly returned. He couldn't remember ever seeing her so radiant! In that tangerine-colored dress, she looked more tantalizing than the most succulent fruit. In fact, Clarke yearned to quench his thirst. "Hey, baby." He glided over to her. "Are you all set?" He cradled the side of her face in his hand.

"I'm all set to go." Melody set her free hand on the one Clarke had up to her face.

Clarke rushed over to get the front door for Melody. As he did, he took a moment to scope out her living room. Sizing up the room, he considered having one of his men return to the house in order to restore the camera feed.

"Shall we go?" Melody asked, perplexed. She stared warily at Clarke, because his eyes were all over her living room, as if he'd never been there before. Melody figured he was probably racking his brains trying to figure out how to regain hidden camera access. She laughed inwardly, because he seemed baffled.

In the event Clarke sent anyone else over, Detective Walker and his crew had replaced the hidden cameras with inaudible and micro alarm systems. The alarm systems were set in place to alert the authorities of security breaches. So, whoever dared to break in again, were risking immediate arrest. Melody thought it was an ingenious setup.

"Of course, darling." Clarke stared alluringly at Melody. "You look good enough to eat," he said licentiously, as Melody brushed past him. His lips grazed her earlobe, in a failed attempt at kissing her.

Melody turned, gave Clarke a beguiling glance and smiled. She walked ahead of him until they reached the limo. Clarke's driver immediately opened up the car door, and Clarke secured Melody inside. He slid in next to her, and snuggled into her.

Melody was distant and pensive, so Clarke already perceived what was coming. No doubt, Melody was going to censure him for causing her breakup with Luke Bryant. So, Clarke didn't say a word, neither did he attempt to pry anything out of Melody on their ride over to the *Autumn Persimmon Restaurant.*

***

Melody thought she was famished enough to devour her order of lemon beef and noodles from the Thai Restaurant. However, she sat at the table picking at her food, and doing all she could to remain poised. The emotional volcano whirring on the inside, demanded release. And yet, she found herself oddly silent. Moreover, the plaster smile had fossilized on her face. The last thing she wanted was to make unnecessary waves, even if her contention for Clarke was growing exponentially. All the same, she had to keep pretending that she was totally in love.

"You're not eating, Melody. Is there something wrong?" Clarke's face strained in angst. At that point, he was just waiting for the other shoe to drop. "Would you like me to order that mocha dessert you enjoy so much?" he cajoled.

"No, Clarke. I'm not very hungry anymore." Melody made her eyes connect urgently to his. She set her plate aside, and crossed her arms over her chest. It was time she told Clarke she knew all about the deal he'd made with Luke last year.

Sensing where Melody was headed, Clarke closed his eyes with a sense of resignation. He decided it was best to come clean, before *she* addressed the matter. "Melody, I have a confession to make." Clarke's face wrenched in solemnity.

"Is everything alright, Clarke?" Melody's heart lashed so potently, she thought it would pop right out of her chest. She reached across the table, and covered his hand with hers. It was the *only* physical display she could offer without falling apart.

"Well, I guess, I should tell you the entire story."

"Clarke, you're scaring me. Please, just say what's on your mind." Melody's face veiled in apprehension and ambiguity.

Clarke kept shaking his head in feigned remorse. "The moment I laid eyes on you at Radical Interiors, Melody, I was in love."

Melody stared at Clarke in skepticism. *What was he getting at?* She decided to allow him to say his peace and not interrupt.

"However, there was one problem," Clarke illustrated. "You were all wrapped up in Luke Bryant."

Melody's jaw dropped and her eyes widened. She couldn't believe Clarke had just said Luke's name so openly. It was the first time he'd ever made allusions to even *knowing* Luke. "You *know* Luke?" she asked coyly, shaking her head in disbelief. Melody couldn't wrap her head around how calculating Clarke was. No doubt, he'd perceived she was about to bring up the incident. So, in order to play damage control, he had to confess, before she could censure him for his gaffe. Of course, it had to be on *his* own terms.

"I knew you were with Luke Bryant. I also knew that I didn't stand a chance as long as he was in the picture."

"Clarke, what are you saying?" Melody set her hand dramatically over her heart. "What happened with Luke? Did you do anything to hurt him or his family?" Her face knotted in dread, and she instinctively pulled her other hand away from his.

"No, never…nothing like that. But I *did* do something you might be angry about." He tried to look apologetic. "Melody, I have to be completely honest. I strategically found out everything there was to know about you. And, from what I understood, you were falling in love with him. As long as *he* lived in Sands Port, I knew that I didn't have a chance."

Melody shook her head, feigning skepticism, as tears glimmered in her eyes. "So, let me guess… You made Luke an offer he couldn't refuse?"

"Melody…" Clarke reached for her hand again, but Melody theatrically shrank back from his touch.

"I only did it because I love you so much." Clarke grimaced mawkishly. "I wanted you so badly, and I was jealous of this kid. He *had* you, and there was nothing I could do to change it."

"So, you *paid* him to leave town?" Melody retorted, pretending to be incensed.

"No, baby, it wasn't like that. When Luke's father succumbed to a stroke last spring…,"

"I *know* what happened, Clarke." Melody's face rumpled in vexation. "I can't believe you took advantage of him and his family that way."

"Melody, please…" Clarke held his hand up in a halting manner. "I would never take advantage of an ailing man and his family. Quite honestly, I saw an opportunity and I seized it." He shrugged matter-of-factly.

Melody stared at him in utter and complete astonishment. Her resentful feelings were quickly reaching the breaking point.

Clarke's face rutted in false appeal and remorse. "Luke's family was in a bad way. His parent's home was pending foreclosure, the house was in a deplorable state, and his older brother had just lost his job."

Feeling conflicted, Melody cradled her head in her hands. She tried to commiserate, but she really had to convey how appalled and disappointed she was. "I guess, you *really* did your homework. You had absolutely no right to barter for my affection. Look, I get it, you're this dynamic business man who's used to getting his way. Still, Clarke, I'm not a piece of property or a bargaining chip," Melody emphasized, miffed.

"Baby, I've never considered you anything but precious. You're definitely not a bargaining chip or an object of barter. Melody, I honestly can't live without you. I know I had no right to interfere with your relationship with Luke Bryant, but I didn't know what else to do. I couldn't even get you to *look* at me." Clarke's face tensed up in frustration.

Melody sat back, and stared suspiciously at Clarke. She couldn't believe his train of thought or his reasoning. Sadder still, was that in Clarke's world, his actions were completely justified. On *his* planet, if a person wanted to be romantically involved with someone, there were no boundaries in as far as what was ethical and what wasn't. Whether or not the object of their affection felt the same way was immaterial.

Clarke had undeniably made a chessboard move by getting Luke out of the way. Melody was quiet. She glared at Clarke with her arms crossed over her chest. However, no matter how heinous she'd deemed his actions, Melody knew she couldn't stay on that chapter. It was time to pull it together, and convince him she was ready to move forward.

"Look, I'm deeply sorry for what I did, Melody," Clarke tried to *sound* genuinely contrite. "I apologize for pulling you away from a good relationship with someone you loved. Perhaps, Luke Bryant made you happier than I *ever* could. I know what I did was wrong. Honestly, Melody, I couldn't sleep at night knowing you were with him. The two of you were growing closer every day, and it was killing me. I love you! Please, don't send me away. You're the most precious thing in my life."

"First of all, my relationship with Luke was going nowhere, and I **never** loved him," Melody *lied*. Her heart splintered over saying those horrible words. The backlash was a vicious sting and burning to the chest. "You didn't have to manipulate things to go your way, Clarke. You could have been honest with me. You should have told me that you were struggling with feelings of jealousy and insecurity," Melody reproached.

"Melody, I'm sorry. I know I took things too far, but that was only because I didn't think you would give me a chance. I tried to tell you how I feel, but it was always about **him**…" Clarke's face turned crimson.

Melody flinched over Clarke's obvious rage towards Luke. Still, it was time to wrap things up before they turned ugly. She had to make Clarke believe that in spite of his controlling behavior, she still wanted to be his wife. It was imperative for Clarke to meet her over at the castle for the wedding tomorrow afternoon. It was the only way the authorities would be able to apprehend him, and make him pay for his murderous and defamatory actions.

"*I'm* the one who's sorry, Clarke," Melody softened. "I had no idea you were feeling so challenged by my relationship with Luke. Still, you had absolutely no right to interfere in my life that way. You had no right to manipulate the matter by propositioning Luke."

"Melody, you're absolutely right. If I could take it back, I would in a heartbeat. Please, don't walk away from me. Please, don't deny what we've built this year. I don't think I'd be able to handle that."

Melody gulped nervously, and tried to weigh her words before speaking. "Granted, I *don't* agree with what you did, but I *am* trying to process why you felt compelled to behave that way."

"You *are* still meeting me at the altar tomorrow? Please, say you're still mine." Clarke entreated, leaning in closer to her from across the table.

"I don't like what you did, but I *did* promise to marry you." Melody squirmed, but glued a fresh smile to her face. Inwardly, she felt like screaming. Clarke was the antithesis of the man she wanted to marry. He was also the antithesis of a human being. However, she feigned total contentment and aplomb.

Melody reached across the table, and covered Clarke's *blood-tainted* hand with hers. She delved into his eyes. "I've told you a hundred times that I'm *not* that kind of woman. I don't jump from one relationship to the next. When I make a commitment it's for keeps." Melody cringed.

Clarke issued a sigh of relief. "So, that means you're going to put on that glistening white gown, and meet me at the altar tomorrow afternoon?" Clarke brought Melody's hand up to his lips, and covered it with kisses. "I love you so much! I'd die if you ever left me." Clarke's face and eyes were imbued in manipulation.

It was at that moment Melody realized that she was indeed Clarke's most prized *possession*. She was just another one if his objects. He would have done *anything* to have her. What he felt for her wasn't love at all. It was the need to possess her, mind, body and soul. His affections were no different from that of race car driver, who coveted an antique or vintage automobile. Understanding just how calculating Clarke really was, made Melody feel all the more repulsed.

He was definitely the kind of man who would need to control and compartmentalize every aspect of their lives. This time around, she couldn't even bring herself to mutter a generic, *"Love you too, Clarke."* Melody would never say those words to him again, and she prayed that tomorrow afternoon would be the last time she ever saw the man.

After she'd heard Clarke's stirring admission, Melody just smiled and squeezed his hand. It was sad that such a clearly gifted man had chosen a lifestyle of criminality and deceit. Melody resolved to pray for Clarke. God was the only one capable of making a difference in his life.

"So, pretty lady, I will respect your wishes. I will get you a dessert to go, and bring you right home." Clarke's eyes speared through Melody's. "I hope you're not put out, because you didn't have an official bridal shower." Clarke veered away from the unpleasant conversation.

"Not at all, Clarke. *You* went ahead, and bought all of the things I had on the registry." Melody gave him a quirky smile. "So, having a bridal shower would have been just a tad bit *excessive*. Besides, I work with most of the women I know, and we're not that close. Serena's my best friend and my family," Melody explained.

"I just didn't want you to feel as if you missed out on anything."

Melody shook her head contrarily. "I don't feel that way at all. But, thank you for considering my feelings. Can we get that dessert now? I'm just a little tired, and I need to rest up for the wedding tomorrow." Melody tried to spark excitement. However, what little verve she had left was quickly ebbing away.

"Of course, darling. I know I have to get you home within the hour, or risk breaking tradition." Clarke laughed, and winked lightheartedly.

"I'm glad we understand each other," Melody tried to sound

cavalier. Again, a half-baked smile adorned her face. She had no idea how much longer she could keep up the charade. That afternoon, Melody couldn't have been any more grateful for silly traditions. The groom wasn't allowed to see the bride twenty-four hours prior to meeting at the altar. So, Clarke couldn't get her home fast enough. She was *required* to meet him at the *Lalique Castle* tomorrow afternoon. Melody prayed that the performance would come to an end over at the castle.

Luke had the restaurant menu pressed all the way up to his nose, while sitting inside of the *Autumn Persimmon Restaurant* in the town of Hartsville. He'd followed Melody and Clarke there. He was still using the first car he'd rented, but his appearance was completely different. This time around, his hair was dirty blond, and long enough to pull back into a ponytail. He also had on a cowboy hat and a full on moustache.

Sporting a tan-colored dress suit, and large-framed transition glasses, he looked like someone else. However, just behind the glasses, tears streamed down his cheeks. The tears flowed from a profound place, where his heart had been severed. Luke had just overheard the better part of Melody's conversation with Clarke Vale. Melody had reassured Clarke that their short-lived relationship, had meant absolutely nothing. Melody had also reiterated that she'd never loved him.

Luke's world was totally shattered. He was frozen at the table, and had no idea how to get his legs to start working again. He didn't think he'd ever be able to recover. How was he supposed to live his life without Melody? He'd barely existed living away from her for an entire year. And, Luke just couldn't submit to that kind of emptiness again.

From that corner of the restaurant, he plainly observed Melody's interactions with Clarke. Luke regretted being on the listening end of their conversation. After Melody said their relationship meant nothing, and that she'd never loved him, Luke had waited for her to take it back. He'd waited for her to say something to indicate that she *had* once loved him. He'd yearned to hear Melody attest to understanding *his* side of the story. He needed to know that she got why he'd accepted Clarke's proposition. However, the longer he'd sat there, the more it dawned on him that Melody wasn't changing her mind.

The Melody he knew would have never considered marrying a man like Clarke Vale, especially after finding out his deceitful tactics to win her. Still, if what Melody had told Clarke held true, Luke acquiesced to the fact that their relationship wasn't as important to *her* as it had been to him.

Regardless, he couldn't bring himself to be angry. Melody held his heart, and she always would. Luke was completely mesmerized just seeing her. Melody's butterscotch skin was radiant and creamy. Even if she seemed a little tired and sad, she was still the most striking creature he'd ever laid eyes on.

It was sinful of him to stare at Melody with such desire, but Luke couldn't look away. Being objectifying was uncharacteristic, but couldn't be helped in this case. He had to take a moment to take in Melody's porcelain skin, her shapely hips, her caramel legs, and her dainty hands and feet. It was also an exercise in futility to stop gaping at her perfect mouth. It was the source from which he'd never quite been able to quench his thirst.

She was so appealing in her little orange chiffon dress. Luke was jealous to the point of combustion. He would have given anything to be close to her again. Seeing her with Clarke Vale was gut-wrenching. Melody's claim to the insignificance of their past relationship, made Luke want to die.

Clarke took Melody's hand, and kissed it repeatedly. For all intents and purposes, he was savoring a rack of lamb. Clarke touching Melody so intimately sickened Luke. He had to look away each time the two had an affectionate exchange.

In spite of the excessive physical displays, Luke perceived how stressful the circumstances were for Melody. *Why was she so determined to marry Clarke Vale?* Luke wanted to single her out to talk, but there was nothing he could say or do to reach her. Melody had made it clear she wanted nothing to do with him.

When Clarke stood to his feet and helped Melody up, Luke felt as if he was watching a movie. Clarke setting his arms around Melody's waist, and pulling her in for a kiss, was like a thousand knives thrust into Luke's chest. Luke trembled, as he watched the couple lose themselves to the act of kissing. His heart peeled back in layers of unspeakable pain.

It killed Luke not to be able to step in and put a stop to it. Melody no longer belonged to him. Even so, he resolved to follow wherever she went. Not only did he *need* to keep her safe, but he was completely lost without her. Even if it was with a broken heart, Luke determined to shadow all of her moves, because there was no place else for him to go.

Melody was his life, and that was never going to change. Luke somehow mustered up the strength to make it out of the restaurant. He sat in the car rental, and watched on as Clarke secured Melody into the limo. Moments later, the limo driver rolled away from the area. Not too long after, Luke himself pulled out of the parking lot, and followed behind them as discreetly as he could.

"Hey, Luke, are you all right?" Sean's voice resonated on the phone. He was checking in on his buddy.

Having gotten the wind knocked out of him, Luke was barely audible. "Hey, Sean. I'm all right."

"You don't sound all right, buddy. Where are you?"

Luke told Sean he was headed away from the restaurant in Hartsville and following behind Melody and Clarke. He also detailed all he'd seen and heard. Tears brimmed over in his eyelids again to relive the experience. It felt as if someone had an icepick, and kept puncturing his heart. It wasn't one paralyzing jab, but many to the chest area.

"Oh, man, I'm *really* sorry, Luke."

"Yeah, I am too, Sean. It's all my fault. It only took one momentously bad decision, and I lost her." Luke was still trying to process everything he'd heard Melody say. Hearing her say she never loved him still resonated.

"Luke, there's got to be some kind of explanation-"

"She doesn't love me, Sean," Luke interjected.

"Listen, we're going to figure this out once Melody's out of danger. As for now, we've got to stay focused. Listen, I finally went to the police, and told them all I know about Clarke's dealings in the Caribbean. They were grateful, but not the least bit surprised. In fact, they thanked me for providing even more proof in the FBI's *ironclad* case against Vale. So, it won't be too much longer, before they put him away."

"You said *ironclad*. Has anyone else come forward with new evidence?" Luke was skeptical.

"Not sure, buddy. What they said was that they finally have *indisputable* evidence on Vale's illegal activities. Of course, that's as much as they would tell me. So, Clarke's days are numbered, buddy."

"Will they be able to stop him before the wedding tomorrow? I hope they get their hands on him before then."

"My guess is that they're probably trying to set him up at the castle tomorrow. So, I doubt he'll even have time to exchange vows with Melody," Sean theorized.

Luke laughed wholeheartedly. "Are you serious?"

"Yeah, the authorities sounded *that* sure. In light of the kind of day you're having, I *thought* you could use a little bit of good news."

Sean's news infused a bit of hope into Luke's flailing heart. Luke hoped and prayed that Melody wouldn't even have to *look* at Clarke Vale tomorrow afternoon. He was encouraged that once Clarke was out of the way, he'd have another chance with her. "Thanks for letting me know, Sean. All the same, I have to make sure our plans don't glitch tomorrow. I don't want Melody getting caught in the crossfire."

"Absolutely… That's exactly what we're going to do. We're going to make sure she's okay when the dust settles. And,

I've got your back, buddy, whatever you decide.

"Thanks, man. That means more than you know."

"By the way, *you* just landed safely in Virginia."

Luke laughed lightly. "Did I have a good flight?"

"You had the best flight. You slept right through it," Sean teased.

"Sean, I can't thank you and *Josh* enough for making such a huge sacrifice. It's the perfect decoy."

"Are you kidding me? It was the most fun Josh had in years. He wants to be in on the next caper. It's all in a day's work, buddy. Everything's going to work out. Just be careful out there."

"Thanks, Sean. Thanks for all of it," Luke said. There was a tiny spark of hope, and Luke prayed for the strength to fan it.

"You're welcome! I will check in on you later," Sean told Luke.

Sean had already made up his mind to pay Melody a visit. He **had** to know what had changed so drastically in her life for her to tell *Clarke Vale* that she'd *never* loved Luke.

He realized stopping in to see her was risky. However, no one knew Luke as well as he did. So, it was a given. Sean grasped that once Melody was safe, Luke would retreat to an even deeper pit of despair than he had last winter. Sean had to make Melody understand that Luke didn't have much of a life apart from her. So, he hoped against hope that it wasn't too late.

CHAPTER EIGHT

"Did I make good time?" Clarke held Melody possessively in his arms at her front door. His eyes were drunk with desire.

"You made *great* time, Clarke." Melody smiled tautly.

Clarke stared down sensitively into her eyes. "Melody, I'm really sorry about what happened with Luke. If I could take it back I would." Clarke's expression was remorseful. "I'm not proud of the technique, but I *am* so grateful to have *you!*"

Once again, hearing Clarke say Luke's name so easily had baffled her. In spite of the mixed feelings, she held her hand out in a halting manner. "That's all in the past, Clarke. Let's just put it behind us." She gave him a reassuring look.

"I'm *all* for that." Clarke hunched down, and tenderly baited Melody's lips. His kiss progressed by levels, and he was quickly beginning to lose himself.

"Clarke," Melody pulled away in an unobtrusive manner, "you've got to save some of that for our honeymoon." Melody felt bilious to even allude to the word *honeymoon*. In fact, she worried that if Clarke didn't stop touching her, she'd be forced to violently pull away. She didn't want to blow her cover, by expressing how repulsed she felt by his vile touch.

Clarke nodded in agreement. "You're right," he whispered into her ear, "I can't wait to have you all to myself tomorrow night."

Melody smiled. "Me too…" She draped her arms about his neck and squeezed. When she released him, their eyes met intimately for a moment. "Goodbye, Clarke!"

"Before I go, there's just one more thing I wanted to…" Clarke finally released his hold from about her waist. He veered, and rushed over to the limo.

"Clarke, what is it?" Melody's mouth gaped, and her eyes widened in surprise, as she stood at the front door waiting on him.

Clarke removed a huge solid gold gift box from the trunk of the limo. It was wrapped in red ribbon. His handsome face was flushed in both anticipation and embarrassment, as he carried it up the walk.

Tears gleamed in Melody's eyes, as she considered the circumstances. They were indeed cruel. Melody couldn't help thinking that Clarke could have been a halfway decent human, if he was uniformly the same man he pretended to be around her. However, his changes were as certain as that of a chameleon's.

Melody estimated how awesome Clarke was at making grand and generous gestures towards *her*. And yet, how heartless and icily cruel he was to others. Clarke could be downright evil, and Melody was perplexed by the disparity. She smiled as he handed her the gift box. "Clarke, what is this?" Inquisition brightened her jewel brown eyes.

"Well, since you didn't have a bridal shower, think of it as a *shower in a box*. I also took the liberty of taking care of that traditional; something old, something new, something borrowed and something blue, pretty lady." Excitement danced on his features.

"That's very thoughtful of you, Clarke. Thank you." Melody's eyes explored his quickly, but then veered warily away.

"You're welcome, pretty lady! I *will* see you at the altar tomorrow."

Melody pointed at him, and nodded in agreement. Not saying a word, she continued smiling.

"I love you, Melody!" Clarke reminded her.

"Ditto, Clarke," Melody responded.

Clarke walked away backward until he got to the limo.

Melody stood out front of the house, and watched the limo roll away. She then dragged the huge gift box into the house, and shut the front door. Without bothering to open up the box, she set it to a corner of the living room. She wanted nothing to do with Clarke and his blood money. Everything he'd touched had been tainted by blood…including her.

Clarke had handled, touched and kissed her all day. She'd shared both physical and emotional intimacy with a man who had innocent blood on his hands. Shock rippled through Melody, and she shuddered. Clarke's hands were imprinted on her skin, and his lips still scorched on hers. Utterly disgusted, the tears she'd held back over at the restaurant, threatened to choke her. Melody set down on the edge of the living room sofa, and wept with abandon.

She'd lied to Luke. She'd told him she wanted distance, even if the only person she wanted to evade was Clarke. Melody tried to take heart, because things were quickly coming to a head. So, there wasn't time for a pity party. Giving up just wasn't an option. In spite of the circumstances, she believed God had a plan.

She sighed, and lifted up her hands in praise to God. Melody thanked God for the victory in the matter. She let it sink in that by tomorrow night, Clarke Vale would be behind bars. Melody made declarations of faith that afternoon. "I thank you, Lord that Clarke and his evil men will be apprehended tomorrow! I also thank you for watching over Luke for me. Father, I thank you for giving me a chance to show him that distance is the last thing I want for us…"

Dazed, Melody stared all about the room. However, she talked herself out of the trance, because she had to keep going. She decided to do exactly what Serena had said. Melody would pack up her things, and spend the night over at Serena and Dane's. She would take refuge in their home, until the storm rolled away.

Melody determined not to leave the Hennessey's, until the limo picked her up to bring her over to the castle for the wedding. The plan was to lure Clarke to the altar. There, the authorities would pounce on him for his innumerable crimes. She didn't have all of the intricacies figured out. However, she perceived that vindication would come in one way or another tomorrow.

Melody pulled out a suitcase from the family room closet. She rushed over to her bedroom, and packed up everything she felt she would need for the wedding. Her wedding gown was in a garment bag, so she gingerly set it inside a separate compartment. It would ensure that the sequins remained intact.

As she set things in order, Melody couldn't stop reliving the wonderful sensation of being in Luke's arms, even for a few moments. Luke telling her he still loved her, and that they belonged together still resonated.

She cringed as the hurtful words she'd told him reverberated. Melody prayed for a chance to explain. She also prayed that Luke would forgive her. Luke had said how dark his world had been without her in it. And, Melody wanted him to know that life without him had been just as unbearable. "Please, don't let him hate me, Lord...," she prayed.

At that moment, the doorbell rang. The sound echoed throughout the entire house. Startled, Melody automatically rushed over to get the door.

"I'm coming, Serena. Would you stop leaning on my bell?" Melody spoke absently, as she pulled the door open. "Okay, here I am, Serena...," her voice trailed, and her heart dipped down to the floor when she saw Sean standing there.

"Sean, what are you doing here?" Melody finally spoke after getting over the initial shock of seeing Sean again. She figured that if Sean was around, Luke couldn't be too far behind. Still, Sean was the last person she'd expected to see. They hadn't spoken in a while.

"Hello, Melody," Sean said plainly. His expression was that of bewilderment. "Can I come in for a minute?"

Melody's face crinkled in uncertainty and suspicion. She was still angry at Sean for not telling her where Luke was for an entire year. Rationally, she got that it wasn't his fault, but she still wasn't over it. "Sure...," she hesitantly acquiesced.

Before closing the door, Melody looked warily from left to right. Part of her wished that Luke wasn't too far away. However, there didn't seem to be any indication he was anywhere near the house. Melody didn't want Sean seeing how vulnerable she still was in respect to Luke. So, she quickly pulled back, and shut the front door.

"How are you?" Melody tried to sound composed. She

fought back disappointment, because Luke obviously wasn't with Sean. Logically, she'd sent Luke away, but Melody still struggled in his absence. She had to keep reminding herself that Luke keeping his distance was a *good* thing. Working past the pain, she tried to keep an open mind.

Sean frowned apologetically, and held his hand out in a halting manner. "First off, I *know* you're angry with me, Mel. I kept Luke's whereabouts a secret for months. You've got to understand that I was only trying to respect his wishes."

Melody softened, as she stared earnestly into Sean's eyes. She couldn't blame Sean for anything, neither did she have the right to be upset. "I'm not angry, Sean," Melody said temperately. "I *know* you were only doing what Luke asked. I get it. You're his best friend, and you were trying to remain loyal to him." She gave him an understanding nod.

Sean sighed in relief. "If you're *not* mad about what happened, Melody, why are you pushing Luke away?" Sean's expression was solemn.

Surprised by Sean's bold inquiry, Melody realized she had to answer cautiously. She couldn't risk endangering any of her loved ones until Clarke was apprehended. Neither could she place Sean in harm's way by confiding in him. She also couldn't divulge everything she'd learned in the past twenty-four hours. So, she closed her eyes, in exasperation, and tried to weigh her words before speaking. "I *didn't* push Luke away. *He* walked away from me, remember?" She shrugged nonchalantly.

Sean's eyes bridged critically to hers. "Melody, you *know* why Luke left. His decision to leave town had nothing to do with the way he feels about you. Luke loves you more than anything!"

Melody zeroed in to hear Sean out. All the same, she had to stand her ground. She couldn't let herself get all soft on the inside, because Sean had just reminded her how much Luke loved her. She loved Luke just as much. But, she needed for Luke *and* Sean to give her a little space to work things out. So, she continued to hammer away. "Did Luke talk to you? Is he still in Sands Port?" Melody interrogated. She had to know what was going on.

"You mean after he *talked* to you this morning?" Sean answered rhetorically, neither confirming nor denying whether or not Luke was still in town.

Melody's head slumped in remorse. It was obvious Luke had taken her advice, and had left town. "Sean, I'm really sorry things played out that way earlier. Luke caught me totally off guard. Showing up here after a year's time the day before my wedding, wasn't one of his best ideas."

"Melody, Luke's devastated over what happened. It's breaking his heart that you're going to marry that *man*." Sean shook his head contrarily. "Clarke Vale is *not* the man you think he is." He sighed in frustration. "Mel, I can't get into all of the details right now, but marrying Vale is a huge mistake."

"Sean, I appreciate your concern. All the same, I'm more than capable of taking care of myself, and making my own decisions. What, Luke told you that I pushed him away? Did he say that I'm so coldhearted I wouldn't give him another chance?" Melody scoffed. Her words and her expression were venomous. She didn't even give Sean a chance to respond.

"I'm well aware that Clarke's no angel. You don't get to be in that position of power without stepping on a few toes…"

"Melody…" Sean's eyes lowered critically into hers. "We're not talking about him stepping on a few toes here." Sean's face flushed red. "The man is downright dangerous. This is no joking matter."

"How dare you come into my home, and say such horrible things about the man I'm going to marry? Look, I'm really sorry things didn't work for me and Luke. I'm sorry things went south right after he left. But, *Clarke* is the one who helped me pick up the pieces when *your buddy* decided to play savior to his family." Melody's eyes shone in affect, and she trembled.

"Melody, this isn't you. I *know* you're still in love with Luke-no matter what you're telling me right now. I *know* you love him, and he's crazy about you. Don't do this. Don't marry Clarke."

"I'm so sorry to disappoint you, Sean. I guess, you didn't know me quite as well as you thought. I know Luke probably told you I'm this heartless monster, because I don't want him anymore," Melody's voice wavered, as she tried to sound vindictive.

"*Did* Luke tell you we had a once in a lifetime kind of love? Well, guess what? Those kinds of romances don't last. We lived out a fantasy for a little while. What I have with Clarke isn't some fantasy. He's the one who stuck around when Luke turned away.

"Do you have any idea what that did to me, Sean?" Melody's face warped in misery and sorrow. Her reaction seemed totally counterproductive to the cause. She was supposed to sound angry and unforgiving. Rather, she was obviously still reeling from Luke's departure last year.

"You're absolutely right, sweetheart. I can't even imagine how it felt to have that happen." Sean kept shaking his head in denial. "I know what Luke did was hurtful, Melody, but Luke's a good guy. He's a *good* man who was backed into a corner. You *know* Clarke tempted him by making that illicit offer. And, here you are singing Clarke's praises, and ready to have his canonized as a saint."

Melody swallowed the chunk lodged in her throat, as tears blurred her vision. "I'm sorry I'm not the person you thought I was, Sean. I'm sorry I hurt Luke. Believe me, it was the last thing I wanted. Now, I've got to do what's best for me." She breathed spasmodically.

Melody realized that her performance wasn't as convincing as she'd hoped with Sean. She didn't have the strength to keep denying she was more in love with Luke than ever. Her tear-filled eyes connected to Sean's, and the look on his face was of compassion and commiseration.

Sean moved in closer to Melody, and cupped her chin. "I know, honey. I know you're hurting. This *isn't* who you are. You don't have to explain anything to me." Sean pressed a kiss to her forehead.

Melody surrendered to tears, and Sean collected her in his

arms. "I'm trying to move on, and do what best for me, Sean," she justified. She was quickly falling apart, but fighting it every step of the way. .

"I know, sweetheart." Sean hushed her. "I know you're trying to make the right decision." He pulled away, and cradled her head in his hands. "Even if you don't love my buddy anymore, please don't marry Clarke Vale. Marrying him will be a colossal mistake." Sean searched Melody's eyes pleadingly.

Melody had no more strength to argue. She just nodded compliantly. She already had in mind what needed to be done, and she couldn't allow Sean or anyone else to hinder the investigation, and Clarke's impending downfall.

"Are you going to be okay?" Sean tested. "Just because you're no longer with Luke doesn't mean I don't care about you."

Melody smiled through the pain. "I know that, Sean. Thank you for coming out here this afternoon. It means a lot to me. But, please trust that I know what I'm doing."

Sean nodded. "I do trust you, Melody. I know you're a great woman of faith. So, I do trust you to make good decisions." Sean looked away for a moment. "I'm just sorry you and Luke couldn't make it work."

"I'm sorry too," Melody said softly.

"He's a good guy, so I don't want you to be angry with him."

"I'm not angry anymore," Melody admitted. She felt totally drained.

Sean gave her a loving hug. "Are you going to be okay?"

Melody nodded. "I'm spending the night over at Serena and Dane's."

"Do you need a ride over there?"

"No. I'm fine. Serena's picking me."

Just then, both Melody and Sean heard a car pull into the driveway. Melody went over to the window, and saw Serena and Dane. They were in Serena's SUV waiting on her.

Melody's phone went off. "Yes, I'll be right out, Reena. Help with my bags...?" Melody questioned.

She was just about to tell Serena that Dane didn't have to come out to help with her things, but Sean graciously offered. "I'll take your bags, Mel." Sean's smile was perfect as always.

"Okay. Thanks, Sean." Melody stared hopefully into his eyes. "That's very kind of you."

"Of course..." Sean searched Melody's eyes, before she veered off to show him where her luggage was. Something in her eyes relayed that she was still the same girl. Furthermore, she was doing everything in her power to make things right. Sean realized that the hope he'd held of Luke getting Melody back was tenuous. However, tenuous hope was better than no hope at all.

Sean stood in the doorway of Melody's bedroom, and saw the large suitcase and the two smaller duffel bags. He smiled quirkily. "Are you sure it's only for one night?" He winked playfully at her.

"I'm *sure*." Melody smiled at Sean, and gestured it was all right for him to come into the bedroom. Just then, it occurred to her just how much she loved and trusted Sean. She felt stirred to tell him the truth, but she desisted. Before long, everyone would know the truth.

Sean carried Melody's luggage out, as she took care of last minute details around the house. Melody made sure to activate her new alarm system. She couldn't risk Clarke sending anyone else over to plant any more hidden cameras. Melody perused the living room one last time before she shut and locked the front door.

Once outside, Melody found Dane and Serena engaged in conversation with Sean.

The moment Serena saw Melody, she rushed over, and threw

her arms around her. "Are you okay, honey? I was so worried about that stupid lunch date." Serena rolled her eyes in irritation. "Dane and I should have followed you out to Hartsville."

Melody gave Serena a knowing look, and shot a quick glance over at Sean, who was still talking to Dane. The strained expression on Melody's face, conveyed for Serena not to discuss the matter while Sean was there. Melody had *scarcely* dodged a bullet with Sean, and the last thing she wanted was make him worry. Sean, in turn, would tell Luke everything, and get *him* all worked up.

"Did you forget anything…makeup, jewelry, perfume…?" Serena got the gist of what Melody wanted to relay.

Melody nodded. "Got it all covered," she said offhandedly.

"So, you're all set then." Serena stared perceptively at Melody.

"I'm good, Reena. Sean just dragged that big old suitcase out of the house," Melody joked. She *wanted* Sean to hear her. Sean and Dane had already shaken hands.

"Yeah, Mel, what was *that* all about? Did you pack like hundred pound barbells in there?" Sean shook his head humorously.

"Whew…" Serena gestured, pretending to wipe sweat off her forehead. "I'm just grateful Dane and I didn't have to carry her bags out. You took one for the team, Sean."

"It was my pleasure," Sean said. He looked over at Melody, and found her eyes. He wanted to tell her she *could* reach out to him if she needed to. Melody's face stretched out into a faint smile, as she stared over at Sean.

Serena guided Melody over the automobile, as if Melody was a woman in her nineties, and used a walker.

Sean shifted back over to the ladies in order to say goodbye. "It was great seeing you again, Melody!" His eyes delved meaningfully into hers.

"Thanks for everything, Sean," Melody emphasized. She

threw her arms about his neck, and held on for a moment. "Don't worry about me. I'm going to be okay." She closed her eyes meditatively.

Sean gave her a loving squeeze. "I truly believe you're going to be okay, Mel. I'll try not to worry about you." He gently released her, and smiled into her eyes. "Sorry I came on a little strong in there."

"You're fine, Sean. You were just looking out for your buddy." Melody couldn't even bring herself to say Luke's name. It was tearing her apart to even think about him. "*I* think you're the best friend and brother he could ask for!" Melody reached up, and pressed a kiss to his cheek.

"Bye, Mel." Sean set his hand caringly to the side of her face. "You know how to reach me, right?"

Melody nodded.

Sean pressed a kiss to Serena's cheek. "It's so good to see you again!"

"Me too," Serena said. "Say hello to Luke."

Hearing Serena say Luke's name was a puncture wound to Melody's heart, but she tried to move past the pain.

"I will tell him you said hello."

Dane was already standing to the side of the rear passenger's side door, waiting to secure Melody inside of the automobile.

"Good to see you again, Dane," Sean said.

"Yeah, we should hang out one of these days," Dane told him. The men shook hands again.

Melody, along with Serena and Dane, watched Sean jump into a pearl-colored Lexus SUV, and pull away from the house.

Dane helped Melody into the car. "Got everything you need, Mel?" He double-checked.

Melody just nodded. Pressing her back up to the soft leather, made her realize just how exhausted she really was. Dane shut the car door, and walked around to take his place behind the wheel. Serena was already sitting beside him.

Serena turned to look over at Melody. She didn't say a word, but she was obviously relieved that Melody would be spending the night over at her house. That meant, Melody would be secure up until the very last minute. Tomorrow would be precarious enough when everything came to a head with Clarke. And yet, Serena was convinced that their faith in God would carry them all through this horrible storm unscathed.

Melody tried to quiet her thrumming heart and racing thoughts. She prayed and asked God for help and strength. She also prayed that the circumstances would progress, and end quickly. All she wanted was to put the horrific experience behind her.

It was also paramount to find Luke when it was all said and done. He *had* to know that she still loved him and *always* would. Before dozing off, Melody couldn't help thinking how blessed she was to have the love of such wonderful people. Serena and Dane loved her, Sean and *even* Luke had said he loved her. So, Melody was determined to protect them all with as much strength as she owned.

***

Clarke was finally able to unwind after a long trying day. It was after ten p.m. on Friday night. He had on his wine-colored silk pajamas, and just about to turn on the late night news. All was right with the world again, so he felt totally relaxed. The countdown was on to meet *Lady Melody* at the altar. That moment couldn't seem to come fast enough. Clarke had made so many sacrifices to have Melody. So, he took a moment to bask in the victory. At that point, no one and nothing would stand in the way.

A quiet and contemplative smile stretched over his face. Clarke remembered everything he'd gone through just to make Melody his. And yet, in spite of it all, he deemed that it was all worth it. Now, he was anticipating having her all to himself, and making love to her for the first time.

Having to wait as long as he had for *anything*, went totally against his nature. So, Clarke realized just how special Melody was. There wasn't anything he wouldn't have done for her. If Melody had asked him to take a spaceship to another galaxy, and to hang out there for a decade, Clarke knew that he would have readily obliged her. Melody had absolutely no idea that he was at her mercy. She had him totally wrapped around her finger.

It was such a serene night. Clarke was grateful that his employees had nothing intrinsically negative to report regarding Melody's activities. He was very much aware that Melody was currently out in Royale Valley at the Hennessey's.

Aside from Tommy's disappearance at the airport, and the failed hit on Carter Stephens, Clarke didn't have a care in the world. Those issues would be dealt with just as soon as he and Melody returned from their honeymoon. They would be flying out to the Fiji Islands for their first adventure as man and wife. Then, Clarke would return to Sands Port to tie up all loose ends. And, no one knew how to tie up loose ends, and settle the score better than he did.

Clarke stepped out into the hallway of the penthouse, and crossed over to the bar for a late night drink. He looked for ice, but the canister was totally empty. Annoyed, he dropped a string of expletives. "Why do I hire these people, if I can't even get ice when I need it?"

He maneuvered around the bar area looking for ice. Luckily, there was a flask full of fresh ice below the serving station. It was a good thing he'd found the decanter, because he was already considering firing *Jose*, the guy who was responsible for overseeing the bar.

Clarke walked completely around the station. Genuflecting to access the container from below the counter, he bumped his head on the wooden edge of the bar, as he made his way up. More colorful language issued from his mouth. Frustrated, he set down on the plush carpeting and rubbed his head. As he sat there, something shiny caught his eye. The object was lodged beneath the lower rim of the dark wood structure.

Curious, Clarke put out his hand, and felt for the item. He was confused as to why there would be a piece of jewelry beneath the lower rim of the station. He hoped his staff wasn't conducting wild parties in his absence. Clarke laughed at the notion, as he picked up the snowflake-shaped diamond earring.

"What's this…?" Clarke's face wrinkled in jeopardy, as he examined the item. At first, he thought it might belong to one of the housekeepers. However, that wasn't the case, because he recognized the piece. The engraved work on the back read: MM. Clarke knew it was one of the pair of earrings he'd given Melody for her birthday back in October.

Clarke studied the item with interest. "How on earth did Melody's earring get back here? That's strange." Clarke felt around the rim of the bar to see if the other earring would emerge. However, he came up empty. The discovery disturbed him, and he couldn't stop wondering how Melody had lost the earring there.

Perhaps, she'd lost it during a visit over to the penthouse. After all, he'd entertained her at his place on a number of occasions. However, Clarke couldn't recall one instance where she'd worn her birthday present. He was a *very* observant man, and definitely would have remembered if she'd worn them on one of their dates.

How on earth did her earring get here? That question needled him. He was irked, because he judged Melody to be careless with such a precious keepsake. Still, what bothered him the most was why the item had been found right across from the penthouse? Clarke just *had* to get to the bottom of things.

Abandoning his desire for a drink and even for sleep at that point, Clarke moved away from the bar, and reentered the penthouse. He squeezed the earring securely in his hand. It still eluded him to recall a time where Melody had them on. Clarke shut the door, and wandered into his private office.

"Yes, Oliver," Clarke called the doorman, "has my fiancée ever rendered a surprise visit to the penthouse?" Suspicion rose up on the inside like a bag of popping corn.

"Not that I'm aware of, Mr. Vale, but we could always check the security tapes."

"Would you be kind enough to review them for me, and let me know if my fiancée stopped in while I was out?"

"I will definitely do that, Sir. But is there a problem?"

"No problem at all." Clarke's laughter was exaggerated. "As you may or may not know we're getting married tomorrow…"

"Of course I know, Mr. Vale. It's the most publicized event of the year-taking place at the *Lalique Castle*! Congratulations, Sir!"

"Why, thank you, Oliver! I will remember to put a little extra in your paycheck next time."

Oliver laughed awkwardly. "Thank you, Sir. I'll get right on those security tapes for you. Is it alright if I call you back in a little while?"

"It's more than alright, Oliver. In fact, I'll be waiting up just to hear from you." Clarke frowned in uncertainty and angst. There were surveillance cameras in the front end of the building and even out in the lobby. However, Clarke did *not* permit them on the upper level, because it was where he conducted his business. So, if Melody *had* paid him a secret visit, she would have had to come through the front desk.

Clarke retreated to his den, and accessed the news. However, he was consumed by the mystery of Melody's lost earring. He didn't *want* to find a reason to distrust Melody, and he hoped there was a very simple explanation as to why she'd lost her birthday present feet away from his penthouse. Perhaps, it was a visit he was overlooking-although he staunchly doubted that was the case.

It was just after 1 a.m. when Clarke finally wandered back out to the bar to fix himself a Cognac. Floating back over to the penthouse, his cellphone went off. "Vale, here," he said calmly.

"Mr. Vale, this is Oliver."

"Yes, Oliver. What are we looking at?"

"So, I *did* find footage of Ms. Melody coming by the penthouse early yesterday morning. Miles was on last night."

Reflexively, Clarke's heart somersaulted to his feet, and the rebound to his chest was forceful. Veins thumped at his temples. "Early yesterday morning…?" Clarke examined.

"That's when she showed up here," Oliver said plainly.

"Right…," Clarke said distracted. The longer Clarke thought on the matter, the easier it was to put the pieces together. Working past his tangled tensions, he asked temperately, "Would you mind bringing the footage up here, so that I can review it for myself?"

"Of course, Sir," Oliver obliged. He setup the footage for Clarke. Oliver couldn't help feeling as if he'd just opened up a can of worms. Religiously, he said a prayer, touching his forehead, chest and shoulders. He also said Hail Mary's for Ms. Melody, and prayed he wasn't making trouble for her. She seemed like a good person.

Clarke was seething when he reviewed the footage. Melody was chatting it up with his hired doorman Miles. She had on dark jeans and her cream-colored blouse. It was the very same outfit she had on when Luke had visited her place. Clarke also zeroed in on Melody up close, and noticed she had the earrings on. So, she'd *definitely* lost it early yesterday morning, but she'd been much too preoccupied to notice.

Clarke didn't want to believe the worst, but the evidence was staring him in the face. Melody had manipulated Miles into letting her come upstairs to the penthouse. Clarke had been left totally out of the loop regarding her visit.

Melody had told him how she'd run around all Thursday in preparation for the wedding. She'd even alluded to being much too exhausted for company, when he'd asked to stop by her place. Thus, all of those missed calls, where Melody had told him she'd been much too busy to even look at her phone-let alone answer it.

Clarke recounted begging her to let him come by for just one kiss. He closed his eyes meditatively, and internalized the shame and embarrassment he felt. He realized just what a fool he'd made of himself. Melody had lied to him. She'd led him to believe that she'd been at home in bed, when all the while, she'd been across town, and had even come by the penthouse. Everything now made sense.

The missing pieces of the puzzle were coming together. He and Darien had made plans to wipe Carter Stephens out early Friday morning. Tears of rage pooled in Clarke's eyes to imagine Melody slinking around, as he and Darien had finalized that deal. *Was it possible she'd witnessed that exchange?*

Had Melody found out about the hit, and told the police? There was no other way Carter would have known what was coming…unless he'd been warned. Clarke kept shaking his head in denial. "You *wouldn't* do anything like that to me, Melody. You said you love me. I love you *so* much!" Tears of rage and betrayal rolled down Clarke's cheeks, as everything fell into place.

Now, it was clear as to why Melody was driving Serena's SUV. Clarke had assumed it was her way to evade Luke Bryant. However, he now grasped that it was a ploy to throw him off. Disillusioned and hurt, Clarke pushed back into his recliner. Just *one* more phone call that morning would confirm all of his suspicions.

One of his contacts kept surveillance of activities taking place in the locale, especially outside of the police precinct. So, Clarke decided to reach out to Vince Brand. Clarke had to know the truth. Had there been a gray SUV, similar to Serena's in the vicinity early Friday morning? Clarke read off the license plate number to Vince. When Vince confirmed that the SUV was spotted in the area early Friday morning, Clarke's heart splintered.

Vince verified that the automobile was parked out in the police precinct lot for a little over an hour.

When Clarke shut down his phone, the painted picture was

complete. While he was under the impression that Melody was safe at home in the wee hours of that morning, she was busy collecting damning evidence against him. Clarke's face turned redder than a crab's, and veins pounded at his temples. In fact, if he'd suffered from gamma radiation poisoning, he would have morphed into a red version of the Incredible Hulk.

"She made a fool of me and went to the police…" Clarke had a crazed expression on his face. "She probably told the police about the hit on Carter. That's why Carter was nowhere to be found yesterday morning. And, the police got hold of Tommy at the airport." Clarke kept shaking his head in skepticism.

"Ha, ha, ha…," Clarke laughed in irony. "Oh, my precious Melody, you're truly a *femme fatale*! What am I going to do with you?" Tears meandered down his cheeks. "Problem is, I don't know how to let you go. You're mine for better or worse, and this is definitely the *worst*. I didn't see this coming at all, but I have a few surprises of my own." His face instantaneously changed from sorrowful to insidious.

"As much as I love you, no one makes a fool of Clarke Vale. It might break my heart, but I know exactly what has to be done…" If all of his suspicions had panned out thus far, it was more than likely that the authorities and the FBI were on to him. He was their prey, and they were just waiting for the opportunity to pounce.

Clarke had to think fast and move even faster. Within minutes, he packed up as much of his belongings as he could into a bag. Ensuing, he gathered up as much cash as he had laying around the penthouse. He also transferred half a billion dollars into a foreign account.

But, he wasn't going away alone. Come hell or high water, he was taking Melody with him. It didn't matter whether she was dead or alive. She was the asset he'd worked so hard to obtain. Clarke had paid the ultimate price to have her, so Melody *belonged* to him.

Once Melody was securely in his grasp, he would teach her a valuable lesson. A few of the women in his past had learned the hard way *not* to cross him, and Melody would be no different. So, along with his carry-on bag and monetary supplies, Clarke also packed a gun set- fully equipped with silencers.

It occurred to him why Melody had so easily forgiven his wager with Luke Bryant. Melody wanted to lure him to the castle for the wedding at all costs. It was there the authorities were planning to ensnare him. Clarke praised Melody's brilliant performance for Luke Bryant. She'd undoubtedly known he'd be watching via hidden camera.

Clarke connected the dots. It now made sense why the cameras over at Melody's were no longer viable. Melody had them found and removed. The authorities had detected and disabled them. Melody wasn't only beautiful, but she was too smart for her own good. Her brains and beauty would be her downfall.

At that point, Clarke perceived *he* was the one being monitored. And so, he had to play it cool. He had to get out of the building just as soon as possible. Before making his escape, he decided to go down to the front desk to have a word with Oliver. Clarke asked Oliver to carry his luggage over towards the back exit of the building. There was a private apartment there, which Clarke had intentionally left vacant for such an event.

Through that apartment was a secret passageway. He was the only one who knew the access code to gain entry. Clarke would need to walk through a very dimly-lit tunnel, but the exit would lead him at least six blocks away from the Waverly Building. However, Oliver didn't need to be made privy to any of that information.

Clarke also asked another favor of Oliver. He requested that Oliver take a trip over to his private parking garage, and to drive his new silver Benz up front. Clarke must have had over a dozen cars in the garage, but he figured the small sedan was exactly what he needed.

Not asking any questions, Oliver obliged him. "Is there anything wrong, Mr. Vale?" He frowned, nonplused.

"No, not at all. Everything's fine, Oliver." Clarke had a cunning smile on his face. "You *know* how it is. My fiancée and I want to steal a few moments alone before the wedding. The press is everywhere. So, I've decided to go on foot. She's meeting me just a few blocks away." Deceit masked his winsome face. "The measures one has to take to avoid the press..." He gave Oliver a clever wink.

"Oh, I get it. I'm a romantic too. It's nice to get away from it all, especially since your wedding's going to be so highly publicized."

Clarke nodded. "You know how that is. So, my fiancée and I just want a few moments of privacy, before they descend on us like vultures tomorrow." Clarke had a treacherous expression on his face, but Oliver was much too gullible to read into his intentions. So, he went out to the garage, and brought the car out just as Clarke had requested.

"Thank you for trying out my new Mercedes, Oliver." Clarke smiled duplicitously. "The reason why I asked you to drive it out this morning, is because it's *yours*!" he announced. "You've been so efficient in helping me, so this is the little extra I mentioned." Clarke's eyebrows furrowed suggestively.

Temporarily rendered speechless, Oliver's mouth gaped in shock. "Mr. Vale, it's *your* new Mercedes." He kept shaking his head in disbelief.

"No good deed..." Clarke's wily expression had even more definition. "You already have the keys, and the paperwork's in the glove compartment. In fact, take an extended break tonight, and test out your new ride."

Moving past his initial reticence and skepticism, Oliver jumped right in. "You don't have to tell me twice, Mr. Vale." He turned away quickly to access the elevator.

"Enjoy the ride, Oliver. You should *definitely* take the scenic route." Clarke's eyes danced in deviousness.

While Oliver set out to test his new ride, Clarke rushed back up to the penthouse, and changed out of his comfortable slacks and sweater. He had to dress down completely. So, he threw on a faded and stylishly torn pair of jeans, a hooded jacket, and a pair of sneakers. Clarke also put on a baseball cap for effect.

Oliver was the perfect decoy. *He* would be the one driving Clarke's new car to throw off the authorities. In the meantime, Clarke went through the secret passageway of the vacant apartment behind the building. He walked quickly through the dimly-lit tunnel, and came out on a local street, blocks away from the Waverly Building. The taxi he'd called for pulled up almost immediately, and Clarke jumped into the car without hesitation.

The cab would convey him over to a private garage downtown, where he kept a number of other cars, most of which had been registered under aliases. Clarke knew that this day might come. So, having cars *not* tied into his name or to Vale Corp, had come in very hand.

So, while Oliver paraded around in his silver Benz, Clarke managed to make it to an undisclosed location, looking like an average Joe. He accessed his private garage, and chose a black town car. He set his luggage and the attaché case, which contained his gun in the trunk, and drove away.

He had to lure Melody away, before the limo made it over to Royale Valley to pick her up for the wedding. In light of the circumstances, Clarke wanted to skip the wedding, and go straight to their honeymoon. There were a *number* of reasons why Clarke needed to have Melody all to himself. So, this was an appointment neither of them could afford to miss.

***

"Is that Vale driving around in that silver Benz at this godless hour?" Agents and officers examined. They were planted in various locations in the vicinity, keeping track of everyone who went in or out of the Waverly Building.

"I don't think that's him," the men examined extensively.

"That's probably one of his men." The agent zeroed in to study the man sitting behind the wheel.

"I don't care if it's *Mickey Mouse* sitting behind the wheel. Tail him," Sergeant Griffith said. He had every intention of following through until the very end. Clarke Vale *had* to go down and fast.

"Whatever you say, Sergeant, it's your jurisdiction," the agents and officers complied.

They continued to tail the silver Benz. However, they'd missed the man on foot, who'd found a secret exit out of the Waverly Building. That man had on casual clothes, and had vanished like early morning mist. Having no other leads, the authorities followed the silver sedan, while Clarke had already ghosted them. Soon enough, they would come to realize that the man behind the wheel, had nothing to do with their investigation. In Clarke's estimation, eluding the authorities, was a total cakewalk.

CHAPTER NINE

"Thanks for giving me a break, Sean." Luke hopped back into the black jeep parked out in Sean's driveway. The jeep was the third of the three vehicles he'd rented out yesterday. He'd just showered, changed, and had finally grabbed a bite to eat.

His new disguise was as a man at least sixty pound heavier. Making him look all the more unrecognizable, he also had a curly red-haired wig, with full on moustache and a beard. Luke was grateful to have gotten a little bit of rest. It was after six in the morning, and he was wiped out. Even so, having taken a powernap, was a lot better than falling asleep at the wheel, which had almost occurred earlier on.

While he'd napped, Sean had kept tabs on Melody. Sean had barely even *seen* his wife Nicole, who'd just finished an overnight shift at Sands Port Hospital. Luke loved the fact that Nicole never questioned his antics with Sean, no matter how outlandish they seemed. While Luke was inside of the house, he'd seen Nicole. She'd floated out into the kitchen for a glass of water. When she'd seen him, she'd taken a good long look, and had simply said good morning. Afterward, Nicole had gone back to bed, without saying another word.

"Don't mention it. Listen, Melody's fine. There's been no activity outside of Serena and Dane's. So, she's safe for now. No one's left the house since early last night." Sean slid over to the passenger's side seat, and allowed Luke to take his place behind the wheel.

Luke sighed in relief. "At least, she's all right for now. As long as she stays over there she should be fine, but I'm not ruling anything out. Sean, I *know* Melody doesn't want me around, but someone's got to stop that wedding." Concern wrinkled his face.

"Luke, I wasn't going to tell you, but…" Sean frowned in jeopardy.

"What's going on, man?" Luke was puzzled.

"Okay… So, when you were over at the car rental place yesterday afternoon, I actually stopped in to see Mel." Sean flinched, because he knew Luke was about to put him on blasts.

"You went to see Mel?" Luke was surprised, and jeopardy strained his face. "Why would you do that and not tell me?" Luke reached up, and started brushing his fingers through the curly red wig, but stopped short, when he realized it wasn't his own hair. Nervous habits were hard to break. He looked over at Sean, and shook his head in skepticism. "Why, man?"

"I *had* to talk to her after you told me what happened at the restaurant yesterday. You were devastated after overhearing her conversation with Clarke."

Luke took a deep breath, and stared Sean squarely in the eyes. "What did Melody say when you saw her?"

"She said all the things she told *you*. Only, she said them to *me*."

Luke held his right hand up to convey that he'd heard quite enough.

"Luke, Melody said a lot of things. She tried even harder to convince me yesterday, but I know something's off. She was so on the defensive about Clarke."

"You don't have to tell me, Sean. It creeped me out seeing her that way, almost as if someone brainwashed her."

"Exactly, buddy. Maybe *Clarke* brainwashed her." Sean shook his head contrarily, still leery of the conversation he'd had with Melody. "Maybe, she's hell bent on defending him, because she's terrified. All I'm saying is don't be so quick to throw in the towel."

"Melody might be scared, but she was decisive. She made up her mind, and nothing anyone says will change it," Luke's voice broke. "It's possible Clarke has her too scared to go against him. Still, if everything goes according to *Clarke's* twisted plan, she's actually going to marry him today. I can't let that happen." Luke's demeanor was cemented in determination.

"Don't worry, buddy. Even if you're *theoretically* out of town, I'm still here, and I'm not going to let Melody marry that monster. You can count on that." Sean patted Luke's right arm.

Luke sent a prayer heavenward. "Not to mention the fact that I haven't really been *me* these past couple of days." Luke showcased his costume and farmer overalls. "I will crash that wedding if it's the last thing I do." Luke's eyes shifted over to the GPS. Intermittently, he checked for activity taking place outside of the Hennessey's in Royale Valley.

"Yeah, we're going to crash it together, 'Carrot-top Santa,'" Sean teased.

Luke set his hand on the fat suit, and rubbed on his fake full tummy. He also reached up, and felt the matching beard and moustache. He *had* to laugh when he caught a glimpse of his face in the rearview mirror. He *did* look like a carrot-top version of St. Nick in those duds. "Well, what do you know? Ho, Ho, Ho.... Santa's busting up that wedding today," Luke affirmed.

"*Dangerous Santa*," Sean teased. "Luke..." Sean's demeanor changed. "I'm going by Serena and Dane's in a little while to drop off Melody's *wedding gift*. It's just another opportunity to talk to her. I couldn't figure her out yesterday."

"Sean, I don't know... What makes you think she'll listen? She refuses to hear one negative word about Clarke." Luke checked the GPS again.

"I just got this feeling she *wanted* to tell me something, but couldn't...if you know what I mean." Sean pouted.

Luke gave Sean a nonplused look. "I pray she *does* talk to you, Sean. I'd like to be close by when you talk to her if that's all right."

"Luke, if you're close by when I go out to Royale Valley, you've got to remain out of sight. Melody can't suspect you're still hanging around. She'll flip." Sean's eyes flashed in warning.

Luke nodded in agreement. "Yeah, I get it. My presence doesn't exactly evoke the same reaction it once did for her. She doesn't *smile* when she sees me anymore." Luke smiled ironically.

"Melody's hurt, Luke. She's only pushing you away because she's scared."

Luke looked down for a moment, but then looked over at Sean. "I *know* Melody's hurt. One bad decision caused so much trouble for everyone." Tears gleamed in his eyes. "It's my fault she's in danger…that we're all in danger. Sean, I wish that I'd waited before taking that offer from Vale."

Sean sighed and patted Luke's arm again. "Luke, you've got to stop beating yourself up about that. We've got to remain focused and levelheaded. There's no time to look back. It's forward moving from this point on.

"I know your faith in God is strong, Luke. You're the one who's always telling me that nothing happens by chance," Sean reminded. "How do you know God's not going to use *this* plan to stop that sleaze, Vale? God has ultimate control. So, everything *will* work out."

"I guess, I *really* needed a reminder. I *will* trust God right now. I trust Him to make a way. God's got Melody. In fact, he's got all of us." Luke tried to move past the negative feelings. If everything worked according to plan, their nightmare was just about over.

Even if his connection to Melody was still up in the air, Luke was hopeful that she'd make it through this situation unscathed. That was all he truly cared about. He wanted Melody safe, and thankfully everything was falling into place.

Melody had to know exactly *why* she was in danger. In light of the circumstances, it seemed she had absolutely no idea that Clarke was-amongst other things, a coldblooded murderer. No matter how Melody tried to spin it, Luke couldn't see her justifying that. Luke acknowledged that his own set of actions, had caused Melody unspeakable pain. Melody was indeed hurting. What he wanted was a chance to take the pain away. His immediate goal was to shield her from harm, and that was something he resolved to do at any costs.

Even so, Luke grasped that it was only a matter of time before the authorities closed in on Vale. Finally, there seemed to be enough evidence to arrest him. Some of the witnesses Sean had connected to down in the DR, were also ready to come forward. They would undoubtedly need protection from the authorities, because Clarke's hand was far-reaching.

Nonetheless, Luke and Sean perceived that someone even *closer* to home had stumbled upon damning evidence against Clarke. Some courageous soul had stepped forward with the proof needed to put Clarke Vale away for good. Luke considered how brave that person was. No doubt, that individual was going to need safeguarding from the authorities as well.

***

"Serena, come on. It's getting late," Melody said. She was sitting at Serena's vanity in her and Dane's bedroom.

Serena had floated into the huge walk-in closet, looking for her makeup bag. It had suddenly gone missing, but she was determined to find it. While Serena rummaged through the closet, she couldn't help thinking how quiet the house was. If things had gone according to plan, Melody's four bridesmaids would have been there getting ready for the big event. However, because the wedding was a total sham, the bridal party had been informed of a postponement until further notice.

There was no need to drag anyone else into their web of danger, especially since no one really knew how things were going to play out over at the castle. So, for now, Serena planned to be the only one by Melody's side when the limo swung by to pick them up. Even if neither she nor Dane would *ever* allow Melody to marry Clarke Vale, Serena figured Melody could at least *look* the part of the blushing bride. Serena wanted to believe that it was practice for when Melody *really* got married.

Melody stared at herself in the mirror in a daze. Her face was flawlessly made up, minus a few accents here and there. She had to make herself stop crying. As it was, she'd already spent half the night in tears. Serena had stayed up with her, and had kept her sane.

There was no turning back at that point. The FBI had frequented the Hennessey house from very early on that morning. The agents were cleverly disguised as delivery people, employees for the power plant, last minute gift-givers and florists, who were delivering flowers for the special event. The authorities upheld that the plan to ambush Clarke over at the castle was still intact. They deemed it to be the perfect decoy.

There were FBI agents dispersed throughout the area-staking out key spots on the castle grounds. The castle was located in *Lalique Falls*. The historic landmark was twelve miles south of Royale Valley. The citadel was breathtaking, and had been restored to its original beauty. The castle was majestic! It was the kind of setting that could only be found in storybook fairytales.

It broke Melody's heart to consider that if the circumstances were ideal, she would have been proud to be holding her wedding at such a prestigious venue. However, there would be no wining or dining that day, because there was absolutely no cause for celebration. Rather, there would be betrayal, a great deal of regret, and the potential for great danger.

Melody's throat felt scratchy, but she choked back tears. All she could think about was being with Luke. More than anything else, she wished today was *their* wedding day, rather than the nightmare it was turning into.

Even if the circumstances were cruel, Melody was very grateful that the authorities seemed to have everything under control. However, the most reassuring feeling was the knowledge that God was with her. Melody had faith that God wouldn't allow any harm to come to her, or to her loved ones.

Still, there was that sinking feeling in the pit of her stomach, and Melody wanted to run away. It took all the restraint she had not to call Sean, and ask if Luke was still in town. Melody wanted to find Luke, run into his arms, and leave everything else behind. The desire to steal away with Luke seemed to be intensifying by the second. Melody fell apart, and had to catch the tears brimming over in her eyelids.

She kept trying to pull it together, because there was way too much at stake. Melody also kept reminding herself that God was working it out, and that the nightmare was almost over. Nervously, she twisted the tendrils of her upswept hair, and applied a little bit more blush to her cheeks. It was just after 10 a.m., and Melody's cellphone went off. She remained virtually frozen, and her heart clumped up in knots, when Clarke's face and name appeared on the screen.

Just then, Serena returned from her excursion. Seeing the look on Melody's face, she tossed the makeup bag on her bed, and rushed over to Melody's side. "Are you okay...?" Serena's eyes shifted over to the phone, and immediately realized the source of the problem.

Melody held her hand up in a halting manner. "I can handle this, Serena." She sighed and paused just before answering. "Good morning, Clarke!" Melody tried to sound chipper.

"Good morning, Pretty Lady! How was your night?"

"My night was great!" Melody looked up at Serena. Serena had her arms crossed over her chest, and an apprehensive expression on her face. "How was yours?" Melody asked.

"Well, any night away from *you* is unbearable. I can't wait to have you all to myself later," Clarke said sonorously. "I miss you so much right now, I think I'm going to lose my mind."

"Clarke, we're going to be together in just a little while. I'm trying to be strong, so you should too," Melody feigned lightheartedness.

"Melody, you have no idea. I'm not as strong as you are, Pretty Lady. In a little while, Wayne's going to drive me over to

Royale Valley. There's just one last thing I forgot to give you, and it's very important," Clarke baited.

"Clarke, you've spoiled me quite enough with all the gifts. Don't you think so?" Melody frowned suspiciously, as she racked her brains trying to figure out what Clarke was up to.

"Spoiling you is my job, sweet girl," Clarke philandered. "You probably look so tantalizing right now. I can't wait to feel you in my arms." Clarke was staying at a low key motel in the downtown area of Sands Port. He was still dressing down, so that he wouldn't be identified. However, it was now time to get dressed for the wedding. After all, he had to *look* the part when he stopped by to pick Melody up at her best friend's home.

Melody gave Serena a look of uncertainty and shrugged. "You want to give me a present *today*? Clarke, you're going to have to let me finish getting dressed, so that I can look pretty for you. You've got to give a girl a little time. Can you have Wayne *drop* it off?" Melody's eyes connected critically to Serena's.

Serena scowled suspiciously, but she nodded in agreement with the direction Melody seemed to be steering Clarke.

Knowing he would be in total control of the situation, Clarke played along. "First of all, it takes no time at all for you to look pretty, Melody. You're beautiful when you roll out of bed in the morning," Clarke vamped. "Secondly, you're right. Maybe, I *am* being just a little bit selfish. I guess, I just wanted a sneak peek. But, I guess I can have Wayne *drop* off my little token of affection in just a little while."

"*Remember* we talked about this? No peeking until we're at the altar." Melody felt queasy, and had no idea how to keep from chucking. Everything about Clarke made her sick.

"I promise to do better, Pretty Lady. I guess, when you're crazy about someone, you try to honor your word," Clarke said with double entendre. Inwardly, his heart was broken because he *did* love Melody. The way he felt about her wasn't logical or pragmatic, and Clarke second guessed himself. *Was he capable of actually doing harm to the person he loved most in the world?*

"That's right, handsome. So, I will see you at the altar," Melody's voice pealed like tiny bells.

"Of course… Your wish is my command, my lovely wife-to-be! So, Wayne should be swinging by there in just a little bit."

"Okay. Thanks, Clarke," Melody said hurriedly. She couldn't stomach any more intimate and endearing exchanges with a murderer. After Clarke said a few more words, Melody shut down her phone.

She looked into Serena's tear-filled eyes, and tried to be brave. "He wants to bring a gift over for me, but I discouraged him from delivering it personally. His limo driver's bringing it over instead."

Serena nodded in agreement. "I got the gist of it, Mel. You *did* the right thing by redirecting him. The less you see of that man today the better." Serena reached down and gently cupped Melody's chin. "You're going to get through this today. I promise. *We're* going to get through it, Mel. This nightmare is quickly coming to an end," Serena heartened.

Still a bit shaky after speaking to Clarke, Melody shook her head in uncertainty. "I pray that we do get through it, Serena. I can't stand another moment of this."

"It's going to be all right, honey. It *is* coming to end." Serena scrutinized Melody's face, and pointed a playful, but accusatory finger in her face. "You've been crying again, Mel, but no more tears. We've got to convince that *devil* that you're over-the-top in love, and elated to be marrying him."

Melody nodded, but ironic laughter issued from the hollow of her throat. "I'm over the top all right. I'm over the top to see him locked up for good. And, I'm *so* over the top done with him."

Serena smiled and winked. "Now, that's my girl."

The doorbell rang just then, and Melody instantly tensed up. "That couldn't possibly be Wayne so soon…? It hasn't even been five minutes…" Her heart had jumped into her throat.

Serena added a few more touches to Melody's make up. "It's all right. I asked Dane to pick up a few things from the CVS up the road. You wait right here." Serena went to get the door.

Melody froze up again, but realized she wasn't glued to the chair in Serena and Dane's bedroom. So, she got up and left the bedroom. She shuffled down the hallway, and wandered into the living room. Serena was standing at the front door, but she turned reflexively when she heard Melody's footsteps coming towards the living room.

Melody watched Serena open up the front door. "Sean!" Serena heralded and threw her arms affectionately around him.

All of the former fears ebbed, as Melody walked boldly over to the door, and stood behind Serena. "Sean...?" Melody's face wrinkled in confusion.

"Hello, Melody." Sean smiled affably, as he stood there holding a huge, red, glittering gift box in his hands.

"Sean, you really shouldn't have." Melody frowned, as Serena ushered Sean into the house.

"Can I get you some something to drink, Sean?" Serena offered graciously.

Wary because Luke was parked only blocks away from the house, and keeping tabs on every bit of activity surrounding it, Sean wanted to keep his visit short. "No thanks, Serena. I just came by to give this to Melody." Sean's eyes searched Melody's extensively.

"Thank you for the gift," Melody said kindly. She was overjoyed to see Sean. Asking him about Luke was on the tip of her tongue, but she couldn't afford to mess things up. In just a few hours, everything would come to a head. So, the further away Luke and Sean stayed, the less likely they were to be in the eye of the storm when it hit.

"You're welcome!" Sean smiled, and inched in closer to Melody. She was standing at the center of the spacious living room. He set the gift box on the living room sofa. "You look amazing!" he complimented.

Melody smiled timidly. "Yeah, well, I'm not even wearing the dress yet."

"Melody, you would look amazing wearing a custodial jumpsuit!"

Melody laughed to remember her ongoing joke with Luke about the green jumpsuit he used to wear when he worked for Sands Port Elementary. "Funny thing about jumpsuits...," Melody started to say, but stopped short. "Seriously, I'm *so* glad to see you! If you hear from Luke, can you tell him something for me?" Her face twisted in remorse.

"Of course I will."

"Can you tell him that it isn't personal, and that things in life play out as they're meant to?" Melody tried to appease, but realized her words sounded trite.

Sean nodded. "I will tell him just that, but there's something *I* need to tell *you* this morning."

Melody's eyes explored Sean's urgently and she gulped. "Okay...," she acquiesced with an anxious expression.

"But I really *need* for you to listen, and not say anything until I'm done."

Melody nodded in compliance. "Okay..."

"First of all, I'm *really* sorry for being so intrusive yesterday. I didn't mean to come off like the best-friend avenging vigilante."

Melody laughed lightly. "I didn't think you came off that way at all. In fact, Sean, I think you're the best friend and brother anyone could ask for. Luke is *so* lucky to have you."

"Thank you for saying that." Sean smiled hopefully.

Melody held her hand out haltingly. "I'm sorry. There I go...talking again. I will shut up."

"Melody, Clarke Vale is a known criminal in the Caribbean and in all of Central American. He knows how to limit his illegal practices in the states, because he's a cunning business man. He works covertly in America-getting crooked men to do his dirty work, but there are a lot of accounts of missing people, hits that were ordered on men and women who crossed him.

"Luke wanted to tell you everything, but didn't get the chance. But, *I'm* here to warn you not to marry this man. Clarke isn't only devoid of a conscience and a mafia lord, he's a murderer." Sean inspected Melody's face for any indication of shock or fear, but she looked totally composed and unaffected. "Melody, did you *hear* anything I just said?"

Melody nodded in affirmation. "Sean, I know. I know all about Clarke. I know he's a *murderer*. He's killed out in the states and abroad. I know it all," Melody confessed. Tears shone in her eyes again.

Confused, Sean drew closer, and examined the sadness on her face and in her eyes. "Melody, you know? And you're *still* going to marry him?" Sean kept shaking his head in perplexity and disapproval.

Melody's tear-filled eyes connected expressly to Sean's. "I'm *not* going to marry him," she said plainly. "Please, don't ask me anymore questions, okay?" Her face creased in jeopardy.

Bewildered, Sean nodded in concurrence. "Okay… You *know* all about Clarke, and you're **not** going to marry him," he said rhetorically, as he tried to process her words.

"I need for you to trust me today, okay? I will say this," Melody paused, "I know exactly who Clarke is. It's because I do know who and *what* he is, I have to convince him that *we're* getting married today." Melody stared solemnly into Sean's eyes. She perceived that if anyone was capable of grasping what she was saying, it was Sean.

"I *understand*," Sean said decisively. It occurred to him that Melody was waist-deep in a plot to bring Clarke down as well. Internalizing that reassured him immensely. Sean didn't want to ask any more questions, but he had to ensure she was going to be okay. "Is there anything *I* can do to help you meet that goal today?" Sean's face rumpled in conflict.

"Yes…" Melody's eyes fastened urgently to his. "You can give me a little space to work it out. Please… And, if Luke's still in town, please advise him to do the same." Melody had to drive the point home. She had to relay that it wasn't a good idea for either of them to get involved, because the authorities had it all under control.

"If that's what you want, sweetheart," Sean said, relieved. He sighed. "You have no idea how happy I am to know that you're not marrying that man. I'm so glad I came by."

"I'm glad you came by too." Melody smiled mawkishly at Sean.

Sean collected Melody in his arms. "I think you're incredibly brave!"

"Right…" Melody guffawed.

"You *really* are. Please, don't hesitate to give me a call if you need me."

Melody squeezed Sean lovingly. "It's all under control. Promise me that you'll stay as far away from this sham of a wedding today as you possibly can. And, promise me you'll keep Luke away too," Melody said thickly, with shimmering eyes.

Sean just gave Melody a heartening smile, because neither he, nor Luke would be able to honor her request. Even if Melody had said that everything was under control, they would have to ride it out till the very end so that she remained safe. "Please, be safe, Mel." Sean pulled away.

"I will be, Sean." Melody searched his eyes once again. "Thank you for everything."

"You're welcome!" Sean said and turned to leave.

Melody followed him to the door. Sean opened up the front door, but turned back to connect to her. "You know where to find me…anytime," he emphasized.

"I know." Melody nodded. "Thank you for honoring my wishes." She smiled faintly.

Sean gave her a well-meaning look. "Bye, Melody."

"Bye, Sean."

Melody watched him turn away, and dismount the steps. Sean jumped into his SUV, and rolled away from the house.

"Is he gone?" Serena floated back into the living room.

Melody shut the front door, and turned to face her bestie. "Yeah, he just left."

"Everything okay?" Serena moved in closer to Melody.

"Yeah, it's okay. Sean's the greatest guy! Being around him makes me feel closer to Luke," Melody admitted.

"Oh, honey…" Serena wrapped her arms around Melody in comfort. "I can't imagine how miserable you feel today, but it's almost over. Then, you can go to Luke, and tell him how much you still love him."

"I want to tell him so bad, Serena. I really wish he was here." Melody grimaced sentimentally. She told Serena all that she and Sean had talked about. Melody waited for Serena to censure her to being so upfront with Sean.

However, Serena agreed that she'd acted wisely. Serena praised her for giving Sean and Luke a little glimmer of hope that things would fall into place. "You did the right thing, Mel. Luke needs to know that the girl he fell in love with is still in there." Serena pointed to Melody's heart.

"I want him to know that I haven't changed as much as he thinks, and that I don't hate him." Melody shrugged, and tried to sound courageous. Inwardly, her heart felt splintered, because she couldn't tell Luke for herself. Still, she hoped Sean had seen into her heart, and that he'd convey to his best friend that she was intrinsically the same girl. Melody wanted to believe that the hope she'd offered was enough.

***

Encouraged by his conversation with Melody, Sean drove away from Serena and Dane's. He couldn't wait to tell Luke everything Melody had said. She knew exactly who Clarke Vale was, and was *in* on the takedown. It was such a relief to know that Melody never planned on marrying Clarke. Sean made a right turn at the corner up the street, and drove a few more blocks over. Luke wasn't parked too far away. They'd agreed that Luke would keep his distance, while he'd visited Melody.

Sean was coming up on an intersection. However, he wasn't allowed to proceed. A black luxury car abruptly pulled out in front of him. And, a burgundy SUV pushed out behind him. Both vehicles had him hemmed in. Sean was about to jump out of the car in order to confront the man in the car in front of him. However, he flinched, when the black luxury car door opened on the driver's side. The man behind the wheel stepped out brandishing a gun. Sean's heart somersaulted in his chest, and took to hammering.

The tall, husky man with a hazelnut complexion, walked authoritatively towards Sean's SUV. It had been all too easy to take out the FBI agents, who'd been parading around the area in order to *protect* Melody and her friends. It was easy as pie to spot them. The man prided himself for his fed-detection skills. Now that Melody and her friends no longer had the protection of the FBI and the police, it was time to take care of unfinished business.

Sean looked cagily behind him at the other car, and realized that both parties were in on the same plot. They were there to ensure he couldn't get away. The man holding the revolver gestured for Sean pull over to the side of the street. Sean had no idea who was driving the burgundy car behind him.

What he *did* know was that they were undeniably Vale's

men. Just then, all of the talks he and Luke had had about faith in God came rushing over Sean. Since Luke's life-altering decision to receive Jesus as Lord and Savior, he'd told Sean incessantly that he needed to do the same. Luke had emphasized how faith in Jesus Christ was the only way to escape the judgment of God upon death. Now, those words resonated with clarity. Without hesitation, Sean whispered a prayer to God, entreating his intervention at that moment. Sean then made a solemn vow to follow Jesus all the days of his life, if God brought him out of this situation alive.

Sean robotically did what the man had asked, and pulled over to the side of the street. The car behind him did the same, but no one stepped out of that vehicle. Sean's thoughts whizzed in uncertainty. He considered quickly pulling out, and driving away. Another exit strategy was to jump out of the car, and take to running. However, he realized that Clarke's *people* wouldn't hesitate to shoot. They would undoubtedly pump so many bullet holes into him, he would look like a block of Swiss cheese.

With a thrumming heart, Sean waited for the man who had the gun to approach. Suddenly, the stranger floated over to the side of the front passenger's side window. He demanded Sean to roll it down. "Hey, there," he said with a nefarious smile. "How's it going?"

Sean's heart plunged to his feet, but he inoffensively rested both hands on the steering wheel, where the man could see them. "Good…," Sean said shakily. "Anything *I* can help you with?" Tears glimmered in Sean's eyes. He was on the verge of peeing his pants, as the stranger fiddled with the gun above the rim of the opened car window.

"As a matter of fact there *is* something you can do to help me." The man smiled artfully. "You're going to stop meddling in other people's affairs, and you're not going to try to stop Melody Maxwell from marrying Clarke Vale this afternoon."

"Stop *who*?" Sean said coyly.

"Listen, *Sean*, *we* know all about your little investigation down in the Caribbean. You also had the nerve to fly out to Central America. Furthermore, you went to the police to detail things you discovered about Clarke Vale." The stranger's eyes flashed lethally.

Sean was terrified. His face was a mask of apprehension and dread. However, he refused to cower to this man-whoever he was. "Yes, I *did* go to the police, because Clarke Vale is nothing but a murderer. Has he sent you to kill *me* too?" Sean asked, finding supernatural courage. "I did what I had to, because someone's got to stop him."

The strange man hung his head down ponderingly for a moment, but suddenly looked up into Sean's face. "That's quite unfortunate. You're so young, and there's so much life ahead of you. And to answer your question, yes, he *has* sent me to kill you." His expression was sadistic. "And, I do agree... *Someone's* got to stop him, but it isn't going to be you."

"Don't do this," Sean said evenly, too incensed to find the heart to beg a criminal for his life.

"We also know exactly how to find that pretty little wife of yours. She works as a PA for Sands Port Hospital," the miscreant said derisively.

"Please, leave my wife out of this," Sean entreated. He was prepared to beg for Nicole's life. "She's done nothing wrong. She doesn't even know…"

"It doesn't matter now," the man retorted. Then, without hesitation, he pointed the gun at Sean's chest, and pulled the trigger. Using a new and sophisticated type of silencer, made the act seem less impactful than a needle stick in the emergency room.

Sean's head hit the steering wheel, as blood seeped through his dark blue T-shirt. Drops spilled over onto the dark leather seat. The man rushed around to the driver's side, and propped Sean up to make it look as if he'd pulled over for a nap. He then shut the passenger's side window, and walked away, as if he'd just finished having lunch. It was all in a day's work as far as he was concerned.

The man justified that Sean Winters had it coming. The kid was one of the people directly responsible for the trouble Clarke Vale was facing. The other responsible party was less than a mile away. And, in just a few minutes, as soon as he got the okay from Clarke, he would go deal with Melody Maxwell.

She was indeed a self-deceived young woman, because she thought she could pull the wool over the eyes of someone like Clarke Vale. She was about to pay dearly for making such a huge blunder. Luckily, Luke Bryant had skipped town before everything detonated. Still, Luke was *also* implicated in the investigation. So, once Clarke found refuge in his subterranean safe house, he would deal with Bryant as well. It was only a matter of time.

Luke had parked on a neighboring street near the Hennessey's waiting for Sean to return. However, he'd been sitting there for quite a while, and Sean hadn't returned, or even called for that matter. Luke felt sick to his stomach, because he'd seen Sean leave the Hennessey's about half an hour ago. At this point he was getting worried.

Luke's tracker was limited to certain areas in the locale, so he'd inadvertently lost track of Sean. So, Luke had no idea if Sean *had* run into a snag on a nearby street. Even so, if Sean had run into trouble, he would have called or texted. Panicked, Luke started driving around. He had to risk it to find Sean. If Clarke's men *were* lurking, Luke figured they wouldn't recognize him in the car rental, and with his Carrot-top Santa getup.

Luke was also about to take another huge risk. He'd made up his mind to use his groundbreaking program, which was still in the trial stages. He felt confident that he could access and utilize the important features. What good was his technological brainchild **Dimension Four**, if he couldn't put it to use now?

Sink or swim, Luke was about to test the intricacies of the technology. **Dimension Four** and its accessories, had the power to locate anything and anyone. It didn't matter where they were. The feature to locate missing people and objects was called **Dimension Find Me**. There was virtually no hiding from **Find Me**, because there was very little it couldn't detect. As long as DNA was present and accessible, *Find Me* had the capacity to unveil the mystery.

Luke decided to test out his breakout innovation. Sometimes, all he needed was to photograph an item belonging to the missing person. Sometimes, it required part of their DNA, such a fingerprint or a strand of hair. Luke immediately zeroed in on the coffee cup Sean had left in the cup holder earlier on. Then, he connected to *Dimension's* satellite on his phone, and scanned in Sean's fingerprints on the item.

In the very same way Siri is used on an IPhone, the program responded to Luke's inquest. *"What is your search?"* it inquired.

"Find Me, locate the individual with this DNA in the area," Luke put in the command. Immediately, the violet and white laser-like lights began sparking and blinking on the phone.

"The person you're looking for is within the radius of...," the automated voice detailed.

Luke's heart raced, and tears immediately glimmered in his eyes. According to *Find Me*, Sean was close by. "Where are you, man?" Luke asked shakily. "If anything happened, you would have called me." Luke felt winded, as he made a right turn up Faber Street. All the way down that block he spotted Sean's automobile. He was confused, because Sean was parked on the side street.

Luke partially shut down the program, but the blinking lights remained intact. "Sean..." Luke's heart lurched, because he realized something was *very* wrong. There was a feature to *Find Me* capable of generating an image of the missing person.

Luke commanded the program to project an image of Sean close up. Luke's heart plummeted when the image was generated. He saw Sean sitting lifeless inside the car, and blood was everywhere. Tears were in Luke's eyes, and his heart flagellated. He immediately called for an ambulance and the police.

Luke quickly pulled up behind Sean's car, and jumped out of the Jeep. Surely, this was one big nightmare. However, the closer he got to the scene, the more he realized that this was no dream. Sean's head was propped to the headrest, and his eyes were shut closed. "Oh, man... Sean, no.... No, this can't be real..." Luke closed his eyes with a sense of despair. "Sean, please...," he pleaded. His face contorted like an accordion. "Please, Lord, no... I'm so sorry, buddy..."

Luke cautiously opened up the vehicle. He set his hand on Sean's chest, and bawled like an infant. Luke's head slumped, when he felt someone tug on his hand. "Huh..?" Luke suddenly looked up, incredulous.

Sean's eyelids fluttered. "Luke, you've got to get out of here," he said faintly. "I'm sorry I couldn't make it back to you."

Hope sparked in the ashes of Luke's despair. He kept shaking his head in remorse. "Are you kidding me?" Hearing Sean's voice was like finding an oasis in the desert. "Please, try not to talk... Save your strength. I've already called an ambulance. They should be here shortly. Please, don't say another word."

"Luke..." Sean gulped, and gathered up what little strength he had left. "You've got to get out of here. You need to go look after Melody, Serena and Dane. If they did this to me, then... They're going after Mel next."

"Sean, please be all right. Hang in there, buddy. Help is on the way," Luke said thickly with fresh tears in his eyes. He hated having to leave Sean in that state.

"Don't let them hurt Melody," Sean said. "Get out of here. Don't worry about me," he ordered.

Luke was torn in a hundred pieces. No doubt, Clarke's men were going after Melody, and he couldn't let that happen. He would fight for her, even if it meant this was his last day on earth. Crazed, he moved away erratically, and jumped back into the Jeep.

Luke sighed in relief when he saw the ambulance lights flashing up the road. It didn't take very long for them to find Sean. Luke was grateful that they'd responded so quickly, and he prayed that God would spare his best friend. Seeing Sean so weak had affected him. Sean had probably been bleeding out for a while.

Tears flowed down Luke's cheeks, because of the uncertainty of the circumstances. As cautiously as they'd planned, something had gone terribly amiss, and Luke had lost his right hand man. Luke also prayed for God's strength and protection, because he was about to go into the lion's den to fight for the woman he loved. Luke *had* to make sure Melody came of this mess alive. However, his own fate still hung in the balance.

CHAPTER TEN

FBI agents and police raided Clarke's penthouse out in Waverly Falls, and turned the entire building upside down. Tenants and guests were forced to evacuate the premises. Building security had given the authorities access to Clarke's penthouse, and they'd searched every square inch, hoping to find even more damning evidence. However, nothing of consequence was recovered. They concluded that Vale had done his homework, because the place had been swept clean.

The authorities were frustrated, and couldn't figure out how Clarke had managed to get away. FBI agents dispersed throughout the *Lalique Castle*, confirmed that Clarke hadn't shown up to assume his role as the dashing groom. However, when the guests began to trickle in, agents and officers, had to tell them that the wedding was canceled. Fortunately, they were able to guide everyone safely off the premises. The guests had indeed been inconvenienced, but they were extremely cooperative. To avoid any unnecessary casualties, all uninvolved parties had to be redirected.

Clarke had vanished like mist on a foggy night, and they were baffled as to how. Still, they rest assured that Melody Maxwell was all right with her friends out in Royale Valley. A number of police officers and agents had been assigned to that area, to ensure that Melody and her friends remained safe. Because of the nature of the case, FBI had to work in conjunction with the local authorities. Bringing a man like Clarke Vale to justice wasn't only a state matter, but official government business.

However, both parties were stumped and miffed. They'd followed a false lead earlier that morning. The building doorman driving around in Clarke's new Mercedes Benz as a decoy, had thrown them completely off. The authorities weren't sure how, but Clarke Vale knew they were on to him. They'd been circumspect in all of their dealings, so taking Vale down should have been easy as pie. They'd had the *Invalable* Clarke Vale exactly where they'd wanted him, but the man had slipped through their fingers. However, they weren't throwing in the towel yet. No stone would be left unturned until he was found.

***

It was half past 1 p.m. Melody stood in front of the full-length mirror in her ivory, floor-length lace, white and silver beaded wedding gown. Her upswept hair shimmered like bronze and copper in the sunlight, and loose tendrils framed her angelic face. Her head piece was encrusted with diamonds and pearls, and her high back-strapped heels, shared the same sparkling diamond and pearl theme. Melody marveled seeing the finished product.

She couldn't stop thinking about Luke. She yearned for him to see her in the gown, and wished he was the one she was meeting at the altar. Crying had become as natural as breathing in the past few days, but Melody blinked back the tears. She had to find a way to pull it together. It was time to move into action with project *Clarke takedown*. Still, she couldn't help yearning for a *real* wedding day with Luke. Melody judged that if she and Luke made it through this horrible storm, they'd get a second chance to get it right.

Serena drifted back into the bedroom, and admired how perfect Melody looked. "Mel, you are an absolute vision! You look like you just descended from heaven!" Serena clasped her hands together, and stared sentimentally at her bestie. She brushed over Melody's gown with care and tenderness. "You're so beautiful!" Her face warped in sadness. "I wish Luke could see you in this gown."

Melody tried to keep a stiff upper lip. "I wish he was here too."

"One day soon it'll be the real thing, and with the man you love," Serena uplifted. She wrapped her arms around Melody in comfort.

"Melody held back tears. "That's all I want, Serena. He's all I want," she admitted.

"And, it's going to happen." Serena gave her a loving squeeze. "I can't wait to see you as happy as Dane and I are," she heartened, and pressed a kiss to Melody's cheek.

Melody examined how flawless Serena looked in her sand-colored gown, which glistened like new stars in the horizon. Her hair was the color of red and gold henna. The lengthy bangs were tightly curled, and cascaded everywhere like a waterfall. "You are the best friend and sister I've ever had! I love you!" Melody stared into Serena's eyes endearingly.

Serena set her hand over her heart, stirred beyond words. "I love you too, honey! You're my family." They hugged again.

"By the way, Reena, you're killing that dress. Poor Dane won't know what hit him." Melody smiled wistfully.

"Melody's right you know." Dane stood in the doorway of the bedroom virtually salivating over his wife. "You take my breath away!" he established. For a moment, he and Serena locked eyes, as if for the very first time.

"Dane, stop staring at me like that." Serena blushed.

"Now, wait just a minute. Let me get a picture of you two." Dane broke free from being totally spellbound. "It *is* safe for me to come in now, *isn't* it?" he teased.

"Yes, baby, you *can* come in now." Serena walked over to Dane, and gave him a reassuring look. Dane had put up with so much on that day. She draped her arms about him, and pressed a sweet kiss to his mouth.

"You look so good, honey," Dane whispered, as he pelted his wife's face with tender kisses.

"Thank you, baby. *You* look like a dream in that tux," Serena said softly, and pressed more kisses to Dane's lips.

"Thanks, baby," Dane said in between butterfly kisses.

Melody stared mawkishly at the couple, and allowed them to have their moment. It always warmed her heart to watch Serena and

Dane together. They had such a great relationship. Having someone who truly loved her was all Melody wanted. So, she questioned how things had gotten so off course in her life.

"Look at Mel, Dane." Serena directed her attention over to Melody. "I don't think I've ever seen a more beautiful bride!" Serena gaped lovingly over at her best friend.

"I might be just a little biased, Mel, but you *are* stunning!" Dane winked at her. "You're too beautiful to be sad today!" Dane moved in closer to Melody and cupped her chin. "You're about to win a tremendous victory over evil."

Melody smiled. "Thanks, Dane, but can I ask you a question?"

"Sure."

"Who says things like that? 'I'm about to win the victory over evil,'" she banteringly paraphrased.

Serena shook her head humorously. "Only Dane talks like that, Mel. My baby's a future pastor," Serena razzed. She cleared her throat, and did her best Dane impression. 'A tremendous victory over evil…' She got them all laughing.

"Now, you guys are wrong on so many levels…" Dane feigned hurt feelings. In the interim, he took a few pictures of Melody and Serena together. He wanted Melody to remember this event-not because it was a *real* wedding. He wanted Melody to remember it as the day God gave her the victory.

As they finished dressing for the wedding, the doorbell rang yet again. The startling noise knotted up Melody's heartstrings. She knew exactly who it was, because it was much too early for the limo to be there. "That must be Wayne bringing by the gift Clarke talked about."

Dane and Serena stood protectively on either sides of Melody.

"Mel, do you want me or Dane to get that? You don't have to go to the door you know." Serena's delved into Melody's eyes with consternations.

"No, Reena. Clarke's very touchy about things like this. So, the last thing I need is for him to doubt anything I do today. I'll go get his *gift*." She rolled her eyes in annoyance.

"Well, we're coming with you," Serena settled.

"Not letting you out of my sight today, Melody," Dane echoed.

Dane walked ahead of the women, and crossed over into the living room. Serena cautiously gathered the borders of Melody's gown in her hands, and followed behind her husband. Dane checked through the window blinds, and saw the black luxury car. "Looks like Wayne's here."

Dane walked over to the front door. He stood to one side of it, while Serena took her place to the other.

Melody stood directly in front of the door. "I've got this, guys. It's okay." She gave them a reassuring look. Melody took a couple of deep breaths, then pulled the door open. "Wayne, why are you so late bringing over Clarke's present…?" Melody started to say, but her voice trailed, when she realized Wayne wasn't the person standing at the door. It was Darien Stiles *dressed* like the Chauffer, and he had a gun pointed directly at her.

Melody screamed, and tried to push the door closed. "Serena, Dane, run…" Melody thrust forcefully against the front door, in an effort at barricading it.

"Melody, what's wrong?" Dane asked, confused. He knew there was someone at the door, but didn't realize there was a gun involved.

"Dane, get out of here. Darien has a gun," Melody shouted, still trying to force the door closed. However, she lost momentum when Darien pried the door open, and thrust past her. Darien immediately struck Dane on the head with the gun handle, and Dane crashed to the floor. Darien then used his free hand to shut the door closed.

Serena screamed, and cupped her mouth in shock. She rushed over to tend to Dane, who appeared to be knocked out cold.

Melody was petrified and tearful, as she connected the dots. Clarke was definitely on to them. She tried to move, but Darien was on top of his game. His facial expression daunted her to even flinch.

Tears of frustration and shock filled Serena's eyes, as she tried to revive her husband. "What do you want here? I knew you were trash dressed in a designer suit the moment I laid eyes on you." Serena glared at Darien. "You get out of here, and leave us alone."

Darien lowered at her and sneered. "You're not the one calling the shots up in here, lady. And, if I were you I'd be *real* quiet." His eyes slid down to his hand, as if to convey he wasn't afraid to use the other end of the revolver.

Melody shook her head in remorse. She couldn't believe what was happening. "You're a disgrace. I was such a fool, because I actually thought you were a good man. Now, I know who and *what* you are. I can't believe I let you to get close to me. What a huge mistake."

"Was the experience as good for you as it was for me?" Darien berated. "I still haven't gotten over those cherry lips." He licked his own lips in a provocative manner, and his eyes delved into Melody's in a salacious manner.

Melody repined and shrank back in disgust, as tears of frustration brimmed over her eyelids.

An inappropriately loud, but satisfying laugh echoed from the hollow of Darien's throat. "That's the one thing I *do* regret. You should have been mine." Darien shrugged flippantly. "But my boss wanted you. I have to say that I *get* why he paid such a hefty price." Darien continued to stare provocatively at Melody.

Melody couldn't wrap her head around the level of his depravity. She was both dumbfounded and nauseated. However, she resolved not to cower or beg. "I can't believe you, Darien. I really thought you were someone different." She stared at him in utter incredulity.

"Never go by appearances, honey. Hasn't your mother ever taught you that?" He stared derisively at her.

Melody blew off his allusions to familiarity, and his illusions of grandeur. There was only one goal at that point. It was to protect her loved ones at all costs.

"Darien, I know Clarke has a matter to settle with *me*. *I'm* the one he wants. So, please leave my friends alone," she appealed. Even if Melody couldn't see Serena's face, she could feel the daggers darting out from her best friend's eyes, and pointed in Darien's direction. Melody perceived that her best friend was trying to figure out a way to fight back. Melody knew that was probably the worst idea in the world. So, she had to act fast, if she didn't want Darien leaving behind any fatalities after he took her away.

"Melody, my Melody… Oh, *my*, how I've missed you! You're even more beautiful than I remember!" Darien's eyes scanned over every inch of her.

"What is it that you want, Darien? You want *me*, so here I am. Let's go right now. Leave my friends out of it," she negotiated.

"I *have* come for you, Melody. I've come to pick you up for the wedding," Darien informed. He then looked down at Serena. "You get up and go sit over there." He pointed the gun towards the sofa.

"I'm so sorry, Serena." Melody's face twisted in misery, as Serena was forced to stand to her feet.

"It's not your fault, Melody." Serena walked deliberately over to the sofa, as she'd been commanded to. She shrugged resignedly. "You won't get away with this," she told Darien.

"One more word out of you…" Darien shook his head contrarily, as he glowered at Serena.

"God is still in control," Serena said bravely.

"Aren't you *brave*? If you keep this up, both you and your husband will be meeting *Him* in person today," Darien barked.

"Where are you taking me, Darien?" Melody tried to redirect his attention away from Serena and Dane. "I know that you're not really here to take me over to the castle for the wedding. Where are you taking me, and what do you want?" Melody gulped nervously.

"It isn't what *I* want, Melody. It's what *Clarke* wants. You're going to take a little ride with us."

"No... Melody no... Don't go anywhere with that..." Serena trembled, and her face was bathed in tears. She leaned forward, positioned to jut out and attack Darien, but she pulled back in frustration.

Darien's eyes impaled straight through Serena's with the gun pointed at her. "What...? You want to hurt *me*? Ooh," he derided, "*I'm* shaking. Now, Serena, this is my final warning. If you don't shut that trap of yours, it's a done deal. Don't test me, girl." He scowled insidiously.

"Darien," Melody petitioned, "*I'm* the one you want. Please... Just take me. Leave Serena and Dane out of this. I'll go wherever you and Clarke want to take me." Melody quaked, but tried to sound courageous.

Melody was still having a difficult time processing what had gone wrong. It seemed Clarke had undeniably managed to evade the police and even the FBI. Their plan was totally botched. That meant, Clarke wouldn't be apprehended at the castle as they'd contrived. Moreover, if God didn't step in, there was no telling what would happen to her. Melody already knew the deal. Women who betrayed Clarke's trust, never lived to tell about it. Her heart sank in terror, as she considered that she would be another one of his victims.

Darien smiled cannily at Melody. "All right, if that's what you want, *Beautiful*!" He shook his head, and stared lasciviously over Melody's entire body. "I can't believe I gave you up." He grunted. "You should have been mine. Still, I *did* tell Clarke you were the type who would someday bite the hand that feeds you."

Melody had the tremors, and tears dripped down from her

eyes like a leaky faucet. Even if she was outraged, Melody perceived she had to play it smart, and remain as calm as possible. Darien's hand never wavered with the gun pointed to her chest. At that point, Serena was crying inconsolably. Melody knew how helpless she felt in the matter. Serena couldn't even look after Dane, who remained unconscious and vulnerable on the living room floor.

"Can we go now?" Melody asked, traumatized. "I'm willing to go wherever you…I mean, wherever *Clarke* wants to take me…"

She held both hands out in entreaty. "Please, let's just go. Don't hurt my friends."

"Melody's going to take a little ride with us." Darien glared icily over at Serena. "Don't worry, sweet Serena, Melody will be just fine. She *will* be fine as long as you, your meddling husband, and her friends stay out of her business. If you even attempt to contact the police, the FBI or whoever is *supposedly* trying to conduct this little sting, it's bye-bye, Melody." Darien smirked. "I can guarantee that you'll never see your bestie again. Are we clear?" he blared.

Melody turned and looked over at Serena. Seeing the look on Serena's face broke her heart.

Serena sobbed, and clutched desperately at her chest. "Yeah, we're clear," she said caustically, giving Darien the death stare.

Serena then looked over at Melody with a sorrowful expression. "I love you, Mel" Her heartstrings tightened, and she couldn't seem to get enough air into her lungs.

Melody stared ruefully over at Serena. "I love you too, Reena! This isn't your fault, and it's going to be all right." Melody's eyes affixed to Serena's, as Darien's blood-soiled hands clamped on her arm.

"We need to go now, Melody. Tell your people to back off, or they will all end up like your friend Sean. Now move…" He tugged on her arm, and pushed her towards the front door.

The front door was now opened, and Melody's eyes shifted

nervously about the quiet street for any sign of Sean. "What did you do to Sean, Darien?" she asked frantically. "What have you done, Darien?" Melody squirmed.

Darien stared intently into her eyes. "Let's just say he won't be taking any trips down to the Caribbean or to Central America any time soon."

Melody's face twisted in horror and misery. "You're an animal and a miscreant. I don't know how I ever got involved with you *or* your boss," she said regretfully.

"As I remember it, you thought I was *charming*," Darien mocked, as he manhandled her in the direction of the waiting black luxury car.

Melody shook her head in both disgust and incredulity. Regret overpowered her like ocean waves, and she was drowning. She tried to scream, but her voice was muffled by the gun pressed up to her back. So, Melody swallowed the pain, and tried to remain strong.

She was moving quickly towards oblivion, but couldn't stop thinking about Sean. Tears pushed through her eyes all the more, as it dawned on her that he was probably dead. The realization tore her apart. Melody felt as if she was trapped in a nightmare, and kept willing herself to wake up. However, the sun searing on her skin, and piercing through her tear-filled eyes, was too sobering to be a reverie.

What made matters worse was that Darien's ill intent couldn't easily be detected. Anyone who saw them together, would have concluded he was the perfect gentleman escorting her to the waiting car on her wedding day.

There was always that one nosy neighbor watching everything happening in the locale. However, on that fateful afternoon, the block was practically deserted. Very little was going on-if anything at all. Melody could have counted on one hand the number of cars parked in the neighboring driveways. Trying to establish some kind of connection, her head shifted nervously about, but no one was around. Melody kept seeing images of Sean somewhere isolated bleeding to death.

The realization of what Clarke's men had done to Sean, killed her. It broke her heart that she was powerless to help Sean at that point. She hoped and prayed that Luke wasn't anywhere close by. All of it was *her* fault. She'd allowed Darien into her life. Melody realized that she'd opened up the doors of danger first with Darien. Clarke must have seen her on Darien's arm, and decided he wanted her for himself. Her affiliation with the miscreant Darien Stiles, had brought all of the other *undesirables* into her life.

Her prince charming had turned into prince nightmare, and her mistakes had trickled into the lives of her loved loves. Now, Sean was hurt and quite possibly dead. Melody sent a prayer heavenward. She prayed that Luke would stay as far away from the mayhem as possible. If anything happened to Luke, Melody knew that she'd go completely over the edge.

Darien *seemed* like the perfect gentleman. His mannerisms were deceptively pleasant, and Melody was totally baffled by it, especially in light of the fact that he'd probably killed several people that day.

Darien opened up the passenger's side door on the right hand side of the vehicle, and tried to force Melody inside. However, Melody slid compliantly into the automobile. Her nightmare was just getting started when her eyes fell upon Clarke. Melody absently sized him up, and assessed to how handsome he looked all decked out in his tux. He also smelled divine. There was an odd, yet satisfying expression on his face. He hadn't yet spoken, but Melody was already squirming in her seat.

"Clarke, we need to call an ambulance for Sean. Please… He hasn't done anything to you or to Darien. If he's in trouble, we need to get him some help." Melody swallowed the lump in her throat. Her red, tear-filled eyes connected desperately to Clarke's. "Please, don't let him die," she entreated.

Clarke reached across the seat, set his hand on Melody's waist, and collected her into his arms. "*Sean Winters* is the last person on my mind right now. We have a date, my dear. We're going to the chapel, and we're going to get married…," Clarke sang like a crazed man.

Melody pulled back in horror, but couldn't yank completely away from Clarke's restraining grip. It was then she was introduced to the compartmentalized part of Clarke-the one capable of committing murder. "Who *are* you?" Her face wrinkled in confusion and hurt.

"I don't think I've ever seen you as stunning as you are today, darling! You've left me absolutely breathless!" Clarke pressed a kiss to her cheek, seemingly anesthetized. He then set his hand sensitively to the side of her face. "Did you *really* think you could keep secrets from me, Melody?" Flames of distrust blazed in his eyes.

"I...I didn't... I wasn't trying to...," Melody shakily refuted. Her heart thudded so forcefully, it felt as if it would pop out of her chest. At that time, Darien maneuvered the car away from the house. "I would never deliberately try to hurt you, Clarke."

Clarke reached into the inner pocket of his tux jacket in search of something. Contempt covered his face, as he pulled an object out from it. "Is that so, pretty lady? Didn't you notice the other one missing?" He held the earring up, and handed it over to Melody.

Melody closed her eyes in resignation and regret. She didn't even bother taking the earring out of Clarke's hand. There was no doubt in her mind when she'd lost it. Up until that point, she hadn't even noticed it missing. There had been so many other things to consider. So, a lost earring was the furthest thing from her mind. She stared penitently into Clarke's eyes. "I'm really sorry, Clarke. I really tried to love you. I wanted us to work, but when I found out that..." She gulped, and her eyes wandered from his penetrating stare.

"That I'm a glorified crime lord, or that I'm some monster, who goes around killing people for the fun of it?" Clarke's demeanor grew more imposing by the second. Tears glimmered in his eyes. "Is that what you think of me, Melody? You think I'm some monster you have to *try* to love?"

Melody was shocked to see tears in Clarke's eyes. Mystified, she assessed that Clarke's opinion of himself was a total disconnect from reality. Yes, he was a philanthropist and aided a number of needy organizations. However, that in no way altered the fact that he was a murderer several times over.

Regardless, Melody made an earnest appeal to whatever remained of Clarke's humanity. "I...I...don't think you're a monster, Clarke. I've seen the good in you..." Melody strove to catch her breath, and spoke spasmodically.

"You've *seen* the good in me, but still went to the police, and told them about my conversation with Darien early Friday morning?" Clarke set his hand on his chin in an introspective manner.

"I didn't know what else to do," Melody admitted. "You and Darien were planning to hurt that man at the airport." She tried to pull away enough to breathe, but Clarke's grasp was more unforgiving than that of a cobra's.

Clarke rocked Melody in his arms in a quiet rhythm. "I thought for sure that I would have found loyalty from the person I love the most." He pulled away, and cradled Melody's moist face in his hands. He shook his head with a sense of compunction. "You have any idea how much I love you?" Clarke's face bridged with Melody's. "You're my heart." He nibbled the corners of her mouth with fond kisses.

Not only was Melody terrified, but she was now confused. She couldn't even pretend to kiss him back. She felt so sick at heart she thought she'd die right there in back seat of the car. And yet, that didn't stop Clarke in his efforts at imbibing her.

Melody couldn't figure out where their conversation was going. She needed to know what was going on in Clarke's head. Was he going to kill her, or was he going to continue kissing her? The entire situation was bizarre. Even if the partition separating the front of the town car from the back was up, Melody knew Darien was the one behind the wheel. They were now on the interstate heading east.

Melody attempted one final appeal to save her life. "I'm really sorry, Clarke. I didn't know what to do after I heard your plans to hurt that man at the airport."

"I understand, my dear," Clarke said in a detached manner.

"That morning was the first time that I'd seen you and Darien together, and realized you were-"

"Acquainted?" Clarke stopped kissing her, but still held her head delicately in his hands. "If you were made privy to our conversation, then you *must* know what I did to get you away from him?" Clarke's eyes critically delved into Melody's.

Melody nodded. "Yes. I *know* about the deal you made with him." Serena had told Melody that Clarke and Darien were affiliated. However, over at the penthouse that early morning, was the first time she'd seen the two men together.

"So, you *do* know how much I love and want you… Ah, but you've disappointed me, pretty lady."

Melody's face veiled in jeopardy. All the same, she realized that it was wise to play along. "I'm sorry for disappointing you, Clarke. It's the last thing that I wanted. You were there for me after…"

There was a warped, yet mawkish expression on Clarke's face. "I wanted so much to be there for you, but now…" He looked away for a moment.

Melody's heart thrashed, as she awaited Clarke's verdict and sentencing. Petrified, she found the courage to ask, "Are you going to hurt me?"

Clarke gasped in injured surprise. "I am *indeed* disappointed in you, Melody, but I don't want to hurt you." He shook his head contrarily.

"Clarke, the FBI and the authorities are probably tailing us. If you don't want to hurt me, then please let me go." New tears rolled down her cheeks.

Clarke's face was a total contradiction. He looked both menacing and solemn, as his eyes fastened urgently to Melody's. "I'm afraid I can't do that, Melody."

"Why can't you let me go, Clarke?" Melody grimaced in melancholy.

"We were supposed to be getting married today, and that's exactly what's going to happen. I've taken the liberty to change the venue. Someone else will be officiating the wedding. We *will* be married later tonight at an undisclosed location. No one's going to stop it," Clarke settled.

For Melody, there didn't seem to be a way to evade the terror. She was going to have to live it out. A thousand questions overwhelmed at once, and it felt as if she was slipping into quicksand. *Clarke was determined to get married...and then what?*

There had to be more to his plan than what he was telling her. She figured that it was only a matter of time before the other shoe dropped. Clarke held Melody quietly and possessively in his arms, as she writhed in misery. Melody kept an inner prayer vigil. God had promised never to leave nor forsake her (Hebrews 13:5). He'd promised his presence wherever she went (Joshua 1:9). So, no matter how hopeless the circumstances appeared, God was with her, even if she'd just stumbled into an entangling web, and had no idea how to break free.

***

Luke jumped out of the Jeep erratically. Like a man on fire, he rushed up to the Hennessey's front door. He could hardly keep a straight thought in his head, because best laid plans had gone awry. His heart was a set of jungle drums, as he rang their doorbell. It was tearing him apart to internalize how critical Sean's injuries were. Seeing his buddy so frail was a direct hit to Luke's heart. Sean could hardly open up his mouth to speak. The circumstances were grim, but the only thing Luke could do was to commit Sean to God's care.

However, at that moment, he had to get to Melody before it was too late. If anything happened to her, he knew there would be no coming back from it. At that point, Luke was no longer concerned if Melody found out that he'd gone against her wishes, and had remained in Sands Port. So far, nothing had worked out in the way they'd planned. For that reason, Luke was trying to control what little he still could.

He hesitated at the door, and listened for noises beyond it. However, only silence hummed on the other side. Desperate, he twisted the knob, and pushed the front door open. Luke was barely in the doorway when someone screamed.

"Who are you and what do you want?"

Luke moved past the doorway, and saw Serena standing to the left hand side of the door. She held a large kitchen knife, and waved it around like a crazed woman. It was even more bizarre that she was all decked out in a sequined sand-colored gown. She would have looked perfect, but her face was caked in tears. Luke instantly put his hands up. With his back pressed up to the front door, he shut it closed. The last thing he wanted was to set Serena off. Because of his getup, she probably had no idea who he was.

Serena breathed spasmodically, and eyed the stranger with mistrust and disdain. "Whoever you are, you need to turn around, and get out of here. Go back to wherever it is you came from. And, tell that murderer you work for that he won't get away with any of it," her voice wavered.

Luke was very cautious in his approach, and his hands remained up in surrender. He kept shaking his head in total skepticism, and tried to deescalate the situation for a traumatized Serena. "Serena, it's me." Luke brushed over his fat suit.

Serena gasped in shock. "Luke?"

"Yes, Serena, it *is* me." Tears flooded Luke's eyes, and he was still trembling.

Serena instinctively dropped the knife to the floor, and rushed into Luke's opened arms.

"It's okay Serena… I promise." Luke squeezed her in comfort. He pulled away, and grasped her shoulders. "What happened here, and where's Melody?" It was at that moment that Luke saw Dane stretched out on the living room floor, just feet away from the door. "Oh my God, Dane…" Luke frowned in shock and angst.

"I tried to move him out of harm's way in case they came back," Serena said frantically.

Luke immediately hunched down. Helping Dane off the floor, he conveyed him over to the couch. Dane was still out cold, as Luke propped his head with a couch pillow.

Dazed and overwhelmed, Serena followed aimlessly behind Luke. She swallowed the chunk lodged in her throat, and met Luke's confused stare. "They took Mel." Serena grimaced in sorrow, as tears rolled down her cheeks.

Luke nodded as if he understood. However, the words were taking a moment to process. "*Who* took Melody away, sweetheart?" Luke took hold of Serena's shoulders, and desperately searched her eyes. "Was it Clarke?"

"I'm sure it was on *his* orders, but Darien Stiles came to the door, and threatened us at gunpoint. He dragged Melody away. There were supposed to be FBI agents and police officers keeping tabs, but I guess Clarke and Darien handled them." Serena flinched.

"So, they took Mel." Luke's thoughts were whizzing. "I can't be sure, but I think Darien also shot Sean."

Now, Serena shrank back in horror. "Sean's dead?"

"Very close to it, Serena," Luke admitted. "I found him a few blocks over, and called an ambulance, but it didn't look good. He's lost a lot of blood," Luke said in a hushed tone, as if that would in some way take away the sting.

Serena shook her head in denial. "There's no doubt in my

mind that Clarke is behind hurting Sean and he authorities. I'm sure, he ordered Darien to take Melody away." Serena was still clearly traumatized.

Luke was in a stupor after hearing that Melody was with Clarke and Darien. A part of him still couldn't process everything which had occurred. Although he was tempted to lose heart, Luke refused to. He didn't care what he had to do that day. He was going to find Melody, and he would find her *alive*.

Just then, Dane began to show signs of coming to. He tried to lift his head, but Serena immediately rushed over to his side. "No, honey, don't try to get up... I've already called for an ambulance," Serena told her husband.

Dane moaned in pain, and kept rubbing his head where he'd been struck.

Serena turned to face a crestfallen Luke. "I don't know what do to. We thought we had it all under control, but somehow Clarke and his lackeys figured things out. Now, they have Melody. Luke, we've *got* to find her. Clarke can't get his way. Please, tell me there's something we can do," Serena appealed. "Please..."

Serena's entreaty roused Luke from his whizzing thoughts. He stared boldly into Serena's eyes. "I don't care what I have to do, I'm going to find my girl today. I *will* get her away from Clarke and Darien." Luke held Serena in his arms in sustenance as she cried. "I'm going to get our girl back," he reassured.

"If *anyone* can find her, you can." Serena overbreathed.

Luke pulled away. "Did Melody leave anything behind-maybe her phone, a comb or hairbrush?" Luke asked intently.

"Why?" Serena asked, confused.

"I need to get her fingerprints, or even a strand of hair from a comb or hairbrush. I know it sounds bizarre, but getting hold of anything containing her DNA is imperative."

Serena didn't even question. "Melody *did* leave her phone behind, and *I* did her hair earlier, so..." Serena rushed over to the master bedroom, and Luke followed. "I don't understand," Serena admitted, as she led the way.

"I realize there's a lot you don't understand. For starters, why I'm dressed this way, but you've just got to trust me, okay?"

"I do trust you, Luke, and I am so happy to see you!" Serena smiled through the tears.

"You have no idea how glad I am to see both you and Dane alive," Luke's voice broke.

Serena's face wrinkled in sympathy. She didn't say anything, as she grabbed the items Luke had asked for. She handed him Melody's phone, and the hairbrush she'd used to do Melody's hair.

"Perfect," Luke said. Without hesitation, he pulled out his phone, and accessed *Dimension Find Me.* The app was violet and white. The design was loops of meshed circles and in the center was a portal. The violet sensor lights blinked on immediately, as Luke scanned both Melody's prints and strands of her hair using the application.

"*Dimension*, find this individual," Luke ordered.

The purple lights turned deep violet, and a luminous white light issued through the portal. *"Based on data you provided, the woman is approximately one hundred miles east of this location,"* **Dimension** replied.

Serena watched on, amazed. "She's alive!" She celebrated-realizing Luke's technology had done something she'd never seen before.

Luke smiled. "Yes. She *is* alive, and she's going to stay that way. One more thing…" Luke fiddled on the phone again. "*Dimension,* I need for you to generate an image of that individual," Luke put in another command.

It took all of two seconds for the program to produce an image. Luke's eyes released fresh tears when he saw Melody. Through the tears he smiled at Serena. "She's okay. She's traumatized and scared, but she's okay!" Luke nodded affirmatively.

"Luke, you have no idea…" Serena rushed over to take a look at Luke's phone.

Luke and Serena saw Melody sitting in the back seat of a car with Clarke. Terror veiled her sweet face, and she was in tears. Clarke had his arms possessively around her, and kept kissing her. The expression on Clarke's face was that of someone who was under hypnosis, or some form of mind control.

"I'm coming to get you, baby." Luke couldn't stop smiling, because Melody was all right.

"Luke, you're amazing! What's **Dimension** all about? I've never seen anything like this before." Serena marveled.

Luke couldn't give away too much about **Dimension Four** for a number of reasons. "It's fairly new, and only a handful of people have access to it," he wisely explained. "Serena, I'm going to find Melody. If it's the last thing I do, I'm going to make sure she's safe."

Serena nodded. "*Now*, I can say that I believe it. Please, hurry…"

Just then, the doorbell rang, startling both Luke and Serena. However, Luke took his place protectively in front of Serena, and crossed back over into the living room. They had to make sure it wasn't another one of Clarke's henchmen.

Luke told Serena to stay back, and gestured for her not to go anywhere near the front door. Serena complied, and hovered protectively over her ailing husband. Both Serena and Dane's eyes remained affixed to the door.

Luke stepped aside, pushed back the blinds, and peeked through the living room window. He saw the ambulance and the paramedics coming up the walk. "It's all right, Serena, Dane… The ambulance is here," Luke turned to address them.

The couple sighed in relief.

Luke opened up the front door to the rescue crew. They stormed inside, and immediately began tending to Dane.

As the first responders helped Dane into the ambulance, Luke got off the phone with the authorities. A feature on his phone, made it impossible for any of his calls to be traced. So, Luke felt confident in telling them that *their* officers and FBI agents, had been taken out by Clarke Vale's men.

Serena told Luke about the nearly failsafe plan to trap Clarke at the wedding. Clarke had evaded them, and had left behind a cold trail. Luke asked the authorities to allocate teams, and have them dispersed throughout different locations on the eastbound interstate

Luke wanted the authorities close by, when *he* found Clarke for himself. **Dimension Find Me** would bring him to Melody in a fraction of the time. The police and the FBI would unquestionably be on the chase for hours. They were suspicious as to how Luke had garnered his information, but Luke told them he was an anonymous caller. Moreover, he advised them to follow his lead. They tried to grill him, but he quickly shut down the phone.

Just before Luke hopped back into the jeep, he checked in on Dane. He hovered over Dane on the gurney. "Are you going to be all right?" He frowned in concern.

"I'll be fine," Dane said. While Luke remained close, Dane grasped his arm, and pulled him close to whisper something in his ear.

"Dane, I can't..." Luke shook his head contrarily.

Dane nodded his aching head in affirmation. "You have to. You're definitely going to need it. It's in the lockbox behind the bar in the dining room. Find it and take it with you," Dane ordered, as they prepped him for the trip over to the hospital.

Serena stood close by, and followed their conversation. She stared into Luke's eyes urgently. "Yes, Luke, you need to do what

Dane says. The FBI and the police will follow, but you're stepping into this danger zone completely alone."

Luke no longer argued. He assured the couple that he'd do as they'd said. Before the ambulance rolled away, Serena and Dane promised to keep Luke posted about Sean. Luke was extremely grateful for this much.

When the ambulance rolled away from the house, Luke went back inside and accessed Dane's gun. He found the key, and lockbox exactly where Dane had said. Luke concealed the weapon in a compartment of his fat suit. He then rushed back outside, and hopped into his Jeep.

"*Dimension*, take me to Melody Maxwell," Luke ordered. The GPS Feature of *Find Me* showed Luke how to navigate out of Royale Valley. Turn by turn, he was led out to the expressway, and headed east. "What's the fastest way to make it to Melody, *Dimension*?" Luke spoke into the phone.

"There's an alternate route that will bring you to her in approximately one hour," **Dimension** calculated.

Luke smiled. "Perfect." The luminescent violet and white laser lights transposed, and diffused inside of the automobile. It looked as if Luke was caught up in a time warp. He knew exactly what the lights meant. It meant, Clarke or Darien had made a sudden stop. Luke hoped their pit stop wasn't a final destination.

Seeing Melody alive in the back of the town car, kept Luke going. She was undeniably horrorstricken, but still breathing. That's all that mattered as far as he was concerned. Luke determined to keep Melody alive and breathing at all costs. His heart was broken, and best laid plans had been completely botched. Sean was wounded in battle, and Luke had no idea if he'd ever see his best friend alive again. Serena and Dane had been victimized in their own home, and Dane was probably in the ER.

Amidst the anguish, Luke sent a prayer heavenward. "Lord, I don't know what to do. I'm doing the very best I can. You promised to always be with us, and to be our help in times of trouble." Luke sniffled, and wiped tears from off his face. "Lord, please help me to make it to Melody before it's too late. I love her more than anything.

"I never thought things would get this hard. You're the only one who can carry us all through this experience. Father, let your goodness and power crush every evil work. Please, look out for Sean, and bring him out of this. Give him a chance. He's more than just my buddy. Sean is my brother…my family."

Luke couldn't even speak coherently, because of his jumbled thoughts. He cried silently, and acknowledged God's presence there. No matter what he went through in life, he knew that he was never left to himself. He trusted in the one who sticks closer than a brother (Proverbs 18:24). As he sped out on the highway, he continued to monitor Melody's interactions with Clarke. Melody was in tears, but Clarke didn't seem to be hurting her in any way.

"Don't worry, Mel, I'm coming, and I'm going to bring you home." Luke pressed down on the gas pedal. "We've worked too hard to lose the battle today. Hang in there, Honey Baby."

Luke tried to stay focused, as he allowed *Dimension Find Me* to lead the way. He was also immensely grateful that God had given him the wherewithal to create such a groundbreaking tool for the 21st Century.

CHAPTER ELEVEN

Slowly, the blindfold was removed from Melody's eyes, and light filtered through the shadows. She made a sudden turn, and saw Clarke standing behind her inside of a very large and lavish bedroom. The walls were painted pale peach, and the accents were gray. The plush carpeting was gray, and the canopy bed was embellished with linen and pillows with the same color theme. Had the circumstances been different, she could have considered this a dream getaway.

However, she knew all too well this was no resort. Rather, it was a very well hidden, off the beaten track safe house for Clarke. This was a world he'd created all for the sake of evading the law. Melody had been blindfolded part of the way over to this place, so she had absolutely no idea where they were.

"Where am I, Clarke?" Melody's voice sounded strained. She had wept, and had pleaded to be released for quite a while now.

Clarke stared down at her with a great deal of involvement. He set his hand to the side of her tear-caked face. "You're here with me, and you're safe. That's all that matters."

Tears stung Melody's eyes all over again, and her face contorted in misery. "What are you going to do with me? Why did you take me with you on this asinine trip?" Frustration reddened her face.

Clarke seemed utterly composed, as he delved into Melody's eyes. "You still don't understand, do you?"

"*What* don't I understand, Clarke?" Melody huffed.

Clarke tenderly brushed over her face. "You don't understand how much I love you-how much you mean to me." He stared yearningly at her. Clarke had wanted to teach Melody a lesson, as he'd done to other women in the past. However, in spite of her betrayal, he couldn't see his life without her.

"Stop saying you love me, Clarke. You don't know what

that means. You've hurt people. You've put out hits on innocent people, because they refused to do things your way. How can you say you love anyone, when you're capable of committing such acts?" Melody's face wrenched in turmoil.

"Because I *know* I love you, Melody. You have no idea all of the sacrifices I've made to make you mine."

"You want to *own* me like one of the classic cars in your collection. I'm this possession-like an object you won, because you were the highest bidder." Tears meandered down her cheeks.

Clarke collected Melody into his arms, and crushed her to himself. "No, darling, you're wrong. I love you so much!" He pressed a kiss to her forehead, and covered her face in gentle kisses. "I love you, and I want you so badly..." Clarke's excursion reached its destination. Finding her mouth, he assaulted it mercilessly with hungry kisses.

Melody squirmed, and shrank back from Clarke's embrace. However, she didn't want to set him off, because she was totally confused about his state of mind. He seemed to be in a daze. He'd just discovered her betrayal. Furthermore, he knew that she'd set him up with the FBI and the police. However, all he wanted was to tell her how much he loved and needed her. Something had to give. And, when it did, Melody didn't want to be around.

As Clarke caressed her all over, Melody's eyes drifted over to the points of exit. There was the door and also three windows. Maybe, they were her ticket out of this nightmare. She tried not to display her repulsion over Clarke's affection. But, he was undeniably a ticking time-bomb, and no one would make her touch the detonator.

Melody was repulsed by Clarke's PDA's. All the same, she knew better than to shove him away. Pulling away had to be done wisely and with finesse. "Clarke, it's been a *really* long day, and a lot has happened. So, can I have a moment to fix my face and possibly change?"

Clarke stopped his kisses midway. "Of course, darling..." He pulled away enough to allow her to breathe. "But, don't change out of the gown. The wedding officiate should be here in an hour or so." He cupped Melody's chin.

"Wedding...?" Melody asked, troubled and scared.

"Yes, of course, pretty lady." Clarke wrapped his arms around her waist, and held on acquisitively. "You're going to become Mrs. Clarke Victor Vale today. This is *our* wedding day, and nothing's going to get in the way of that." Clarke's eyes took on a lethal quality. "Make no mistake about it, Melody, you *will* be mine."

Melody flinched. She was both shocked, and in denial over what she'd just heard. She stared at Clarke in the way one would at a clown performing a tightrope act. "We don't have to get married right away, Clarke. You have me *all* to yourself now. We can do it another day. Besides, I'm really tired," she stalled.

"I'm afraid it *does* have to be today, Melody." Clarke's grasp tightened about her waist, as he searched her sad eyes. "Take all the time you need to fix your face, and take a little powernap if you need to. But, we *are* leaving the country tonight."

"Leaving the country?" Melody flinched, stunned. Her face wrinkled in jeopardy, and she instinctively tried to pull away from Clarke's voracious grip.

"Yes, Melody, we're leaving for Ticino, Switzerland tonight. We should be in the city of Lugano early tomorrow afternoon. I don't think the authorities will be looking for me in such an obscure little town."

"What about Vale Corp?" Melody grasped at straws.

"Vale Corp and its subsidiaries can pretty much function on their own. I'm just taking an extended sabbatical away from it all." He softened, cupping Melody's chin. "Now, I *know* that it wasn't *your* plan to go to the police, and have the FBI dragged into the matter. I don't blame you at all, Melody."

"I would never deliberately hurt you," Melody placated.

"I realize that. You did what anyone else would have under

the circumstances." Clarke's eyes searched hers intuitively.

Still bemused by Clarke's bizarre behavior, Melody tried to explain the matter away. "I didn't mean to make trouble for you, Clarke, but I *can't* go to Switzerland with you tonight. And, as much as I respect you, I really don't think we should get married." Melody withdrew. Her eyes still explored Clarke's in uncertainty, as she waited for the other shoe to drop. She needed to know Clarke's *true* intentions.

"What's the matter, darling, don't you *love* me?" Clarke's face took on a sinister quality.

And there it was, the loud thump of the shoe. It seemed to fall right on top of Melody's head. "Clarke, you're running away from the law, and you want to take me with you. We would be fugitives. I don't want to live my life that way," she appealed.

"I'm sorry things have to be this way. When you make a commitment to someone, it's for better or worse. I'm committed to you, Melody, and I've *never* gone out on a limb for anyone in this way. So, you're *going* to be my wife today. You *will* go wherever I say, and we will stay together no matter what." Clarke shook his head defiantly. "I'm *never* letting you go."

Aghast, Melody pulled back. It was *now* she understood Clarke's mindset. He was determined to have her no matter what. Up until that very moment, she hadn't internalized the extent of his fixation. This was just another move on his chessboard. Clarke had systematically moved everything and everyone out of the way, so that they would be together, and he refused to concede.

Melody pushed away, and drifted backward. "I need a moment. I need to use the restroom now, Clarke," her voice cracked.

"Of course, darling." Pleasantness masked his face. "Take a moment to freshen up, but please don't be too long."

"I promise not to be too long," Melody readily complied. She walked backward, distrustful of every move Clarke made. Finally, she turned, and opened up the door to the adjourning bathroom. She had to take a moment to pull herself together, because her entire world was spinning out of control.

Melody stepped into the peach-colored bathroom, and looked at her face in the mirror. She'd cried so much that her eyes were bloodshot. Makeup had calcified on her face. And, around her eyes, were blotches of compromised mascara. Melody buried her face in her hands, and cried as she assessed the reality of her nightmare.

Sean was probably dead, and she didn't know how things had fared for Serena and Dane. Maybe, *they* were dead too. She was beginning to grasp that Clarke and his flunkies took no prisoners. So, Melody doubted that Clarke's men had left Serena and Dane alive. Melody also feared for Luke. She had no idea if he'd taken her advice to leave Sands Port. Imagining Clarke's men finding Luke and hurting him, was too bitter a pill to swallow. Melody couldn't help thinking maybe *he* was hurt somewhere and needed help.

"Psalm 50:15: "And call upon me in the day of trouble, I will deliver you and you will glorify me," Melody repeated, as she washed her face with trembling hands. "…in all these things we are more than conquerors through him that loved us (Romans 8:31-39)…" Melody recited passages of scripture to reaffirm her faith.

She was also reminded of what Psalms 91:14 read: "…Because he has set his love upon me, therefore will I deliver him. I will set him on high because he has known my name. He shall call upon me and I will answer him. *I will be with him in trouble*…," Melody must have repeated that portion of scripture a dozen times, "I will be with him (her) in trouble…"

"Lord, I know you're with me now. Please, bring me out of this situation. Please, watch over Luke, Serena and Dane, and please give us a miracle for Sean. Sean did the right thing by investigating Clarke's criminal activities. So, he shouldn't have to pay with his life. Father, please make Clarke choose to do the right thing for the first time in his life. You're in control of everything, even over the actions of the wicked.

"I also pray mercy for Clarke, in spite of how evil he is. As long as he's breathing, he can always choose to receive you into his heart as his Lord. Help Clarke to see that you, Lord Jesus, are the only way. Take a hold of his heart, and make him a better man. I would pity him if I wasn't so angry."

Melody had freshened up by taking a moment to call out to her heavenly father. He was her strength, her shield and protector. She trusted him to make a way, and to untangle her feet from this vicious snare. Melody patted her face dry with a clean towel, then brushed over the wedding gown delicately with her hands. She couldn't escape just how pristine it still looked. It had remained untainted, in spite of the tumultuous set of circumstances.

Cagily, Melody stepped back out to the bedroom. She expected to see Clarke standing there, but he was gone. Surprised, she collected the fringes of her gown, and rushed over to the window. There were two on one side of the large canopy bed. Melody tried to pry the first one open, but it was tightly shut. She repeated the process with the other two windows on the opposite side, but to no avail.

It was too obvious, but she decided to take a chance with the bedroom door. Melody slunk over, and took hold of the knob. She flinched in shock when it turned in her hand. Opening it up, a cool rush of wind struck against her face.

Looking both ways, she drifted out of the bedroom. Taking baby steps, she glided out into the vast hallway. She judged that this house or development was colossal. The corridor stretched out into eternity. The ceilings were high, and chandeliers symmetrically hung above. Melody floated down the passageway on bare feet. For the first time since she'd been abducted, she actually felt the taste of freedom.

As she set out to make a right turn at the end of the hallway, Melody encountered an obstruction.

"You have someplace you need to be?" the baritone voice inquired. The man was tall, brawny, had dark hair and gray eyes. He was wearing a smoke-gray designer dress suit. He forcefully pulled Melody against his hip, and kept a vise grip hold on her. "Listen to me, *beautiful*, be a good girl, and go back to your room. We wouldn't want you getting *hurt* or lost out in these big bad woods, now would we?" He displayed the gun tucked to the side of his slacks.

Melody gasped. "I was just looking for Clarke." She trembled like blades of grass on a windy day. She now realized that Clarke had his men surrounding every inch of the immense complex. This little excursion was something Clarke had thought out extensively. He'd obviously spared no expense.

"Well, you just go on back to your room, and I'll tell him you were looking for him. Besides, he should be right back." His smile was laced with venom.

"Thank you," Melody squeaked. "Can you let me go now?" She flinched.

"Yes, of course, *beautiful!*" He gently released his hold on her, but gave her a stern warning. "You stay in that room until Mr. Vale brings you out of there. I don't want to have to use this." He pointed to the gun on his hip. "Are we clear?"

Fresh tears spilled over Melody's eyelids, and she swallowed hard. "Crystal." Her heart plummeted to her feet, as she shakily veered in the opposite direction, and rushed back down the hallway. Melody managed to find her way back to the luxury room, which was nothing more than a gilded prison cell.

She shut the door in utter frustration, floated over to the bed, and surrendered to it. Tremulously, she continued quoting passages of scripture, as she wrapped her arms about her lower abdomen. Rocking back and forth, she tried to retain her sanity. Melody resolved not to give in to despair, even if the waves of hopelessness threatened to submerge. She was confident that God would bring her out of this situation in one way or another. Once God did bring her out of it, she'd be able to testify of his faithfulness yet again.

***

Dimension's intense violet and white lights dazzled with intensity.

The field encapsulated Luke like millions of shooting stars falling from the sky into the Jeep. The lightshow was the program's way of indicating that Melody was nearby. According to **Find Me**, she was less than half a mile away, but it hardly made any sense.

Luke had followed the GPS, and it had led somewhere out in the woods of Morgantown, Maryland-at least one hundred miles away from Sands Port. The area was for the most part rural. Only a few farmhouses lined the dirt roads here and there. The remote area was in the middle of nowhere, and appeared to be deserted. So, Luke was extremely frustrated. Even so, he had to follow through, because **Dimension** had been accurate so far.

Dusk was quickly turning into the penumbra of nightfall. It was now dark enough for outsiders to see the blinking light show inside of the automobile. That was the last thing Luke needed. So, he dulled the lights, but left the portal open. The portal was a mesh of white spinning circles with a gateway in the center. The passageway was a dark blue vortex capable of absorbing and *transporting* matter, and even the human body if activated.

However, the **Power Portal** was something Luke hadn't yet experimented with. Moreover, he didn't know if it would work in time to be of any use. If it worked in the way in which it was designed to, it had the potential to convey him over to Melody at record speed. However, it was extremely risky. There was the very real danger of getting caught midway. If caught midway, a person *could* eventually find their way back, but the process could potentially be lengthy. And, *time* was something he was short on.

Luke felt as if he'd covered the area in vain. As he continued down the backwoods, up ahead, at a clearing, he saw a large dilapidated farmhouse. His trusty new friend, **Dimension** indicated that he was closer to Melody than ever. "Bingo." Luke teared up, because he couldn't wait to find her and bring her home.

At a distance, Luke decided to go on foot. So, he parked the Jeep as far away from the old farmhouse as possible. He figured it would be a lot harder for Clarke and his men to detect him, if he slunk around on foot. Also, on foot, there was a lot more he could do with **Dimension Four**. Luke's heart lashed, as he made his way through the provincial area like a man possessed. Only feet away from the house, he put in another anonymous call to the authorities.

Luke clued them into his position out in Morgantown, and asked that they follow his lead. Again, they were curious as to how he'd obtained such information, but Luke shut down his cell, and continued moving towards the old house.

The shadowy night sky appeared ominous, and thick leaden clouds floated above, as Luke cautiously tread over to the frail structure. For all intents and purposes, he was a skulking thief. There was no way he could risk running into Clarke Vale or any of his men. He avowed not to let anything or anyone stop him from finding Melody.

There was nothing special or distinct about the old farmhouse. Luke guardedly tugged at the rustic cast iron door handles, and encountered very little resistance. So, he pulled the heavy door open, and stood warily to its side, leery of venturing in. Luke accessed *Dimension* again. "Are there any cameras or recording devices nearby?"

"The recording devices are not present in this farmhouse, but I do detect a few not too far away," **Dimension** informed.

"Is there a way to go inside without running interference of detection?"

"Of course there is, Master Luke! You created me. Use the **Vortex to Vanish** *feature. So, even if there* **are** *cameras in close proximity, you'll be a ghost."*

"*I* programmed all that into you, *Dimension*?" Luke smiled, amazed.

"Yes, of course you did. Should I go over the list of things you programmed me to do?"

Luke laughed. "No. That won't be necessary. The *Vortex to Vanish* feature is about to come in real handy."

Luke accessed the translucent button. The vortex lights swallowed him up, and created an invisible capsule around him. So,

even if there were cameras, or in the event he stumbled across
Clarke's men, they wouldn't be able to see him. However, he first
had to locate them. Luke wandered into farmhouse, and drifted into
the barn. There seemed to be nothing unusual about the place.

Bales of hay were scattered throughout, farming tools,
equipment and chopped wood everywhere. It all looked legitimate.
However, Luke knew not to take anything at face value, because he
was dealing with Clarke Vale. Confident, he set the phone in the
pocket of his extra-large overalls. Dane's gun was positioned only
inches away from it. Luke sighed and whispered a prayer. The last
thing he wanted was to have to use a gun.

Getting down on his knees, he felt around the stretches of hay
which lined the barn floors. Luke was in search of a doorway or an
opening. **Dimension** insisted that this was where Melody could be
found. But, where could Melody be in the middle of bales of hay
and farming equipment? Moreover, why would Clarke bring her to
such a dismal place?

Luke crawled on all fours, and continued to feel his way
around. However, he was coming up empty. Ensuing, he bounded
back to his feet, and brushed over the walls. **Dimension Find Me's**
lights blinked with greater intensity, so Luke felt hopeful that he was
getting closer to finding his girl. He pounded the base of his right
palm into his forehead. "Come on, Luke, think…"

"God, please show me how to get to Melody. Every minute
I spend out here is one closer to losing her." Tears shimmered in his
eyes, as he began to examine the farming tools and equipment. In a
far right hand corner of the barn was a tractor. Luke warily
examined the tractor. It was different from the rest of the farming
paraphernalia, which looked rusted and worn. This dark forest-green
and silver tractor shone like brand new.

Luke rushed over to the machine and hopped inside. He
turned the key in the ignition, and cut the engine on. The tractor
roared to life, but it wasn't the only thing which had been turned on
or activated. Awestruck, Luke watched as a huge, wooden cylinder
emerge from the hay-stretched flooring. The cylinder made that part
of the floor collapse. It was like an elevator springing up from the

ground. His jaw dropped in utter shock, as he observed the manifestation.

Hopping off the tractor, he rushed over to the cylinder. The apparatus looked extremely crude-almost like first model elevators. However, the old, wooden capsule pushed back its wooden constraints, and revealed a clear, glass receptacle, which looked like a single revolving door. And just like a revolving door, a compartment of the cask opened up. Undaunted, Luke slipped right inside.

He kept shaking his head incredulous that he was inside of the cask. He was taking a huge risk. However, he didn't feel the least bit frightened or intimidated when the cask closed up, and began its descent deep into the ground.

There was very little scenery for Luke sequestered in the tube. However, he trusted that if Clarke and his men had used the device to transport themselves and Melody to an underground location, it would bring him straight to them.

The machine plunged feet into the ground, and felt like a dipping roller coaster ride. When the glass cylinder came to a halt, it automatically opened up. Before Luke could even size up what appeared to be some underground complex, he caught sight of Clarke and three of his men. Their guns were drawn.

Knowing that he was encapsulated by the vortex and invisible to the men, Luke quickly took cover behind an entertainment center, as the men fired their guns where the cask had opened up, and had dropped him off.

"What's going on, Blake?" Clarke's face wrenched in irritation. "There's no one on this thing. How was it activated, and came down here on its own?" Clarke moved warily over to the cylinder. His heart flagellated, as he kept the gun pointed.

"I don't know, Mr. Vale," Blake answered. Blake stood about 6'2". His complexion was ginger, and he had a muscular build. He was also well-dressed in a tailored black business suit. "Maybe, it was an animal."

Luke smiled cunningly, and slowly began to move around.

"An animal...?" Clarke growled. "An animal knows how to use an ignition key?" He stared all about the expansive area, more paranoid than ever.

"Maybe, it was raccoons, boss," another one of Clarke's *brilliant* associates conjectured, waving his gun around nervously. This was a kid no older than twenty-four.

"And, maybe I'm a clown for the local circus," Clarke sneered.

"Maybe it's the wedding officiate. He probably turned on the ignition to get into the tube, but couldn't managed to get in on time." Baffled, Blake rubbed his head.

Clarke sighed in relief. "It's possible, but I'm not sticking around long enough to find out. That old fool should have been here already. Melody and I will be leaving right away. I can't risk the authorities getting anywhere near this complex. Melody and I will get married abroad. Do you have my luggage ready as I ordered earlier?" Clarke lowered at the third man. He was white, short and stocky.

"It's all set, Mr. Vale. Now, will you be using that private jet?"

"Of course, you idiot! Did you think I'd be flying commercial?" Clarke glared at the man. "Now, you go and get Melody's luggage, so that we can get out of here right away."

"Yes, Sir," the third man said compliantly. "Darien's taking care of the jet situation as we speak." The man's arms were now resting at his sides, and his gun was pointed down towards the glistening wooden flooring. They were all convinced that an *animal* had started the tractor's ignition, since they didn't see anyone step out of the cylinder.

"Well, tell Darien to speed things up."

"Sure, boss."

"You two stay here. Don't budge from this post. I'm going to *get Melody*. Bring the suitcase I packed for her, Blake. As soon as she changes, we're getting out of here." Clarke still stared cagily about the place.

Luke heard the magic words, and began shadowing Clarke's every move. Stealthily, he glided over and went to stand behind the man.

"Who's there?" Clarke made a sudden turn, and pulled his gun out again.

Luke snickered, seeing Clarke squirm. Perspiration beaded over Clarke's usually placid demeanor.

"The two of you don't move, and keep your eyes peeled to the transporter." Clarke literally shuddered. There was a bit of a draft, but he had no clue where it was coming from. Trying to work past his suspicions, Clarke veered, and began to move away from the commodious room.

Luke examined the place. It was a very sophisticated compound. He had to give Clarke some credit. Clarke wasn't just your run-of-the-mill criminal. He was a mobster with a plan, and he had the resources to back it up. It seemed the man had thought of everything.

You thought of everything, Clarke, but you didn't factor me into your plan. Luke followed after Clarke. For good measure, as Luke passed through the passageway, he held his hand out, and deliberately knocked down a very expensive vase. The object crashed to the floor, and broke into a hundred pieces.

Clarke made a sudden turn to see where the noise had come from. However, faster than he or Luke could blink, shots were fired in their direction. Luke was already well out of the way, but Clarke barely managed to evade the hailstorm of bullets.

Outraged, Clarke decided to address his incredibly *bright* flunkies. "Why on earth would you idiots want to shoot at me?"

"Uh, we didn't mean to shoot at you, Mr. Vale. The vase got

knocked down and…"

"Of course the vase got knocked down, because you idiots were shooting at it," Clarke bellowed.

Luke was tickled by their stupidity. The temptation was to keep playing mind games with Clarke and his men. However, Luke was convinced that they would eventually self-destruct. He also regretted that Clarke hadn't taken a bullet to the backside.

"Clean up this mess right away," Clarke blared, with a face redder than sugar beets. Annoyed by the turn of events, he turned away, and continued down the stretch of hallway in front of him.

Luke quietly pursued behind Clarke. He was grateful that they were now walking on carpeting instead of the glossy hardwood flooring in the other room. The pathway was winding, until Clarke turned right at a corner. There was a door just up ahead. Luke hung back while Clarke stood in front of it.

Clarke kept looking suspiciously over his shoulder. His head shifted from left to right, as he fiddled with a key to undo the lock. However, Clarke stood temporarily frozen in the doorway. He seemed to be utterly entranced.

Luke realized why Clarke was suddenly captivated, because he was also experiencing the same dilemma. Luke saw Melody standing by a window in a sizable luxury room. She looked more resplendent than an angel in her wedding gown.

Luke's heart thrummed, just as it had the first time he'd laid eyes on her. She was literally making him forget how to breathe. Melody's face looked astonishingly serene. In spite of all she'd gone through, her upswept hair and curly bangs looked impeccable. For a moment, Luke imagined Melody all decked out to meet *him* at the altar. Just then, it dawned on him that he *wanted* to be the man she wore a wedding gown for.

"My darling, there's been a change of plans," Clarke told Melody. Stepping fully into the bedroom, he shut the door behind him.

Unbeknownst to Clarke, Luke had glided into the room right before he'd shut the door. Luke's eyes fastened to Melody, as she listened to Clarke's breakdown of their new plan. Luke was chomping at the bit to make his presence known. He wanted to reassure Melody he was there, and that she was safe. However, he had to wait until he had a moment alone with her.

"Darling, we have to leave the country right now. Something's come up," Clarke reiterated.

Confusion and disbelief wrinkled Melody's sweet face. "I thought we were waiting for a wedding officiate to marry us tonight, Clarke? You said we'd be in Switzerland in the *morning*," her voice wavered. "Why do we have to leave right now?"

Clarke wrapped his arm possessively around Melody's waist, and cupped her chin with his free hand. "I know I said we'd be married, then leave for Switzerland in the morning. But, there's a great deal of uncertainty in risking that. Also, I'm afraid there's been some kind of security breach. It isn't safe for us to stay here any longer."

Melody kept shaking her head contrarily. "Clarke, please, let me go home. I promise I won't tell *anyone* where you're going. I won't get in the way of your plans. Please, let me leave here," Melody appealed, desperate and petrified.

Clarke possessively grasped hold of her shoulders. "I'm sorry, darling, but that's just not possible. As I've said before, you're mine, and no one's going to get in the way." He caressed her face, as one would a small child. "Do you understand?" his tone was mellifluous.

Melody turned away defiantly. She trembled with tears shimmering in her eyes.

Luke stood only inches away from the woman he loved, and it took all of the restraint he had not to make contact with her. He wanted to tell her there was no need to cry. Stirred by her sadness, he moved in instinctively to touch her moist cheeks. However, as if he'd been electrically shocked, Luke flinched.

Clarke walked around to have word with Melody again. So, Luke quietly and quickly shifted out of the way.

"Please try to understand, baby. I love you so much! I just want to be with you. You told Bryant yesterday morning that you love *me*, and that the two of you were history. Did you mean that?" Clarke appealed.

Piqued, Melody looked up, glaring at him. "How do you know I said that to Luke?" she asked cuttingly. She wanted to cue him in that she was aware of his camera antics over at her house. Recounting how deeply she'd hurt Luke still seared Melody's heart to the core. She'd annihilated him because Clarke was watching.

Clarke smiled shrewdly, and tried to cover up his lies. "Well, we talked about it yesterday afternoon over lunch," he justified.

"Right...," Melody said glibly. "I *did* say that at lunch yesterday." She chose not to argue with him. Inwardly, she was falling apart, and didn't see a way out of her current ordeal. Besides, she didn't have the strength to go back and forth with Clarke on the technicalities. Itemizing his crooked actions took way too much energy. So, it seemed a total waste of time to call him out on *all* his lies.

Tears pooled in Luke's eyes to see the defeat and despair on Melody's face. He was still confused about the things Melody said to him yesterday morning. It was difficult to tell, but he wanted to believe Melody still cared. He could only hope. Even so, he couldn't keep torturing himself by wondering. Luke wanted Clarke out of Melody's face, so that he could have a moment alone with her. It sickened him to watch the man touching Melody so intimately. Clarke's arms fastened about her waist with a cobra-like clasp.

Luke had to look away. He couldn't stand to see Clarke so close to Melody. Suddenly, there was a raucous knock on the bedroom door. Luke sighed in relief, because the clatter forced Clarke to remove his blood-ridden hands off of Melody. Clarke rushed over to the bedroom door.

While Clarke spoke to some goon at the door, Luke moved in

closer to Melody. He tenderly caught a tear which had rolled down her cheek. His touch was like a whisper, but it was enough to startle her.

Melody gasped, but didn't make a sound. She stared suspiciously about the room. She couldn't be sure, but someone or something had just touched her. She had no real time to process the incident, because Clarke rushed back over to her, holding a fresh change of clothes and a pair of boots.

"Sweetheart, I need for you to change into something more comfortable. Our flight will be quite lengthy, and we have to leave just as soon as possible."

Clarke examined the clothing. He was balancing in both hands; a pair of jeans, an off-white sweater, a pair of chocolate-colored UGG Boots, and a black leather jacket. "I'll give you a moment to get dressed. I'll be back to get you in a few minutes. Don't worry, I've already packed a suitcase for you. Anything else you might need, we can purchase abroad."

Melody's thoughts whizzed, after hearing Clarke detail their itinerary once they got to Switzerland. She kept nodding absently to everything he said. Clarke floated over to the canopy bed. He set the clothes on it, and the boots to its side.

"Melody, I'll be back in exactly ten minutes." Clarke's demeanor and his words seemed strained. At that point, he was standing in front of the bedroom door. "Are we clear? Please, don't try to resist what's happening. This is really for the best. I *know* I can make you happy. Just give me a chance."

Melody stared at him in utter denial. The entire experience felt surreal, and she kept expecting to wake up at any minute. Clarke eyed her for a few seconds before he stepped out of the room, and shut the door.

As soon as she was sure he was gone, Melody wrapped her arms about her lower abdomen, and bawled. "Lord, please, help me… Please, get me out of this situation. Please send someone to help me, or show me how to help myself." Melody tried not to falter.

Luke frowned in misery, because Melody was so heartbroken. Because she'd turned in the opposite direction, he waited for her to veer back over towards himself. The last thing he wanted was to startle her from behind. The moment Melody turned, Luke delicately inched in closer to her. In a subtle way, he wrapped his arms about her waist, while setting his other hand over her mouth, so that she wouldn't scream. "Melody, please, don't scream."

Melody froze instantly. Her heart lashed so forcefully, it felt as if her chest would explode. Someone or something had gotten a hold of her, but she couldn't see anyone there. Melody now *willed* herself to wake up from the nightmare. She could have sworn she'd heard Luke's voice. *Am I losing my mind?*

"Melody, it's me, honey," Luke said deliberately, trying not to frighten her.

"What…?" Melody gasped in shock, as she tried to process what was happening. So, it wasn't in her imagination after all. Melody set her hand on whatever or whoever was there. She outlined the shape of the invisible mass. Someone was undeniably there. They smelled clean and musky like Luke used to, but the body felt all wrong.

"Melody, it's me. Please, don't be scared," Luke reiterated, seeing the confused expression on her face.

"Luke…?" Melody continued to outline the stranger's form. "I don't understand. Where are you?" She was stumped.

"I'm standing right in front of you, honey."

"I can feel you but…Luke, is it *really* you?" Melody's voice wavered, and fresh tears meandered down her cheeks. "Whoever you are, this is *really* cruel." She swallowed the dryness in her throat.

Knowing there were no hidden cameras in that room, Luke reached into the pocket his fat suit, and deactivated the ***Vortex to Vanish*** feature of ***Dimension.*** It was at that moment he knew for sure that Melody could see him. "I would *never* deceive you." He set his hand tenderly to the side of her cheek, and brushed caringly on it.

Melody baulked in shock and bewilderment. "Luke…? But how…?" She reached up, and felt his gruff beard, and examined his fat suit. Looking past the disguise, Melody searched the stranger's eyes, and realized she was staring into the eyes of the man she loved.

She automatically threw her arms around him, and bawled. "I thought something horrible happened to you. I thought they hurt you like they hurt Sean. Oh, Luke…," Melody spoke choppily. "Oh, Luke…" She held on to him for dear life.

Luke wrapped his arms around Melody, and held on to her acquisitively. "I'm still here, honey, and I'm not going anywhere." He was overjoyed to have her in his arms. Luke gently cradled her head in his hands, and bathed her face in tender kisses.

"I *know* what they did to Sean." Melody's face wrenched in reproach, as her eyes connected critically to Luke's.

Luke's head momentarily slumped. It was difficult not to give in to feelings of despondency. "Sean was only trying to…," his voice cracked, as he stared into Melody's sad eyes.

Melody brushed tears away from Luke's eyes. "Is he…?" She couldn't even bring herself to say the defining word.

"Pretty close to…" Luke kept shaking his head in denial.

"I'm *so* sorry, Luke." Melody grimaced in sympathy and commiseration.

"I'm sorry too, honey. Sean didn't deserve that." Luke realized he had to stop the landslide of grief, and caught himself. "Sean was actually worried for you," Luke told Melody. "He was hurt, but he wanted me to look after you." Luke sensitively explored her eyes.

"I hope Clarke and Darien pay for the rest of their lives for all they've done." Melody sulked, but then redirected. "But are *you* safe here? Are you sure they didn't see you?"

Luke gave her a heartening smile. "Trust me, they have no idea I'm inside this bizarre underground complex. They're not the brightest bulbs in the box."

"But they *are* wicked. I hope they all wind up with consecutive jail sentences." Melody seethed.

"They will. I will *see* to it that they do," Luke said emphatically. "But right now, honey, we've got to get out of here." He cradled Melody's face in his hands again.

"That can't happen fast enough for me. I'm *so* happy you're safe." She stared wonderingly into Luke's eyes. Hers reflected the love she still felt for him, but Melody pulled back, too afraid to express her heart. She'd hurt him so much. "I thought you left town." Melody's face rumpled in guilt.

"Leave *you* alone in Sands Port in the hands of a ruthless killer?" Luke's eyes delved weightily into hers. "*Never…*" He still blamed himself for putting her in harm's way. Taking Clarke's incendiary offer, had forever altered the lives of his loved ones. So, Luke had to find a way to make things right.

"There's so much I still don't understand, Luke," Melody admitted.

"I promise to explain everything later. Right now, I need to get you out of here." Luke looked all about the room, and his eyes settled on the bedroom door. "And based on what that nut job just said, there's very little time to make that happen."

"You heard all of that?" Melody squirmed in shame over the matter.

"Yes, I did, but I'm not going to let him get anywhere near you."

"But how are you going to get us out of here? Clarke's men are swarming the place, and they're all armed." Melody frowned in angst. Her greatest fear was that Clarke and his men would barge in at any minute and hurt Luke. "I know Clarke won't hurt *me*, but he won't hesitate to hurt *you* if he finds you here. I don't want anything to happen to you." Melody worried that Clarke would come back, and find Luke there.

Luke was stirred by Melody's concern. The tiniest spark of hope ignited in his heart that she still cared. "Don't worry, honey. Clarke and his men can only hurt us if they can *see* us…"

Luke pulled away from Melody for a moment, and issued a fond wink in her direction. He then accessed the *Vortex to Vanish* feature of *Dimension Four*, and blinked out again.

"How are you able to disappear like that, Luke? Luke…? Luke…?" Stupefied, Melody's eyes shifted everywhere. "Where did you go?"

"I'm right here, honey." Luke suddenly reappeared.

Melody's heart skipped a beat when Luke popped up again. She smiled. "Now, I'm *really* confused." She shook her head in skepticism.

"I promise to explain everything later but for now…" Luke cautiously set his hand on Melody's waist, and secured her hand in his. He then pulled her to himself as closely as he possibly could. She had to be in the field of the vortex, so that they'd both be encapsulated. "Now, *you're* invisible just like me," Luke said winded, and overwhelmed by his love for her. It had been such a long time since they'd been this close.

Their faces bridged, and their lips were a whisper away. Instinctively, Luke leaned in to kiss her, but then pulled back. It took a lot of self-control to abstain from tasting her dulcet mouth. However, there was a time and place for everything, and this was neither the time nor the place for a kiss. Besides, so much had transpired in the past year, which had driven a wedge between them. Luke was honestly scared to kiss Melody, because he still questioned where they stood. He *sensed* that she still cared. However, caring about him and loving him were two different things.

Luke's heart twisted in knots to even consider letting Melody walk away. Nonetheless, his objective at that point in time wasn't to try to win her back. When it was all said and done and they were both out of harm's way, if Melody said the word, he'd move heaven and earth to have her back in his arms. However, it had to be something they *both* wanted.

Luke wanted Melody so badly, he was willing to do *whatever* he had to in order to win her back. If Melody gave him a second chance, he would hold on for dear life, and never let go…not ever. Yet and still, at that juncture, he had to ensure that they both had a future, and that they'd make it out of this bizarre situation unscathed.

Melody had to fight the urge to kiss Luke. Their faces bridged like two pieces of land above a body of water. Engulfed in a virtual field of violet and white lights was strange. But, being in Luke's arms felt safe and familiar.

It was instinctive to give in and press a kiss to his mouth. Melody felt as helpless and mislaid as a little girl. Realizing she was losing control, she moved awkwardly away, so that she wouldn't surrender to the lure of indulging in the honey stream of Luke's mouth. "Are you sure they *can't* see us?" she tested.

Luke smiled and nodded. "I'm *pretty* sure." Luke explored the sweet features of Melody's radiant face. Oh, how he'd missed her!

"Luke, I'm scared…"

"You don't have to be, honey. I've got you. Do you trust me?" Luke's voice was throaty, as he cupped her chin.

Melody nodded. "I trust you," she said softly, staring wonderingly up into his eyes.

"Now, let's get out of this nightmare. You might want to change out of that gown like Clarke said." Luke pointed over to the change of clothes on the bed. "It'll be easier to move around in them."

Looking away from Melody for even a second was a real challenge. Luke felt like a man brought over to a buffet table after an extended period of fasting. He was ravenous, and couldn't stop ogling *everything* Melody.

Melody nodded again. "It would make sense to change, but we don't have much time."

"It'll be fine. You can change in the bathroom. If Clarke rears his ugly head, stall him, and tell him to give you a minute."

Melody felt a shift in her universe, as she stared into Luke's amazing teal eyes. Also, the feel of his hand on her waist was sheer heaven. More than anything else, she'd missed his kiss and his tender touch. And even in his middle-aged, portly man disguise, he was still absolutely irresistible.

Moving past her fascination, Melody redirected. "Can you help me out of the gown?"

"Of course," Luke said. His heart raced, and he gulped nervously, when Melody veered, so that he could undo the clasps on the wedding gown. His hands brushed delicately over the soft feel of lace on Melody's back. Luke worked through strong feelings of desire, and moved about quickly to help her. He watched Melody slip into the bathroom. Soon after, Luke knocked discreetly on the door. She opened it up, and took the change of clothes and the boots he proffered.

Luke stood in front of the bedroom door, and listened for activity beyond it. He also kept his eyes on the bathroom door, anxiously waiting for Melody to come out. The moment Luke moved away from the bedroom door, he heard footsteps drawing closer. Irrefutably, it was Clarke coming back for Melody.

Luke rushed over to alert Melody. "Mel, I hear footsteps. I think Clarke might be coming back. So, I'm gonna blink out for a while."

Melody's heartstrings tightened in her chest over Luke's disclosure. She was sickened over the realization that Clarke was coming back. Her worst nightmare materialized when she heard his voice.

"Melody, darling, are you all set to leave?" Clarke surged thoughtlessly into the bedroom.

"I'm almost finished dressing, Clarke. Please, just give me another minute or two," Melody said sweetly, through the door.

Luke observed how panicked and frazzled Clarke was. Luke had never seen the man lose his composure. It was an artificial experience to say the least. Luke stood just outside of the bathroom door, and Clarke stood only a few feet away.

"Of course, you can finish dressing, darling…but please hurry. In a few minutes, we'll be boarding the jet." Clarke moved about anxiously. "The flight strip is at another location, so we need to get out of here quickly."

"I understand, Clarke. I'll be out in just a minute." Melody wondered what was going on inside of the bedroom. She was terrified that something would go wrong, and Clarke would find Luke there. Melody also worried that Luke's technology would in some way glitch. So, she remained prayerful the entire time. She tremulously slipped on the jeans and the sweater. Melody took deep breaths in order to remain calm.

At one point, she cracked open the bathroom door to see if Clarke was still there. Much to her chagrin, he was there pacing nervously beyond it. When Clarke saw her head through the ajar door, he offered an uneasy smile. Melody gave him a pseudo smile just before she shut the bathroom door. Melody sent a prayer heavenward. Her prayer was for Clarke to leave the bedroom, so that she and Luke could get out of there.

Luke remained perfectly still, and even tried to control his breathing. His face reddened in frustration, because Clarke refused to leave the room. The man had told Melody he'd give her a minute to finish dressing, but he wasn't going anywhere.

In light of what was happening, Luke had to find a way into the bathroom. He had to connect to Melody before it was too late. In order to disappear, they both had to be in the direct field of the vortex. Also, if Melody stepped out of the bathroom, Clarke would forcefully usher her away, and ruin their plan.

Luke observed Clarke pacing agitatedly, while intermittently checking his watch. It was obvious he wasn't going anywhere, until

Melody got done dressing. So, Luke had to find a way to get into the bathroom without scaring Melody. It was much too risky to have her come out to Clarke.

"Darling, are you all set?" Clarke asked temperately. However, his face and eyes were no longer crimson. He was so miffed they'd turned into a plum color. In spite of his clearly rattled display, he still tried to project total placidity.

Melody didn't know what to do at that point. Luke was just outside waiting for her. But, how were they supposed to make a connection, with Clarke breathing down her neck? She hadn't blinked out as Luke had, and Clarke was much too clever to miss a beat. Tremoring like a bass speaker maxed-out in volume, she inched closer to the bathroom door. "I'm almost ready, Clarke."

Distressed, Melody knew she had to come up with a way to let Luke into the bathroom, without stepping out herself. Melody wrung her fingers together nervously, as she conspired. Something suddenly occurred to her. She realized she could ask Clarke to get her boots. She'd tell him that she'd forgotten to bring them into the bathroom, even if they were already on her feet.

In a very delicate way, Melody opened up the bathroom door again. She stuck her head out, so that Clarke wouldn't see the boots on her feet. "Clarke, can you get the boots for me? I forgot to bring them in here." Melody's face crinkled in angst. She breathed a sigh of relief when she felt Luke brush past her, when he slipped into the bathroom.

"Of course, darling," Clarke reassured.

Melody shut the bathroom door again, while Clarke walked around the bed to look for the boots. "Muffin, I don't see them out here..." Clarke knelt down to check under the bed.

"Are you all set?" Luke pulled Melody into his arms again, and drew her into the field of the vortex. The lights engulfed them both.

Melody nodded. She was more than ready to wake up from the nightmare. And as long as she stayed close to Luke, she was hopeful that they could escape.

Luke nodded affirmatively, and activated the *Vortex to Vanish* feature.

He set his finger on his lips to relay that they not make a sound. Melody's eyes stayed critically connected to Luke's, because she trusted him to guide her out of that horrible place.

Luke held Melody's hand, and indicated she stay as close to his side as possible. He pulled her to the far right hand corner of the bathroom, to the side of its sizable claw-footed tub.

"Melody, sweetheart, I don't see your boots out here. Are you sure you didn't bring them in there with you?" Clarke knocked on the bathroom door. "Melody…?" Clarke was puzzled, because there was no answer.

Melody and Luke remained as still as they possibly could. Luke supported Melody by the waist, and Melody's head rested just beneath his chin. Melody's body pressed up to his, was something Luke hadn't experienced in such a long time. It was literally making him insane, despite the current dangers they faced.

Melody tried to stifle her breathing, as her face brushed up against Luke's chest. Regardless of the uncertainty and the peril, it felt like paradise being in Luke's arms again. Melody had only dreamed of this moment every night for the past year. She couldn't have imagined her dream becoming a reality under these conditions.

Luke's eyes affixed to Melody's, as they listened and waited for Clarke's next move.

"Melody…?" Clarke knocked frenetically on the bathroom door. "Honey, are you in there?" Clarke broke out of his even-tempered veneer and barged in. "Melody, where are you?" His eyes were bright with shock and fear. "Melody…?" Clarke rushed towards the center of the room, and collected her wedding gown in his hands from off the floor.

"No, no this can't be happening. Melody!" Clarke bellowed.

By then, Luke and Melody had already slipped past him, and

were out of the bedroom. Luke guided Melody down the long stretch of hallway. They stepped aside, and remained perfectly still when they saw Darien coming towards them.

"What's the problem, Clarke?" Darien met Clarke down the hallway, and saw how crestfallen he was. "Why are you holding Melody's wedding gown? Where is she?"

"She's gone, Darien."

"What do you mean…gone? There's no way of leaving here except for the three points of access."

Clarke's face and eyes were imbued with rage. "Don't you think I know that, Darien? I know that better than anyone else, but Melody *is* gone," he said tautly.

"Unless Melody is secretly a magician, she couldn't have vanished."

Clarke pointed an accusatory finger at Darien. "I'm telling you that's exactly what happened. Now, I need you, Blake and the other idiots I hired to mind this place to find her. Find her now, and bring her back to me. I've already turned that bedroom upside down looking for her."

Darien was flabbergasted. However, Clarke was his boss. So, he had to do what his boss had said, even if Clarke's tale of Melody's sudden disappearance made absolutely no sense.

Darien perceived that Clarke was coming apart at the seams. That had to be the case, because in the past, Clarke would not have tolerated betrayal of any kind from a woman. However, Melody Maxwell had found a way to bring him to his knees. It was indeed a sad sight to behold!

Melody and Luke had evaded Clarke's men, and only feet away from the cylinder transporter. Clarke's goons were scattered throughout the compound frantically searching for Melody.

Melody's arm was linked to Luke's, as she watched him fiddle around with the glass conveyor. He spoke into his phone, and asked his program to help him decipher a code to get the transporter working. She was more than just a little bit impressed by Luke's brilliance and ingenuity.

"***Dimension***, is the activation button for this conveyor down here?" Luke kept his voice to a bare whisper.

As Luke awaited an answer from his trusty pal, ***Dimension***, Melody couldn't help noticing the blue portal enmeshed in the vortex field. "What's that for, Luke?" she asked, riveted.

"That's the ***Power Portal***. It can transport anyone or anything from one place to another," Luke said in a hushed tone.

"Activation is biometrically discerned by the voice or fingerprints of the main user. I don't have access to either of those at the moment," Master Luke," ***Dimension*** detailed.

Luke sighed in frustration, because they knew exactly who the *main* user was. It was the same man he and Melody were trying to get away from.

Luke went on to explain to Melody how the ***Power Portal*** worked. "The portal has the capability to transport us someplace else, but I'm not sure *where* we'd end up. It's risky, honey." He searched her eyes apologetically.

"We're already taking a huge risk, Luke. If that portal can get us out of this underground pit, we have to try." Melody stared at him pleadingly.

"Are you willing to take that chance with me?" Luke asked, amazed by Melody's faith.

"I *trust* you. I *know* this will work."

Luke smiled at her hopefully. "All right, honey, we ride or die…together." He squeezed her hand.

"Together…," Melody echoed. She felt more than safe with Luke, and trusted him completely. If he'd gotten them this far, she was confident of the effectiveness of his revolutionary technology.

"*Dimension*, how far away from this complex can we get using the portal?" Luke spoke into his phone, but his eyes remained fastened to Melody the entire time.

"*How far would you like to go, Master Luke?*" *Dimension* replied.

"Can it bring us over to the Jeep parked half a mile away from here?"

"*Of course it can. Use the Portal Find Me feature. It's the gray button beneath the Find Me feature,*" *Dimension* reminded Luke.

"Okay…" Luke wrapped his arms around Melody, and issued a command to the *Find Me* feature. "Are you okay?" He enfolded Melody closer to himself, and squeezed her hand.

"I'm okay." Melody set her arms about Luke's potbelly, and clung to him for dear life.

"I'm going to get you out of here, Mel." Luke pressed the gray triangle located beneath the main *Find Me* button. "Bring us back over to where I parked the Jeep," he issued the command.

The vortex lights grew brighter and more dominant, as the portal opened up and sucked them in. For all intents and purposes, they were particles on a carpet, which had just been suctioned up by a vacuum. Luke and Melody felt as if they were caught in a wind tunnel. Melody held on tightly to Luke and closed her eyes, as she felt herself being imbibed by the vivid indigo light. The whirlwind spun around them, but they were totally unharmed by its consuming luminescence. The portal's atmosphere was cool, drafty and a little scary.

"Just hold on to me, honey. You should be just fine," Luke's voice was a booming echo in that void.

"Luke, this is amazing!" Melody perceived that they were indeed being transported away from Clarke's imposed prison of a compound. "This is like Star Trek, only much more sophisticated.

You are amazing!"

"I guess it *is* like the 'Beam me up, Scottie of the 21ˢᵗ Century.'" Luke's smile was irrepressible. He was over the moon, because Melody seemed to be so impressed. Sporadically, she opened up her eyes to look around, but the windstorm was a bit intimidating. So, she continued to cling to him for dear life. Luke prayed that this untested feature of **Dimension Four** wouldn't fail them.

The lights within the portal created a cyclone-like effect, and snaked around them. The lights also blinked faster than anything Luke had ever seen. It was almost as if he and Melody were soaring through the galaxy. Suddenly, the portal lights dimmed to violet and gray, as the roiling wound down. Luke felt pressure to the chest, similar to the way he imagined a tennis ball would feel, thrust out from an automatic ball thrower.

"Can you feel that, honey?" Luke's voice roared, as if he was speaking from a chamber of some kind.

"It feels like I'm being squeezed out, like toothpaste from a tube." Melody kept her eyes opened this time around. "But, it feels wonderful." There were tears in her eyes as a result of the excessive draft, and also because she felt so safe and happy to be there with Luke. She hoped for a chance to tell him that she'd meant nothing she'd said the day before.

Luke had to know the truth. The truth was that she loved him now more than ever, and that was *never* going to change.

Luke covered Melody's head protectively, as he felt them drawing closer to being ejected from the portal. "Hang on, honey," he whispered into her ear. Raising his voice inside the portal, sounded like he was trying to speak while submerged underwater.

"Luke…," Melody cried out, alarmed. She buried her head in his chest, and wrapped her arms more securely around his waist.

"I've got you, honey. You're okay… You're okay…," Luke placated, as their bodies were being jammed through the portal. "It's okay…"

Suddenly, there was a sense of release, as if huge hands had finally eased their grasp on them.

Luke and Melody found themselves out in an open field. An onyx sky dusted with crystals above them, and a cool gentle breeze infused the night air.

Luke kept his arms securely around Melody, and he laughed when he saw the jeep feet away. "Mel, you can open your eyes now." He tenderly cradled her head in his hands. Hunching down, he pressed a fond kiss to her forehead. He was on cloud nine that they'd made it out to the clearing.

"We made it?" Melody slowly opened her eyes, and took in the scenery. Tears flooded her eyes to see the jeep. The night sky never looked more glorious!

"Yes, we're out of that godforsaken place." Luke stared suspiciously around. "But, we've got to keep moving. Clarke and his men aren't too far away." He shut down the portal, and closed up the vortex. He and Melody were now visible. Luke helped Melody up to her feet, and took her hand in his. Without hesitation, they began running towards the jeep.

They were within reach of the automobile, when they were overtaken by a host of police cars with muted sirens. There were also unmarked police vehicles.

"Luke, what's going on?" Melody pressed in closer to him. Her heart thrummed in angst and uncertainty.

"It's all right, honey. We're safe now. I clued the authorities in as to where they'd be able to find Clarke and his men."

Melody and Luke saw at least a dozen men issue out of from the myriad of parked cars. Luke felt out of sorts when they rushed over to them. He was still holding Melody's hand, but he had to let go, when the authorities ask him to put his hands up in surrender.

"What is your name, young man?" one of the officers asked Luke. The man's face gnarled in rage, as one of the agents patted Luke down. The man found the gun Luke had stashed in the pocket of his fat suit.

Melody flinched when she saw the gun. However, she figured that Luke had probably brought it along in case he'd needed to use it. "Luke, you don't have to explain anything to them, because you haven't done anything wrong." With her hands pressed up to his flanks, Melody held on protectively to Luke.

"It's all right, Mel. Everything's going to be okay," Luke whispered to Melody over his shoulder. He then addressed the FBI agent's query. "My name is Luke Bryant."

"Luke, you have the right to remain silent…," the police went over the drill with Luke.

"No. Let him go. He hasn't done anything wrong!" Melody fought.

"Young lady, you're going to have to come with us," an agent told Melody, and began dragging her away from Luke. "Let him go," Melody argued. "He hasn't committed any crime," she disputed. Melody cried all the more when she watched them handcuffing Luke.

"Luke…," Melody screamed. "Luke…." She tried to break free from the acquisitive grasp of the agents detaining her.

"I'm okay, Mel. You go on with them. Let them get you out of here. I'll be okay. You don't have to grab her that way," Luke shouted at the men who were hauling Melody away. "You're okay, Mel. I promise…" Luke watched them coerce Melody towards an unmarked FBI vehicle.

"Luke…," Melody cried. "Please, let me go." She tried to shove away.

"Melody, you're safe now. You're going to be all right. Let us get you as far away from this place as possible," Agent Morgan told Melody. His hand was like a vise around her arm.

"What about Luke?" Melody glared at him. "What has he done?"

"Melody, I'm afraid that is classified information. I *will* say this. Your friend has tampered with this investigation. We also have reason to believe that he's gotten hold of classified information."

"What do you mean? If he hadn't shown up here, I wouldn't even be alive. He hasn't done anything wrong. Please…," Melody appealed.

"Melody, your friend will be just fine, provided he can answer some key questions." The car began to roll away.

"Luke…," Melody cried out, as the agents pulled away from the locale.

"It's okay, honey," Luke placated. And, then Melody was gone. Tears of frustration pushed through his eyes over the circumstances. *He'd* wanted to make sure Melody made it home safely. And, Luke felt as if that right had been stripped away.

"Now, *Luke*, we need to know how you were able to find Melody on your own. How were you and Melody able to appear out in that clearing, when we couldn't even *find* a location for Vale?" Agent Sturgis stared at Luke in skepticism.

"I can bring you straight to them. *Someone* tipped me off," Luke said truthfully. That *someone* was his trusty new technology. What was really *classified* was **Dimension Four**, and Luke couldn't afford to have that information leaked out to the authorities.

"No doubt, you can lead us to Vale and his lackeys. Still, how were you able to find them, when *we* couldn't?" Agent Sturgis rubbed his head in perplexity.

"Just lucky, I guess," Luke said glibly. "Look, am I under arrest here or what?" He was becoming increasingly more annoyed over their incompetence.

"We need for you to lead us to Vale and his men. Then, we have a few questions for you." Sturgis's face tensed up again in mistrust.

"What? You think I'm some kind of government spy?" Luke

shook his head inanely over how ridiculous they were.

"We're not sure what to think at this point, but we do need your help in bringing Clarke Vale in."

"I have no problem helping you out, but you need to take these handcuffs off, if I'm *not* under arrest." Luke stared at the men in incredulity.

Sturgis ordered that the cuffs be removed from Luke's writs. "Take us to Vale," he ordered Luke.

"Gladly. Just so you know, Vale was finalizing plans to take a private jet to Europe when Melody and I found our way out of his compound. You've already wasted time busting *me*, when you could have already found Vale and his cohorts." Luke soothingly rubbed on his wrists.

"Okay, you've proven your point. Now, take us to Vale, kid."

"First off, you and your boys need to turn off the flashing lights. The last thing you want is to have them all scurrying away to leave that complex." Luke floated over, and jumped into one of the unmarked vehicles. The officers and agents followed his lead, as he detailed the exact location of the seemingly abandoned old farmhouse.

"You're something else, kid," FBI Agent Calder told Luke. He stared Luke down in utter disbelief. He was baffled at how the kid had pulled the wool over the eyes of the notorious Clarke Vale.

Luke instructed the authorities to leave the cars a distance away from the abandoned property. He also warned that if they used the cylinder transporter inside of the barn as a point of entry, they would instantly be killed upon their descent to the compound.

In the meantime, Luke accessed the **Dimension** app again. He quickly typed in an order for the program to show him other access points into Clarke's intricate safe house. He recalled Darien telling Clarke that there were *three* points of access.

Luke trusted the program to show him an alternate way

inside of the labyrinth. The fact that he'd vanished before stepping out of the cylinder had saved his life. However, Luke couldn't promise the same level of protection to the police and the FBI.

Dimension highlighted the three points of access, and displayed them on Luke's phone. When the men asked what was so pressing on his phone, Luke told them he was playing Minecraft. Luke already knew that the safest access point was the water well located towards the back end of the farmhouse.

The well was a cover for a second transporter. It was also considerably larger than the cylinder Luke had used. It had the capacity to transport three men at a time. But none of that would even matter, if Clarke was already on his private jet. Time was running out, and they had to move fast before Clarke and Darien fled the country.

CHAPTER TWELVE

Following Luke's lead, FBI and police used the transporter behind the old farmhouse to lower themselves into Clarke's underground facility. The men asked Luke to remain outside, and not to interfere with the takedown in any way. However, Luke had already accessed the *Vortex to Vanish* accessory of *Dimension Four*, and had blinked out.

Luke then solitarily used the transporter. Before long, he saw the officers and agents navigating through the expansive and winding complex. Their guns were drawn, as they cautiously turned every corner. But, Luke rushed ahead of them-scanning out the halls, and checking for traps or snares set by Clarke or his men in order to trip them up.

A good distance ahead of the police and the FBI, Luke stumbled upon Darien Stiles. Darien was moving quickly, and carrying an attaché case. There was no doubt in Luke's mind that Darien, along with all of Clarke's minions, were now aware of a true security breach. So, they were all scrambling to get out of there.

Luke bridged the gap between Darien and himself, and he jumped the man. Luke allowed Darien to yelp once, but then set his hand tightly over Darien's mouth, so that he couldn't make another sound.

"What the...?" Darien's head kept whipping from side to side in utter panic. "Who's there?" he muttered. Luke could audibly hear the man's whisking heart.

The FBI and the police had undoubtedly heard Darien's notable shriek. It was the howl of a man who thought he was under paranormal attack. Just as Luke had planned, the men came rushing down the sinewy hallway, and found Darien Stiles wrestling with *himself.*

A dozen agents descended on Darien like locusts and restrained him. However, the men were confused as to why Darien was on the floor unable to help himself. They had to wonder if the man was suffering simultaneously from a psychotic break and sudden paralysis.

Luke stood a few feet away, and watched them read Darien his rights.

Darien's face was a mask of vexation, bewilderment and fear. "You've got nothing on me," Darien said smugly as they cuffed him.

"We've got a lot more than you know, Mr. Stiles. How does murder one, conspiracy to commit murder, extortion, blackmail and drug dealing sound? We could keep going-then again *who* has that kind of time? We've got bigger fish to fry."

"Like I said, you've got nothing on me, and you *won't* be doing any fish-frying-at least not today," Darien blared as he was led away. He wouldn't stop talking, so one of the cops placed a stretch of duct tape over his mouth.

Luke watched on with tremendous satisfaction. "One down and another one to go," he said quietly, as he forged on ahead of the men. Luke wasn't the least bit concerned with Clarke's henchmen, because he knew for sure that they would trip themselves up. Luke was only interested in finding one person. It was the man responsible for hurting Sean, who'd destroyed his relationship with Melody, and who'd berated him and his family. Luke's goal was to bring down the miscreant, who had the audacity to threaten the life of the woman he loved.

Luke roamed the spiraling corridors, and wandered back to the place where the glass cylinder had first transported him. Three of Clarke's men were buzzing around like bees, doing all they could to destroy what appeared to be documents. Two of the men carried briefcases. They were all set to abscond. Luke staked out the luxurious room, and randomly began knocking things down.

"Huh...? Who's there?" Blake, *supposedly* the smarter one of the three, pulled out his gun and began shooting into the open air. His *genius* coworkers pulled out their guns, and had a shootout jamboree, as Luke knocked over lamps, sculptures and books. He watched the men succumb to mental breakdowns -pumping bullets into the air, and emptying their gun chambers.

Luke's intention was for Clarke's cronies to use up their rounds shooting at nothing, while simultaneously clueing the authorities in as to where to find them.

"Freeze, dirt bags," Agent Sturgis, and half a dozen other men infiltrated the area. They overtook the three men, who'd implicated themselves by excessively firing their guns.

Luke smiled gratifyingly, as he watched Clarke's men apprehended and handcuffed. Still, only *one* thing could top his sundae with a cherry. He had to find Clarke. There was no way Clarke was getting away. For Luke it was personal. Clarke had endangered all of their lives, and had ordered Darien Stiles and his men to hurt Sean.

Luke wanted Clarke to pay for what happened to Sean. So, he sped all around that property to see where the mastermind of the operation could be hiding. Like a man possessed, he powered through the meandering passageways by leaps and bounds. Luke remembered Clarke telling Melody that the private jet was at another location. He hoped and prayed that Clarke hadn't yet found his way out of the complex.

Luke must have gone in and out of a dozen rooms, but had turned up empty. Still, he was determined to find Clarke-that was if Clarke was still around.

Luke came to a corner of the immense development, and stumbled upon a room with a set of double doors. On the right hand side of the door was a security keypad. Luke asked **Dimension** for help in disabling the security feature. He scanned the security pad's picture into the system. Within seconds, luminous silver light covered the metal block. For a minute, the keypad fused with the silver lighting, and appeared as fluid as mercury. There was a humming noise and some heat just before the security pad was immobilized. Moments later, Luke let himself into the room.

"I just hit the jackpot." Luke floated into what appeared to be a library. Clarke was petrified standing at a corner of the room. Terror danced on his face and in his eyes, because the double doors had been opened. If Luke didn't know better, he would have thought that Clarke had just seen a ghost. Clarke's mouth gaped in shock, as he scurried over to the set of doors to see who was behind the compromised security feature.

Luke's smile was irrepressible, as he watched Clarke suspiciously look both ways before shutting the set of doors again.

"Where's Darien?" Clarke grumbled, as veins pounded at his temples.

At the far right hand corner of the library were Clarke's bags. He was all packed up and ready to take flight. Luke shifted over, and went to stand feet away from him. He couldn't help noticing how jumpy Clarke was. The man kept checking his phone like a nervous pigeon.

Apparently, he hadn't gotten the email that his men were apprehended. He had no idea that he'd be waiting on Darien *indefinitely*. Luke decided to mess around with Clarke for a little while, because the man obviously wasn't going anywhere. When he got done tormenting Clarke, the man would fall into his own trap.

Luke walked over to the bookshelf, and dropped one single book on the plush Asian carpeting.

Startled, Clarke turned reflexively, as his mouth gaped. His heart hammered. "Who's there?" he asked tremulously, staring all about like a demented man.

Luke slid over to the adjourning shelf, and knocked over another book. He watched on, tickled, because Clarke seemed to jump right out of his skin.

"What's going on here?" Clarke scowled, and his eyes flashed. "Who are you, and what do you want?" He did an entire 180 degree turn.

As other objects flew across the room, Clarke's head whipped back and forth, like someone engaged in watching a spirited game of tennis.

"Huh…?" Clarke's face turned as white as a bleached

blanket, and he dropped his phone in fear and shock. "I refuse to believe this is happening. What's going on here?" His knees knocked together so loudly, Luke couldn't help thinking that a woodpecker had found its way into the library.

"Clarke…," Luke said using a ***Dimension*** accessory to distort his voice.

"Sweet mother of God, please have mercy on me. What's happening?" Clarke's erratic movements thrust him up against one of the bookshelves. "Who are you and where are you? How do you know my name?" His expression was bordering catatonia.

"Clarke…?" Luke's voice resonated inches away from Clarke's ear.

"Ah…, get away from me." Clarke jumped, and scurried to the other side of the library. He pulled out his gun, and fitfully began shooting into the air. "Who are you, and what do you want from me?"

"I think you already know. You've been very, very bad, Clarke. Now, it's time to get what's coming to you. Did you really think you could go on stealing from, and murdering innocent people without having to pay the piper?" Luke taunted.

"I've never *deliberately* hurt anyone." Clarke's face had turned as scarlet as a white beet-stained bowl. "People always wind up betraying me. It's not my fault that they've gotten caught in the crossfire."

"Clarke…?" Luke toyed. "You're about to meet your maker…"

"Oh, God, no…!" Clarke aimed his sophisticated Hollow-Point revolver at nothing in particular all set to shoot. Falling to his knees, he squeezed the trigger a number of times. "You're not going to take me alive. You won't get me…whoever you are… I'm Clarke Vale and I am invincible."

Luke bobbed and weaved out of harm's way, but continued to torment Clarke. It dawned on him that the didactic speeches of morality weren't necessary. Clarke was unraveling before his very eyes. So, Luke just kept on reiterating, *Clarke*… in different corners of that room.

Clarke finally dropped his chamber-depleted gun to the floor, and surrendered to crying like a child. "Please, don't let me die, God. Please, forgive my mistakes…" Clarke covered his face with both hands.

Luke got a yearning for popcorn, as he watched Clarke lose it. It was so much better than a movie! Luke's back was pressed up to a bookshelf, and he nodded in satisfaction and closure. It was only a matter of time before the authorities heard noises in the library, and Clarke's blubbering. Luke crossed his arms over his chest, and silently counted down; "Four, three, two, one…"

At that very moment FBI and police raided the security-compromised library. And, Clarke was poised on his knees to be apprehended.

"Clarke Victor Vale, you have the right to remain silent. Anything you say can and will be held against you in a court of law…," the police read Clarke his rights, as four other men restrained him.

Clarke didn't resist, but stood to his feet compliantly as they cuffed him. "What exactly am I being arrested for?" He stared accusatorially at the men.

The FBI and the police stared amongst themselves in total incredulity. Some of the men shook their head humorously.

"You *really* want to go there, Vale?" One of the FBI agents asked.

Clarke's face stretched into a temperate smile. "Why not…?" He shrugged.

"Okay, let me just tell you this. You see all these books?" An officer Mattock pointed over to the myriad of books on the shelves. "Well, what we've got on you is more than enough to fill up every book in this place." All of the men chortled, and shook their heads comically over Clarke's innocent act. "Let's go, Vale. This is over."

Luke preceded the men outside of the library. He went to stand at the very end of the hallway, and watched as they led Clarke away. "Thank you, Lord!" Luke lifted up his hands in praise to God.

He then accessed his phone, and recorded the unprecedented moment. Clarke had evaded arrest for years, and this was definitely a milestone. Luke was also grateful that God had used *him* systematically to bring it to pass.

As much as he wanted to relish the moment, he now had to find his way back out to where the FBI and the cops had ordered him to stay. He had to make them believe that he hadn't budged an inch from that spot. Luke stood a good distance away from the fake well with his arms crossed over his chest. His mannerism and expression were cavalier, as he watched the authorities emerge from the compound using the transporter.

A total of eight suspects were brought out of the development restrained in cuffs. Clarke Vale himself was the last one to be brought out.

As they led Clarke way, he caught sight of Luke standing in the distance. "*You*...?" he growled and lowered at Luke.

Luke feigned a tipped hat in Clarke's direction, but didn't speak. This was the moment he'd waited on for months. It was indeed poetic justice to see the authorities pressing Clarke's head into the back seat of an unmarked FBI car. Luke saw them repeat the process with Darien Stiles, and the other mobsters. They'd all run out of luck on that day.

After the riffraff had been tucked neatly way, Agent Sturgis and Kane directed their attention over to Luke.

Luke put on his best poker face, and stared them directly in the eyes.

"You sure you've been here this entire time, kid?" Sturgis's eyes narrowed suspiciously into Luke's.

"I'm just happy you got your man. This has been a long time coming," Luke evaded.

"You have no idea, kid. Today we went fishing, and caught eight big ones," Kane said.

"Am I free to go now?" Luke asked, totally distracted.

"I'm afraid you've got to come with us," Sturgis told him.

Luke's face wrinkled in annoyance. "What are you charging me with? I haven't done anything-"

"You've interfered with a very sensitive FBI and police investigation."

"How have I interfered?" Luke stared at them in disbelief.

"We have a whole lot of questions for you. For starters, how you knew this old farmhouse was a cover for Vale's complex. We had absolutely no leads-even using our own state of the art technology. I know you said you got a tip, but there's got to be more to it than that." Sturgis kept shaking his head in skepticism.

"Look, there was a lot at stake, so I *had* to find this location. Vale and his men shot my best friend this afternoon. I have no idea if my best buddy...if my *brother* is still alive. Come hell or high water, there was no way I was going to let them hurt Melody Maxwell." Luke pointed a liable finger at the agent. He was totally incensed they were detaining him.

"So, if it's all the same to you, I'd like to leave. I need to see about my friend, and to make sure Melody's all right."

"Luke, *kid*..., believe me, we won't keep you a moment longer than necessary. We just need to sit with you for a while to examine a few matters."

"Can we examine those matters out here...now? What is it that you want to know-how I was able to find Vale's compound?" Telling them the truth about ***Dimension Four*** just wasn't an option. Luke knew if he disclosed that information, it would be opening up a whole new can of worms with the FBI. So, he had to tread cautiously.

"I did *not* interfere with your investigation. I'm the one who clued you all in about the mass takedown of your men earlier on. I'm also the one who asked you to follow this lead. I *know* who Clarke Vale is, and I had to get Melody away from him. I just followed an anonymous tip. That's how I was able to find her."

"How were you able to get into the compound without being detected?" Kane demanded.

"There's a camera-sensitive device on my phone. It helped in avoiding detection," Luke said truthfully. The authorities really didn't need to know anything more than that.

"One of our men will be driving your jeep back down to Sands Port, and we're going to need to see your phone for a minute."

Luke shrugged in a nonchalant manner, and handed the device over to them. He figured that they'd want to see it. So, he'd already set up the abort feature of the *Dimension* App. Temporarily aborting the app, meant there would be no trace of it on the phone, until he chose to restore it. Only Luke's DNA could reactivate it.

"So, you have my phone… Can I go now?"

"Luke, I'm sorry that your friend's in critical condition over at the hospital, but we're still going to need for you to come with us. Promise we won't keep you too long. You're not the only one with casualties today, kid. We lost at least five of our own," Kane said thickly.

Luke softened, as he internalized the onslaught carried out by Clarke's men earlier on. Sean had also gotten caught in that crossfire. Realizing that arguing with the FBI was a total waste of time, Luke acquiesced. "You've got one hour. If by then you can't come up with a viable reason to detain me, I'm walking," Luke said boldly. He didn't even blink as he delved into Agent Sturgis's eyes.

"Let's go, kid. It's been a long messy day for all of us." Sturgis looked over at the waiting vehicles. "It's time to throw out the trash."

"So glad it's finally trash day!" Agent Kane concurred.

Luke voluntarily followed behind Agent Sturgis, and Agent Kane trailed behind Luke. Luke was hesitant. On the one hand, he was immensely relieved because Melody was safe, and that Clarke and his men were being brought in. And yet, on the other, he was peeved because of this unexpected detour. All the same, he tried to play it cool on the drive back down to Sands Port with the authorities.

Luke prayed for God's peace and temperance. He took deep breaths in order to remain calm. Assenting to the fact that the authorities were only following protocol, Luke tried to see things from their perspective. Truth be told, if he was a police officer or an FBI agent, he too would have had questions in respect to the way things had played out that day.

Dwelling on the moments shared with Melody earlier on kept Luke sane. It was hard not to belabor the closeness they'd experienced. Their precarious set of circumstances had provided a new sense of codependency. Now more than ever he was in love. Furthermore, Luke knew that he wouldn't have wanted to face a life-threatening crisis without Melody by his side.

He would never forget how they'd successfully used the **Power Portal** together for the first time. It was an experience he wouldn't have wanted to share with anyone else. In a tactual sense, he could still feel Melody in his arms. It had been equally wonderful to feel hers around him.

But, the question remained. *Did she still love him?* It was hard to tell. Melody was relieved that Clarke's men hadn't hurt him. *But was she still in love?* As much as Luke wanted to believe that she was, her words on Friday morning still resonated. She'd said they were over, and that she no longer loved him.

Luke hoped he could find a way to get Melody to believe in him again. There had to be a way to rekindle what they once had. He loved her so much that he'd never stop trying. All the same, Luke realized that Melody needed a breather. She would undoubtedly need time to process all she'd just gone through with Vale. If she needed time, Luke resolved to give the space she needed. However, he determined not to let her slip away again. His aim was to win her back, even if it took the rest of his life.

***

Melody paced up and down on the slick tiled flooring at the police precinct in downtown Sands Portville. It was where the authorities had brought her, after they'd dragged her away from Luke in the middle of nowhere near Clarke's development. She wrung her fingers nervously as she traipsed the glossy canvas.

Police officers and FBI agents had questioned her for hours regarding the abduction. They were curious to know how things had played out inside of Clarke's compound. Melody had told them all she knew. However, she refused to disclose anything having to do with Luke's classified technological breakthrough, **Dimension Four**. Now that she'd had a moment to process, she could hardly believe any of it herself. She and Luke were *invisible*. They'd slipped into a *portal*, which had transported them safely away from Clarke's horror show of a complex.

Melody would *never* divulge that secret, until Luke said it was okay to do so. He'd said that **Dimension** was still in the trial stages. So, Luke wasn't quite ready to share the mystery with the world at large.

"So, everything you've told us so far is *all* you know about that underground development and Clarke Vale's dealings?" An FBI Agent Grant, asked Melody for the umpteenth time. His eyes searched hers critically.

Melody stopped shuffling midway. Exasperated, she shrugged. "What do you want me to say? I've told you all I know. I was blindfolded when I was brought down to that hole in the ground. And, I've explained the details of how Luke found me." Saying Luke's name softened Melody's tone.

Just then, the office doors opened, and revealed Serena and Dane. They both rushed over to connect to Melody. Tears of joy shone in Melody's eyes to see her friends. She was so grateful that they were all right.

Melody closed her eyes meditatively, and thanked God. She was stirred to see the bandage on the right side of Dane's forehead. In spite of all the couple had endured, they were unharmed. It was a miracle, and Melody couldn't stop thanking God.

Melody collected Serena in her arms, and held on for dear life. "I'm so happy you're here." She trembled in Serena's arms.

"Oh, honey, you have no idea how *good* it is to see *you*!" Serena folded Melody protectively in her arms, and cried as they hugged.

Melody allowed herself to cry in her best friend's arms. Breathing spasmodically, her words were choppy, as she tried to express her heart. "I thought I'd never see you guys again. I had no idea what Clarke had planned..." Melody gasped. Dane found the ladies, and draped his arms around them in comfort.

"You're okay, honey. Oh, God... Thank you, thank you..." Serena kept repeating as they sustained each other. All three were in tears.

Melody crushed Serena and Dane in her arms. She closed her eyes musingly, relieved and grateful. "I'm so sorry... I'm so sorry for all the trouble I've caused for everybody." She grimaced in guilt and shame.

"Don't you dare apologize to us, Melody Christine," Serena chided. She pulled away, and pointed an apprising finger at her best friend. "You had no way of knowing what was going to happen and neither did Luke. So, I don't want to hear either of you blaming yourselves for anything having to do with Clarke."

Melody frowned in misery again. "Luke risked his life to get us out of that complex, Serena. Were it not for him, I'd probably be headed to Switzerland with Clarke right now."

"How *did* Luke manage that?" Dane shook his head, stumped.

Melody stared all about the expansive office. Police and agents were still buzzing about like bees, so she decided not to discuss the details. She veered back towards her friends. "I can't talk about it here. I can say this. Luke's not ready to share his special gifts with the world."

Serena gave Melody a knowing look and winked. "You're right. It's something he's still working on, and until he's ready to put it out there… But *I* will say this…" Serena smiled through the tears. "He's a genius, and he loves *you* more than anything."

Melody smiled mawkishly, as she clasped her hands together. "And, I love him now more than ever! But, I'm still upset about what happened the moment we escaped from the compound. Luke didn't do anything wrong. I know he's probably fine, but I just need to hear from him. We went through a lot together today."

"The FBI probably have a gazillion questions. They don't understand how Luke was able to find you when *they* couldn't. Even so, if anyone knows how to handle himself it's Luke. I'm sure you'll hear from him just as soon as he's free to call you." Serena gave Melody a heartening smile.

"I'm counting on it, Serena. I doubt, we'll ever forget the challenges we faced today." Melody shook her head, mystified.

"No, I doubt any of us can forget, Melody," Dane agreed. "Luke's going to be just fine. And, don't worry about the gun. It's registered to me. *I* encouraged Luke to take it with him in case he ran into trouble," Dane reassured.

"I'm just glad he…*we* didn't need to use it." Melody sighed, relieved. "Did you stop in to see Sean?" Melody's face contorted in dread, and her heart lashed as she awaited an answer.

"Yeah, right after Dane was discharged, we stopped into the ICU. Sean's barely clinging to life." Tears glimmered in Serena's eyes.

"But he's still alive?" Melody nodded in hopefulness, and blinked back tears of her own.

"He's strong, so there's always a chance. We're going to turn Sean's condition over to God. God's the only one who can step in and intervene," Dane solemnly expressed.

"But he's still alive," Melody affirmed, for her own sense of sanity. Tears rolled down her cheeks. "Luke should know that Sean is still alive." Melody closed her eyes meditatively and whispered a prayer. "Lord, I believe you're able to heal Sean completely. You are the healer and restorer. Please don't let us lose him…"

It broke Melody's heart to consider how much Sean had suffered. Both Luke and Sean had made so many sacrifices. They'd placed themselves in the direct eye of the storm to ensure her safety. Now, all she cared about was *theirs*. Melody wanted Luke to know how much she still loved *him*. She had to tell him that she'd never stopped. Moreover, she had to explain that she was no longer upset about the wager, and helping his family during a dire set of circumstances.

"Mel, Sean's in God's hands, and Luke knows how to take care of himself." Dane gave Melody a sympathetic look.

"I know that, Dane. Still, I can't rest until I know for sure that Clarke and Darien were apprehended. They were planning to leave the country." Melody brooded over the horrific experience of being trapped underground, as she stared between Serena and Dane.

There was a roar of laughter and celebration amongst the police and the FBI. Melody, Serena and Dane's faces wrinkled in confusion and uncertainty, as they warily examined the agents and officers. At that moment, there was a broadcast interruption on CNN. The red lines at the bottom of the screen were daunting, and solemnness cloaked the face of the middle-aged anchorman with platinum- colored hair. "We interrupt our regular scheduled program for an important update…"

Silence permeated the entire office, and all eyes fastened to the large flat-screen television mounted on the wall in the center of the room.

Melody, Serena and Dane held their breath to hear what the pressing matter was.

"Founder and CEO of Vale Corp, along with several of his employees, were apprehended earlier this evening in what police and FBI are calling the biggest organized crime bust of the century…'" The police and the agents whooped and hollered in celebration and victory.

"Oh, thank you, Lord!" Serena lifted up her hands in praise to God.

"They got him, Reena." It took a moment for Melody to process. "Luke did it!" Tears of joy gleamed in her eyes, and she couldn't keep a stiff upper lip. She was caught up in the overwhelming hugs of her dearest friends. "You mean it's really over?"

Serena laughed heartily. "Yes, honey, that's exactly what it means." Serena pulled away, but kept a firm grasp on Melody's shoulders. "You're right. *Luke* did it. He was probably the one who helped the FBI find Clarke and his men."

"Wow, I guess Luke is something of a hero!" Dane marveled, unable to stop smiling.

Melody listened with great pride and amazement, as the anchorman went over the details. He explicated how the authorities were anonymously led to an underground development, where Clarke and his men were planning their greatest escape yet. Without equivocation, Melody knew that the anonymous tip had come from the man she loved. Her heart inundated with even greater love for Luke, and she couldn't wait to see him.

The news anchor went on to expound how the mighty Clarke Vale had been brought down. "Apparently, Vale was under suspicion for years for his shady practices in the pharmaceutical world. The tycoon who'd made billions through his enterprise, also generated wealth through other illegal underground drug activities. It is purported that Vale is also responsible for the dispensation of lethal generic medications in different parts of the world-including but not limited to; the Caribbean, Central America and the

Philippines…"

The report was indeed gratifying, but Melody had tuned out after she'd heard the word, *apprehended.* Using Serena's phone, she dialed the only phone number she had for Luke. However, Melody didn't get an answer. In fact, she was informed that the number was no longer in service. It was pressing for her to connect to Luke, but Melody tried to remain calm. She had to believe that he would reach out, once he was free to contact her. She prayed for a quiet heart and mind, as she awaited his call.

Her sole purpose at that point was to leave the precinct. She was grateful that Serena and Dane were there to usher her away from all of the madness.

Melody approached Agent Morgan. He was one of the agents *directly* responsible for pulling her and Luke apart earlier on. Serena and Dane trailed behind Melody, but they were close enough to hear what Melody was about to say to the agent.

"Am I free to leave now?" Melody's voice sounded strained. She'd cried and screamed so much that she was barely audible. "My friends are here to pick me up." She stared intently into the man's face.

Jim Morgan nodded affirmatively. "Just as soon as you sign some paperwork, you'll be free to go. Melody, don't think for one minute we don't understand how dangerous all of this has been for you. You really put yourself on the line and-"

"Don't give me too much credit. And, if it's all the same to you, I would prefer that you all kept my name out of the papers and away from the press."

The agent nodded compliantly. "Of course. Whatever you want…" Agent Morgan pulled out of his rolling chair, and told Melody he'd be right back.

"I really appreciate that," Melody said, before the agent veered away.

Agent Morgan didn't say a word, but rather gave her an

affirming nod.

Melody turned to look over at Serena and Dane. She indicated that she still had paperwork to sign, and then she'd be free to leave. Moments later, Agent Morgan brought over the paperwork on a clipboard. Melody read over everything quickly, and signed the forms in all of the highlighted spots.

Agent Morgan told her that they would be keeping tabs on her, in the event Clarke's cohorts felt the need to follow his initial orders. Although, they doubted Clarke's *employees* would continue his twisted ministry, now that Clarke himself had been arrested. All the same, they weren't taking any chances.

Agent Morgan warned Melody that Clarke was capable of continuing his shady practices even behind bars. Apparently, men like Clarke never knew when to accept defeat. No matter how ominous it all sounded, Melody felt secure in the victory God had given her and her loved ones. So, she would boldly and confidently move on with her life.

It felt good to feel the night air on her face, as Melody hopped into Serena's SUV. She pushed back into the soft leather seat and sighed. She was also exhausted. Not hearing from Luke was tough, especially after the way in which they'd been pulled apart in Morgantown.

Negativity tried to stifle the joy of their battle won. *Perhaps, Luke had only stuck around to make sure she was okay. Now that he knew for sure that she was, he no longer needed to stay connected to her... It was quite possible that he'd changed his mind about their relationship. Melody considered that she'd crossed a line by saying so many hurtful things to him. Maybe, Luke had met someone else out in Virginia, and he wanted to give that person a chance...*

Melody blinked back tears, as her thoughts tried to get the better of her. She had to reign in her fears, and remind herself that God was in control. He was *always* in control of every given situation. After all, if God had had brought her and Luke out of the compound alive, she knew she could trust him to carry her through *anything.*

Melody tried to take heart, as Dane drove them away from Sands Portville. She was determined not to think the worst. She would wait to see how things played out. All she wanted was the chance to say I love you. It seemed simple enough, but the circumstances had made something so elementary extremely complicated.

***

The next morning, Melody pulled into the parking lot of Sands Port Hospital. Even now, her adventure with Luke the day before seemed surreal. Clarke and Darien were in custody, awaiting arraignment with no bail set. In spite of such a tremendous victory, Melody had trouble sleeping last night over at Serena and Dane's.

Spending the night away from home wasn't the problem. What had kept Melody up for most of the night was missing and longing for Luke. Now that they'd reunited, Melody didn't want to be away from him ever again. However, she hadn't heard from him, since they'd been pulled apart last night in Morgantown.

Luke hadn't called or texted, and it bothered Melody. She was sure Luke still had her phone number, even if she didn't have an updated number for him. The only person who probably knew how to get in touch with Luke, was in the ICU of the hospital fighting for his life.

Melody wiped tears away from her eyes, as she got out of the car. Sunlight exploded in the panorama, but it was still brisk and windy out. Melody had on an olive green parka with a fur-lined hood. It was cool enough to tuck her jeans into comfortable boots. The gales of wind were forceful. So, Melody was grateful that her hair had been pulled back into a ponytail.

Everything that took place the day before still resonated. The more Melody thought about being invisible with Luke, and traveling through a portal, the more she doubted any of it actually happened. Even so, Melody couldn't deny the events, because she was free, and

Clarke was now behind bars.

Melody pushed through gusts of wind to make it to the hospital's main entrance. Not only was she fatigued, but she was heartbroken over her circumstances. However, her visit to the hospital that morning had very little to do with herself. She was there to see about Sean. Sean was a casualty of Clarke's reign of terror, and Melody couldn't help feeling in some way responsible for what happened.

As she tread the ground floor lobby, Melody wondered if Luke had skipped town. If he had, she couldn't say she blamed him. Luke's job to ensure her safety was over and done with. So, he owed her nothing more. Perhaps, Luke had taken her at her word, and had left Sands Port. After all, she was the one who'd told him to leave.

Melody slipped into an elevator. As soon as the doors shut, she buried her face in her hands and bawled. She regretted not telling Luke the truth. Worse yet, she didn't even get a chance to say goodbye. Now that the nightmare with Clarke was over, she had no idea where to find Luke. She couldn't tell him that life without him was totally unbearable. She'd tried to protect him at all costs, but had inadvertently pushed him away.

The elevator conveyed Melody up to the second floor. The green light on the number pad blinked twice just before the doors opened. Melody strove to pull herself together. Pulling out tissues from her pocketbook, she thoroughly wiped her tear-stained face. She then walked up to the Nurse's Station to inquire about Sean.

"Room 243U," the nurse told her. She was a beautiful girl, with dark hair and electric blue eyes.

"Thank you." Melody offered a faint smile.

Turning on her heels, Melody floated down the hallway, in the direction in which the nurse had indicated. She realized she had to tuck in the hurt of her current struggle. All the same, it was difficult to stop thinking about the feel of Luke's arms around her. Having such a powerful inclination was foreign. She kept reliving the sensation of his tender touch, and the sweet kisses he'd decorated on her face.

Luke was always so loving and kind, even the times where she had failed to be. He'd planted fond kisses to her face and forehead, when they were reunited in that underground pit. Luke had held her gently in his arms in the vortex field, and within the portal. Luke had also given her a forehead kiss, once they were freed from the magnetic grip of the *Power Portal*, out in the open field.

Why didn't I tell him that I was more in love than ever? Of course, at the time, they were facing uncertain danger. However, Melody was convinced that Luke would have stuck around, if she'd told him the truth. Now, things being what they were, it was too late. As it seemed, he was giving her the space she'd requested.

Melody stood in front of the ICU hospital room door. Through the square glass slot at the top of the door, she could more or less see what was happening inside. Peripherally, she saw Sean. He was on the hospital bed connected to a monitor and wires. However, Melody froze when she saw who was visiting with him.

Luke was there with Sean's wife Nicole. The two were in tears, but also smiling. Nicole threw her arms around Luke's neck, and clung acquisitively to him. Luke crushed her in his arms, as they swayed in a loving comprise. Melody watched on for a moment. The pair seemed happy, so Melody surmised that there was good news about Sean. She hoped against hope that was the case, as she quietly observed Luke's interactions with Nicole.

Melody evaluated how amazing Luke looked in dark jeans, and a cream-colored sweater. Even if his face hinted at a five-o'clock shadow, he looked more winsome than ever. Melody's heart skipped a beat upon seeing him. She loved whenever he was just a little unshaven. She laughed in irony to recount his disguise, as the redheaded, portly man with full on beard and moustache. Luke was somewhat thinner than she was used to seeing him, but that took nothing away from how naturally toned and rugged he was. His olive sun-kissed hair and skin gave his eyes an arcane quality, and his muscles rippled with every graceful move.

Logically, Melody grasped that she didn't need to feel jealous. Luke was only comforting Nicole. All the same, Melody

felt *envious*. Nicole undoubtedly needed all the support in the world.
However, Melody wanted to be the one in Luke's arms. She hated
feeling like a spoiled and selfish child. On that note, Melody
stepped aside to allow Nicole and Luke a little time with Sean.

Being intrusive was uncharacteristic, so she decided to wait
before making her presence known. Walking away from Luke-even
for a minute was hard, but necessary.

Melody wandered down the long stretch of hallway, and
found the second floor café. There, she purchased a cup of coffee,
and floated back over to the ICU waiting area. She kept reminding
herself that it was respectful to give Luke and Nicole some alone
time with Sean. In a short while, she'd walk back over to the ICU
room and try again.

Melody sat in the near-isolated waiting area sipping coffee.
At least, now she knew where Luke was, and that he was all right.
Even so, it was torture waiting for a chance to speak privately with
him. Melody prayed for the courage to tell him how she felt.
Temperamental tears shone in her eyes. It dawned on her that she
might have lost her *heart*, after being pulled out of the lion's den.

CHAPTER THIRTEEN

"I'm so glad you're going to make it, buddy!" Tears were in Luke's eyes, as he squeezed Sean's hand in celebration. "You really had me going there for a minute."

Sean had lost an exorbitant amount of blood, and was extremely weak. However, he'd made it through surgery. The surgeon who'd removed the bullet from his chest had marveled. He'd explained that for one reason or another, the bullet was contained. There was some damage to the surrounding tissue in the chest area, but nothing too major. The surgeon said Sean was lucky, but Sean knew that it was only by God's grace he *was* expected to recover.

Luke had come by the hospital quite early that morning to donate blood to his buddy who needed a transfusion. They both shared the AB blood type.

"You know what they say. You can't keep a *good* man down," Sean said faintly and winked at Luke. His grasp on Luke's hand was still frail.

Nicole pressed closely to Sean's side, and gently plowed her fingers through his perfect blond hair. She hunched down, propped her head to his and cried. "I love you so much! I can't believe I almost lost you," she murmured.

"I wouldn't leave you, baby. You're the reason why I fought so hard." Sean gently lifted her downcast face, and pressed his lips affectionately to hers. "I love you more!" he emphasized.

Sean's eyelids fluttered, because it was still a struggle to keep his eyes open. He tugged on Luke's hand. "I made a deal with Jesus, while I was sitting in the car on that street bleeding to death."

Luke took a moment, and examined Sean in amazement. He shook his head wonderingly and smiled. "What did you bargain?"

"I promised that if he'd let me live, I'd turn my life over to him." Sean smiled faintly.

"So, you need to pay up." Tears of affect shone in Luke's eyes.

"I already have," Sean told him.

"Actually...*We* already have, Luke," Nicole said. "You see, I kind of made the same deal with God. I told Him that if he spared my baby, *I* would go back to the church. It isn't right for us to call on *Him* when we're in trouble, when *He* wants us to connect to him every day." Nicole swallowed the chunk in her throat, as tears escaped the corners of her eyes. But, she brushed them away quickly.

"Aside from me seeing this guy's eyes opened this morning, I don't think I've ever heard better news!" Luke smiled irrepressibly. "Jesus is the way! He's the only thing that makes sense in this crazy and often cruel world. Personally, I know I couldn't make it without Him..." Suddenly, Luke had a rush of memories of the day Melody had shared her faith with him. He was overwhelmed by feelings of nostalgia, and perceived Melody had no idea how much her faith had revolutionized his world, and that of his loved ones.

"I know *you're* different since you asked Jesus into your heart," Sean told Luke. "I guess, it took something this drastic to make me want to be different too."

"God *always* finds a way." Luke nodded, and winked cleverly at his buddy.

"I'm *beginning* to realize that." Sean smiled musingly.

"So, Luke, what's the deal with you and Melody?" Nicole's face wrinkled in concern.

Luke shook his head contrarily. "I really don't want to be that selfish guy who can't wait to get my hands on her, after she's just gone through the ringer." His expression was solemn at that point.

"She *never* loved Clarke to begin with, Luke. Melody loves *you*!" Sean said deliberately.

"It would be so nice to hear her say she does...just once..."

Luke's eyes shimmered affectively.

"She really doesn't have to say it, Luke. It's on her face every time your name comes up." Sean swallowed hard. It took all the strength he had to enunciate those words.

Luke smiled mawkishly to consider that Melody *did* love him. "She's all I want, but I can't move in on her so soon," he reasoned.

"I get what you're saying. Melody's been through a lot. She needs a little time to process everything that's happened," Nicole said thoughtfully.

"Have you spoken to Mel since yesterday?" Sean's voice wavered.

"There hasn't been any time. I was interrogated all night by the FBI and the police. They took away my phone, and denied any communication with the outside world. What matters to me is that Mel is safe. I know for sure she went home with Serena and Dane last night. So, later today, I had planned on stopping by their place. I need to say *goodbye* for a while." Luke's face rumpled in misery. Sadness overwhelmed like a soaked-through piece of cloth.

"You're *sure* you want to say goodbye?" Sean's eyes found Luke's.

"What I *want* and what *has* to be done are two different things. I can't just jump in there, and make mad declarations of my love for her, when she's barely out of the flames of this ordeal with Vale. Melody needs time. It took all of the self-control I had not to *show* her how I feel yesterday. I felt like an addict trying to resist my drug of choice, while locked up in a pharmacy. But, I knew that I had to pull back.

"We've both been through so much. It would be selfish of me to assume that we can just pick up where we left off a year ago, just because Clarke's out of the way."

Luke brushed through his curly hair, as was his nervous habit.

"You're right, Luke, but you *need* to let her know that you're not giving up."

"She's my entire world! How can I *ever* let her go?" New tears formed in Luke's eyes. "But love isn't selfish. I will try to give her time to move past all she's gone through."

Sean nodded. "But, not too much time, buddy."

"You *know* that I'll be keeping tabs on her *every* move." Luke smiled sadly.

"I still can't believe that the authorities detained you for such a long time, when all you were trying to do was help *them* out." Nicole scowled in annoyance.

"I felt like I was on a spaceship being probed by aliens. That office was like a totally different planet," Luke said, only half-joking. "Still, I'd do it all again in a heartbeat. Melody's safe, and those dirt bags were finally brought in. You should have seen the look on Vale's face when he realized that *I* had something to do with his arrest. It was classic." Luke shook his head humorously.

"How I wish that *I'd* been there." Sean's smile brightened.

"I'm just glad you're around, baby," Nicole told her husband. She then turned to Luke. "We have so much to thank *you* for." She set her hands sentimentally on her heart.

Luke deflected. "It's no big deal. The authorities were rattled because I found Clarke before they did. They had a hard time wrapping their heads around it."

"You didn't tell them about **Dimension**, did you?" Sean muttered.

"Of course not… What they don't realize is that **Dimension Four** is what's *really classified*."

"You're a wonder, my friend. I can't believe how ingenious you are." Sean gave Luke's hand a gentle squeeze.

Luke smiled. "I still can't believe any of it myself.

Dimension is a gift from God," Luke deflected, and gave God the glory. "There's no way I can take credit for such a mystery."

"But, God trusted you with that gift, buddy, and I couldn't be prouder!" Sean gave an affirming nod, and smiled.

"Neither could I." Nicole gave Luke a heartening smile.

"Aw, come on, guys. You're *really* embarrassing me here…" Luke's cheeks flushed red. Luckily, his phone rang at that moment, and cut through all of the awkwardness.

Luke checked the number, and saw that the call was from Burbank, California. It was undeniably a business call. *Dimension Four* and its accessories, were still under negotiations with a number of software companies.

Sean and Nicole's eyes fastened to Luke's, as they goaded him to answer the call.

Luke held his right hand up in a halting manner, and excused himself for a moment. He walked a few feet away, and answered the phone. "Yes, of course, I understand…"

Sean and Nicole listened attentively to Luke's end of the conversation.

"I have every draft and outline you might need. You're offering me what…?" Luke's face and eyes were imbued with excitement. "You mean as soon as possible…? I would have to take the first flight out…?"

The smile on Luke's face radiated brighter than a silver coin in the sunlight. "Yes, Sir, I *will* be there. No, I *haven't* settled on a company yet… Absolutely," Luke confirmed. "Thank you, Sir. You as well…"

Luke shut down his phone, and tucked it into the pocket of his jeans. He then veered to look at Sean and Nicole. There was an indomitable smile on his face. Brushing his fingers through his curly mane with nervous energy, he coasted back over to Sean's hospital bed. "I can't believe this. I can't believe any of it. This is mind-blowing." He kept shaking his head in disbelief.

"What is, honey?" Nicole frowned in uncertainty.

"Come on, buddy. Don't leave us hanging." Sean stared expressly into Luke's eyes.

"Okay...," Luke leaned up to the edge of the hospital bed, "that was a Mr. Nolan Mayer from **Valhalla Software** out in Burbank. Get this... They want to offer me a sweet deal on **Dimension** and its accessories." Luke's face and eyes radiated with intensity, and he could hardly stay still.

"What's a 'sweet deal'?" Sean's voice seemed stronger.

"Let's just say that it can be in the ballpark of...billions of dollars. **Realms United** was offering me 1.2 billion for it, so I'm guessing *Valhalla* wants to top their offer."

"That's amazing, man!" Sean beamed. "You should go for it."

"Luke, that's fantastic! Sean always told me how gifted you are. I guess, all those years of hard work paid off." Nicole noticed the troubled expression on Luke's face. He was pensive and sulking. "What's wrong?"

"I have to leave right away." Luke stared from Sean to Nicole with a conflicted expression.

"You *should* go," Sean rallied.

"If I leave now, I won't even get a chance to say goodbye to Melody. Not to mention the fact that I'll be worried about *you*," Luke told Sean. "My flight leaves in just a couple of hours. *Valhalla* has already booked it."

Luke felt torn. As much as he wanted to go out to California and finalize a deal, he wanted to see Melody one last time-if only for the sake of saying goodbye. Notwithstanding, Sean was still quite fragile. So, he wanted to stick around to ensure his buddy's complete recovery.

"Luke, I *know* you wanted to see Mel before you leave, but you can always call or text her if you need to. This is a once in a lifetime opportunity," Nicole explained.

"Nikki's right, buddy. As soon as you secure this deal, you can take the first flight back to Sands Port. In fact, what you'll be doing is to secure a future for the two of you."

Luke smiled musingly, and imagined being able to offer Melody the kind of life he'd always wanted to. "Thanks for making me see it that way, buddy."

"You go out there and wow them all, Luke! Don't worry about me." Sean waved his left hand dismissively. "I'll be okay."

"With the help of God, and with *me* by his side, Sean's going to be just fine." Tears gleamed in Nicole's eyes, as she stared lovingly down at her husband.

"I'm really beginning to believe that." Luke hovered over Sean for a little while longer. "You *will* let me know if you need anything…anything at all." Luke was still hesitant.

"Of course, we will. Now, go on and get out of here. You have to keep us posted on how things go," Sean said with renewed strength.

"I will text you right away." Luke nodded, as tears brimmed over in his eyes. He hated the thought of leaving his best friend in such a frail state.

"*We're* going to be *fine*, Luke," Nicole said softly. Tears were in her eyes as well. "I know you want to be here to make sure my baby's okay, but God's got this," she enlivened.

Sean nodded in concurrence. "You *have* to do this, buddy. If anyone deserves this break it's you."

"I guess, I should go and make the flight." Luke lingered for a moment.

"I guess you *should*," Sean urged.

Luke walked around to the side of the hospital bed, and drew Nicole into his arms. "My buddy's so lucky to have you!" he told her.

"*I* feel the same way. In fact, the two of you make *me* jealous most of the time," she teased, and pressed a kiss to Luke's cheek.

"You never have to be jealous, baby." Sean stared sappily up into Nicole's eyes.

Luke laughed over Nicole's comment, and got Sean laughing as well. "There's no way I can compete with *all* of this." Luke showcased Nicole like an object on a gameshow. Just then, a light rap came to the hospital room door.

"I guess, you've got another guest." Luke was still laughing over his own silly joke. Not even bothering to check through the square slot, he thoughtlessly pulled the hospital room door open. He found himself taken aback and winded, when he saw Melody standing on the other side.

Luke's heart dipped down to the floor in utter captivation. "Melody…" His expression was of pure shock. Luke tried to speak, but the words eluded him. If his desire for Melody was strong before, he was now on fire. The magnitude of his desire for her overwhelmed him. Luke realized that his love was stronger than ever.

"Luke…" Melody gasped, surprised to see him. She hadn't expected to see him so readily. Tears glimmered in her eyes. She pursed her mouth to speak, but found herself unable to. Being in Luke's presence again was overwhelming. Like a little child watching a shooting star dart out from the sky, Melody felt just as awestruck.

Neither Melody nor Luke spoke. However, like a well-rehearsed dance, Melody threw her arms about Luke's neck, as Luke possessively slipped his arms about her waist. The two held each other potently, and swayed in a quiet rhythm.

"You're such a sight for sore eyes! I hated what happened last night. I wanted to make sure you were safe," Luke said throatily, as he buried his head in her shoulder.

"Because of *you* I *am* safe. I can't thank you enough for..."
Tears rolled down Melody's cheeks. Reminiscent of happier days,
her fingers plowed fondly through Luke's hair. Luke's arms around
her waist were gentle and protective. Melody had missed being in
his arms to the point of tears. "I don't know what I would have done
if you didn't find me. Thank you…a million times…"

"You don't have to thank me for anything." Luke pulled
away, but tenderly cradled her face in his hands. "For you, I would
fight Goliath!" His eyes delved intently into hers. "I'm just happy
you're safe, honey." Their chemistry was so palpable, Luke found
himself magnetically inching in closer. Melody's touch was making
him forget how to breathe. He wanted to relish the feel of her hands
on his skin.

"I kept praying for God's help, and I'm *so* glad he sent you.
I had no idea what Clarke was going to do next," Melody admitted.
"I was so scared." She caringly fondled Luke's face and his hair.

Luke stared admiringly at her. "You never have to be scared
again. As long as I'm around, I will *never* let anyone hurt you."
Luke smiled into her eyes.

Melody's heart plunged in excitement and anticipation.
"Having you in my corner means a lot more to me than you'll ever
know." She inched in closer, and buried her head in his chest. For a
moment, she basked in the warmth and safety of being in his arms.
Luke held on to her just as potently. However, Melody couldn't be
sure, but she felt him slipping away. So, she hesitantly began to ease
her hold on him.

As they pulled back, they were still close enough to nestle.
And, the lure for a kiss was like ocean tides trying counter the effects
of the moon. Melody did all she could not to succumb to that desire
before she and Luke got a chance to talk things through. So, she
pulled away completely, and her eyes fastened urgently to Luke's.
"Do you have a moment…?" she asked reticently.

"I wish I did, honey, but I'm already behind schedule.
There's this business trip, and my flight leaves in just a little while.
Was there something you wanted to talk about?" Luke cupped
Melody's chin, and stared at her pertained.

Melody's heart plummeted. "Business trip…?" she said, dazed. "You're going away?" she asked thickly, overwhelmed by shock and sadness. Melody struggled not to fall apart right then and there.

Luke frowned in regret and nodded. "I'm afraid I have to for a little while. We can talk later. I'll text you my number. Feel free to call and text me anytime. Like I said, I'm *always* around if you need me. I'll always be your *friend*…" Luke inched back in order to look into Melody's sad eyes.

It was difficult to know what she was thinking. She was obviously just as sad as he was, but Luke *wanted* her to say that she still cared. He had to know if she still loved him as much as he loved her. Inwardly, he was screaming for Melody to give him a reason not to fly out to Burbank that morning. He battled himself not to take her in his arms, and keep her forever.

Melody was devastated. Not only was Luke leaving Sands Port again, but he'd just alluded to always being her *friend*. Her worst fear had become a reality. Luke was doing exactly as she'd told him. He was leaving town. She tried to blink back the sting of tears needling in her eyes, and forced a smile. "*Friends*…right…"

Luke set his hand to the side of her face, and stroked it sensitively. "I need for you to take care of yourself, okay?" He hunched down, and pressed a kiss to her cheek.

Luke then took Melody in his arms once more, and crushed her to himself. It was tearing him apart, but he wanted the moment to last. However, Luke realized that he had to go before he lost his nerve. Heavy tears clouded his vision, and he trembled like a man locked outside of his home on a bitterly cold winter night. Luke cradled Melody's head in his hands, and pressed a number of kisses to her forehead. "Bye, Mel," he said thickly, as his wistful eyes connected to hers.

"Bye, Luke," Melody said, feeling adrift. Luke slipping from her grasp was more than she could bear, so she gently pushed away. "Safe flight…" She forced a smile.

Luke felt even colder when Melody took away her addictive

touch. Nevertheless, he smiled through the tears and the pain. "Thank you."

Luke stood there for a moment feeling totally lost. However, he forced himself to turn away, and scurried down the hospital hallway. He couldn't risk looking back for a number of reasons. He was falling apart. His face was bathed in tears, and he couldn't stop shaking. Moreover, he realized if he *did* look back, there was no way he'd be able to walk away from Melody again.

Melody's face rumpled like a misshapen lump of clay. She shuddered as if she'd just walked miles through a horrible snowstorm. She sobbed, and pounded her fist to the side of the hospital room door.

Nicole unobtrusively stepped outside of the ICU room, and found Melody. She really didn't have to say a word, because she and Sean had heard the gist of her conversation with Luke. Nicole grimaced in hurt and commiseration, as she took Melody's hand in hers. She then guided Melody comfortingly into her arms. "It's okay... It's all right, honey... Everything's going to be all right. He isn't going away forever. He'll be back soon." Nicole pacifyingly rocked Melody in her arms.

Melody screamed silently into Nicole's chest, and wept with abandon. There were no words to express the level of pain she felt. For all intents and purposes, she'd been punched in the gut, and had just gotten the wind knocked out of her. She'd hoped that Luke would have stuck around to help her piece her life back together again.

However what little hope remained, had been sucked out, as if a tornado had swept through. Melody clung desperately to Nicole, and mourned the shards of her broken world. Luke was gone, and she had no idea when he'd return. He was gone, and he'd taken her heart right along with him. Melody knew that only God and time could buffer the gaping wound which had replaced her heart.

***

The lavish décor of Luke's private suite at the *Majestic Rendezvous Hotel* in Burbank, was by far the most extravagant place he'd ever been. The oceanic beachfront view, decadent amenities, deluxe spa, sauna and Jacuzzi, were the epitome of excess and indulgence.

Room service had just come through, and there was champagne on ice. However, Luke stretched out on the comfortable king-sized bed staring idly up at the ceiling, as tears rolled unremittingly down his cheeks. The meeting with *Valhalla Software* had ended hours ago, but he was still wearing his business suit.

Taking *Valhalla's* offer of 8.5 Billion to develop **Dimension Four** and its accessories was more than lucrative. So, in the weeks and months to come, Luke would be working on perfecting the technology. He would also be proactive in keeping **Dimension Four** updated and far ahead of the competition. So far, his cutting-edge program had been unmatched and unparalleled.

The 8.5 billion would be transferred into a number of Luke's new accounts as early as tomorrow morning. Luke was immensely grateful to God for all of the blessings. Becoming a billionaire overnight far exceeded any dream he'd ever had. And, if everything worked accordingly, he'd be in position to secure a good life for himself and his family.

Luke had called his parents earlier on, and had told them he was out in California on business. However, telling his parents how much money he was now worth, wasn't something he could just spring on them. His dad was still undergoing post-stroke rehabilitation. From extremely modest beginnings, Luke didn't know how his parents would process that kind of information. So, he planned to break it down to them gradually and wisely.

This was by no means an *ordinary* blessing. So, Luke readily gave God the glory for equipping him to create such a unique means of biometric transport, and a number of unprecedented modes of communication. It boggled his mind to even think about it. After all the near misses, his life was finally moving in the right direction.

At last, he was getting the recognition he deserved for his hard work. And yet, in spite of it all, he was absolutely miserable. None of it even mattered, if he couldn't share the good news with Melody. He wanted to tell her that his dream of a breakthrough in software engineering had finally come true. But, Luke didn't want to start crowding her. He'd promised to give her a little time and space to heal. Suddenly becoming wealthy was never something Luke had aspired to, but it was a gift from God. Still, what good was having any of it, if he couldn't share it with the woman he loved?

Luke hadn't stopped beating himself up over the conversation he and Melody had earlier on out in Sands Port. Luke couldn't help thinking that he'd messed up. Their talk had ended on the wrong note, and Luke hated himself for not making time to talk to her. At that point, he'd probably never know. Maybe, Melody had wanted to tell him that being apart was killing her, in the same way it was him. '*I'm always here if you need me. I will always be your **friend**...,*' resonated in Luke's thoughts.

Luke buried his face in his hands and wept sorely. "I don't want to be friends, Melody," he muttered. "I love you! I want you to belong to *me* forever. I don't want anybody else to ever touch you, to kiss or to love you...

"Oh, God, what have I done? Lord, what have I done? I don't want to go back to living without her. Life without Melody in it is too hard. Please, fix what's broken, and help us find our way back to each other. Please, Father..."

Inwardly, Luke felt empty and cold. So much so, he couldn't even find the strength to change for bed. He also had absolutely no interest in the room service dinner. It took a while, but he managed to get off the bed. Peeling off his dress suit, he slipped quietly underneath the covers, and cried himself to sleep.

***

The offer of a new job out in Burbank, CA as an interior designer for a string of new offices, seemed to come at just the right time. Melody was actually considering the move. The invite had been issued through her boss at **Radical Interiors... Portals Unlimited** had gotten a hold of Melody's work portfolio. They seemed impressed by many of her past projects, and were eager to meet.

"Are you sure you packed all of the important things, honey?" Serena asked Melody for the umpteenth time. She was helping Melody pack up for the initial interview. However, Serena was quickly becoming emotional again. She moved around nervously, and set some of the outfits Melody wouldn't be bringing along in their proper place. However, she froze in front of Melody's sizable walk-in closet and fell apart.

Melody grimaced in hurt, and tears immediately began shimmering in her eyes. She stopped zipping up her suitcase midway, and rushed over to her bestie. "Reena, please don't do this to me. You're going to get *me* started all over again." She gently set her hand on Serena's arm.

Serena turned to face Melody, and hugged her protectively. She couldn't stop trembling. "I can't believe you're actually *thinking* about leaving Sands Port…leaving *me*." Serena's face warped in hurt, as she caringly brushed her fingers through Melody's hair.

"Reena…," Melody said feeling conflicted. She pulled away from Serena's grasp, and floated back over to the bed. She sat down, and gesture for Serena to come sit beside her. Serena despondently hauled over to the bed.

"Try to understand. We've already been through this." Melody blinked back the tears. "It's only an offer. Nothing's set in stone, sweetie. I'm *thinking* about it, because it would be nice to get away for a little while. It's been a rough few weeks."

The sadness Melody tussled with was palpable. Three weeks had passed since she'd said goodbye to Luke at the hospital. Although, there were some highpoints in respect to their ordeal. Sean was now at home, and recovering nicely from a *near-fatal* bullet wound. Clarke, Darien and their minions had been arraigned. They were still in jail, and no bail had been set, as a result of their myriad of crimes. Also, Clarke and his cronies were definitely flight risks.

Melody was thankful to God for bringing her through that nightmare. She was even more grateful to be safe. However, her heart remained broken and raw, because Luke was gone. Since saying their goodbyes that morning at the hospital, Luke had texted her a few times. His messages were generic for the most part. He always wanted to know how she was doing after all she'd endured.

Melody had returned Luke's texts in a similar way. She always emphasized how diligently she was trying to move forward, after making such a huge gaffe with Clarke Vale. Melody felt silly to consider telling Luke how much she still loved and needed him, especially when it was obvious he no longer felt the same way. Everywhere she turned in the town of Sands Port, was a painful reminder of their failed relationship. Even being at home was tough, because of the precious memories, and the milestones she and Luke had shared.

"Even before Dane and I met, it's been you and me against the town of Sands Port." Serena pouted. "I know this is an amazing once in a lifetime offer, but I just can't help…" Serena buried her face in Melody's hair.

"I'm only going to check it out. It's only for a few days, Reena." Melody wiped her tear-streaked face and eyes. "I just need a change of scenery for a while. It's so hard being around here." She quickly scanned over the space.

Serena pulled away, but took both of Melody's hands in hers. She swallowed hard and nodded in agreement. "I know, sweetie. Everything around here reminds you of Luke."

Melody reclaimed her hands from Serena's grasp. She covered her face, and sobbed. Melody gasped. "I miss him *so* much, Reena." She breathed spasmodically. I can't believe he's not here with me." Her face twisted in melancholy.

"Oh, honey, I'm so sorry. I'm sorry Luke left that morning. I thought for sure the two of you would have found a way…" Serena frowned in commiseration.

Melody took deep breaths. "I thought so too." She shrugged, and tried to pull it together. "I guess, he just didn't want to look back."

Serena kept shaking her head contrarily. "I don't think that's the case, Mel. Luke loves you so much!"

Melody shook her head in skepticism. "I don't know about that, and I blame myself. I *told* him to leave. I took a knife, and cut his heart out that morning. He'd driven all the way down from Virginia to warn me about Clarke. He was *only* trying to protect me."

"And *you* were trying to protect *him*, Mel. I'm sure Luke realizes that now. So, please stop blaming yourself. I still have faith things will work out. What you and Luke have is true love. And, when it's as true as it is for the two of you, you can't run away from it."

"I sure hope you're right, Serena." Melody kept shaking her head in uncertainty. "I don't want to spend another year like the one we just spent apart."

"*Portals Unlimited* is in Burbank." Serena considered.

Melody nodded. "I don't think Luke lives too far away from the *Portals* building."

"Well, since you're going out there anyway, you should look him up. It's a big city, but I'm sure you won't have any trouble finding him." Serena smiled.

Melody shook her head contrarily. "I can't just go out there and look him up."

"And why is that, Melody?" Serena crossed her arms over her chest cheekily. "Love isn't proud. I know you love Luke as much as he loves you. You have this opportunity, and you should make the most of it. Look him up, Mel. You've got nothing to lose."

Melody doubted, and sadness settled on her face like overcast clouds. "I don't know how he feels about me anymore. Sometimes

I think he's no longer interested, because I got involved with Clarke. He didn't date *anyone* else while were apart. Maybe, he just doesn't see me as the same person."

"Shut up, Melody Christine! Stop this right now. That's the dumbest thing I've ever heard. Luke told you how he feels that morning. He said you would *always* have his heart. He's not the kind of guy to drop those words on a girl unless he means them. Luke risked *his* life to bring you out of that horrible underground complex. What more proof do you need to know that he's head-over-heels in love with you?" Serena shook her head, marveling.

Melody didn't say a word. She pondered everything Serena said. Maybe, it was irrational, but her worst fear was going out to see Luke, and finding him with someone else.

Luke wasn't only good-looking and charming, but he was also incredibly kind. It really didn't take much for him to attract women. Melody knew just how difficult it was to resist him, because she'd initially tried and had failed. Melody considered how awkward it would be if she *did* look him up, only to hear he no longer felt the same way.

"You don't have to be scared, Mel. Whatever happens, you already know Luke would *never* deliberately hurt you." Serena brushed caringly on Melody's arm.

"I know Luke would never *deliberately* hurt me, Reena. Maybe, that's the reason why he decided to leave. It's possible that he left, because he didn't want to have to tell me he wasn't feeling it anymore…feeling *us*." Melody sulked.

"Mel, you're so *wrong*. Pray about it and go out there. Maybe, Luke needs to know *you* still feel the same way about him. He told you how he feels, and *showed* you by putting both his heart and life on the line. The *least* you can do is to look him up while you're out in Cali." Serena gave Melody a questioning look.

Melody hesitantly nodded in agreement. There was a spark in the shadows of her sorrow. "Does that mean I have your permission to go?" Melody gave Serena a quirky smile.

Serena pointed a liable finger at Melody. "You have my permission to go…but you better come back." She threw her arms around Melody, and crushed her in them.

Melody squeezed Serena lovingly. "Of course, I'm coming back. Thank you. Having your approval, means more to me than anything. I love you!"

"You're lucky I love you too!" Serena pulled away, and pressed a kiss to Melody's cheek.

***

Melody checked her phone, and realized that the indicator reflected Mountain Time out in California. Back in Sands Port, it was a little after two in the afternoon, but it was just after 11a.m. out in Burbank. She'd just claimed her two pieces of luggage from Baggage Claim.

Melody scanned the area for representatives of **Portals Unlimited** in the expansive Burbank Airport-also known as The Bob Hope Airport. She'd heard much about the bustling and booming locale, and she honestly wasn't disappointed. Watching patrons step on and off ramps and escalators with their rolling suitcases and backpacks, was like watching a well-oiled machine. And, Melody breathed it all in, while on the escalator headed down to the ground floor terminal.

She was barely off of the contraption, when she was approached by a representative of **Portals Unlimited Software Co**. Melody couldn't say she wasn't impressed by his promptness and professionalism. She smiled openly at the young man, who seemed to have been waiting on her for quite a while.

"You must be Melody Maxwell!" he announced, as he simultaneously relieved Melody of her bags. He couldn't have been more than twenty-five years old. The young man was also extremely handsome. His dramatic dark hair, and piercing blue eyes were such a contrast. He reminded Melody of a Ken doll. And, in his coffee-colored suit and straitlaced mannerisms, he could have been a doll or a robot.

Melody was more than just a little bit impressed. "I *am* Melody Maxwell. I would shake your hand, *if* you weren't holding my luggage," she broke the ice.

The young man laughed lightly. "*I* would shake *your* hand, if I wasn't holding your luggage." He smiled affably. "I'm Peter Lawton! And, at the '*Portal Master*'s' request, I'm here to officially greet you to California! It's nice to finally meet you, Melody! I've heard many great things about you!" Peter stared pleasantly and confidently into her eyes.

"Is that *so*?" Melody surrendered to a deliberate, but skeptical smile.

"It *is*, and I'm looking forward to showing you around. Hope you had a pleasant flight."

"I did, thank you. I only have one question." Her face wrinkled in confusion.

"Anything…" Peter extended.

"Who is the *Portal Master*?" Melody asked, feeling completely out of the loop.

"If you choose to accept this offer, he will be *your* boss. He likes to be called the *Portal Master,*" Peter informed.

"I see…" Melody frowned in perplexity.

Peter moved quickly and efficiently towards the exit doors. "Come with me, Melody!"

Melody followed Peter outside of the airport. Almost instantly, another gentleman-clearly Peter's driver or chauffer-came and relieved him of Melody's luggage.

Melody was humbled by the grandeur of the California skies. The bustling airport terminal reminded her of New York City.

However, the western skies were more impressive. The cotton white clouds were almost within reach, the panorama was a rich blue, and the sun glimmered fluorescently.

Peter opened up the luxury limo door, and secured Melody inside. Melody rested on the tawny leather seat, and pressed her back into the soft material. It felt nice after having been stuck on a plane for hours, even in first class.

"So, I guess I *should* tell you a little bit about **Portals...**" Peter took his place in back of the limo next to Melody.

Melody smiled politely. "That would be nice."

The driver took his place behind the wheel, and cautiously began pulling away from the busy airport terminal.

"First off, can I pour you a drink?" Peter cordially extended.

The fully stocked bar was tempting, and Melody *was* a little thirsty after the five and a half hour flight. "Ginger ale would be nice, thank you." Melody stared into Peter's intent eyes. They shone even more vividly in the sunlight. She smiled, and shook her head approvingly. "I guess, I'm getting the royal treatment today."

"My boss has spared no expense. He's truly impressed by much of the work you've done in the past, and you're his first interviewee for this challenging project." Peter seemed excited, as he poured ginger ale into a clear cup with ice in it.

Melody sipped on her drink, and rested the cup in a napkin on her lap. "What's the *Portal Master* like?" She was curious, and felt just a little bit intimidated.

Peter smiled musingly. "He's the best boss you could possibly have! He's more like a *boss buddy*. He's young, and this is all brand new to him, but he's doing an awesome job! He's a genius, but he's extremely modest and down to earth. He's the kind of guy you would want to hang out with, shoot a few hoops with on a Saturday morning, or throw back a few cold ones with at a bar on a Friday night."

"He *sounds* really cool. I can't wait to meet him!" Melody

nodded affirmatively.

"I hope you *do* get to meet him. Truthfully, he's been in over his head for the past few weeks. Let's just say that laying the foundation for ***Portals***… has kept him more than just a little bit preoccupied. He wanted me to make sure all your needs were met once you got here.

"Trevor here…," Peter pointed over at the chauffer, "will be taking you over to the Paradise Hotel first. My boss has set up for you to have lunch, and to rest up before your 2:30 p.m. meeting. Is that all right with you, Melody?" Peter's expression and his eyes were earnest.

"That's just fine. I guess, that's the only time he has available to *squeeze* me into his busy schedule." Melody tried not to worry at that point.

"Not at all, Melody… My boss isn't that way. He likes to give his clients and employees his *undivided* attention. I think you're going to like him as much as we all do." Peter nodded. "If you have any questions or concerns, please don't hesitate…"

Melody felt a little overwhelmed by everything Peter had told her. It seemed that his boss already had *her* on his payroll. This *was* a once in a lifetime opportunity, but Melody was still on the fence about making such a radical commitment.

She also couldn't help thinking that the *Portal Master* was in all likeliness very aggressive. It was exciting to consider the prospect of working for ***Portals.*** All the same, Melody was distracted. She kept wondering if there would be time to drive out to visit Luke later in the day. In light of everything Peter had told her, if she *did* accept the position, she'd be tied up with work and meetings the entire week. She prayed for the strength and wisdom to take everything in stride.

Potentially moving to a new city, and working for a new company was a bit much to take in all at once. Furthermore, the way in which Peter had described his boss, gave Melody the impression that the man was a bit presumptuous and even pushy. She hadn't yet agreed to anything. Uprooting her entire life *was* a big deal. She was going to have to find a way to get that point across to this *Portal Master*.

***

Pampered, was the only way to describe how Melody felt after an early afternoon massage, and having lunch brought up to her elegant hotel suite. The beachfront view was absolutely breathtaking! And now, Melody was all dressed up in a shell-colored business suit and stylish black pumps. Her hair was pinned up in the back, bangs framed her sweet face, and tendrils cascaded over her shoulders. She *looked* the part, but wondered if she was ready for her interview with the CEO of **Portals Unlimited**-the one Peter Lawton kept referring to as the *Portal Master*.

Melody shook her head in skepticism over the entire matter. It seemed bizarre for a business mogul to be called by that name. Even if Peter had raved about his boss, Melody was convinced that her potential boss was a rich, over-privileged kid, who'd probably gotten a loan from his wealthy parents, in order to impress his equally rich friends by starting his own company. *What kind of man calls himself the Portal Master, anyway? Sounds just a little arrogant and narcissistic to me...* Melody brooded on her way over to the **Portals** building.

When Trevor pulled up in front of the impressive high rise, Melody was awestruck. The structure appeared to be a block of shimmering obsidian. Trevor came to open up the door for her, but Melody hesitated-taking in the view like a child would at the circus. The building was a shimmering jeweled tower, and the words **Portals Unlimited** glinted like marcasite stones in the intense California sunlight.

"You should see how it looks when it's all lit up at night," Trevor said and winked at Melody.

Melody was so transported, she was oblivious to the hand Trevor had extended to her. "I'm sorry. I guess, I'm just a little taken aback by all of this. Is this all new?" she inquired, unable to stop marveling.

"It isn't a new building, but it *has* recently been remodeled, and enhanced to fit the vision of the new owner."

"Wow!" Melody gaped. "The building itself looks like a construction of onyx stones."

"It *is* breathtaking!" Trevor agreed. He took Melody's hand, and helped her out of the vehicle. "I think that's what the new owner was going for. He's just a kid you know." He looped his arm through hers, and guided her over to the front doors.

"So, I've heard…," Melody said passively, as Trevor escorted her inside.

If Melody was impressed by the outside of the building, she was blown away by the futuristic and galactic backdrop on the ground floor. She perceived that she'd probably see things she'd never had before on this little excursion. Melody thought about just how much Luke would love the building, and she couldn't wait to tell him all about it. She imagined having Luke by her side, as they took a tour of *Portals* together. How she wished he could be there with her! No doubt, Luke would have totally been in his element. In fact, he could have easily *schooled* the CEO of *Portals* with his incomparable genius.

"Now, I'll be waiting right down here for you once your meeting ends," Trevor said. In a teasing manner, he waved his hands over Melody's face. "Hello…"

"Huh…?" Melody snapped out of her daydream. She'd slipped into *Luke World* once again, and had lost her way. "I'm sorry, Trevor. What did you just say?"

Trevor smiled curiously at Melody. "*Whoever* you're thinking about is *quite* lucky."

Melody laughed nervously. "I…I wasn't… You were saying…?" she evaded.

"I said, I'll be down here waiting when you're ready." Trevor smiled curiously.

"Okay. Thanks, Trevor." Melody's cheeks turned scarlet. She couldn't deny the fact that Luke was on her mind all day every day. In fact, Melody was hoping that her interview would be brief. Taking a drive over to Luke's later was all she could think about. The urge was so strong, she could no longer keep her wits about her. She wanted to text him, but still had misgivings.

The plan was to ask Luke for his address, because she planned on sending him something through the mail. Then, she'd go out to his place and surprise him. His address was in Burbank. So, Melody considered having Trevor drive her over. No sooner than she came up with the idea, Melody rethought asking Trevor to take her anywhere. This was business, and she couldn't use the company car to handle her personal affairs.

Melody's thoughts raced, as she stepped into the lobby elevator. **Portals Unlimited** encompassed the entire building. However, in the invitation letter, Melody was told that the head of the company would meet with her on the fourth floor. Before the elevator doors reopened, Melody pulled her phone out from her pocketbook. At first, she was hesitant to execute her plan, but then she risked shooting Luke a quick text message.

She hoped for a prompt response, so that she'd be free to follow through with her plan. Melody felt good about taking the initiative to text Luke. Once the elevator stopped on the fourth floor, she took a deep breath, and sent a prayer heavenward. "Lord, please let Luke respond to my text. It would mean a lot if we saw each other today. I didn't think it was possible to miss someone as much as I miss him.

The doors opened up to the most elegant, otherworldly and cosmic office Melody had ever seen. Quite a number of employees buzzed around -looking busy and focused. Like Peter, they were young, well dressed and well-presented. The futuristic and eclectic designs on that floor were enough to make Melody's firm back out in Sands Port look like a hut. And, **Radical Interiors**, was by no means anyone's shack.

"May I help you?" the beautiful, perky young lady sitting

behind the main desk immediately piped up.

Melody was a bit startled by her voice, because she'd been so absorbed taking in the breathtaking environment. Melody tried to remain focused. She stared into the face of the young lady-who was even more beautiful up close. There was something very genuine about her smile. "Good afternoon! I'm Melody Maxwell, and I have a meeting with…"

"The *Master*," the young lady filled in.

Melody nodded, still incredulous over their boss's arrogance. She tried not to roll her eyes in annoyance to hear this seemingly smart and beautiful girl refer to her boss as '*The Master*.'

Melody smiled till her face hurt. "Yes. My interview is scheduled for…"

"I know all about it, Melody! We've been expecting you. It's so nice to finally meet you!" Arianna heralded. She *was* truly excited to meet Melody, because Luke had spoken incessantly about her. And now, Arianna got to see for herself why Luke was so captivated. Melody was quite beautiful!

It took a lot for Arianna to live down Luke's gentle rejection. After kissing him at his farewell party back at Body Electric Era, she was mortified. However, she soon realized that Luke wasn't the kind to sweat the matter in the least. In fact, shortly after the incident, she'd agreed to dog-sit Luke's buddy Cupid for a while.

Arianna fell totally in love with Cupid after keeping him for close to a month. Cupid lived up to his name as the sweetest, most fun-loving dog. Besides, Cupid got along famously with her Yorkshire Terrier Boxie. Luke never brought up the kiss they'd *almost* shared at that party, and never made her feel weird. Arianna would probably always have a crush on him. It was hard not to, because he was the *perfect* guy. Goodness knows! No one else deserved the kind of blessings that were pouring into his life.

Luke had also changed her entire life. Arianna had dreaded Luke's departure from BEE. So, Luke had been kind enough to hire her a few weeks ago to join his brand new company, **Portals**

Unlimited. Arianna was blown away. It was an offer she couldn't refuse, and she'd immediately said yes.

Luke had flown her out to California, and had set her up in a lavish condo on the beach. Now, she was his Assistant Director for the incredibly radical and unstoppable *Dimensions* brand, which was revolutionizing time and travel. Arianna realized she would probably *never* hold Luke's heart. Yet and still, it was so worth it to be a part of his life. He was *good* people.

Arianna sized up Melody curiously. She considered that Melody Maxwell had no idea how lucky she was. It was also funny that she had no clue that Luke Bryant and the *Portal Master* were one and the same. Arianna smiled musingly, as she studied the appointment calendar.

Luke had insisted no one call him by name, until he got a chance to connect to Melody for himself. It was quite mischievous of Luke to withhold certain details from Melody. However, Arianna was *so* on board, because she wanted to see him happy. Luke had been sad for far too long.

"I know you were scheduled for the interview at 2:30, Melody, but there's been a slight change of plans." Arianna's face warped apologetically.

Melody sighed, and braced herself for the worst. All she wanted was to get the interview over and done with, so that she'd be free to go visit Luke. Passively, she glanced at the phone screen in disappointment. There were no alerts or notifications from anyone.

Melody also felt mislaid over the circumstances. "There's been a change of plans?" she repeated cagily. "I don't see how that's possible. Your boss scheduled this appointment three weeks ago. Is everything all right? I've heard how swamped he is with work…"

"I'm so sorry for the inconvenience, Melody. My boss *is* just a little bit busy nowadays…" Arianna scanned over the calendar again, then suddenly stared into Melody's eyes. "It's not a *horrible* change. It's just that he wants to meet with you at the house of one of his clients. I think he might need your expertise on it."

Melody was worried at that point, but she tried not to come apart at the seams. She *had* to find a way to tuck in her personal feelings, and zero in on this opportunity. So, even if she probably wouldn't get to see Luke later on, she had to be professional about this job opportunity. Melody issued the most genuine smile she could. "Where is the client's home located?" she asked politely.

"Beverly Glen is about half an hour away, but my boss has already gone over the details with Trevor."

"I wish someone would have gone over the details with *me*," Melody muttered.

Arianna's face twisted in commiseration. "I'm so sorry for the trouble, but Trevor will bring you over to the house. My boss and the owner will meet you there."

Melody's attitude softened, because Arianna was being so kind. She offered a sincere smile and an apology. "I'm sorry that I'm just a little bit flustered. This entire experience has been a little bit much," she admitted.

"That's understandable, Melody. But, once you meet my boss, I promise you'll feel right at ease. He's the greatest!"

"Everyone keeps telling me that... I don't think I got your name." Melody smiled pleasantly at Ariana again.

"I'm Arianna Ward."

"Arianna, it's nice to meet you!"

"Nice meeting you too, Melody," Arianna said cheerfully. She already liked Melody.

"If I *am* hired, will I be seeing you around here?" Melody asked with a twinkle in her eye.

Arianna nodded. "You certainly will. I just moved out here from Virginia-in fact just a few weeks ago."

"That's great…," Melody's voice trailed, because thoughts and images of Luke overpowered her. "Must be exciting…"

Melody caught herself from drifting too far away.

Arianna smiled openly. "It's the most exciting thing that's ever happened to me, and I am so grateful."

Melody nodded in agreement when she thought of Luke. "A good friend of mine used to live out there."

"It's a great place to live, and the beaches are awesome!" Arianna exclaimed.

"Maybe, I'll get to visit one of these days." Melody tried to work past the Luke movie playing in her head. Not making everything about him seemed close to impossible, but Melody realized she had to do better. "Arianna, it was nice to meet you! I hope I get to see you again," she said amiably. It felt as if she'd just made a friend.

"Likewise, Melody and don't worry. I know how frustrating this must be. I promise once the technicalities are out of the way, and you get to know the *Portal Master*, everything will be all right," Arianna enlivened, with a sincere smile.

"That's what I'm hoping." Melody nodded in agreement. "So, I'm headed back downstairs to Trevor?" Melody affirmed.

"He knows all about the changes, and he's waiting to drive you over to Beverly Glen. Be safe, Melody."

"Thank you, Arianna." Melody stared earnestly into her eyes.

She then turned away, and hiked back over to the elevator. The doors opened up, and she slipped inside. Before the doors shut, she waved over at Arianna. Arianna waved back cheerily. Melody resolved that she was going to like Arianna Ward, no matter what happened.

How she would feel about the CEO of *Portals Unlimited* remained to be seen. Nonetheless, she couldn't think about *him* at the moment. She was preoccupied fighting back feelings of sadness on the limo ride over to the house in Beverly Glen. Luke hadn't responded to her text.

Even if she tried to be strong, she couldn't blink back the tears. Maybe, Luke was over her. It was only by God's grace Melody didn't fall apart. This was a unique venture, and a once in a lifetime opportunity. So, she couldn't afford to mess it up. Still, it was difficult to push through with a broken heart.

"Cold, Melody?" Trevor asked from the front of the limo, because he heard Melody sniffling.

"I *am* a little cold," Melody mumbled, trying to reign in her emotions. Trevor was kind enough to lower the air conditioning, but that did very little to mitigate her sorrow.

***

The New England type house out in Beverly Glen, was Melody's dream house! She had always wanted to design a luxury beachfront home. It was exactly the kind of house she'd fantasized about out in sunny California. The house had more space than she would even know what to do with.

As Melody explored, she was inspired with ideas and possibilities for the commodious bedrooms, the bathrooms, the deck, den, pool areas, private theater, gym and the high loft. She was already taking notes, and drawing patterns in her sketchbook.

All fixtures and amenities were brand new. However, the house was only sparsely furnished. The family room was accommodating and roomy. There was a sofa, an armchair, a loveseat, and a fireplace, primed and ready to use. A huge, high definition flat-screen television was mounted to the wall. Melody remarked that only two of the nine bedrooms were furnished. Their adjourning bathrooms were also guest-ready.

Melody tried to work up excitement about the prospect of designing the house, but the anticipation was quickly ebbing away. Through the large casement windows, she could see that the sun was about to expire in the vast California vista.

As beautiful as it all was, Melody struggled with feelings of discouragement. There was only one redeeming aspect of that moment. If she *did* fall apart, no one would be around to witness it. It was almost eight p.m., and she'd been waiting at the house for hours. The darkening skies were a painful reminder that she wouldn't get to see Luke at all. Apart from that, as it would seem, not only was her new potential boss young, rich and spoiled, but Melody was willing to add *rude* to the list.

Arianna had called to check in on Melody a few times. She'd pleaded with Melody not to leave the house. Arianna told Melody that the *Portal Master* was running behind schedule due to an unforeseen set of events. Melody had tried to keep her wits about her, and had feigned diplomacy. However, she was upset.

She kept thinking that the CEO of **Portals Unlimited**…was more than just a little bit ill-mannered. He'd not only kept her waiting for hours, but he hadn't even called her for *himself* to apologize.

"I can't believe this, Serena. I thought for sure something was going to get done today," Melody complained over the phone. She was sitting on the comfy sofa in the family room nervously twisting the tendrils of her hair.

"Honey, I'm sorry you're having such a rough first day-"

"It was actually nice earlier this afternoon. My flight went fine. Peter and Trevor met me at the airport, and brought me over to the hotel, where I was catered to and spoiled the entire afternoon. But this guy… I don't know who he thinks he is. I *get* that he's nouveaux rich, but that doesn't give him the right to treat someone so horribly."

"Mel, wait and see what happens. I can't even imagine how frustrating it's been waiting on this man for hours, but I'm sure there's a good reason. I doubt he's the narcissist you're making him out to be. His company's just getting off the ground, so he must be up to his ears in work."

Melody sighed. "I guess, you're right. He's not the one I'm mad at anyway. It still feels like I've been bouncing around all day and..."

Melody was projecting her hurt feelings on this young kid, when the real issue was her failed plans to see Luke. Sadder still, Luke hadn't responded to her text. So, the excitement and anticipation of seeing him had dwindled, pretty much like the waning sun in the panorama.

"I know you're really sad about Luke. I also get how hurt you are, because he didn't text you back. Mel, knowing Luke, there's a good reason. He would *never* slight you that way. He's never treated you that way in the past. So, I can't see him starting to now. Mel, have a little faith. That man loves you *so* much! Hang in there, sweetie. Call me later."

"Okay. Bye, Reena," Melody said, feeling dispirited.

Hearing Serena say Luke loved her sounded so odd at that point. She and Luke had shared the truest and purest love she'd ever known. However, choices made a year ago, individually and collective, had left them both forever altered. Moreover, even if it seemed as if Luke was over *her*, Melody knew she'd never be over him. Her love for Luke was just as strong as the misery she felt because they were apart.

Clarke Vale's schemes had destroyed her relationship with Luke. Quite honestly, there were moments where Melody still struggled to find purpose for what happened with Clarke and Darien. Her association to those criminals, had set her relationship with Luke on a downward spiral. However, God never failed to remind her that he'd used *her* to bring down their evil empire.

Now that the world was a much safer place because Clarke Vale, Darien Stiles and their cronies were behind bars, Melody's heart was still shattered by the experience. She kept trying to get inside Luke's head to figure out what he was thinking. *Maybe, Luke couldn't see a future together, so he decided to move on.*

"I think I should go, Arianna," Melody said demurely. It was after eight p.m. at that point, and Arianna had just called to check in on her again. This time around, Arianna was calling from home. Her care and concern meant a great deal to Melody. Still, not only was Melody upset, but she was tired of hanging out in this huge house all by her lonesome.

Arianna sighed, frustrated and rankled by the turn of events. "I guess, I can't say I blame you. It *has* been a while now." Worry creased her usually unperturbed demeanor. *Luke, where are you?* She brooded. "So, Melody, I'm tentatively penciling you in for first thing tomorrow morning. I'm so sorry things went so awry on your very first day."

"Not at all, honey. It's not your fault. I guess, the *Portal Master's* bitten off a little bit more than he can chew. Look, I get it. This is a brand new enterprise, and it's probably hard for him to even squeeze in a minute for himself, let alone for me."

"He's been working so *hard*, but don't give up, Melody. It will be so worth it when you do have your sit-down interview with him."

Melody smiled hopefully, and tried not to take things personally. Perhaps, if she was *lucky*, she would get to meet this elusive man in the morning. "From your lips to God's ears… Thanks for everything today, Arianna. You've been great, but I'm going back to the hotel. Oh… I think a car just pulled up. Maybe, it's Trevor. Arianna, I've got to go. See you in the morning. Goodnight."

"Okay. Goodnight, Melody," Arianna sounded disappointed. She hated that Luke hadn't found a moment to connect to Melody on her first day out on the West Coast. Luke had talked about, and had extensively planned for her first day there. However, Arianna realized how hectic the beat had been for Luke lately.

Bounding off the sofa, Melody grabbed her pocketbook and her phone. She was grateful Trevor was back. Now, she could go back to the hotel, and nurse her wounds from the disappointments of her day. She walked over to shut down the lights in the next room, when she heard stirring at the front door. It sounded like someone using a key.

Melody gasped in shock, and a chill rippled through her. On

the defensive, she set her things on a plant stand. She was unsure as to why she felt so rattled. Perhaps, it was because she'd been there *alone* for hours. Melody's hand rested on her neck, and her heart thudded in angst. Maybe, it was the owner of the house-or dare she believe even the *Portal Master.*

Feet away from the door, Melody stalled. Her heart was in her throat in suspense, as she waited to see who was on the other side. The knob twisted in the stranger's hand. However, when the door swung opened and the intruder was revealed, Melody was both stunned and scared. If she was frozen before, she was a glacier at that point, when her eyes fastened to Luke's. She thought she would pass out. .

Melody's heart thrummed as she scrutinized him. This was the most beautiful she'd ever seen him! In his dark gray business suit, he should have been featured on the cover of GQ or Esquire Magazine. Luke was also the perfect calendar post of a dream man, even if he was still a little on the thin side.

Luke's light brown hair had been highlighted by the sun. And, his bronzed skin made his eyes look more turquoise than teal. Melody was swept away, and desire she'd never experienced before radiated through her like fire.

She felt so inept standing there just staring at him. Melody finally found the courage to speak. "Luke… I don't understand. What are you doing…? I mean…" She just kept shaking her head doubtfully.

Luke hesitated before shutting the front door. He was entirely hypnotized by the object of his affection. Tears of joy gleamed in his eyes, and a slow meaningful smile colored his symmetrical face. For all intents and purposes, he'd just been released from prison. Seeing Melody was like seeing the sun and stars again on the outside. The potency for her touch and kiss defied explanation. She was more than stunning in her professional business attire, and pinned up hair. Cinnamon tendrils cascaded down her shoulders and back, and framed her angelic face.

"Hello…," Luke said deliberately. His heart raced like a machine, and his stomach sank to his feet.

"I don't understand…" Melody's face wrinkled in confusion. In spite of how intimidated she felt because he was suddenly there, she still found it impossible to resist the magnetic pull compelling to draw closer to Luke. "I came out here on business and…" The closer she got to him, the more gauche and shaky she felt. Automatically, Melody reached out to touch him, but instinctively flinched.

"I *know*, Mel. You came out here to interview with the *Portal Master,*" Luke said softly as his eyes delved into Melody's. He didn't think it possible to crave someone as desperately as one did a needy drug, but he was wrong. Luke was beyond saving, because Melody was his addiction, and loving her was his fix.

Melody's face twisted in confusion. "You know him…?"

Luke smiled, and looked down for a moment. When he looked into her eyes again, he modestly revealed, "Melody, I *am* him."

Luke eliminated the space between them, and closed in on Melody by degrees. "I'm so sorry I kept you waiting, honey. It's been an unbelievable day. I also *just* got your text. My phone was off for most of the day, because I was tied up in meetings. *So* sorry for everything…"

Luke ogled Melody, as one would watch a celestial or paranormal manifestation. He was utterly enthralled.

Melody gasped, amazed. "What…?" She kept shaking her head, nonplused. "*You're* him? Luke, I don't understand."

"I know I have a *lot* of explaining to do. But, first, come here…" Luke set his hand possessively on Melody's waist. Gently pulling her into his arms, he held her meaningfully. He took a moment to inhale, and released a yearning sigh. "I've missed you so much!" He breathed into her hair.

Melody trembled in his arms. Her eyes released their tears, as she plowed her fingers through his curly bed of hair. She pulled away, and cradled Luke's tear-stained face in her hands. "I've missed *you*. I didn't think it was possible to miss anyone the way

I've missed you."

Luke nodded and smiled with shimmering eyes. "You have any idea how *hard* it's been being out here all alone, how hard it's been staying away from you?" His face warped mawkishly, as he explored her sad eyes.

Melody nodded. "I think I might have some idea," she said wispily. It felt so good to be in Luke's arms and to be this close. All the same, Melody felt overwhelmed by guilt and shame recounting how much she'd hurt him. Her face warped in remorse, and she cried. "I'm so sorry. I'm so sorry for what happened that morning...all the horrible things I said to you." Tears rolled down her cheeks.

Luke delicately collected her face in his hands, and brushed over her cheeks with his thumbs. "It's all right..." He pelted her face in loving kisses, until his lips found hers. He then began to drink slowly, but exigently from the ambrosia of Melody's mouth.

Luke baited her mouth in gentle nuances, and avidly brushed over her lips. Then, his embrace keenly progressed. He was a man parched in the desert, who'd just stumbled upon a source of water. He drank violently, finding it almost impossible to quench his thirst. Luke knew that he would never be satisfied, even if their kiss lasted an eternity. Their scintillating kiss blazed more fiercely than billions of stars.

Like the first time they'd shared a kiss, Melody was overwhelmed. Safe in the harbor of Luke's arms, she forgot the misery of the past year. He held her protectively and ministered his unique brand of tenderness and love. Melody didn't have to wonder if her still loved her. His great love for her emanated through him like fire. It was in his eyes, his kiss and in his smoldering touch.

Their soul-quenching kiss was meteoric. Luke was in tears in the aftermath of the gentle detonation. "Do you still love me, Melody?" his voice wavered, as he held her face protectively. Luke felt that she did, but he direly needed to hear her say it.

Melody's eyes glistened in affect as they delved into his. "I love you, Luke! I love you more than anything! I've never stopped…not once… I hated being away from you. I hated letting anyone else touch me…" She trembled, and surrendered to his arms.

"I love you more than life itself, honey baby! I know *exactly* how you feel." Their faces bridged, as they breathed in butterfly kisses. Luke smiled. "I don't want to live without you anymore," he said throatily, and pressed more kisses to her face.

"I don't want to be without you either, Luke. I love you so much! I'm so sorry about what happened with Clarke. I'm sorry for all of the horrible things I said. I didn't mean…"

"You don't have to explain, honey baby." Luke kissed her tears away. "I know you were doing what you thought was best for me at the time. I get that Clarke was watching every move you made. So, you had to send me away. You were magnificent by the way." He gave her a playful wink.

Melody laughed, as Luke lavished kisses on her face. "It was the hardest thing I've ever had to do, but there was just no other way."

"I'm so grateful to God! He's blessed me with someone who loves me enough to break my heart just to keep me safe."

"*I'm* the lucky one. God gave me someone who risked his own life to save mine. When you came by the house that morning, all I *wanted* was to be close to you," Melody admitted. It killed me to spend an entire year apart, and not be able to show you how much I missed you. Not be able to…"

Melody tenderly held the side of Luke's face in her hand. She then reached up, and bridged her lips arduously to his. She thirstily indulged from the source of his mouth. However, Luke held her with even more intensity. "I love you," she reminded him in between kisses.

"I love you, Melody! Don't ever go away. Please, don't ever leave me again." Luke swayed her body in a quiet rhythm, as she fondly caressed his face and hair. For a while neither spoke. They just savored being each other's arms again. God knows, they'd waited far too long.

"So, you see, I *had* to keep my identity under wraps, honey," Luke whispered into Melody's ear, as they cuddled on the sofa. He held her protectively in his arms, and brushed through her soft hair.

Melody turned to face Luke, and pressed her hands to his chest. She kept shaking her head in denial. "So, you bought out **Valhalla Software**, because **Dimension Four** is much too huge to be contained?"

"Something like that." Luke smiled, and pressed a kiss to her forehead.

"I really had no idea all of this was you." Melody looked around at the impressive house. "Why didn't you tell me?"

Luke smiled artfully into her eyes. "I wanted to *surprise* you."

"When we talked at the hospital that morning, I thought you were leaving because you didn't love me anymore."

Luke gently took her face in his hands, and stroked it lovingly. "Mel, I told you when I came by the house on the morning I returned to Sands Port, that I would *never* stop loving you. I wouldn't even know how to do that," Luke's voice broke. "For me, there's just no one else. You've been through so much, so I wanted to give you a little time. I didn't want to be selfish."

"I doubt that you even *know* what selfish means." Melody pressed her lips to his.

Remorse clouded Luke's features. "I hated walking away from you, and not being able to help my family. Mostly, I hated making a deal with that monster Vale. It was the *hardest* thing I've ever done." Luke explored her eyes with growing love. "Can you ever forgive me for making that awful bargain?" Luke pouted in remorse.

Melody pressed more sweet kisses to his mouth. "There's nothing for you to apologize about, Lucas William Bryant. You were doing what you thought was best for your family." Sadness veiled Melody's face, and new tears formed in her eyes. "I would *never* hold that against you," she whispered. "I just wish that you'd come to me. We could have worked it out together..."

"At the time, I thought it was much too soon to be leaning so heavily on you." Luke was solemn. "You and I were just getting started."

"I *wanted* you to lean on me. Being away from you, felt like the world caving in on me." Melody stared yearningly at him.

"Being away from *you* for an entire year, was like I stopped breathing for a while." Luke propped his face to Melody's. "I made some choices during that awful time that I'm not very proud of." Luke looked away in shame.

Compassion and understanding were in Melody's eyes, when she gently prodded Luke to look at her. "Oh, Luke..."

"I took to drinking for a while." Luke blinked back tears. "Being away from you was *literally* killing me. I love you so much, honey baby, and I always will."

Melody pressed her face up to his, and kissed his tears away. "So many nights I cried, and I prayed for God to bring you back to me. I fell asleep most nights clutching the locket you gave me." She planted a kiss on his nose.

Luke sighed, and just relished being close to her again. "I'm not going to suddenly wake up, and find out that this was all a dream, am I?" his voice broke. "Having you in my arms again was my recurrent dream for the past year. It killed me every time to wake up, only to realize you were miles away."

"I'm here, Luke and I'm not going anywhere. I promise." Melody squeezed him in a lasting hug. "And I'm *so* proud of you, and totally impressed by ***Portals***... I couldn't have imagined. I knew that you'd be successful one day, because of how gifted you are, but..." Melody stared all about the room, marveling.

Luke laughed. "Yeah, I guess, I just don't do in between. I'm either really poor or..."

"I can see that," Melody teased. "But I *do* miss my poor guy-the one who worked for Sands Port Elementary, and wore the green jumpsuit." Her eyes gleamed in joy and affect. It was taking a minute to internalize who Luke *really* was.

"I still have the jumpsuit, and I can put it on for you anytime you want." Luke's demeanor danced in mischief.

"You promise?" Melody pressed more kisses to his face.

"Would I ever lie to you?" Luke's voice resonated. He took short desiccated sips from Melody's mouth. "You think you could get used to the new me?" Luke's entire face radiated, as he explored Melody's eyes.

"You mean the *Portal Master*?" Melody set her hand on her chin ponderingly. "Oh, I don't know…"

"You mean, you *don't* like the Portal Mas…?" Luke was silenced by Melody's sugary kisses. "Let's get this straight. I like the *old* Luke, *new* Luke, *poor* Luke, *rich* Luke, *brawny* Luke, *skinny* Luke and I even like…" Melody feigned pretention.

"Yes!" Luke cheered, and pulled her enviously into his arms. "You *do* like the Portal Master!"

"He's all right…I guess." Melody burst into laughter, as Luke pelted her with kisses. "Okay, okay…," she submitted. Melody lost herself in his eyes. "I am *so* in love with the *Portal Master*!" Tears flooded her eyes again, as she caressed Luke's face and hair.

"The *Portal Master* loves you more than life itself!" Luke's voice dithered as he squished her in his arms again.

The two held each other silently, and talked about the future. At times, the intensity of their love was so tangible it was immobilizing. They'd spent an entire year apart. Life had thrown so many challenges their way, but somehow they'd survived, and had made it through the darkest night. Their love had been strengthened by their struggles.

"So, are you going to take the job?" Luke asked, holding

Melody securely in his arms.

Melody turned to face him, stunned. "You *really* want to hire me to design offices for ***Portals***?" Melody lifted her head above Luke's chin to connect to his eyes.

"Of course, I do. That's why I extended the invitation. "That is… if you want to… No pressure, but you *did* promise me your expertise if I ever needed it." Luke smiled into her eyes and nestled her.

"I *did* make that promise to you on our second date, didn't I?" Melody remembered their second date at her house back in Sands Port. They'd decided to have dinner, after having spent the entire day at the beach. "So, let's talk business," Melody propositioned.

"So, lets… I see a cylinder-shaped flying saucer in the middle of my office, alien effigies all over the place, and an aurora borealis type portal gateway for business clients and…" Luke's squinted his eyes and arched his brows in quirkiness.

Melody stared warily at him, but then rose playfully to the occasion. "I think I can actually work with that."

"Seriously… Mel, I asked you to meet me here, because I not only want you to design offices for ***Portals Unlimited***, but I'd like for you to design this house." Luke's eyes skimmed over the expansive house.

"This house is amazing! I've always wanted to work on a project like this," Melody appraised. She was totally fascinated by her surroundings. "As long as it's okay with the owner, I would be honored to do it." Melody smiled in earnest.

"So, what do *you* think? Do you think you'd be okay with it?" Waggishness played on Luke's face.

"Luke…?" Melody stared curiously at him.

"You said you'd be okay with the project, as long as the *owner* agreed to it." Luke's demeanor and voice changed as he pulled away. He stood to his feet, and gently pulled Melody up off of the sofa. "So, are *you* okay with it?"

"Luke, what are you saying?" Melody's heart skipped a beat.

Tears shone in Luke's eyes, as he took Melody's hands in his. "I'm saying that this is *your* house, Mel."

So stirred by Luke's revelation, Melody eyes released pent up tears, and she quavered like Jell-O. She examined the luxurious backdrop. "You… I mean, you want me to live here?" Melody gasped to catch her breath.

"Uh-huh." Luke delved earnestly into her eyes. "I would *love* it if you lived here…with me." He stared longingly at her.

Melody kept shaking her head in denial. "Luke…I don't know what to say. This is too much…"

"*I* know exactly what to say, Melody. Spending an entire year apart from you almost killed me. Even these past few weeks have been sheer torture. I've been counting down the days, the hours, minutes and the seconds till you'd come out to me."

Overwhelmed, tears rolled down Melody's cheeks. "You tricked me." She shook her head incredulous.

"Are you mad at me?" Luke stared yearningly and apologetically at her.

Melody shook her head contrarily-too emotional to speak.

"As I was saying before I was so *rudely* interrupted." Luke jestingly cleared his throat. He was unable to contain the powerful current flowing through him. "I don't want to be without you, Melody. I know that our relationship has been tried, and stretched to the limit this year. The one thing I'm sure of is that everything we've gone through, has only deepened my love for you."

Luke grasped Melody's hands in his again, and searched her eyes earnestly. "Being pulled apart this year, only made me realize that I never want to be away from you. I *can't* live without you, Melody!"

"I love you so much, Luke! I never want to be away from you again." Melody's face warped sentimentally.

"When I asked you to live here with me, I don't know if I made myself clear. So, please allow me to clarify." Luke got down on one knee. "So, Melody Christine Honey Baby Maxwell, will you marry me?" Maudlin, Luke's eyes shimmered affectively. Melody was everything he'd ever hoped to find. God had honored his prayers, and was granting him a second chance, and he would *never* let go.

Melody was astounded, and rendered speechless yet again. Tears rolled down her cheeks, and she trembled emotionally. She kept shaking her head in disbelief. "You want to get married?" She stared dubiously at him.

"I want to be married to you more than anything, baby."

"Luke...." Melody reached for his hand. She helped him up to his feet, wrapped her arms possessively around him and cried. "Of course, I will marry you." She covered every inch of his face with tender kisses. "I love you so much!"

"I love you more, Honey Baby! You've made me the happiest man alive!" He swayed her in his arms in celebration. "She said yes! Melody said yes!" Luke cheered.

Melody gushed, but her tears turned to those of gladness. Luke picked her up off the floor, and swung her around in their new home. She couldn't believe any of it was happening. She'd prayed for such a long time for this moment, and God had finally made it a reality. Just when she'd thought he'd forgotten all about her, God had surprised her with the greatest blessing of all. The Lord had restored the most precious gift she'd ever been given. It was the gift of Luke's love. Melody would hold on to him with everything she had, because she would never love anyone else.

Moments later, Luke asked Melody to wait in the family room. There seemed to be one more trick up his sleeve. Laughter and excitement crackled like electricity when Luke asked her not to move, and to keep her eyes closed.

Melody grudgingly shut her eyes. "Luke, stop torturing me," she complained. "I don't think I can handle anything else." She shook her head humorously. "You really got me good this time."

"Hang tight, my love. There's just this one last thing I forgot to do." Waggishness sprinkled over Luke's face, as he stepped out of the house for a moment. Luke found Trevor waiting to the side of the limousine. He handed the driver a fold of bills for keeping watch of Cupid, while he and Melody had enjoyed some alone time.

"Thanks for doing this, Trev. I really appreciate it."

"Not a problem, Luke. It was my pleasure! How did things go with Melody?" he asked expectantly.

"Well, things are *still* going, but she said *yes*," Luke revealed with a hopeless smile on his face.

"Congratulations!"

"Thank you. You're free to leave for the night if you'd like. *I'll* take care of Melody."

"No doubt you will, Luke." Trevor winked. He walked around to take his place behind the wheel of the limo, while Luke opened up the back passenger's side door to get Cupid.

"Hey there, buddy! How are you? I haven't seen you since this morning." Luke rubbed playfully on Cupid's collar. The dog jumped out from the back seat of the car, and immediately pounced on Luke. Cupid barked delightfully to see his best friend.

"I'm happy to see you too, but guess what? We're going inside to surprise Melody." Cupid bounded excitedly at Luke's side, as Luke moved away from the limo. The two tread up the house walkway. Luke heard the limo pull away, but he didn't bother looking back.

"You want to surprise Melody with me, boy?" Luke spoke to Cupid like the *dog whisperer*.

"Roof…," Cupid barked frenziedly.

"You're going to be *so* happy, because I know you haven't seen her in over a year." Luke conveyed Cupid all the way up to the front door of the house. Cupid barked up at him, but Luke gestured for the dog to remain quiet, by setting a finger over his lips.

Cupid seemed to understand, and remained perfectly well-behaved when Luke led him over to the foyer. Luke knew that Cupid would go berserk the moment he saw Melody. Luke wasn't the only one who was *mad* about her. He floated back into the family room, where Melody remained poised with her eyes closed.

"Mel, you can open your eyes...," were all the words Luke managed to get out.

Cupid's tail whirled like helicopter blades, and he couldn't stop barking and salivating. The dog leaped over all the furniture, and rushed over to Melody-literally tackling her to the floor in the same way he had the very first time he saw her. The dog celebrated over Melody, and lavished his soggy kisses all over her face.

Melody was in tears, as she held Cupid by the flanks, and shifted her head from side to side to avoid his mushy brand of love. "I can't believe you're here today. I have missed you so much!" Melody positioned herself to sit upright again. She ruffled Cupid's mane, and planted three kisses on his nose. "You are such a sight for sore eyes! You're even more beautiful now...yes you are...yes..." Melody fondled his collar, but felt something odd attached to it.

Luke watched on totally tickled by the scene. He knew exactly how to get Melody's goad, and things were falling right into place.

"What's this, boy?" Melody questioned, but she looked over at Luke, who was standing feet away. "Luke...?" Her face wrinkled in confusion, as her fingers brushed over Cupid's collar.

Luke shrugged coyly with a blank expression on his face.

Melody kept shaking her head nonsensically. She turned the collar to find the buckle feature. It was then, she noticed that Luke had attached a ring on Cupid's collar. "Oh, Luke..." Melody's face warped in corniness.

Luke glided over to Melody, and sat closely to her on the hardwood floor. "Now it's official. You'll always have my heart." He kissed her repeatedly.

"Oh, you… What am I going to do with you?" Melody cried, as Luke slipped the nearly 30 carat diamond ring on her finger. It was breathtaking, and she knew he'd had it custom made just for her. She was trembling again. She grasped Luke's face in her hands, and covered it with loving kisses.

"I hope you decide to spend the next fifty years or so with me," Luke's voice broke- totally lost in Melody's embrace.

"You've got me for as long as you want me," Melody said, breathless.

"I guess, I've got you forever then," Luke said hoarsely, and pulled Melody exigently into his arms. He held her acquisitively, and explored every inch of her dulcet mouth. This time around, Cupid didn't try to come between them. The dog was just overjoyed to be with two of his favorite people. So, he merrily pranced around wagging his tail.

"I can't believe you remembered." Melody was pleasantly surprised, as she saw Luke slip the Blue Ray disc into its compartment near the flat screen television.

Luke carried a freshly made bowl of popcorn over to the coffee table, and sat on the sofa next to Melody. "I *did* promise that I wouldn't watch this movie again, until *you* watched it with me." Sappiness covered his winsome face.

"You've waited over a year to watch the second part of this movie with me?" Melody pressed a kiss to Luke's cheek. Luke stretched out on the sofa, and secured her in his arms. Melody rested her head under his chin in anticipation of the movie, *The Other Side of the Mountain Part 2*.

The film was the second installment, chronicling the life of Jill Kinmont Boothe. Kinmont Boothe was a championship skier, who fell off of a mountain during a competition in Alta Utah in 1955, and was left paralyzed. In this second allotment, Jill meets and marries her husband John Boothe.

"I would have waited forever to see it with you, but I'm *so* glad to have you by my side tonight." Luke caringly pressed a kiss to Melody's forehead.

"Is it any wonder why I'm so in love with …the ***Portal Master***?" Melody beleaguered. Her eyes flickered in playfulness and excitement. Luke's love overwhelmed her, and she was delirious.

"I thought you loved *me*?" Luke teased.

"I do love *you*…ah but the *Portal Master*…," Melody razzed on him.

"Ah, man… I know I shouldn't have introduced the two of you." He feigned hurt feelings.

Melody shook her head humorously. "I'm sorry, but there's just something about him."

"*Really*…?" Luke got a puzzled expression on his face, as he feigned jealousy.

"Oh, yeah… It's all about the *Portal Master*."

Melody laughed and affectionately raked her fingers through Luke's curly bed of hair. His loving grasp only tightened around her, once the movie started. She felt secure and deeply loved. It was difficult to take it all in, but she would never stop thanking God for his many blessings.

Other titles from Higher Ground Books & Media:

Destiny Revealed by Marjorie Joseph

Of Love & Witches by Marjorie Joseph

Erin & Oliver by Marjorie Joseph

Max by Marjorie Joseph

The Bottom of This by Tramaine Hannah

In the Wash: The Rona Shively Stories by Rebecca Benston

The Music Murder Industry by A.R. Ratliff

Jack Kramer's Journey by Frank Adkins

The Power of Knowing by Jean Walters

The Real Prison Diaries by Judy Frisby

Add these titles to your collection today!

http://www.highergroundbooksandmedia.com

HIGHER GROUND BOOKS & MEDIA IS
AN INDEPENDENT PUBLISHER

Do you have a story to tell?

Higher Ground Books & Media is an independent Christian-based publisher specializing in stories of triumph! Our purpose is to empower, inspire, and educate through the sharing of personal experiences. We are always looking for great, new stories to add to our collection. If you're looking for a publisher, get in touch with us today!

Please be sure to visit our website for our submission guidelines.

http://www.highergroundbooksandmedia.com/submission-guidelines

---

HGBM SERVICES IS OUR CONSULTING FIRM

AUTHOR SERVICES

HGBM Services offers a variety of writing and coaching services for aspiring authors! We can help with editing, manuscript critiques, self-publishing, and much more! Get in touch today to see how we can help you make your dream of becoming an author a reality!

*****

We also offer social media marketing services for authors, small businesses, and non-profit organizations. Let us help you get the word out about your book, your projects, and your mission. We offer great rates, quality promos, consistent communication, and a personal touch!

http://www.highergroundbooksandmedia.com/editing-writing-services

Need Bulk Copies?

If you would like to order bulk copies of this book or any other title at Higher Ground Books & Media, please contact us at highergroundbooksandmedia@gmail.com.

We offer discounts for purchases of 20 or more copies. Excellent for small groups, book clubs, classrooms, etc.

Get in touch today and get a set of great stories for your students or group members.